WITHOUT
QUESTION

WITHOUT QUESTION

EVELYN CRONK

LEVEL
BEST BOOKS

Historia
ESTABLISHED 2019

Author Photo Credit: Mark Shröeffel

First edition

ISBN: 978-1-68512-528-8

This book was professionally typeset on Reedsy.
Find out more at reedsy.com

To my sister Helen

Praise for Without Question

"A dramatic and engrossing love story spanning two continents and a world war."—Kathy George, author *Sargasso & Estella*

"Isabella Clemens's simple life is catapulted after events that leave her desperate for answers. Her journey for the truth is a good read and entertaining."—Jennifer LaFountain (NetGalley Reviewer)

"*Without Question* draws in the reader with an engaging story, well-developed characters, continuously intriguing action, and highly descriptive environments. Evelyn Cronk creates ambience with beautifully poetic writing. There is extraordinary sensitivity in conveying Isabella's internal thoughts. Introductions to location immediately enable the reader to fully envision that specific place. None of this is surprising when we learn that the author wrote "Without Question" as the basis for a limited television series. The visuals are so strong and the structure so dramatically absorbing, that it should make a powerful and popular screen production. Here is a new author whose work stands head and shoulders above commonplace novels. Read it!"—AW (NetGalley Reviewer)

Prologue

Mézières, France January 1944

Sunshine blinds the captives as they stumble on frozen feet from the shuttered church. Overnight frost has polished the ice-covered cobblestones to skating rink perfection. Leisure far from their minds, the men and women, all with their arms tightly bound, struggle to keep upright. Armed soldiers shape them into lines against the church wall. The sun on their faces cannot comfort them. After their night of terror in the church, they understand their fate.

Across the shadowed square, the watching villagers stand in silent horror as they realize the meaning of the early morning summons. Cries rise in their throats only to be stifled by the fear of further reprisals. The captives, each one the onlookers' family or friends, have only minutes to live.

Two men, one Australian, the other English, are amongst the hostages. Dressed as French workmen, unshaven with berets pulled down over their foreheads, they look like the villagers around them. They are allied airmen who, like hundreds of their comrades, are attempting to escape across France from their downed plane.

I

Part One

Chapter One

Mt Buller Victoria, July 1980

T hrough driving snow, Isabella Clemens sees the man at the head of the tow queue. She's struck by his stillness; she feels the presence of a panther. He looks straight at her, calls 'single'—etiquette for finding a partner to ride the ski lift. He beckons her towards him.

An unseen hand of fate pushes her forward. Her skis hiss in the fresh snow as she crosses the open area between the queue and the lift. As she slides to a halt beside him for the lift take off, she sees he is tall and broad-shouldered, dressed in a stylish ski suit and hat. Dark-lensed snow goggles hide his eyes. She can only see his wide, rather sensuous mouth that greets her with a smile.

They ride the lift in silence; it would be useless to speak. As soon as words leave her lips, they would fly away in the wind to land in a snowdrift with piles of other lost words. At the top of the slope, the gale is ferocious. She slides off the lift turning her face away from the sleet rattling against her goggles and stinging her cheeks. He skis to her side and leans in close to speak to her; the color of his voice is of a foreign country. She looks up, startled. She's so intent on placing the accent, she doesn't hear the question.

He repeats. 'Will you ski with me? I ski alone this afternoon.' He adds, 'My name is Eli.' The smile follows.

Her brain tries to sort the messages—why is her heart tumbling like this? All she can say is, 'Isabella... I'm called Bella.'

From the lift station, they ski across the plateau toward the lee side of the mountain. As they push across the empty space, a horizontal blast of wind knocks Bella sideways. Ahead of her, the swirling cloud is about to swallow Eli. She pushes harder. She doesn't want him to disappear. They ski over to the lip of the ridge into the large bowl called Federation.

Down, down they ski. In the shelter of the bluff, the wind drops, and they are skiing in a white and silver world. A still, silent world except for the sound of their skis whispering on the untracked powder snow. Down, down, down. He skis with a lazy ease; she keeps up. Bella follows him turn for turn; their pace is good; they're well-matched. She feels in tune with this stranger. Small bumps give them jumps to perform. He's making very short turns down the fall line now. She finds his rhythm; it suits her style. She follows him closer and closer.

He leads her over to the far side of the run, close to the trees. *Ah*, she thinks, *he knows where to find the best snow*. He turns to see if she's following. He smiles again. She hopes she'll see that smile a lot more often. Away from the power of the tearing blizzard, Bella enjoys the duet they're performing. They ski like violin and bow. Eli turns left towards one of her favourite trails, a white ribbon winding through the canopy of tall trees.

The trail enters a wide bowl, like an amphitheatre draped in white velvet. They are alone on the slope. Large moguls carved by skiers, slice and dice the snow. With a complete lack of caution, they bounce from mogul to mogul. Bella's knees and thighs scream stop! But she can't stop now. They reach the bottom lift station and slide onto the take-off area after a greeting from the lift operator, who tells them they're mad to be out in this weather.

They smile at each other; if this is madness, she hopes it continues. She knows nothing about this man; only his name, Eli, sounds very biblical. How does one know anything about someone you've just met? He's a blank screen that waits for the images and sound to move across it, to tell her his story. Until then, she feels the mystery of him.

This lift is a T-bar on a steep narrow track, it is a challenge to ride even in fine weather. The journey up the glass-smooth trail is difficult. They watch their ski tips in front of them to avoid shards of ice. One slip could unbalance them and throw them off the lift. To make it easier, Eli leans into her shoulder and puts his arm around her; he is taller than her, but not by much. She can feel his warmth. As they near the ridgeline, they can feel the ferocity of the storm they'll ride into; they put their heads down and wait it out. Finally, when Bella thinks she can't stand any more of this wind-borne punishment, they reach the top and slide off the lift. They ski to the sheltered side of the lift station to catch their breath.

'Where to, Eesabella?'

She laughs. 'I need a brandy.'

He puts an arm around her shoulder. 'Are you cold?'

'No, not cold. You set a cracking pace down there.'

The smile appears. 'You had no trouble keeping up.'

'Let's go to Goldies,' Bella points to another trail. 'We can get there without going back over the top into the wind.'

They push off and take the run to the café. They pull up, stamp out of their skis, and head for the warmth inside. As he opens the door, he pulls off his hat and goggles. Her first sight of his face. He has high cheekbones and golden freckled skin. His hair is brown with auburn tints, and sits close to his head in tight, crinkled waves. The lines in his face tell her he could be a few years older than she.

It's his eyes. Tawny amber shot with green flecks; Bella has never seen eyes like these. Is this a moment I'll never forget? she asks herself. She feels his gaze as he helps her peel off her outer shell jacket. He takes in her deep red, figure-hugging, one-piece ski suit zipped up to a high black fur-lined collar. She wears a matching fur hat, and her hands are encased in black leather gauntlets. A tartan-padded gilet gives her extra protection from the cold. He takes her damp gloves and hat and hangs them with his own on the wire cage surrounding the heater.

In the café, they find a table near the fireplace and order coffee and brandy. An awkward silence sits between them. He gazes at Bella; her emerald-green eyes are friendly but watchful.

'You are beautiful,' he says.

Isabella shivers, and not from the cold. 'Oh,' she blurts out in surprise.

They both laugh, the ice breaks. Their order arrives, and they wrap their hands around the warm mugs.

'How long are you staying Eesabella?'

'I am here for four weeks to ski and to write.'

'Writing? Is that—your job?' he asks.

'I'm a freelance journalist. I write for music and lifestyle magazines.'

'Ah, I see. Do you write by commission or generate your own articles to sell?'

Bella is pleased with this question. It shows this man thinks a bit more than the usual reply from the uninitiated who think she has a totally exciting life.

'Both,' she replies. 'I enjoy finding stories and developing them. Also, I get to travel a lot.'

He orders another brandy. A brief silence whilst they size each other up; she's not uncomfortable with his scrutiny, which is unusual for Bella. She prefers to be the observer, not the observed.

'Where do you come from?' she asks. 'I can't place your accent.'

'I grew up in Israel, but I live in Melbourne now.'

'What do you do?'

'I've a business of my own. I build infrastructure. Dams, roads and bridges.'

'Why do you live here?'

'I wanted my children to have a few years at school here. In Israel, they experienced much danger and uncertainty in their lives.'

Bella feels her heart catch… 'How old are your children?

'Mikael and Veronique are twins; they're fifteen. They're at high school in France now.'

Children have mothers. Mothers are most often married to the children's fathers. She dives right in.

'That must be hard on your wife, having her children so far away.' A pause, she feels Eli is assessing his reply.

'Eda returned to Europe with the children. She didn't like living so far away from her family, especially as I travel so much. So, we separated.'

'You must miss them.'

'I talk to them every week, and my work takes me to Europe. I visit them quite often.'

Her curiosity satisfied, Bella says. 'We should go. The last lift closes at 4:30.'

'Yes,' he replies, 'I don't fancy a long climb to get back in this weather.'

As they're leaving the café, Bella is crestfallen when he mentions he must return to Melbourne that evening. She's sure this will be the last she sees of him.

Chapter Two

Mt Buller Victoria, July 1980

Early evening, the lodge manager calls her to the telephone, it's Eli. 'The road off the mountain is closed from a rockslide. I can't leave until tomorrow. Will you have dinner with me this evening?'

Bella dresses in navy blue corduroy trousers, a cream polo neck jumper and adds her favourite Norwegian fair isle knitted jacket with pewter clasps. She pulls her curls into a bunch, shrugs on her goose-down walking coat, woolen hat, scarf, and gloves, and is ready to go. As Eli drives to the restaurant, she takes in his fashionable but understated après ski clothes and likes what she sees. At Fanny Adams, the smartest restaurant on Mt Buller, Eli is clearly well-known. They are given a table away from the noisy heart of the restaurant. Candlelight enhances his amber eyes, and Bella starts to feel a little mesmerized by this stranger who has skied into her life out of a blizzard. He orders dry martinis and for dinner, with her approval, oysters czarina and chateaubriand for two.

'Do you like red wine?' he asks as he scans the wine list.

'Oh yes, my family home is in the Yarra Valley.'

'Excellent,' he replies as he passes the list over to her.

Bella chooses a shiraz from Tarrawarra Estate, a vineyard near her home that she knows well.

Eli orders champagne to drink with the oysters which they eat slowly, savouring the velvet texture, fresh from the sea flavour, and the tang of the caviar.

After some polite conversation about the political landscape, Eli says. 'Tell me about yourself.'

Bella is used to being the interviewer, not the subject, but she takes a breath. 'I was born in London. My mother died there when I was two years old. My father Howard, who is a war correspondent, was always somewhere else, so he brought me home here.' Bella tells him of her early life with her aunt Fiona and her grandparents on the family farm at Yarra Glen.

'What was that like? With your mother dead and your father away, did you miss them very much?'

She thinks for a minute. 'No, I guess it was normal for me. And, being a war baby, many children in our neighborhood were missing a parent and living with grandparents.' She smiles. 'I had everything a girl could want. I had the farm animals, my own horse, and we have always had beautiful German Shepherds.' She tells Eli that Max and Mischa are the latest generation of dogs whose ancestors have been in her family since her great-grandfather smuggled two pups home to Australia after serving in France during World War One.

She continues. 'I was a boarder at St Margaret's in Berwick. From early on, I loved writing stories. I guess I got that from my father. I was lucky to have a teacher who encouraged me.'

Bella tells Eli that each year, she spent part of her school holidays in London with Howard, travelled in Europe, and shared many experiences with him. 'He comes home for short trips during the year and stays longer for summer.'

'And after high school?' Eli enquires.

'An Arts degree at Melbourne University. After I graduated, I got a cadetship with *The Age* newspaper and worked my way up to become a feature writer. I loved working there, but after a few years, I decided that I wanted the life of a freelance writer. I'm like my father, I have his wanderlust.' She smiles at Eli, 'I've had a fortunate life and, I'm sure, it's a lot different from your growing up?'

'Yes, in every way,' Eli agrees. 'Except living on a kibbutz, I had plenty of animals around. Sadly, most of them were raised to be eaten.'

Bella nods. 'At university, many students went to Israel to work on Kibbutz during the holidays. Their tales of life as Kibbutzim fascinated me.' Bella tells him she would like to visit there on assignment. 'Were you born in Israel?'

'Yes, it was Palestine then. My mother left Germany when she could see that Adolf Hitler's ambitions could be lethal for our family. My sister Maya was two years old, and Mother was pregnant with me when she sailed to Palestine in 1937. She couldn't convince her family to leave with her, so we were the only survivors.' He pauses before he continues, 'My birth father wasn't Jewish; he chose to stay in Europe. I never saw him again.'

Bella is aware this is a painful history Eli shares with so many Jewish families. 'Do you have any other family?'

'Yes, after my father divorced my mother for being politically 'undesirable,' she married a wonderful man. I couldn't have had a better father.'

'Are they still alive?'

'My mother Sofia is. Sadly, my stepfather, Menachem, died.' Eli stops, and Bella gets a strong feeling not to push any further just now.

Over the next three weeks, Eli arrives on the mountain each Thursday and stays until Sunday. He is always polite in a European way that charms Bella. They ski each day, delighting in their well-matched ability. The weather and snow are perfect, so they explore every run on the mountain and all the connecting trails through the forests. Bella comes to appreciate his self-deprecating humor and especially his apparently endless fund of insightful observations about the world around them and humanity in general. He is never bombastic or forceful in his views and listens to her intently, drawing her out gently so that she becomes more confident with him.

Bella works hard when Eli is in Melbourne so that she can spend more time with him. This isn't a fast romance. In fact, she wouldn't describe it as a romance at all. It's more a growing friendship. She realises she doesn't want to go back to a time before Eli came into her life. He is warm and affectionate with her but has never tried to seduce her.

As Bella's time at Mount Buller draws to a close, she wonders if she'll see him again. Although they have become comfortable with each other, he hasn't mentioned spending time together in Melbourne. Intuition tells Bella to be patient, which is difficult for her, with her Clemens curiosity.

Chapter Three

Mt Buller Victoria, July 1980

Bella awakes to a full-on blizzard. Howling winds and driving snow rattle the window; she places her hand on the glass and feels the cold seeping through. Eli phoned yesterday to say he is detained in Melbourne but will see her on Saturday. Bella and the other guests settle down for a day inside. Mid-afternoon the power goes out; the only warmth is the open fire in the lounge. Snow drifts bank higher against the windows, cutting down the daylight. Bella helps to light the old gas lamps, which give a warm, soft light. The lodge grows colder; fortunately, there are gas stoves for cooking. Towards evening, the guests drag bedding into the main room. The bedrooms are too cold for comfort, let alone to sleep. Bella settles in for a night of indoor camping.

The door opens; Eli enters. With a brief nod to Bella's companions, he takes her hands and pulls her up from her beanbag.

'I came early; the road will close if this weather keeps up. Would you like to come to my place? It's much warmer.' He looks around and smiles, 'Besides, one less person here will leave more room by the fire.'

Bella is bemused; he's never invited her to his chalet. She dresses warmly, and then, in the foyer, he wraps her in a blanket. She doesn't resist when he picks her up and carries her through the driving snow to his Range Rover.

He whispers as he tucks her into the seatbelt. 'I couldn't leave you alone here in this weather.' He kisses her cheek. 'Hold on tight, the track is very rough.'

The windscreen wipers can't keep up with the snowflakes pelting against the glass. The wind is blowing the normally somnolent snow gums into shapes resembling whirling dervishes. Bella feels the rumbling snow chains on the Rover's wheels biting into the drifting snow. Eli is concentrating so hard on keeping to the road that she doesn't wish to start asking him questions about her apparent abduction. She knew there was no turning back; she liked this man. The attraction she felt from the first moment she saw him had grown at a faster pace than she would have liked to keep her feelings in control.

Eli turns off the road and drives down a narrow track. At the end, deep in the snow gums, is a cedar shingle-covered chalet. He comes around to the passenger's side and scoops her into his arms; she can feel his strength. She realises she has longed for him to hold her. No man has ever managed to have this effect on her. With her arms around his neck, Bella has never been so near to him and breathes in his mix of maleness and a subtle cologne.

Inside, he puts her down in front of a wide stone fireplace, which warms the room. Gas lamps glow on the walls here too. Bella looks around; she likes what she sees. A deep leather couch and a long dining table speak of entertaining and sharing happy times. Persian rugs in rich jewelled colours cover the slate floor. Everything in this room has a sheen that shows an exotic yet understated style.

'Eli, this is beautiful.'

He smiles, 'I'm pleased you like it.' He piles cushions on the floor in front of the fire. He takes her hand and draws her down. On a low table, a bottle of champagne peeps out of an ice bucket. Firelight reflects in the champagne flutes. Plates of the food of Eli's Israeli homeland sit on the table with flat bread to scoop up each taste sensation.

'Do you like this food?' he asks her.

'Yes, very much. I buy food like this at Rubin's in Acland Street.'

Eli smiles. 'I go there too; Rubin was in the army with me.'

'Tell me about your life in the army?'

'You know we have National Service in Israel?'

She nods.

'I was drafted straight out of school into the army. The training was excellent and enabled me to study engineering at Haifa University.' He pours more champagne and tells her that he saw active service in the Six-Day War between Israel and the Arab coalition in 1967 and again another stoush with the Arabs in the 1973 Yom Kippur War. He looks thoughtful for a moment, then says. 'Let's not have a history lesson tonight,' and gently pulls her closer to him.

Bella doesn't resist. 'Being here makes me feel as if I'm somewhere else entirely.'

'Yes, I've recreated a little bit of my home in Israel.'

Eli covers her in soft blankets, and they talk. Sometime during that long, wild night, she falls asleep in his arms.

A noise wakes her. Eli is moving about; she can smell coffee. She wraps herself in a blanket and draws back the curtains to see a leaden dawn struggling to emerge from the dense cloud. The overnight blizzard has changed the landscape to a still-life painting of velvet whiteness. Whilst they slept, the wind has blown itself to exhaustion; the stillness is eerie. Ice-laden snow gums are resting from their efforts to withstand the storm; their boughs bent to meet the deep snowdrifts. Bella sees some tiny animal tracks, possibly a pademelon, looking for food for her family.

She feels cocooned and safe here with Eli; the power and telephone are still out of order. He stokes the fire, returns to their nest, and draws the blankets around them. For the first time, she feels his skin. They're slow to get to know each other; an unspoken wish to please each other makes them shy. For such a strong man, he's so gentle. For such a contained man, he makes love to her as she has never been loved before.

They stay there wrapped in each other's warmth, sleeping, waking, eating, loving. Bella knows that nothing in her world will ever be the same again. It's as if this first day opens a door that she steps through, leaving her past life behind.

Chapter Four

Bella and Eli 1980

Eli's first visit to Bella's home at Yarra Glen gives her a new insight into the man she loves. She is touched to see how he gives her aunt Fiona the gentle respect he clearly feels for her. After some initial barking and suspicious sniffing, Max and Mischa sit back on their haunches and allow him to introduce himself.

Fiona laughs. 'You must be alright Eli, Max and Mischa aren't normally so welcoming.'

'Fiona, I confess I like animals a whole lot better than I like some humans.'

Fiona smiles, 'I agree.'

With this icebreaker, they show him around the beautiful old property. Bella watches him absorb the very essence of Yarra Glen and its inhabitants. Surrounded by gardens, a vineyard, and the farm beyond, *Ceres* is a well-known Hereford cattle stud. Bella explains to Eli it was her grandparents' property. The old bluestone house is Howard and his twin sister Fiona's lifetime home. It would've been their younger brother Tom's home too, but he was killed in World War Two. Fiona has lived her life unaware of any need for a husband. Bella's arrival had filled any empty space in her heart. Fiona has provided the anchor point for the family since Tom's death and the death of Bella's grandparents.

Bella and Eli spend most weekends at Yarra Glen. Within a short time, Bella can see how much Eli and Fiona grow to enjoy each other's company.

Bella watches her aunt get to know Eli in the best way Fiona knows. She saddles up her mare Luna and takes Eli riding around the paddocks on Howard's roan gelding Struan. One morning at breakfast, Fiona says.

'Eli, would you come over to the O'Connell's with me this morning. I'd like you to meet Balthazar.'

'Sure,' replies Eli, 'is he a neighbor?'

'You might say that,' Fiona laughs. 'Balthazar is Joe O'Connell's horse. A six-year-old grey who needs a new home. At eighty-six, Joe feels he needs to give up riding. He wants Balthazar to live here with our horses. I think he'd be a perfect fit for you.'

'Great, let's go now.' Eli hugs Fiona.

Bella is delighted. She understands that Fiona's gesture is about as close as she can come to giving her approval and acceptance of Eli as part of the family.

Bella watches Fiona and Eli working the cattle; they work well together. He works with a thoroughness that she knows matches Fiona's own standards. Bella doesn't make any comment on this unusual position of trust bestowed by Fiona.

Eli's knowledge of machinery is as good as any mechanic. Bella passes the workshop one day and hears Fiona and Eli's voices. She watches them working on Grandpa Clemens old Land Rover. Eli underneath with his legs protruding and Fiona, leaning over the engine well, holding a light. Bella can't hear their words, but their tone and occasional laughter tells her everything about their friendship. She wonders how much Howard will see that Eli has done to help Fiona when he comes home.

They enjoy driving the old Rover across the paddocks to barbeque by the river with their neighbors. Bella notices how much Eli enjoys these days. He is more relaxed here than in social settings in Melbourne. She puts it down to the company of the no-nonsense country folk who are their friends.

Some days, they pack a picnic and drive the Rover into the nearby Yarra Ranges to hike the trails criss-crossing the country. Bella loves the tall forests of Mountain Ash layered with fern glades. Both fit and agile, they walk for hours and climb slopes and rocky crags until they reach a break in the trees, giving them views of the whole Yarra Valley. Bella has walked these hills all her life with her father and Fiona. She is happy that Eli has absorbed her love of this country and made it his own.

They walk in silence, appreciating the natural bush sounds. Eli prefers it that way, and, after all, they have no need to disturb the peace. Bella notices that in the dense bush, Eli has an instinctive and unerring sense of direction. And, for such a large man, he walks quietly without making any disturbance where he places his feet. She asks him.

'How do you do this? It's as if you don't have a body.'

'Practice,' he replies, 'on patrol, you can't let the enemy hear you coming.' His stillness in the bush is complete. Once, she lagged looking at a clump of wild orchids, and when she tried to find him, she became alarmed as he seemed to have disappeared. She stopped on the track, straining her eyes to find him in the dappled light of the sun filtering through the high forest canopy. She found him quite close but camouflaged in the trees. He was looking straight at her.

'Oh, you frightened me; you look like a huge brown bear waiting to pounce! I'm going to call you Mr Bear from now on.'

He smiled at her. 'Well then, you are my Mrs Bear.' These became the private names they used for each other.

Bella and Eli grow to love each other deeply; life becomes an endless conversation between them. It feels natural for Eli to share Bella's townhouse in Armadale. She has never paid much attention to making this her home, Yarra Glen fills that place in her heart. Eli regards it as a blank canvas, he takes her to furniture markets and antique dealers in Melbourne and country towns. It becomes a shared interest, and piece by piece, they create their home.

She is fascinated by his small collection of handwrought pieces of silver created by a local Israeli compatriot, Ben Arieh. And two Atlas Mountains Moroccan fossil bowls. They are exquisite; each one has fossils embedded in the bowl. When she runs her fingers around the polished rim, these treasures give Bella a complete sense of timelessness and almost a meditative state and understanding of the transience of the world she lives in.

'Eli, these are beautiful; where did you find them?

'I have dealers looking out for things for me,' is his cryptic reply.

For two people from such different backgrounds, they blend like a fusion of gold and silver. Each retain their individuality, but together, they glow. They exude a quiescence and gracefulness that can make people turn their heads but hesitate to intrude upon them.

Their love is complete. They're able to talk to each other in their minds and hearts even when apart. Outwardly, they aren't very demonstrative with each other, but in private they can spend hours entwined reading and talking. Sometimes when Bella is writing, she looks up and watches Eli reading. She feels a sense of peace in his presence and a quiet joy that she has found the man she wants to share her life with.

Bella learns that Eli is quite socially withdrawn and dislikes crowds and noise. She understands how much he needs to be at Yarra Glen to balance the demands of work and city life. He has few long-term friends in Melbourne but, given he only came to live in Australia five years ago, this isn't surprising. Melbourne is a lot about relationships formed as far back as school days, Eli's roots are in Israel. He makes calls to Israel in the evenings, but as these are conducted in Hebrew, Bella has no idea of the context of the conversations unless Eli tells her he was speaking to his sister or gives her snippets of news of his friends or family.

Occasionally, they meet with other Israelis in Melbourne, but these outings often leave Bella feeling an outsider. She understands this is the same experience Eli must feel amongst her lifelong friends and colleagues. None of this matters to her; they have each other.

He isn't like her friends' partners; he doesn't easily gravitate to the groups of men around the barbeque. Eli doesn't do well at dinner parties either—he's too silent and watchful at a time when good dinner party performance is an entree to social acceptability. One evening, not long after Eli moved in with her, she invited friends to meet him. He was enthusiastic and helped

18

her prepare the food. He was an excellent and attentive host but seemed at a loss to join in the conversation. Over the course of that dinner and other occasions, she realized that sometimes, Eli's separateness was hard for her friends to understand.

One evening, a close friend corners her in the kitchen and asks, 'Why don't you settle down and marry someone of your own kind?'

'Because I'm happy,' Bella replies. 'And what do you mean by my own kind? White middle-class Australian Protestant with an arts degree?'

Seeing the look on her friend's face Bella stops, because that exactly describes her friend and her husband. She realises how few of her long-term friends have moved away from their apparent cultural and class background. She reminds herself that her journalism career possibly gives her a different life view than her friends. She hopes in time, they will get to like Eli for himself. She returns to the dining room with the next course in time to hear another woman, the new partner of one of her friends saying.

'Are you an Israeli secret service agent?' She's a bit tipsy and adds, 'what're they called, Moshaaad? Y'know those dudes who raided that airport and blew up planes to rescue the hostages. Where was it?' She looks around for someone to support her.

Eli replies quietly. 'Entebbe Airport in 1976.'

Cassie isn't going to drop this. 'Were you one of them? One of those dudes that killed the hijackers?'

Bella feels the guests hold their breath; this hasn't been said as a polite enquiry but as a challenge.

Eli smiles and says, 'I'm an ordinary soldier. In Israel, we all serve at some time in our lives unless we get dispensation on religious grounds.' He continues. 'Cassie, I don't think James Bond has done us any favors. We look for spies everywhere.'

Everyone laughs, the moment passes, and Bella breathes again.

Later, in bed, Bella tucks herself under Eli's arm and says, 'I'm sorry about Cassie putting you on the spot like that. I think she'd drunk too much wine.'

'My life has been so different; there's no way for some people to understand that,' he's silent for a minute. 'I know I need to lighten up, but life in Israel is far more intense than here. We live under constant threat of incursion from our neighbors. My friends there are all very politically aware and can get very argumentative. I'm not like that, so you see,' he pulls her closer and kisses her hair, 'I'm fairly silent no matter where in the world I happen to be.'

'You're not quiet with Fiona, and I'm sure when you meet Howard, you won't be quiet with him either.' She tickles his ribs.

'Ah well, Fiona is different. And I'm sure Howard will be too.'

'Why is Fiona different?'

'She's the mainstay in your life, and I care for her deeply. But more than that, I think that Fiona, after her lifetime on the land and the loss of Tom, understands more about me than I understand myself.'

Bella holds that thought close.

Chapter Five

Yarra Glen, Howard and Eli

A fax from her father waits for Bella when she returns home from work. She smiles as she reads that he intends to come to Yarra Glen for three months. "I need to help Fiona more; she's not getting any younger. After the low rainfall, we'll be hand feeding." states the letter. She rings Fiona.

'Dad's coming home to help you,' she says with a smile in her voice.

'Hmmph,' snorts Fiona, 'I heard from him too. Dry seasons haven't worried him in the past.'

Bella can hear the radio playing jazz in the background; her aunt will be in the kitchen. The newspaper will be on the large table open at the daily crossword, half filled out but with a sprinkling of earth from freshly picked vegetables scattered across the page.

'He can't resist coming home to meet Eli.'

'Of course,' says Fiona.

'Dad isn't used to me having someone who shows signs of staying around.'

'He wasn't easy on your boyfriends, was he?'

Bella thinks for a minute about the young men who would meet Howard for the first time and be clearly intimidated by him. 'That's an understatement.'

'I'd better get busy with some cooking. Your father eats everything in the freezer when he's here.'

'Especially your lamb curry, the slow cooker will be in overdrive,' says Bella.

They both laugh. 'I'll pick him up at the airport.' Bella hangs up.

Bella turns off the road into the lane leading to the property. She is happy to have her father home. Whilst he is here, Bella wants to ask about her mother. Howard has always deflected Bella's questions, so over time, she had stopped asking. Now that she is making her life with Eli, she needs to colour in a picture of her mother.

She sees her father's head turn as they pass through the newly repaired wooden gates and the refurbished sign *Ceres* on the gatepost.

'Someone has been busy,' Howard comments.

'Yes, Eli loves working with wood.' She smiles inwardly at the surprises in store for her father.

Bella and Howard ride around the property. The homestead, outbuildings, pasture, fences, gardens, and the livestock are all in top condition. He doesn't comment until taking coffee with Bella and Fiona on the verandah, he says. 'I am impressed. You've achieved so much since I was last home.'

Fiona replies. 'You can thank Eli, he's so capable. I'd hate to be without him in our lives now.'

Bella watches the two of them and feels such love for them. As they've aged, their resemblance has become more striking. They are tall, still slender, and carry themselves ramrod straight. Both have silver hair and intense blue eyes, and their gaze is as unwavering as their opinions. Fiona is one of very few people who can get anywhere near telling Howard Clemens she doesn't agree with him and stand her ground.

'I think we'd best buy in some feed to get us through this dry.'

Fiona nods.

Howard continues. 'I'll check the tanks today; I'd rather buy in water before it gets scarce... and expensive.'

Fiona says. 'Eli and I are planning to cut some fire breaks along the northern boundary. There's a lot of fuel on the forest floor. If a fire comes down those slopes and jumps the road, we're in trouble.'

Howard pauses before he replies, 'I'm going to have a yarn with the Country Fire Authority. Is Dave still running it? I want to get our fire plan into place.'

'Yes, he is,' replies Fiona. 'Why don't we get the crew over for a barbeque and invite our neighbors so we're all on the same page.'

'Good plan.'

Fiona adds, 'Eli has serviced both the tractors and all the pumps. He's sorted and checked the hoses, rakes, and hoes. And repaired the old Furphy tank. You'll find the equipment ready and loaded onto the tandem trailer in the small barn.'

'I saw that. I wondered if you'd done it all. Well, he'd better be here for the meeting then.'

'I'm sure he will be,' replies Fiona. She turns away to hide a smile.

Bella gathers the cups and leaves her aunt and father talking. She wonders if he's a little piqued to come home and find he's been a bit replaced.

The first weekend Howard meets Eli, Bella hopes her father can see her happiness. She knows that Howard will only accept Eli in his own time. They ride through the vineyards and the nearby mountain trails. Bella watches Howard and Eli as they spur their horses to gallop up a rise, Howard comments. 'You're a fine horseman Eli. Where did you learn to ride?'

Eli smiles. 'My parents were friendly with the local Bedouin. When I was young, I rode with their children.'

Fiona asks. 'Was that unusual for the Bedouin to mix with the Israelis?'

Eli replies. 'Our Kibbutz was in an area that the Bedouin liked to camp through winter. We had good water to share, and they bought our vegetables.' He shrugs, 'We had no cause for argument.'

'A pity more Arabs and Israelis can't find that peaceful place,' Howard observes.

'Yes, I was fortunate to be brought up in that environment,' Eli pauses, then says quietly. 'I found it hard to go out into the wider world and encounter prejudice against the people I believed to be my friends and neighbors.'

'Did that make army life hard for you?'

Eli sighs. 'Yes it did. I wished the army could be a less adversarial organization. All that manpower and resources mostly used to destroy, not to build.' He falls silent as he looks across the valley, then says, 'But Howard, you have spent much time in conflict zones. You must abhor the waste as I do.'

'Too much time,' Howard replies. 'And yes, I detest the useless destruction of lives and property.'

'Why do you keep reporting in war zones? Surely, by now, you could take an easier path.'

Howard replies. 'Soon I'll need to but, I still want to tell the world the truth about the uselessness of war. And, of course, we have this new threat called terrorism.'

Both men fall silent. Purple shadows are lengthening across the valley, and the first tendrils of evening chill start to wrap around them.

Bella turns her horse's head and says, 'Last one home has to feed the horses.'

As dusk falls, Eli walks to the fence line dividing the homestead gardens from the paddocks and hills beyond. From the veranda, Bella watches the silent man gazing out at the peaceful scenery made even more beautiful by the setting sun. She doesn't intrude on these quiet minutes; they are Eli's alone. His stillness gives an illusion that he is blending into the landscape, almost in a meditative state. This continues for many minutes before he turns back towards the house. Bella realises that Howard is standing beside her, watching Eli too. When they meet on the verandah, Eli says. 'It's the tranquility. I've never known such peace.'

Bella knows that Howard understands exactly what Eli means. She is touched when Howard replies.

'Yes, I know. No bombs.'

Eli says, 'It's as if the serenity comes up from the earth.'

She understands that there's been a shift in Howard's attitude when he puts a hand on Eli's shoulder, and they go inside to join Fiona. She knows her father well enough to understand that there is a difference in his attitude towards Eli compared to other men in her life. Bella can see Howard clearly respects Eli for his obvious care of her. Eli returns this respect. She can also see Howard is very much aware of Eli's unspoken, but determined, "This is our life; please allow us to get on with it as we choose."

At dinner, they share a wide-ranging conversation in which Eli reveals an excellent grasp of world affairs. But Bella notices that whenever Howard tries to steer the conversation to Eli's life in Israel, Eli politely restates that he was a structural engineer working on infrastructure projects. Bella serves dessert and wonders what her father is trying to find out.

Howard rises and goes to the drinks tray. 'A Drambuie, Eli? Or can I interest you in this?' asks Howard, holding up the bottle of Arak.

'That's a long way from home,' says Eli. 'How did you come by it?'

Howard pours and hands the glass to Eli. 'My colleague Ariel Achmed gave me some while we were reporting from Tel Aviv during the Six-Day War.' Howard pauses and then says, 'Were you in Israel in '67?'

Bella observes the silent contest playing out before her.

Eli gazes into the fire; then looks up at Howard and says, 'yes I was.'

'And 1973 for the Yom Kippur war?'

Eli replies with a nod. His eyes don't leave Howard's face.

Howard's next question surprises her. It's unusually direct for her subtle father.

'What branch of the Israeli Defence Force do you serve in Eli?' asks Howard. 'Are you Special Forces?'

Bella catches her breath. Still serving? She thought, or rather assumed, that Eli was retired. She'd never asked him; she feels a frisson of tension before Eli replies.

'Yes, I'm a Sayeret. A commando.'

Stunned, Bella asks, 'Are you still active? You've never told me that.'

He reaches over and takes Bella's hand. 'My life is with you now. I don't think about it, so we don't talk about it.'

Bella has a fleeting thought about the journey of getting to know someone. She sits back and listens.

He turns to Howard. 'Yes, when I left full-time service, I stayed in the reserve.'

'That's interesting,' says Howard. Doesn't that go against your views on war?'

'Outwardly yes, but I have a strong commitment to peace-keeping duties. I put my engineering training to good use re-building infrastructure damaged through war or natural disasters.'

Bella feels an iron fist squeezing her heart. 'If there is a war, could you be called up?'

'Yes, I can,' Eli smiles, 'but don't worry, it's unlikely I'd be jumping out of aeroplanes anymore. They keep us older guys around to help train the younger ones.'

'I'm pleased to hear that,' says Bella tartly, wondering why she'd never got him to tell her this before. What else doesn't she know?

'What rank are you, Eli?' asks Howard. 'Could I guess colonel?'

'About that,' says Eli, finishing his Arak and rising. 'Thank you, Howard, I'll turn in now. Bella and I have an early start.'

As Bella says goodnight, she catches her aunt's smile and realises Fiona shares her thoughts that Howard has finally met his match.

Chapter Six

Bella and Eli

During their first autumn together, they find an old Couta boat for sale on the Mornington Peninsula. Owned by a retired fisherman, it has been neglected since he stopped going to sea. The old man is grateful that Eli wants to restore his beloved boat and sits down to yarn with them. He tells Eli and Bella the history of these boats, which were originally built for fishing for Barracouta along the coast of Bass Strait. Eli tells them the shape reminds him of the ancient fishing boats on Lake Tiberias in Israel. Like these Couta boats, they are being rebuilt on traditional lines and used for recreational sailing.

On the drive home, Eli tells her. 'Historically, in Tangier, my adoptive father's family were seafarers, so sailing was in his blood. Holidays were rare for us, but he would take my sister and me to the lake to sail. We loved it.'

'Did you take Mikael and Veronique sailing?'

'They went to the cadets' program at Brighton Yacht Club but,' he pauses and says sadly, 'I didn't spend enough time with them in those days.'

Bella, remembering her own mainly absent father, doesn't press Eli. She understands that without Fiona and her life on the farm, she would have missed her father's presence more than she did. She doesn't want to make Eli feel sad about that time. She is touched by this rare insight into his childhood.

They work together, Bella learns from Eli's craftsmanship that brings the old boat back to seaworthiness. He christens her *Isabella,* and like skiing, sailing becomes a shared passion for them.

Eli is competitive and loves to win the Couta Boat races at the Sorrento Sailing Club. He takes to the combined challenge of racing tactics and reading the local weather patterns as if he had been sailing on Port Phillip Bay for years. She notices that, apart from herself as crew, he prefers giving a berth to the younger sailors. He is more at ease with young people than with adults. He is a patient skipper who imbues confidence in his crew but teaches them to be respectful of the sea and its moods. She wonders if he's trying to make up for time not spent with his own children.

In the clubhouse after sailing, Bella notices that Eli doesn't mix comfortably with the other members. Like all pack animals, they seem to sense that Eli isn't one of them. His separateness would concern Bella more if she didn't have the balance of seeing he and Fiona totally at ease with each other. Also, on her visits to Eli's workplace, Bella sees that his staff all like and respect him enormously. Clearly, he is in command, like a general with his troops, but the aloofness and separateness he shows in social situations, is replaced by a more relaxed manner with his workers.

As well as Europe and Israel, Eli's work projects take him to far north Queensland, the Northern Territory, and Western Australia. Whenever she can, Bella travels with him; she loves seeing remote parts of Australia. They drive for hours, then camp under the stars. At night, he stands outside the rim of the firelight, gazing into the darkness. One night, he takes her hand and leads her away from their camp. The desert cold hits her as soon as they are away from the fire's warmth. The blackness is total; the myriad stars look like diamonds scattered on velvet. He reminds Bella of a desert lion; he has such a powerful sense of alertness.

'Tell me more about your time in the army?'

Eli sits down and puts his arm around her. She loves this feeling of closeness in the vast desert night.

'We spent a lot of time on night patrol in the desert. Our survival depended on being prepared for attack, so our training to be able to anticipate this was crucial. We had to learn to see in the dark.'

'Does this have anything to do with your dislike of bright lights and loud noises?' she asks.

'My darling, I can't tell you about the noise of battle.' He falls silent.

Bella is used to this reticence. Howard changes the topic when the conversation turns to World War Two and more recent conflicts. Bella only finds out about Howard's work in war zones by reading his articles.

Bella and Eli travel together whenever possible and meet up with Howard in London. On one trip to Switzerland, Bella is disappointed when a planned catch-up with Eli's children, Mikael and Veronique, is cancelled. They must attend the funeral of their grandfather in Germany. Eli is apologetic as he knows she is looking forward to meeting them. Another time, they are called away to see their sick grandmother.

During Eli's absences, friends invite her to meet "someone interesting whom I'm sure you'll like Bella." Bella accepts some invitations; she's warm and engaging, but any men hopeful of getting to first base with Bella come up against an invisible shield. Eli teases her about her well-meaning friends, but their obvious concern for their friend Bella's unusual partner doesn't worry him.

After a beautiful autumn weekend at Yarra Glen in May 1985, Eli arrives home on Monday evening and says he needs to fly to Queensland tomorrow.

'I'm preparing a tender to build a road to a new mine near Rockhampton. I want to survey the area.' He pours her a glass of wine and adds. 'I need to stay in Queensland long enough to see local suppliers to negotiate prices.'

Bella talks to him about the feature she's doing over the coming fortnight. 'I'll be busy. I want to get this assignment done before Howard comes home so I can spend more time with him.'

When Bella drops Eli at the airport, he kisses her and says, 'I'll see you in three weeks.' He looks into her eyes, pulls her to him, holds her close, and whispers, 'I love you. I'll always love you.'

Bella feels his tenderness and, feeling his heartbeat, a fluttering sensation pulls at her stomach. Is it the love that flows between them? She feels an unbreakable silver thread, a thread that moves with them whether together or apart. She takes a deep breath and, after he disappears through the entrance, she drives away.

II

Part Two

Chapter Seven

Iris Magazine Office, Melbourne, August 1990

D ressed in a full-length camel hair coat, a tartan scarf and matching hat, and leather gloves, Bella strides down St. Kilda Road with her long-legged gait. Her feet are shod in her favourite high-heeled leather boots. Clamped on her face are her signature Rodenstock sunglasses that are, along with her collection of Bally shoes, one of her few fashion indulgences.

It's a sharp winter morning; the chill south wind blows the remaining leaves off the Plane trees lining this boulevard. The morning sun has a bright glare but casts hard-edged shadows. She enjoys these brisk walks from Flinders Street station, past the Arts Centre, and on to her office building. She's about to start a new assignment, and the subject is one close to her heart. Three years ago, Bella gave up freelancing after a job offer to join the Melbourne bureau of *Iris* magazine, an international publication specializing in high-class photojournalism. She loves the work and enjoys how every assignment opens another world to explore.

The job has been a lifesaver. Bella's memories of her life in the two years after Eli disappeared in 1985 remain raw. She had adopted a solitary, gypsy lifestyle and couldn't settle. After two years, the act of pitching stories and always being on the move had palled, and inner peace eluded her. Her father helped her realise that she needed to get some structure back into her life. She agreed to Howard introducing her to his long-time friend,

Lord Douglas Storm, known to all as Storm, the British owner of Power Press, one of the biggest magazine companies in the world, and owner of *Iris*. Bella liked him from their first meeting.

Three years later, she acknowledges that her father's advice to help heal her life was good. *Iris's* editor, Meg Peterson, is a forthright woman of angular lines and a blunt-cut Mary Quant hairstyle that marry with her sharp intellect. But both her style and her personality hide her huge commitment to social justice and compassion for humans and animals alike. She has a real feel for a good story. Bella has a strong respect for Meg, and they have become friends.

Bella enjoys working with her colleague, Scott Sinclair. Like Bella, his background is on the land. The youngest of four sons, he knew from an early age that he would need to make his career away from the family farm. A love of art and Australian landscape drew him to photography. The bush has never left Scott; he still looks and dresses like a country person in moleskins, checked shirts, bush jacket, and RM Williams boots. It also suits his laconic nature. Fashion photography, with the intensity of personalities, would be torture for him. Photojournalism fills every part of his love of traveling and his creative soul. Bella thinks they are a great team. They like to be where the story happens, to find eyewitnesses, and gather their material. Her writing is skillful and creates word pictures. Scott's photography has an unerring eye for composition and fine details that give life and depth to his images. His pictures marry with her words in a perfect partnership. Since working together, they've shared top-level assignments all over the world, their stories for *Iris* are syndicated by other magazine editors in the Power Press network.

In the office, coffee in hand, Meg outlines the story. 'International Missing Persons Week is coming up.'

Bella doesn't react; her heart thumps.

Meg continues. 'The objective is to create awareness of the plight of those left behind,' she pauses and looks at Bella. 'Most often with unanswered questions.'

Bella nods but doesn't speak.

Meg continues. 'In this rapidly expanding computer age, international sharing of information is gathering momentum. This will impact on the ability to trace missing people.' She places a paper on the table between them. Bella picks it up; it's about the work the International Red Cross Tracing Service have performed helping people to reconnect after war or disaster for over a century. She puts it down without comment.

'Storm will run our stories with his own in the UK.' Meg tells them that Storm believes this series must be international because it might even persuade people who have moved countries to rethink and maybe get in touch. 'It's big, and I'm thrilled that he's included us.' Meg places a folder on the table.

'The Salvation Army also helps people reconnect. Their work is not as widely known as the Red Cross, but the series will build an awareness of their work. It's hoped that the stories will enable some missing persons to choose to reconnect directly or they may choose to simply leave a message with a service saying that, for their own reasons, they do not wish to reunite with their families. Even knowing if someone is alive, that alone can assuage a lot of unresolved grief.'

Silently but fervently, Bella agrees with this statement. She asks herself; can she do this?

'So, Bella, given your own experience, I'll understand if you don't feel up to it.'

After a pause, Bella says, 'Yes Meg. I'm up for it.'

'Are you sure?' says Meg.

'Yes,' says Bella, adding, 'it might help...'

Bella recalls the endless frustration of trying to find any information, even a birth certificate for Eli, with so little to go on. He'd told her he was born in Haifa, and although she knew his birthdate, her enquiries, made more difficult by language barriers, were littered with false hopes and dead ends. Yes, she is very familiar with the work of the Red Cross and other agencies.

She made telephone calls all over Israel to people who shared his surname. Every call met with polite answers that no, he wasn't related. Too late, she realized that she'd never sought details of his older sister Maya. She had accepted pleasant but short greetings on the telephone when Maya called. Bella assumed she would travel to Israel with Eli, and all these details to build a picture of Eli's life would fall into place. Somehow, there had never been the opportunity to make this trip. Now she wonders why.

Scott's voice brings her back to the present. 'Bella, do you feel like telling us about Eli's disappearance?'

'Yes, Bella,' says Meg. 'I've never heard the full story.'

Bella nods, it's time. Scott sits next to her and takes her hand. She's a bit startled because, despite their warm relationship, he's very much an arm's length guy. She feels a rush of affection and squeezes his hand gratefully.

She describes taking Eli to the airport, completely unaware that when he disappeared through the terminal doors, it would be the last time she would see him.

'I never minded Eli's absences. I was an only child, so aloneness had never worried me. And I had Fiona and Yarra Glen. I was busy working, catching up with friends, and I truly didn't have any thought that anything was wrong.' She looks down, and her voice falters as she tries to find the words to tell them how every piece of certainty she had about her life with Eli was shattered by the home invasion.

Chapter Eight

Bella Tells Her Story - Melbourne 1985

B ella parked her car next to Eli's Range Rover and turned to enter the house when a voice behind her whispered.

'Put your hands above your head, flat on the door!'

Ice-cold shock gripped her as she heard the garage door close, locking her in with no way of escape.

'Where is he?' growled the man.

'Who? What are you talking about? Who are you?'

She turned around to see four more armed men behind the leader, all wearing dark clothes and balaclavas. Anger replaced the shock. 'What do you want?'

'Where's Eli Fossbach?' her interrogator barked.

'He's not here. Get out. Now!' She screamed, 'Help me! help!'

A stinging blow to the side of her head dazed her; she fell against the door. Rough hands hauled her upright.

'Let us in, or see this?' the man said, pointing to another man brandishing a small steel battering ram. 'He'll use it.'

Bella had to unlock the door and let them into her home. While her questioner pushed her into the living room, the other men dispersed around the house. They went from room to room; she wondered what they were looking for. She heard them talking but not in English.

The leader stood opposite Bella. He was her height, so she could see his intense dark eyes through the slit in the balaclava; she felt fear tugging at her stomach. This was an unfamiliar sensation for Bella, and she didn't like it.

He pushed her hard, and she fell heavily onto the couch. He leant down closer, too close; she could smell him, a sour and fetid smell that turned her stomach.

He barked aggressively. 'Where is he?'

Bella tried to muster a shred of defiance, but her voice cracked as she said, 'I don't know.'

Another slap across her face, and another, made Bella realise that this man could hurt her very badly.

'Somewhere in Queensland,' she said.

'What's he doing there?'

'He's quoting for an infrastructure project for a mining company.'

'I can tell you,' the man leant in close, his dark yes menacing. 'He's on one of his Mossad witch hunts, and you know where he is.' He raised his hand again. 'Tell me now.'

'Mossad? What rubbish! He is Israeli, but he's an engineer.' She touched the side of her face; it was swelling, and it hurt.

The man nodded to someone else. She was pushed forward, her arms pulled behind her and tied, then she was pushed sideways. Her legs were tied too and raised onto the sofa, and then she was gagged. This was the most terrifying sensation of all.

She waited; waves of fear washed through her as she listened to the noises upstairs. Her brain told her that if they left her alone, any damage to the house could be repaired. This logic didn't help much; to quell the rising panic, she focused on the men. She willed her journalist's brain to remember details. Height? Build? What were they wearing? dark clothes. All of them had black tracksuit pants and tops. Balaclavas covered their heads. Shoes? all dark sneakers. Any logos or distinguishing features? nothing. She hoped a neighbor saw these strange men and would call the police. How long have these people been watching her? She would never be home at this time except a dental appointment gave her the opportunity to come home and make an early getaway to Yarra Glen for the weekend. An hour passed before the sounds faded, and the silence told her she must be alone.

Her face was so swollen she could only see out of one eye. Bella tried to think how long it might take for Fiona to call her if she didn't arrive at Yarra Glen by evening. Fiona was her only hope of rescue. Bella could see the clock on the VCR under the TV; the minutes and then one hour, two hours, three hours ticked away. The phone rang several times, but as the answer phone was connected, she could hear Fiona's voice on the machine, growing more agitated.

She rolled off the couch onto the floor, but the heavy coffee table in front wouldn't allow her to move very far. She tried to get onto her knees and crawl to the doorway, but she kept falling forward, and the effort made her choke on the gag. She fell on her side and concentrated on trying to breathe through her nose and not to vomit, which would suffocate her.

Her thoughts about Eli swirled in confusion. She was conscious that he hadn't rung her, apart from one call in the first week, which was unusual. She thought back to that call; it wasn't any different to any other. He talked about the survey and was his usual loving self. When she hung up, there was absolutely nothing to give her any feeling of disquiet. Until today, she believed he would ring her at Yarra Glen so he could chat to Fiona too.

Where was Eli? Had anything happened to him, and he couldn't call her? She'd never asked him if he had her contact details in his wallet. From her position on the floor, Bella scanned the room; she loved how Eli had decorated it. Bella's first clue to Eli's heritage had been his chalet at Mt. Buller. It remained her favourite place to be with him; it was where they found love.

Here in Armadale, Eli had achieved the same comfort but with some beautiful pieces of artwork that added subtle touches of sophistication. Each piece had its own story woven into their lives. She remembered where each one came from, their mutual excitement at each 'find.'

The afternoon sun slanted onto the handmade silver plate from Israel that he had given her for a birthday; the light made it glow, like her deep love for him. An overwhelming feeling of drowning washed over her. If

Eli was lost to her, how would she survive? Bella realized she had never given thought to a time that she and Eli might not be together. They had woven their lives together as beautifully as the Persian rug she was lying on. Exhausted, Bella couldn't think anymore. She craved sleep, hoping that she would wake up and find that today had never happened.

Outside the sitting room window, the sun set, casting shadows across the room. As darkness fell, Bella finally heard a key in the lock and Fiona's voice. 'Bella, Bella!'

Instinct had made Fiona fearful; she had brought the dogs. In the hallway, Max and Mischa pushed past Fiona and rushed to Bella on the floor, whining and whimpering. In the narrow space, they got as near to her as they could and licked her face and her hands. Max sat back and made a heart-piercing howl. Tears ran down Bella's cheeks as the light flicked on, and her aunt cried out. 'Bella, Bella! What's happened to you?'

Chapter Nine

Armadale 1985

Her home was a crime scene, and a complete mess; every room was devastated. Fortunately, Bella didn't see much of this as she was taken out to an ambulance. Later, Fiona took her to Yarra Glen, until her home was made liveable after the police completed their forensic work.

The next day, the police came to interview her. She was shocked when the detective said.

'We have to refer this case to ASIO Miss Clemens.'

'ASIO…the security service, why?' Bella said, then she sat back. She was completely drained of any energy to resist. And, to resist what exactly? She hadn't heard from Eli, and by then, she was desperate to try to find out anything she could. The police were interested that the intruders turned the house over so thoroughly. She couldn't help them with any answers as to what the men were looking for.

The ASIO agents arrived at Yarra Glen on Monday. Bella met them in Howard's study. The senior man handed her a card.

Ron Blakely
Specialist Intelligence Officer
Australian Security and Intelligence Organisation

'Call me Ron,' he offered from a face as closed as a steel door. He read the copy of Bella's police statement. She couldn't add anything else to it, but he was more interested in Eli than any further details about the attack on her. He questioned her about the day Eli left and the weeks leading up to his departure.

'Nothing was unusual at all.' Bella concluded after she recounted the events and details of where she believed to be his destination and the purpose of his trip. 'It was no different to any other time he's taken a business trip.'

'Miss Clemens, can I call you Isabella?'

'Bella,' she says in a low voice.

Ron continues. 'None of the airlines have any record of Eli Fossbach flying to any Queensland port on that day or the next day either.'

'But I saw him go through the doors at the Ansett terminal.' Even as she spoke, Bella realized that if that day was Eli's first step into an unknown life, this statement meant nothing, just a simple red herring and possibly the first of many.

Ron Blakely broke the silence. 'How do you get in contact with him while he's away on these trips?'

'I don't need to. He rings me when he can get reception on his mobile phone.'

The two agents exchanged a glance. 'His mobile phone? – What kind of phone?'

Not sensing the agent's interest, she replied. 'It's a portable Motorola; he transfers it between vehicles.' She remembered him saying as he hefted the heavy unit, *"They'll have to make these things smaller one day."*

She watched as they took notes, then Ron asked her. 'Where are all his business records? Did you see the intruders remove anything from the house?'

'No, I couldn't. I was tied up in the sitting room, and besides, everything like that would be at his office. Have you been there?' Bella continued, 'I'd planned to ring there today if I didn't hear from him over the weekend.'

'The place is empty; the gates are padlocked,' Ron Blakely countered.

This revelation shocked Bella. She felt a punch in her stomach. Winded, she tried to remember how long it has been since she was last there. She rarely had any reason to visit.

Despite her anxiety about Eli, Bella's curiosity allowed her to let this story unfold. She said, 'I don't believe you. He has staff and equipment there, and they've always got contracts to complete.'

'I'm happy to take you there now. We can continue this conversation in the car,' he replied.

'How long has Eli been in Australia, and did he emigrate?' Ron asked as they drove away.

'I met him at Mount Buller in 1980. He came here shortly after the Yom Kippur War. He wanted to make a better life for his wife and children.'

'Wife and children?'

'Yes twins, Mikael and Veronique.'

'Where are they?'

Bella tells him what she knows of Eli's family, which she realizes in retelling, is not very much.

'Did you meet these children when you travelled with Eli?'

Bella paused. The intelligence officer had unerringly hit on a tiny fissure, a hairline crack in her life with Eli. Twice, they had made plans to see Mikael and Veronique in Paris and each time, it hadn't worked out. It always seemed plausible that they had to be somewhere else.

'No, I didn't.' she related her memories of the aborted meetings. 'I truly didn't think anything of it.'

'Did he talk to them on the phone? Did you talk to them?'

'Yes, he did, but they mostly spoke in Hebrew. I would say hello sometimes.'

'Is he divorced?'

'Yes.' Bella was feeling nervous. It was like feeling a gust of wind blowing through the window. The wind pushed at the foundations of the beliefs she had built to contain their life together.

'We know that Eli travels to Israel and Europe quite frequently. Why?'

'Business... He buys equipment in Sweden and Germany. He has a business in Israel doing the same kind of work. His brother-in-law is his partner.'

'What is his name and where does he live?'

'His name is Jacob… and he lives in Tel Aviv… I think.'

'Have you met him?'

'No… only Eli's mother, Sofia, when she came to Melbourne for a visit.'

She tried to remember details about Sofia. She was an elderly, motherly woman. Bella wanted to get to know her, to ask her about Eli as a child. To ask about their lives in Israel, anything to color in the scant picture of the man she loved so much. But Sofia only spoke Hebrew, French, and some German. Their communication relied on Bella's limited French. She dragged her thoughts back from that visit to the present.

'How do you know this "family" were real? We have reason to believe they were a cover created for this man.'

'A cover? ridiculous. Why wouldn't I believe him?'

She understood that her answers were not building a full picture of Eli or her relationship with him. She wouldn't be doubting Eli for a minute, but the attack on her and his absence worried her desperately. Like a house of cards, the walls of their life together toppled. In shock, she realized she may have been living with a man who was someone else. A stranger.

Chapter Ten

Melbourne 1985

At the yard, Ron Blakely unlocked the gate. The silence was so profound she could hear the traffic on the freeway a block away. The place looked abandoned; leaves swirled in the forecourt untended by Harry, the yardman. No equipment lined up in the service bay, none of the drivers in the tearoom to wave and call out greetings to her.

They crossed to the office building. Though still furnished, the rooms were empty, no paperwork files, folders, or books. The work-in-progress boards were clean and blank. No Janet, the receptionist, or Mrs Morris, the office manager and bookkeeper. No Hamish, Eli's bluff Scottish foreman.

Bella was devastated; her legs shook. To get control of herself and the situation, she sat down at the meeting table.

'D'you believe me now?' Ron asked.

Tears prickled Bella's eyes; she felt her heart pounding and had difficulty breathing. 'I don't understand how he did this. Or why? How long did it take to clear a place like this? Where are his staff? What did he do with his staff?'

'That shows how little you know the man you've been living with, Miss Clemens. He gave everyone a week off, bought them a holiday at the RACV Resort at Inverloch. Bused them and their families down there and cleaned the place out while they were away.'

'When was this?'

'The last week of the school holidays.'

'So, what happened when they came back?'

'There was a stranger with two armed guards who paid all their entitlements and cash bonuses in lieu of notice before seeing them off the premises.'

'Why didn't anyone call me?' Bella asks.

'Because he'd given the office manager a false phone number and address for your home.'

'That's impossible, why would he do that? And he couldn't clean out this place by himself.'

'He didn't. The neighbors tell us there was a very well-oiled operation of military precision here cleaning this place out.'

This rang true. Bella had seen Eli in well-oiled military precision mode at construction sites. 'Where would he have got the people to take everything away?' She looked around the empty yard and thought about all the heavy equipment. Where was that?

'You haven't been listening to me, have you?' Ron Blakely continued. 'I tell you; he got a team of his terrorist trainees here to do it as an exercise.'

This statement broke Bella's calm. She ran outside and vomited. The agent gave her some water, and they drove back to Yarra Glen in silence. Bella didn't want to talk; she wanted to turn her life back three days and go on without this nightmare. She tried to focus and asked with more calm than she felt.

'Mr Blakely —Ron, the men who attacked me referred to Eli being on another "Mossad witch hunt." What could they mean? Why were they looking for him?'

'Bella, we don't know who they were. We're trying to find out. Because of their violence, we need to find Eli before they do.'

'Why did you say, "his terrorist trainees?" Are you telling me that Eli is a spy?'

The officer explained. 'We believe that Eli came to Australia as an undercover agent for a foreign agency. We don't know who. At best, he was operating for friendly powers. At worst, he might be acting for an unauthorized agency. It's impossible for ASIO to know yet, but,' he lowered his glasses and looked hard at her, 'we will find out.' He explained that their intelligence was that he was working against the interests of the Australian government.

'I can't believe any of this. What do you mean?'

'I'm not able to tell you any more now, but we believe his business that takes him away so much could be a cover for his activities.' He concluded. 'We believe that Eli was ordered to leave Australia very quickly.'

For the first time in this whole dreadful afternoon, Ron's voice loses its tough edge. 'I'm sorry, Bella; I don't think he'll be back. If he does return, we'll find out. I strongly advise you not to hide anything from us.'

Bella couldn't eat or sleep. She sat watching the telephone, willing it to ring and for it to be Eli, her beloved Eli. He couldn't be who these people said. It's all a terrible mistake. She believes they must know more than they told her. She stayed at Yarra Glen with Fiona; she couldn't face returning to Armadale. As time passed with no news of Eli, Bella felt she was watching her life depart on a moving train, taking her heart with it and leaving her to go on without it.

One morning, she looked in the mirror. She had lost so much weight that her gaunt face and shadowed eyes were totally unfamiliar; her self-control shattered, and she howled. The door pushed open, and the dogs crowded in, their eyes full of concern. They were by her side constantly. At night, she had only to reach down to stroke a silken head lying beside her bed. During the daytime, she tried to be calm as she could see that Fiona was very distressed and trying, in her practical, loving way, to keep Bella focused on getting through each day by doing tasks around the farm.

When Howard arrived home, she felt his love and deep concern. She was touched that he didn't make judgmental statements about Eli as he set about helping her to try to accept the situation, at least until some more information might help them to understand.

Grief continued to hit her when she least expected it. The anger and hurt were physical feelings that left her feeling weak and breathless. The telephone became an instrument of torture when it rang. Will it be Eli? It must be him! It never was. He had gone.

Chapter Eleven

Iris Office August 1990

She looks up to see her friends watching her. Meg pours coffee. Bella takes a large gulp to shake off the memories.

'You know I accepted everything Eli told me. I never doubted anything about him.' Bella stops, thinking she's said all she can say. But then she continues, determined to finish her account. 'Over the next weeks, I realized he'd left me, never to return. That kind of pain is hard to heal. I think it would have been easier if he'd died.'

Scott puts his arm around her and draws her towards him. Bella feels the pleasure of his arms around her and leans into him. Scotty seems to be showing a different, softer side of himself today.

Meg says, 'Okay, the job's yours if you're up to it.'

Scott says, 'We should film the family interviews. I want to try out my new video camcorder; it's perfect for this work.'

Meg adds. 'The police are on board. They welcome any publicity about missing persons because it can trigger people's memories and bring in information.'

As they research the article, Bella and Scott are overwhelmed by the number of disappearances reported each year. The National Missing Persons Co-ordination centre becomes their main source of information and contacts.

Bella pins the photos of their subjects onto the corkboard, stands back and says to Meg and Scott, 'These four families agree to be interviewed for the story. Each has a family member who disappeared without warning and has never contacted family or friends.' She points to other photos grouped around each subject. 'Each of the missing people present a different challenge to understand the circumstances of their disappearance.' She turns back to Meg and Scott.

Over the next weeks, with every interview they do, Bella recognizes the families' emotions of grief, despair, loss, confusion, and anger that she understands so well. They all live with the terrible fear of death or misfortune, having befallen their loved one.

The assignment is a test of Bella's mettle. Scott's quiet strength keeps her going; without him, she isn't sure she would see it through. He seems to know when to be supportive and when to make her laugh, to take her out of herself. After two months of research and interviews, they travel to the scene of one disappearance, Perisher Valley in New South Wales.

Scott rolls the camera, Bella records her intro. 'Today in brilliant sunshine, I'm at Perisher Valley, one of Australia's most popular ski resorts. Mount Kosciusko dominates the skyline. As far as I can see, snow covers mountains and valleys. It looks like endless folds of white velvet.' She pauses, looks around and continues. 'This beauty can be dangerous. A plaque on this seat,' Bella turns to show the carved wooden seat, 'commemorates the life of a thirty-two-year-old skier named Simon Spencer who disappeared in a blizzard in 1987. We hope by retracing his steps that day, we might gain some insight into what happened to him.'

Scott cuts the camera, and Bella sits down on the seat. It is the work of an artisan with a love of nature's colours and shapes. Simon Spencer's family commissioned it. Bella thinks the seat is a metaphor for the families of the missing who wait for answers that might never come. Waiting for any answers to give them some peace. Is his family able to live in peace? Isabella wonders. She knows that she has never truly known peace since Eli left.

She remembers interviewing Simon Spencer's family; their distress is so much like her own. Their lifelong love of the mountains and skiing here at Perisher will be tinged with the memories of their loss forever. Snow always brings back memories of meeting Eli for the first time and how much they loved skiing together. Skiing always gives her the feeling that she'll turn at any minute and find Eli beside her. He skied with a lazy ease, so irritating to people who struggle to learn. She often feels a breath-squeezing rush—there he is! Thank God, there he is! But it's never him. It's always a shadow or a mischievous doppelganger bent on startling her.

Scott calls out. 'Bella! Stop daydreaming and come over here.'

Bella rises and poles her skis over to Scott.

He kneels on the snow. 'This is the T-Bar line that Simon Spencer took to the top that day. I'll get a low angle looking up the track through these rocks.'

'Great, I'll be behind you, so you won't slide backwards.'

When he's in position, she kneels to check his angle through the viewfinder. 'Perfect! Imagine what the narrow part up there with a sheer drop to one side, would have been like to ride during a full-on blizzard.'

'No thanks!' He stands up, 'I'll get some close-ups looking through the snow gums, and then, if we move over to the ridge there, we'll get a great wide shot.'

They move towards the edge of the bowl. Leaning forward to peer through the viewfinder, she can see the shot is a vast, un-tracked moonscape of mountain ridges. If Simon Spencer had ventured out there in a whiteout, he could have fallen and ended up in the dense forest below the snowline.

When she's sure Scott is safe, Bella steps out of her skis, sits on the seat, and eases off her boot buckles. Today, in the white brightness, it's hard to imagine the blizzard that spirited Simon Spencer away.

Bella looks at her notes. Why was he out here alone in that snowstorm? Why had he left the lodge without notifying anyone of his plans? He was an experienced skier; he must have known this was breaking mountain safety law.

Bella recalls the police interview transcript. The operator on the top station of this lift was the last to see him. He recalled telling Simon this would be the last ride for the day, given the wind strength and chill factor. Since then, not even an article of Simon's clothing or equipment has been found to give silent witness.

She makes a note to do another search through the records of interviews taken at the time. Had he left any unspoken clues for others to decipher? Has something been missed that has been hiding in plain sight?

These thoughts trigger her own memories of the incessant questions she'd asked herself after Eli's disappearance. She'd gone over and over everything time and time again. Had she missed something?

Elis's last words to her were, 'I'll see you in three weeks.' These words have haunted her ever since. Were they spoken in truth? Or were his words a lie to distract her from his real intentions? She has spent these years living as two people. To the outside world, she looks as she always did. Inside, Bella feels like a petrified forest. Like the snow gums that were burnt in a vast bushfire here at Perisher Valley. They stand naked, contemplating their past life when their abundant silver-grey leaves shimmered in the wind.

Bella knows that it would be different if Eli had left her a note or sent one on. She would have been able, despite the shock and the pain, to accept the parting and get on with her life. She shares this need for answers with everyone in the Missing Persons story. This dreadful yearning is like a constant gnawing sensation in the stomach.

If people who plan their disappearance could understand the effect on the people who love them, would they still do it? Is their need to disappear greater than knowing they will inflict pain on those they leave behind?

Scott finishes his shots, packs his gear, and skis over to where she sits, her mind still far away in time, he trips into her thoughts. 'Did wild Dingoes get him? he nods his head towards the vast wilderness, 'or is he in the south of France?'

'Do you mean Simon or Eli?'

'Either or both, come on, let's go.' He leans down to snap her boot buckles into place and helps her with her backpack. They ski down trails winding through the Snow Gums. The sun melts the ice coating the branches, shivering cracks free the tree's limbs, and fling ice shards into their path. Bella thinks about how the mountains reflect her life. One moment, the sky is clear and bright. Then, almost without warning, clouds and mist can roll in. She can have moments of insight, a feeling of being near to an answer, only to have it fade away to nothing.

Scott shouts, 'Bella, for heaven's sake, what's wrong with you today? You cut me off.' He makes a wide turn away from her.

'Sorry, Scottie, I'm seeing ghosts.' Bella calls out.

'We did try to warn you.' Scott tucks his skis in behind hers.

'I know. It seemed so clear then…I'll be okay.'

'Has anyone ever seen Eli?' Scott asks as they perform the acrobatics required to jump onto the moving T-Bar with their bulky packs.

'Nothing firm; he could be anywhere. I contacted some of his Israeli friends in Melbourne. No one had heard from him except one, Daniel, who told me he'd heard that Eli died and is buried in Haifa,' she replies.

'That must've been a shock.'

'It was.'

'Did you follow that up?'

'I tried to; I asked Daniel to see if he could find out more, but I didn't hear from him. Then, one day, I called, and his number was disconnected. He'd left his job too. So that was that. It's not as if we were very friendly. I went to the house, but the new tenants had no idea about them. I tried the real estate agent but drew a blank there too.'

'How long is it since Eli disappeared?' asks Scott.

'Five years. Long past time it should still affect me.' Her ski pole jabs into the snow of its own accord as she says these empty words. 'It's like living in a parallel universe.'

Scott turns to face her, he says. 'Bella, can you start to accept that, for whatever reason, he's chosen not to live in your universe?'

She looks up at him. His eyes are hidden by the dark lens of his goggles, but she can feel his gaze.

'I don't want you to keep living like this,' he says in a low voice as he turns away. They reach the top lift station and slide off the T-bar. Scott says.

53

'Time for a coffee run?'

As they push off, she says. 'Y' know Scotty, I've never changed the front door lock. If he is out there somewhere, he still has a key.' Bella often wishes she could escape the hold that Eli still has over her heart. She still feels that at any moment, he could open their front door and walk back into her life.

'Change it immediately,' Scotty advises with an unaccustomed touch of asperity in his voice as he skis off down the run.

Chapter Twelve

Melbourne September 1990

Howard Clemens takes the train from Yarra Glen to Flinders Street; he enjoys this quiet time to put his thoughts in order. He left London for this extended stay at home, planning to tie up a lot of loose ends. Like many expatriates, he feels a sense of divided identity and difficulty reconciling both halves of his life. At seventy-three, he is fit and mentally sharp. However, as his London medico points out to him, it might be time for him to plan for his next stage.

He's happy at home at Yarra Glen with his sister Fiona. The farm, the animals, and the vineyard all bring him back to his roots. Of course, being closer to Bella is another reason to settle down here. He's been thinking a lot about her; he's looking forward to having dinner with her this evening. He's immensely proud of his daughter, both as a person and her career.

After Eli disappeared, she was so lost, he was heartsick watching her struggle with her grief. He had arrived home at Yarra Glen shortly after the home invasion to find his daughter completely devastated and Fiona worried and confused by Eli's disappearance. Howard realized how much Fiona had come to value Eli as her friend and that she was grieving too.

At the time, Howard made his own enquiries with ASIO and shared with them what knowledge he had of Eli's history. An unforeseen and unwelcome consequence of this contact was that ASIO had invoked the National Security Act, which, in effect, prevented him from ever telling

Bella and Fiona anything he might know or find out about Eli. This caused him deep inner conflict as he watched his two loved ones struggle through the aftermath.

Sometimes in the night, he'll wake with a start and must take deep breaths to banish the ghosts of his past actions and their consequences. It's not only Eli; it's time now, time to tell her about her mother; Alexandra Monerayo-Clemens. He's put this off for too long; he justifies this by telling himself that he didn't want to cause Bella more upset after Eli disappeared.

At the time, unable to do anything to help his daughter, he knew from his own experience that work would help her through. Good sustaining, challenging work with a great team of people. Not the flim-flam stuff she'd been doing as a freelancer.

She's gone ahead since joining *Iris*. He'd hoped she would take up the offer from his old friend Lord Storm, but he kept right out of it, because he knew she wouldn't go along with anything that she thought had been set up via his 'old boys' network. Storm rose to the occasion, not that he needed much convincing, especially after his Melbourne Editor at *Iris*, Meg Petersen, met Bella.

Now, all Howard worries about is how long Bella's friend and workmate Scotty will wait in the wings for her until she deigns to notice him. He decides he'll broach this topic at dinner. Howard sometimes wonders whether the life he has led has fed his daughter's restlessness. He leaves the train to walk to his club to have a few drinks with old cronies until he meets Bella this evening. On the way, he decides to make a detour to see another love. This love predates even Alexandra and Bella.

Howard arrives at the entrance to Dyson's. The manager greets him, and after a brief chat, he walks through the showroom of classic cars towards a car at the rear. Gleaming red, long, and low-slung, she looks exactly like her namesake, the Jaguar. Even stationary, her attitude is one of an animal leaping upon its prey. He opens the door and lowers himself into the ribbed leather seat; he doesn't see her often enough these days; he loves this quiet time with her. At his age, so many friends are dead. It's a relief each time he comes to find her still here, as beautiful as the day he first met her. He anticipates every visit with the hunger of an impatient lover.

Reaching into the glove box, he removes a leather folder, opens it, and reads the service entries. He first fell in love with her in London, and knew that he had to make this beauty his own. Together, they'd crossed the channel on many sorties to Europe for business and pleasure. Stamps from the Jaguar service dealers dotted around Europe: Paris, Biarritz and Rome. Each one notes a milestone of time and place. Before the Spanish Civil War, he would drive through the night, crossing borders to find news to report.

Howard and Hemingway, old sparring partners, both competed and colluded to find stories; it didn't matter; they wrote for different news barons anyway. They worked together like a pair of stealthy wolves to track down their prey and get their stories on the wire before anyone else. The outbreak of World War Two stopped all that. He took this beauty to England for safekeeping.

He puts his head back; his thoughts drift to a meeting with another beauty. Alexandra had changed his life forever. Minutes pass, and his thoughts are far away at another time; the city noises fade beyond his hearing. His eyes close; he's back in the Rivoli Bar in the Ritz Hotel in London in July 1944. He was meeting his younger brother Tom and his friend David McKenzie for dinner. In those rationed times, The Ritz, still managed a decent meal and a glass or two of good Bordeaux.

At the outbreak of war, Tom was already in London reading for admission to the London Bar. He didn't go home to Australia to enlist, waste of time to sail home, and dangerous. He wanted to get into action as quickly as possible. Tom and David had enlisted in the RAF. They were on final leave that night, so time together was precious.

Howard was early for the rendezvous. He sat with a gin and tonic, people-watching. His never-ending fascination for this activity had plenty of scope in that crowded bar. The patrons were intent on having a good time. They pushed away any thoughts of the war outside the sandbagged walls and taped, shuttered windows. His gaze rested on a young woman sitting by herself across from him. Howard thought her profile is the most perfect that he had ever seen. She was beautifully dressed in a suit and hat that clearly hadn't been purchased with rationed clothing coupons. She exuded style, from her perfectly coiffed hair to shoes and a handbag that could only be the finest Italian creations.

Howard moved across to her. 'May I introduce myself? My name is Howard Clemens.'

'Normally no, as I am alone. But in the circumstances, yes.' She held out her hand. 'My name is Alexandra Monerayo.'

She piqued his interest on two counts. One, her accent, and two, in those days of wartime, this kind of formality was unusual.

'And what circumstances make my approach acceptable, Miss Monerayo?'

'My mother is about to arrive, and I'm sure you are not here to be alone either.'

'No, I am waiting for my brother and our friend to join me. Do you mind telling me where your accent comes from?'

'My mother is English; my late father was Spanish. I grew up in Barcelona, but I attended university at Cambridge.'

Howard offered her a cigarette and lit it for her. 'Did the outbreak of war prevent you from going home?'

'Do you always cut to the chase like this? I've heard that Australians are very direct. You are Australian, aren't you?'

'Yes, I'm from Melbourne; I'm a War Correspondent.'

'Yes; the war did prevent us returning to Spain.'

'Is it difficult to be separated from your family for so long?' Howard was fishing for information about this good-looking woman.

'No, my mother is enjoying indulging herself here. Barcelona society is very conservative. Is that your brother over there staring at us?'

Howard turned around. Tom and David were sitting at the table Howard had vacated to introduce himself to Alexandra; both men had large smirks on their faces. Clearly, they're enjoying watching him, in Tom's words, "chatting up a Sheila." Howard handed Alexandra a business card. 'I would like to be able to meet you again. Please will you call me? Do you have a card? I could call you. That would please your mother more, wouldn't it?'

'Yes.' says Alexandra, slipping a card into his palm as she rose. 'Here's mother.'

A middle-aged woman, also very well-dressed for wartime, looked Howard up and down. Alexandra says, 'Mr. Clemens, I would like you to meet my mother, Clara Monerayo. Mother, this is Howard Clemens; he is an Australian War Correspondent.'

Clara held out her hand. 'Are you joining us, Mr. Clemens?'

'Thank you, no, Senora Monerayo. I am meeting my brother and our friend.'

Howard joined Tom and David. He endured quite a lot of ribbing about 'Don't let the grass grow under your feet, do you?'

He fell quickly and hard for Alexandra. She had graduated from Cambridge and was looking for work. Her multi-lingual skills were ideally suited for the Ministry of Information, and Howard, with his contacts, secured her an interview. She was hired. Soon after, Clara and Alexandra were bombed out of their London home, so Howard offered them his spacious apartment in Florin Court. He was away so much that the place was most often empty. Whenever they managed time together there, Clara visited friends in the country. Wartime cut across the accepted courting rituals.

Alex was completely unlike any other woman Howard had met. She was willful, obstinate, and very passionate. It was that passion that blinded Howard to qualities in Alexandra that, given different times, he may have stood back and taken a good look at. He didn't. He adored her and proposed marriage.

Howard opens his eyes; he comes back to the present. As he has countless times before, he thrusts those images behind him. The awakening, the realization of how she had played him, made him dance to her tune, came later.

Since Alexandra's disappearance, he had through a confluence of circumstances, embarked on a life of secrets and evasions that had become second nature to him. He did this to protect his only child from knowing the truth about Alexandra. He'd told Bella that her mother had died, which was the reason for bringing her here to live with Fiona at Yarra Glen. A lie he had, out of shame, perpetuated in all the years since. He shakes his head and says in a low voice.

'Damn you, Alexandra. Damn you to hell!'

The terrible outfall of this was that he kept his life in London and his life in Australia separate. This visit home is to clear up the tangled mess he could leave behind him. It's time to bring the two halves of his life together. And Adeline, his colleague and dear companion. Had he the right all these years to keep her apart from his life here? Like a shaft of piercing light, Howard is confronted with the realization that he has been a selfish and cowardly person. He'll tell Bella some of it this evening, and then, tomorrow, when they are with Fiona at Yarra Glen, he'll tell them everything.

A thought comes to him: Eli. As part of this, possibly the hardest part, he will tell Bella whatever he can about Eli. Enough is enough. He'll face the consequences of breaching his security undertaking later. Maybe if he can give her any peace about Eli, she might start to look at Scotty differently.

Having made these decisions after keeping everything locked away for so long, he starts to feel a peacefulness he hasn't felt for forty years. He puts his head back onto the worn leather car seat. Without warning, an intense pain in his chest makes him gasp. As it worsens, he realises this is it. No coming back from this one. He tries to call out, but his voice is only a whisper. 'Dearest Bella, I'm so sorry. I wanted to make it right …'

Chapter Thirteen

Iris Magazine September 1990

Bella is pleased with her story on Simon Spencer's disappearance at Perisher Valley. It has enabled her to reflect more on her own experience with Eli. Interviewing the relatives and friends of missing people has made her aware she needs to move on. She's seen clearly how some people have allowed the disappearance of a loved one to define their life, freezing it at the point of loss. She knows now it's imperative that she follows the example of other interviewees who have been able to build a life that encompasses their pain and puzzlement while allowing them to start again.

She's thinking how pleased Howard will be to hear this at dinner tonight, given his ongoing counsel to open herself up to the future when Scott puts his head around the door. Her face lights up, and she beckons him in, asking, 'What've you got to show me?'

She gasps as Scott lays out a series of stunning photos from their Perisher trip. Vast, trackless peaks and valleys stretch to an infinity horizon. His photos of snowscapes, crags, and boulders evoke a Lunar landscape.

'Superb Scotty,' she moves next to him and puts her arm around him in a small hug. 'Thank you so much, these pics are perfect.'

Pleased with her reaction, he kisses her lightly on the cheek; he asks her to help him narrow down the shots to the best ones for her story. Chatting away, they choose the images that will work best and pin them on the corkboard, moving them around to form a montage and discussing the captions. Time flies by as heads together; they finetune the interaction between words and images.

'I'm still wondering whether Simon Spencer chose to go missing,' says Bella, picking up a photo of him. 'He has such a friendly, open smile that it's hard to believe he was hiding something. And the laughter lines at the corners of his eyes show someone who was usually happy and joyful.' She puts the photos down and picks up one of Simon in a group of friends. 'His family had owned the lodge he was staying at since he was a child. He grew up on that mountain. I can't imagine him getting lost there.'

Scott checks their notes. 'That photo is the one taken at a party not long before their trip, isn't it?'

Bella nods. 'Yes, and everyone there agreed he was in good spirits and was looking forward to the week skiing.'

They keep working, attaching transcript cards of relevant conversations, moving them around to find a progression, a sequence.

'I wonder if he injured himself skiing and died of exposure, then wild animals took his body?'

'Yes, but the lift operator told him it was 'last ride' due to the weather. He saw Simon turn right off the T-bar, onto the home trail towards the Front Valley. Simon was the last passenger. The operator stopped the lift, stepped into his skis, and followed him only a couple of minutes later.'

Scott taps the enlarged map of the Front Valley ski trails. 'Did the lift guy actually see him ski all the way down Front Valley?'

'No, he said the fog swallowed Simon somewhere near here.' Bella circles the area on the Perisher map.

'Could he have taken another lift up and gone over the back?' asks Scott.

'No, the higher lifts had already closed. The only way he could have got any higher was by walking up the hill. Also, the ski patrol swept the slopes from top to bottom as the lifts closed to move on any slow skiers.'

They move across to the next map, showing the higher slopes and the access trail to the Guthega area. Following the trail with her pencil, Bella says, 'It's a huge climb from where he was last seen to here. It'd be almost impossible to traverse in bad weather with little visibility.'

'Why would you do that anyway,' says Scott, who disliked trudging up hills on his skis.

'Beats me. The only reason could be that someone was waiting for him at Guthega,' says Bella, pointing to the Guthega ski area.

'Did the police follow that up?' asks Scott.

'The road to Guthega was closed due to snowfall at 3:00 pm that day. The timing for him to get from where he was last seen to Guthega, just doesn't fit.'

Scott nods. 'That leaves the only possibility that Simon left by the Ski Train to Bullock's Flat before the police were alerted.'

'The Ranger found his car was still at Bullock's,' Bella mused. 'Of course, he could've been picked up and away from there before anyone missed him.'

'If that's so, he had some hours head start. Every avenue, including this, was covered in these police reports.' Scott picks up the transcript copy and leafs through the pages. 'If he did, that puts his disappearance into a well-planned operation. So, what are you thinking?' he asks.

'These stories are for the ones left behind. The survivors. God knows that "survivor" is not the right word. I can tell you; one doesn't "survive" this kind of experience at all.' Bella thinks before she continues. 'We can't provide any answers, and it would be wrong to make wild guesses. We can only hope that whatever we write has some key to an answer for these people. Something that might open their minds to a possibility that hadn't occurred to them.'

'Yes,' agrees Scott, 'we can't speak for the missing. Unless they return to speak for themselves.'

'Also, I want to write about how important it is to move on.'

Scott looks up, surprised. It's the first time he's heard Bella say this. In the past, she has said she'd never let anyone close enough to hurt her again. Maybe there's hope for him after all.

Outside the window, the light is changing as a storm blows up the bay en route to the distant hills fringing the city. This matches how Bella feels inside. She lives with the conflict of her outer world and her inner world, trying to function as a normal person. Her inner world is still suffering the pain of the unexplained. Also, the pain of rejection in such a brutal way. Bella believes she shares this with the interviewees. The feeling that Eli didn't value her enough to tell her he was leaving, leaves her crushed. How else could he leave her without a word?

As they delve deeper into the final shape of the story, Bella glances at her watch and stands up. 'I've got to go; I'll be late for dinner with Dad.' Her office phone rings as she picks up her jacket and bag. She's so late she's torn about answering it. She picks up and listens; her face pales. She picks up a pen, writes out an address, and then says, 'I'll come immediately.' Her face stricken and unsteady on her feet, Scott moves to her.

'Bella?'

'Howard has had a heart attack!'

'Oh, Bella! Scott picks up his keys, 'let's go.' He puts his arm around her as they leave.

They arrive at the address. It's Dyson's, a well-known classic car business, but why is Howard here? Bella can't stop to wonder about that right now.

Robert, the manager, introduces himself. As he leads them towards the rear of the premises, he says, 'I came to see if Howard wanted to take the car out and could see something was terribly wrong.'

As soon as they see Howard sitting in the driver's seat of a red Jaguar, Bella realises he's dead. Along with the intense shock that hits her, a lightning sliver of memory flashes before her. *She remembers her father driving this car, wind rushing through her hair as she nestles into a woman wearing a fur coat. A little girl's voice cries, 'Faster, Daddy, faster!'* Within seconds, the image fades, and grief takes over. She turns to Robert; he's saying something to her, but she can only see his lips moving.

'I rang the medical clinic next door. The doctor came straight away, but it was too late for CPR. Howard wasn't breathing. I'm so sorry.' He handed Bella a wallet. 'I hope you understand. I had to find a contact number for you.'

Numb, Bella calls Fiona; the sound of her beloved aunt's voice unleashes Bella's tears as she tells Fiona the shocking news.

'Bella, where are you? I'll drive in immediately.'

'No, Fiona! Please don't try to drive.' She listens to her distressed aunt as she tries to find a handkerchief. 'Yes, Dad's here in town. He's sitting in an old Jaguar in a classic cars showroom!'

'An old Jaguar? How can that …?' Fiona stops herself and then asks. 'Has a doctor been called?'

'Yes, Doctor Franck is here. He's arranging to move Dad. I'll speak to him as soon as you promise me that you won't leave home. I'll come to you. Okay?'

'As long as you don't drive either! Will you ask Scotty to pick you up, please?'

'He's here with me. We'll let you know when we're leaving.' Bella hangs up and turns to find Robert.

She returns to the car to sit with her father. She's touched to see Scotty has pulled up a chair and is sitting close to Howard as if they were continuing one of their conversations. She slides into the passenger seat and takes Howard's hand. He looks so peaceful, which comforts her.

Bella asks Robert, 'Why is my father sitting in this car?'

'Howard was an old friend of my father, Jack Dyson. When your father was home, they often took the car out for a spin.' Robert smiles, remembering the two setting off as if they were young bucks going to a party. 'Jack died five years ago; it was always a pleasure for me when your father visited and told me about their younger days. He had an enormous attachment to this car.'

'It's in beautiful condition. How old is it?' asks Scott.'

'It's an original Jaguar SS100, built in 1936.' Says Robert. Then, after a moment's silence, Robert adds gently. 'I think you may find some answers in the service book on your father's lap.'

Bella nods her thanks and leans across to pick up the book. On the first page, the dealer stamp says, 'Bartram's of Piccadilly' and gives the purchase date as the 7th of August 1936. The owner's name is Howard Clemens.

'Oh Dad, what's this all about?'

The service book shows maintenance performed in London and Europe from 1936 to 1946. From 1947, all the entries are here, at Dyson's. Bella places her head on her father's shoulder as tears run down her cheeks. *She has another flash of memory of being in this car. This time, she can see the woman. Her hair was dark and framed a beautiful, rather exotic face.*

Her father lifted her high up in his leather-clad arms; he lowered her over the side of the car onto the whispering silk of the woman's dress. He smiled at her; his eyes were laughing. She loved touching his hair that sat flat on his head in waves like the sea... Most of all, she liked the smells. His hair, his skin, and clothes.

Now, sitting so close to her father, she can smell his Pinaud hair tonic, still the same as she remembers from so long ago. Bella closes her eyes and allows herself to drift backwards in time.

She nestled into the woman's lap; fur-clad arms held her. Bella traced the shape of the black spots and rings on the animal's pelt with her small finger. Wind ruffled her hair, as they travelled at great speed in the fast, growling car. She heard laughter and smelt perfume. Her little girl's voice cried, "Faster, Daddy, faster!"

Bella sits up. 'Scott, this car. I remember this car...and my mother, the woman who was in it with Dad and me, she must've been my mother!'

Scott reaches over to take her hand. 'Just sit with your memories. Close your eyes.

The images flicker into her mind's eye. *Then Mother wasn't there anymore. Life darkened as if someone has turned out the sun. No more rides in the fast, red car with her mother and father laughing. Instead, Bella's little life was placed in the care of nanny Brown. Life became very ordered. After a time, Bella and her father travelled by ship for many weeks to a place called Australia. Bella still has* a penchant for whispering silk dresses, fur coats, and fast red sports cars.

'Oh Scott, this is the first time I've ever remembered my mother like this. I've never seen her before.'

'Bella,' Scott says gently, 'you've had a huge shock, and finding Howard here in this car is sure to have triggered something.'

'I need to find out more about her.' She looks at her father and says, 'I've always wondered why he wouldn't talk about her.'

She kisses her father on his cheek and tucks the owner's manual and her father's wallet into her handbag. Scott puts his arms around her as they sit together and wait for Howard to be moved before they leave for Yarra Glen.

Chapter Fourteen

Yarra Glen Victoria September 1990

It's difficult for Fiona and Bella to say farewell to Howard in a way that does him justice. He always told Bella that his experience as a war correspondent meant he'd seen too many people fighting each other in the name of the same God to have any belief in organized religion. He'd often said, "God and I have come to an arrangement—I don't interfere in His business if He doesn't interfere in mine."

They receive countless phone calls and letters of condolence, and numerous enquiries about the funeral arrangements. Bella's childhood friend Jane O'Connell at Yeringa Farm comes to their rescue, offering to host the funeral. Bella is touched by her friend's kindness. The O'Connell and Clemens families have been friends and neighbors for generations. Nowadays, the old home is a beautiful boutique hotel and winery. Bella and Fiona opt for the more casual cellar door area at the vineyard.

Howard's funeral is on a crisp afternoon. A cold snap has frosted a dusting of late snow on the peaks of the surrounding, blue-tinged mountains of the Yarra Ranges providing a stunning backdrop to the vineyards and, the barely budding trees lining the fences. Late morning, Scott drives Fiona, Bella and Meg over to Yeringa and helps them set out seats in the large barn overlooking the vines and the ornamental lake. As they're laying out cups and glasses, Meg looks out the window to the drive; a taxi pulls up. 'Bella, someone is here early.'

Bella comes to the window, and they watch as a tall, silver-haired man dressed in an impeccable grey suit, alights.

'Goodness,' Meg says. 'It's Storm!'

'Did you know he was coming?' Bella asks.

'No,' Meg replies. 'Scott, where are you? Storm has arrived.'

Outside, the two women hug Storm and plant a kiss on his cheek.

'Steady now, ladies, what's all this for then?' Despite his words, he looks pleased as he reaches out to shake Scott's hand.

Scott says. 'Why didn't you tell us you were coming? We could've met you at the airport?'

'No need, thanks, Scott. With good flight connections, I could get here today and then go on to Sydney for a meeting tomorrow. It's all worked out rather well.'

'Certainly has,' says Bella. She feels an ache of sadness and tears feel close. 'Come inside and meet Fiona.'

Storm puts his arms around Fiona, and the two share a quiet moment. 'Oh Fiona, you must be so sad. Now that I see you, it's like seeing Howard again.'

'Well, we are twins.' Fiona smiles through some errant tears she hasn't managed to restrain. 'Scotty, please will you take Storm's coat, I'm going to make him a cup of tea. Or perhaps something stronger?'

Storm nods, 'something stronger please.'

When they're sitting down, Bella says, 'Storm, I know this is a big ask without notice, but do you think you could say a few words? There's no one here who has any connection with Dad's life outside Australia.'

Storm draws some paper out of his pocket. 'I thought you might ask, so I came prepared. There's nothing like a thirty-six-hour plane flight to focus the mind.'

Bella feels touched that Storm has thought of this, even more so that he has made the effort to be here. She doesn't know him other than as a boss. She likes and respects the way he runs the company and cares for his staff. But he seems to be today, exactly the right person to be here as a friend, for

Fiona and for her. 'Thank you, Storm. I'm so grateful, and I look forward to it.'

'Me too,' smiles Fiona.

'Great,' says Scott as he pours Storm another stiff scotch.

The day is wonderful in every detail. The choice of venue is perfect; a kilted Scottish piper plays on the terrace as the guests arrive. Inside, a large open fire warms the space, and the room is lit by hand-crafted iron chandeliers, which give the old hand-made brick and timber interior a glowing patina of warmth and welcome. Champagne flows, and delicious canapes are served. Laughter and clinking glasses give the day a real party atmosphere. 'After all,' Scott says to Bella, 'we are celebrating Howard's life.' She thinks that even Howard, who deplored any "fuss," would be very happy with this send-off.

Speeches are short and pithy. Each one captures the essence of the multi-faceted personality of Howard Clemens. A school friend spoke about Howard's prowess and cunning in chess tournaments and always cleaning up the writing prizes so that no one else ever got a look in. As would be expected, a journalist friend spoke about Howard's ability to consume red wine at the traditional long lunch and still manage to return to the office and deliver a brilliant piece of copy by deadline.

Storm's speech shifts the tone away from the vaguely "student roast" style of the earlier speakers. Bella observes this man who plays an important part in her life. He certainly has presence. Charismatic is a good description of him; the room is completely silent as he speaks. Bella marvels at how much he knows about Howard's life. Like the earlier speakers' anecdotes, she is hearing about the father she had known and loved all her life but in truth, had known so little about him.

Storm concludes: 'Howard Clemens was a rare being. Despite all his years as a roving correspondent in many dangerous locations and devastating human situations, he never became cynical or battle-hardened. He had an unusual understanding of those whom we might judge or perceive as our enemies. He had an uncanny ability to see both sides of any situation and to get to the heart of the matter. And to communicate his findings to us in clear language and beautifully written articles.'

The piper pipes Howard down the long drive. As the hearse turns into the main road, the keening sound of the old Scottish lament brings long-delayed tears to her eyes. After the guests have returned to the warmth, Bella and Scott stand in the driveway; damp cold settles on her shoulders, moist drops shine on her dark jacket. She still can't grasp how Howard, who had filled the corners of her life for all her life, in a heartbeat is gone. Eli had also filled the corners of her life; he has gone too. She's touched by Scott's quiet presence. He puts an arm around her shoulder and draws her closer. She leans into his warmth. then they turn to join the crowd of people inside.

A fiddler plays some Scottish reels and folk songs that make them all want to sing and dance. Feet are tapping everywhere. Someone forms the crowd into an old-fashioned barn dance; Bella, Scott, and Fiona are whirled into the circle, and away they go. The tireless fiddler keeps playing tune after tune. Fiona and Bella take a break to make sure they speak to Howard's eclectic mix of friends. Dressed in a dark suit and winter coat, one man stands out amongst the colorful characters from Howard's life. Bella wants to speak to him, but before she has a chance to do so, he disappears.

Meg and Scott drive Fiona and Bella home. They share a light meal and recount snippets of news about Howard gathered from people they spoke to.

Remembering the strange man at the funeral, Bella asks, 'Did anyone talk to that man who left early?'

They all shake their heads. Meg says, 'He looked like a banker or solicitor to me.'

'Not our solicitor,' says Bella. 'I saw Jock dancing a jig with Mary from next door.'

'Howard would've loved all that; it wasn't like a funeral at all,' says Fiona, wiping away tears.

'I did see Storm talking to him,' Scott chimes in.

'I'll ask Storm when I get to talk to him.' Meg gathers up the plates.

The moment passes, and they forget about the man.

After Meg and Scott leave, Fiona and Bella take Max and Mischa for a walk. Bella sniffs the crisp air perfumed with the musky aroma of wood smoke. The last rays of sun are sliding off the hills into the shadowed valley. The dogs seem to sense their mood and walk beside the two women instead of their normal dash from side to side of the avenue, hunting rabbits.

'I'm surprised at how many people came today. I was so grateful for Scott's help. He seemed to sort people to introduce to me, as well as our working dogs.' Even today, Fiona's sense of humour doesn't desert her.

'I'm not sure that Scott would like to be classed as a good working dog, but I know what you mean. Wasn't he marvellous?'

They walk along the rows of vines. Fiona breaks the silence, asking Bella. 'Have you ever thought of making a relationship with Scott?'

Bella pauses, then replies. 'He's never really given me the impression he'd like our relationship to be any different. We're friends and workmates. That's it.'

'For goodness sake, do you really believe that?' asks Fiona, incredulous. 'If you do, you've got more of your father's pigheadedness in you than I thought.'

'I like it the way that it is.' Bella's face reflects the straight-mouthed look her father could adopt.

Fiona recognizes the look; she pushes on anyway. 'How would you feel if he met someone else?'

Surprised, Bella looks up; this's an unfair shaft from Fiona. 'That's a bit rough! Putting me on the spot like this.'

'Well, Bella, if I don't, who will?'

Bella thinks for a minute, and then, with a passion in her voice that surprises her, she says. 'The short answer is, Aunty dear, I wouldn't like it.'

'I thought so. You should do something about it.'

'I still miss Eli; you must know that.'

'I know, dear girl, but time is marching on. Eli hasn't let you know what happened to him, and you aren't getting any younger.'

'So, this is all about getting some little feet pattering around here, is it?'

'Well… partly, but it's more about you getting on with your life and finding happiness again.'

'Fiona, you're incorrigible. Get Max and Mischa to make another litter of pups to keep you happy.'

'That's not the same thing at all.' Fiona replies.

Inside, with the curtains drawn and the fire stoked, Bella asks. 'I know we've talked over the years about my mother, but we never seem to get anywhere. What do we know about her? I only know her name was Alexandra Monerayo. I remember I had a tough time getting Howard to tell me that until I wanted to get my Australian passport. He had to send me a copy of my birth certificate.'

Silence. The clock ticks, the fire crackles. Flickering firelight bounces off the crystal brandy decanter on the silver tray refracting rainbow glints.

'All I know is that Howard married your mother in London during the war. I received a card months after the wedding. Haven't you seen it, Bella?'

'No, I don't think so. I'm sure I'd remember that.' Bella replies.

'I'll look for it. It didn't say much; for someone who wrote volumes for his work, your father didn't say much about his own wedding!' Fiona pauses, Bella waits.

'After he brought you here, I did try to talk to him, but he wouldn't talk about her. I guess I gave up, and life continued,' Fiona smiles, 'after all, we had you here with us, and that was more than enough. With Tom dead and your father living overseas, your grandparents and I thought we'd never see grandchildren here.'

'Fiona, did you mind inheriting a child that you would have almost sole responsibility for?'

'You brought us such joy. I still remember you arriving. A little tot dressed in an English coat with a velvet collar and patent leather shoes. You had on a beautiful, blue-smocked Liberty print dress and looked like something out of a magazine. Heaven knows where those clothes came from with post-war shortages in England. We certainly didn't have such gorgeous children's clothes here then.'

'But Fiona, what about your own life?'

'Oh Bella, I was over thirty! In those days, that was considered properly on the shelf. Mostly by my own doing. I didn't want to marry. Back then, it wasn't acceptable for single women to have children, so a ready-made child was a true blessing.' Fiona laughs, 'I admit that at first, we thought that Howard had only brought you for a visit. It was a double joy for us to find out he wanted to leave you here with us.'

'What was I like?'

'You were so quiet. I remember your huge eyes following everyone and everything. But you didn't speak.' Fiona recounts that when Bella finally did, she had a very proper English accent and was very polite. They were absolutely charmed, but when they asked some neighborhood children to a tea party, they were quite shocked that Bella didn't seem to know how to play with other children.

'Howard admitted that most of the time, you had been looked after by a nanny and that your mother believed children should be seen and not heard. He said he travelled so much for his work that his wife had been lonely, so she spent a lot of time out of the house and away from her child. Thus, the nanny.' Fiona laughs, 'It didn't last long. Soon you were running around in little corduroy overalls and knitted jumpers your grandmother made, and gumboots. The little English doll child disappeared very quickly!'

'Oh Fiona, I couldn't have had a better mother than you. Tell me again about when he arrived with me, please. Something else might pop into your memory.'

Fiona sighs. 'He was my brother. I loved him, but it was strange the way he arrived back here with you. We received a cable from the ship to say he would be disembarking in Melbourne in five days. And bringing you!' Fiona laughed. 'Not a word about Alexandra. We were completely mystified.' She relates how they had all busied themselves making a suitable bedroom for their small visitor.

'Howard's news that Alexandra had died in an accident was such a shock. I remember thinking how awful to have endured that frightful war, then to find happiness, marry, and have a baby only to be knocked down by a lorry. It was such a tragedy.' She shakes her head, remembering. 'He said he couldn't send you to Alexandra's family, and he was always traveling on business in Europe or Africa. And he wanted you to grow up here. Of course, we didn't mind. It was easy to agree to keep you. As I said, you were a gift to us.'

'How did he seem? Was he terribly sad?'

'Y'know Bella, that struck me at the time. He was quite calm and recounted about Alexandra's death in a very matter-of-fact manner. Almost like he was reporting it for a newspaper.'

'How odd,' says Bella. 'But then, knowing Howard and our family's tendency not to show any emotion, Why should we be surprised?'

The two women sit quietly gazing into the firelight. Bella breaks the silence.

'You know when I saw dad in that Jaguar, I had a flash of memory from my childhood,' says Bella. 'I'm sure I remember driving in it with him and my mother when I was little,' she pauses, 'I used to have dreams about being in a car with my father, or I thought they were dreams.'

'That would be right. I'm really surprised about the car. Howard bought it new in London before the war.' says Fiona. 'He shipped it out here when he came home with you. I remember asking him why he'd brought it all the way back but never drove it. He said, "Too many memories." It disappeared and I assumed he had sold it.'

Like a curtain blowing in the wind revealing an inner room, another memory comes to Bella. 'Fiona! What about the apartment in London? Was that Dad's apartment? Did he ever say he'd sold that? I can remember being there.' Bella stands up and moves to the fire. She stirs the embers and adds another log before she turns to Fiona. 'I remember the big rooms with tall windows that looked out over a large garden square. There was an older woman too. Who was she? I've never thought of that place again. I can remember that the two women left, but nothing else. Then, the nanny cared for me. She was serious and starchy; her clothes crackled. Why didn't I ever ask him about those women?'

Fiona thinks for a minute. 'I don't know if he still owned that apartment. Howard used his club as his mailing address for years. I forgot about the apartment and assumed he'd sold it.'

'He was always staying at the club whenever I met him in London. I stayed there too. I loved it, such a quaint, old-fashioned place.' She laughs, remembering the cavernous dining room with starched, white tablecloths and a vast array of silver cutlery for her to navigate. 'He travelled so much that I thought it suited him perfectly.' Bella could feel her throat closing. At last, she feels she can cry, like a true Clemens; she hasn't allowed herself this simple emotion. Fiona sits next to her and puts her arm around her. They sit in their own thoughts for a while.

'It's frustrating that dad wouldn't talk about my mother,' says Bella, pacing up and down in front of the fire. Agitation and tiredness are making her thoughts difficult to organize.

'He must have had his reasons,' says Fiona. 'He only told our parents the bare minimum too.'

Bella tops up their brandy glasses. Her father's death has opened some closed doors in her heart and, her memory. 'I've always felt that my mother abandoned me. Why would I feel that? And now, I'm angry with him. He's left me with too many questions.'

'I think that's a fairly normal part of grief,' says Fiona.

'This keeps coming up in our Missing Persons interviews. Everyone expects you to get on with life. How can you? You feel as if you were not worth anything to the person who abandoned you without any explanation.'

Fiona tells Bella. 'I felt abandoned when Tom didn't come home. I was angry. I felt that everything about "right being on our side" in that war, was meaningless propaganda. Our parents never moved from their belief that Tom had died a hero fighting for King and Country. A hero! For Christ's sake! Who wanted a dead hero for a brother? I wanted him here at home. I spent years angry at the waste of his life.'

Now, it's Bella's turn to put her arms around Fiona. She'd never heard Fiona say anything like this. There it is again: this worn-out family idea that emotions and feelings are best kept to oneself. Never exposed or shared!

'I guess Grandpa and Grandma had to believe that. Accepting Tom's death would be worse if they didn't believe in the cause.' Bella smiles, remembering her aunt used to take her to the anti-conscription marches in Melbourne during the Vietnam War.

'Fiona, how did your views sit with Howard? After all, war reporting has been his core activity since Spain and World War Two'

Fiona laughs. 'I never told him. When he came home, there was always so much happening around here. Today, we would say, "It was all about him." Then, of course, he was like a visiting prince.'

They smile, remembering how his visits would disrupt the pace of their lives. They loved him and looked forward to his arrival. Howard's energy was palpable and swept everyone along with him. They sit in silence, enjoying the rich flavour of his best Courvoisier.

Bella smiles. 'It was like a royal visit when he came home.'

'Remember those dinner parties?' Fiona shakes her head. 'They often went all night, and then, we cooked breakfast!'

Bella replies, 'I remember the arguments and table thumping got louder with the red wine and port. No one, least of all Howard, ever wanted to concede a point so everyone could go to bed.'

Fiona says, 'I always felt a guilty sense of relief, a return to normality, when Howard left.'

Bella laughs. 'Me too.'

Fiona continues, 'We'll have to look for his will. It would be much better to do it together.' Fiona rises from her chair. 'Do you mind if I turn in? It's been a big day.'

Bella helps her upstairs; Fiona has coped with the funeral today with her usual warmth and dignity. As they kiss goodnight, Fiona says.

'Howard wanted you to settle down with Scott.'

'So, you two talked about it, did you?'

'Oh yes, from time to time.' Fiona smiles at Bella as she closes the bedroom door.

Downstairs, Bella pours herself another drink and stares at the fire. She takes her father's wallet from her handbag she looks through the contents. Not much. Howard wasn't one for credit cards; he preferred the flourish of the traveler's cheque. In a back section, she can feel something. She draws out two small black-and-white photos. She switches on the desk lamp and picks up Howard's magnifier. Bella feels her heart twist; in the foreground is the Jaguar. Leaning against it is a beautiful woman in a fur coat. In her arms a small girl.

The background shows this photo was taken in London on the Thames River embankment. The Houses of Parliament are opposite. The other is the same young woman standing on a balcony wearing a summer frock and a wide-brimmed hat. This is no ordinary balcony; the stonework is sculptured in a most unusual manner. The scene is familiar but so unexpected. Bella knows she has visited this place, but where and when?

'Dad, why couldn't you tell me about my mother?' All her life, she has believed she has had strange dreams. In fact, they weren't dreams; she was remembering her mother. A brush of sadness paints another layer over the unfamiliar canvas Bella's life has become since Howard's death.

Chapter Fifteen

Yarra Glen

Bella loves Howard's study; nothing has changed since she was a child. Tall bookshelves line the walls. The deep Chesterfield sofa and creaking leather armchairs give her the feeling they could tell their own stories about Howard and his visitors. Piles of books and magazines wait on a low table.

Long windows and French doors facing east, north, and west give this room year-round light. Outside, the terrace looks towards the blue-green mountains of the Yarra Ranges. In summer, Wisteria tumbles over the pergola.

On the desk, Howard's Empire portable typewriter sits, waiting for him to return and clatter out another story. He'd carried that to every assignment from World War Two until this last trip home. Howard wasn't one for replacing good, reliable machines with something new. Bella finds its travelworn case and locks it up. Oh, how final that feels.

In winter, when there wasn't much to do on the farm, Howard would light the fire, he'd stretch out on the sofa and plow through the pile of reading he'd selected. Those days are Bella's best memories with her father; she'd take her schoolwork and sit at his desk. Howard played records on his stereo; he taught her to appreciate all types of music.

On the drinks trolley, nestled amongst Howard's single malt Scotch whiskeys, is his favourite Arak. His Israeli friend and colleague Ariel

Achmed had introduced Howard to this potent brandy. If she unscrews the cap, she knows the pungent aniseed aroma will make her eyes water. Ariel visited Yarra Glen a few times; she remembers him well. She makes a note to write to him; there are many letters to write to people all over the world.

Howard always included Bella in conversations with his guests. As the exchanges grew livelier, she would refill their glasses from this trolley and open the windows as the room filled with cigar smoke. Those visitors had nurtured her curiosity. They'd included her as if she was one of them, asked her questions, and drawn her out of her teenage self. They listened to her answers and gave her a real sense of being able to express herself, to use her voice, and to be able to hold her own in many situations.

Bella feels privileged to have enjoyed this informal but essential part of her education; her career path started right here in this room. Those times formed her interest in journalism. She hasn't entirely followed her father's footsteps; her convictions and ambitions are her own. He had allowed her to run her own race. He never influenced or interfered.

She looks back over the past years at *Iris*, working with Meg and Scott, and understands that without this job, she'd still be working the often-isolated life of a freelancer. She wonders how she would've survived. When she took the job at *Iris,* she was still grieving deeply for Eli. Bella realises that although she needs to know the answer to Eli's disappearance, with the help of a job she loves, she has pulled her life together.

She thinks about Scotty and, for a minute, allows herself to think about him as someone more than a workmate. Bella realises that she does enjoy, and even looks for chances to feel Scotty's warmth near her. This feeling has grown on her and confuses her a little. Where has it come from? Why now? Does Scott feel the same? What, if anything can she, should she do about this?

Bella stokes the fire; she adds enough wood to keep the room warm for the afternoon. Fiona will be home soon to start their work finding Howard's will and sorting through his files. She places the fire screen on the hearth and goes to the kitchen and, whilst waiting for the kettle to boil, she looks out on the old kitchen garden. It's still essentially the same as it was planted by her great-grandmother. She makes her tea and goes outside into the bright chill of the early spring day.

On one side, the vegetable garden, with its raised box beds, is enclosed by mesh to keep away the ever-present rabbits. Fiona's beloved Orpington chickens live in their own secure fox-proof run within this enclosure. The hens, with their luxuriant red-brown plumage, are guarded by a fierce rooster who takes his duties seriously. They run to the fence and cackle a greeting. Bella walks around the rest of the open space. It is a sea of Fiona's spring bulbs blooming in profusion. Glenclova and Avalon daffodils, Paper White Jonquils, and clumps of cheerful Ixia are everywhere. Purple, blue, and white Iris announce their superiority by waving their tall, queenly blooms above the other plants. Unconstrained by garden beds, every year, they appear in the lawns, under trees, and in clumps anywhere they find to push their heads above the ground. During the flowering season, Fiona doesn't mow the grass, so the back garden resembles a multi-coloured carpet.

Tall trees form a windbreak on two sides of this tranquil place. A cold wind is causing the treetops to sway and sigh. Bella pulls her cardigan close and, holding her teacup to keep her hands warm; she walks down to the fence that divides the garden from the paddocks. At the fence line, she can see their herd of Hereford cattle. She loves these red-brown and white creatures with their beautiful faces.

She thinks about her father and how much she'll miss him. Howard never remarried despite many opportunities. He combined his love of travel and writing until his death. Howard always said he wasn't cut out for retirement, but then, this visit home, he was talking about the possibility of working less and spending more time here.

At the fence, her chestnut mare, Lotte, welcomes her with a whicker. Fiona's white Stock Horse, Luna, puts her head up and trots over, too. Lotte nudges Bella's shoulder. She is reminding Bella that a lump of sugar or a carrot is expected. Struan, Howard's big roan gelding, follows. At seventeen hands, he's a large horse and needs a strong rider. She'll talk to Fiona about whether they should find a new home for him, but Bella can't bear to think about that. It was bad enough when, after Eli had been gone for a year, his beautiful grey, Balthazar died. At the time, Bella wondered whether the horse was grieving for Eli as she was.

In her own grief at Eli's disappearance. Bella hadn't fully understood that Fiona might also be grieving for the loss of a friend and helpmate. Fiona's sadness when Balthazar died was so deep that it went beyond her normal love for the farm animals. Bella realized Eli had filled an empty place in Fiona's life and, with Balthazar's death, like herself, Fiona had lost another connection with Eli. Some weeks after, when Bella was saddling up Lotte, she saw that Balthazar's saddle and bridle were no longer in their place in the tack room. Neither was Eli's Drizabone or his Akubra hat hanging in the mud room at the back door. Fiona had bought them for him one Christmas. Bella remembers Eli's delight at receiving these quintessentially Australian items. He and Fiona had laughed and hugged each other. Bella understood these gifts were Fiona's way of saying. "You are part of our family. This is your Australian life. You belong here."

When Bella tentatively mentioned the saddle and Eli's coat and hat to Fiona, in true Clemens style, Fiona's only comment was.

'Bella, I've come to realise that Eli came from a different world. Something called him back to that world. We mightn't ever find out what happened.'

At the time, Bella had been too consumed by this fresh loss to really think about her aunt's words.

She knows Eli loved it here much more than the city. Howard and Eli went about the property on horseback, with the dogs following them. They became friends despite the differences in age, and backgrounds. After Eli disappeared, Bella would look out expecting to see them riding in the vineyard. They were both laconic men; neither of them ever wore their private thoughts and feelings on the outside. Bella remembers asking both Howard and Eli, on separate occasions, what they found to talk about? They both replied, "world affairs." Subject closed. Neither man was good for close questioning, so she never thought anything more of their relationship. She was relieved that Howard finally approved of her man. Now, with hindsight,

Bella wonders if her father and Eli had any relationship other than what she saw. She can't explain why she thinks this, but she now sees so many scenes from the past when her father and Eli seemed to be deep in conversations that they would stop when she approached them. Why would that be?

The wind coming off the snow-capped hills drives her back to the warmth of Howard's study. Sitting here today, Bella realises she has never asked herself what Eli may have felt. Had she failed him in some way? Was he looking for something more than Bella could give him? Bella thought that their relationship was complete, and they were happy. She reflects on her current assignment. Some of the partners of the missing tell her they believed they had happy, stable relationships. This experience has made her question how well we can know anyone. Especially people like Eli, who'd arrived in her life out of a blizzard.

Fiona comes into the study, peeling off an ancient plaid coat, red mohair scarf, and matching hat. Fiona also adheres to the Clemens family criteria: never replace any item that still has any wear in it. Time for Bella to stop all this musing; she smiles as she looks at her aunt. Outwardly, Fiona looks her usual calm self, still tall and without any hint of a bend in that proud old spine. Storm was right when he said at the funeral that to meet Fiona was to see Howard again.

Bella realises that she has, over the years since Eli's disappearance, taken her aunt's strength for granted, and now, especially since Howard died, she must be much more aware of the impact of this loss on Fiona. Apart from all this tidying up of Howard's life, they need to talk about how to go on from here with managing the property. Since Eli disappeared, Fiona has hired seasonal help as needed, but this wasn't the same as when Fiona shared all the planning and management with him. Bella feels a fresh wave of guilt that she had so underestimated what Eli's loss had meant to Fiona. And now Howard, too; he discussed and shared farm management decisions with Fiona from wherever he was in the world. She forces her thoughts back to the tasks at hand.

Fiona reaches into the pocket of her cardigan and places a small buff-colored wartime lettercard on the desk in front of Bella. She recognizes her father's elegant script.

Dear Mum, Dad & Fiona

I hope this news will bring you some happiness whilst we wait for news of Tom.

In fact, Tom being posted as missing has prompted me, in these difficult times, to marry the woman I love sooner than later.

Her name is Alexandra Monerayo. I'm sure you will love her as I do. We send our love to you until we can meet. Howard.

Bella looks up. 'So, the wartime censors didn't even let you know Tom was missing or the name of your newest family member.' She turns the card over, but no more information is available other than the address.

'Yes, I'd forgotten that until I found the card to show you.'

'Did he write again with more details?'

'No, the shock of the confirmation of Tom's loss took over from that.'

'Yes, I can understand that.' Bella places the card to one side.

'Did he write anything else about what they were doing?'

Fiona laughed. 'No, not much point because the censors would make a meal of any detail about names or places. Anyway, he was busy. We did get a Telegram announcing your arrival; that was very exciting.'

Fiona opens Howard's deed box. On the top is a copy of his will. Dated ten years ago, it's straightforward; Howard's share of Yarra Glen is left to Fiona and Bella jointly. Any liquid assets held at the time of Howard's death, after some minor bequests, are to be shared equally. Attached is a list of names and contacts for Howard's solicitor, accountant, banker, stockbroker, doctor, and other professional individuals and bodies who might need to be notified. All very concise and in keeping with the precise Howard Clemens.

'Nothing unusual there,' says Bella placing the documents to one side. 'I hoped to find a letter telling us something more about himself.'

'He didn't expect to die so suddenly,' is Fiona's logical reply. 'I'll make an appointment to see Jock about probating this will.'

'There's no mention of anything he might own in England,' Bella observes as she scans Howard's contacts list. 'Ah! There's a solicitor mentioned here, Simon Faulkner, at a company called Pitman's in London.'

'We'll take this to Jock first; he'll know what to do.' Fiona attaches the list to the will and tucks them into an envelope.

They sit for a minute contemplating this tidy summary of a huge life. They both know this will is the tip of an iceberg. Everything to do with this man whom they are mourning, is in the stacked, packed shelves, drawers, and cupboards surrounding them. His writings are his living legacy.

Next out of the deed box is Howard's marriage certificate. 'Fiona, look at this. Howard Clemens, aged twenty-six, married Alexandra Monerayo, aged twenty-five, in London. The date is the 31st of December 1944 at the Chelsea Registry office.'

Bella gently runs her finger across the names as if by this gentle touch, the names might come alive, that her mother's forgotten voice might speak to her. 'Alexandra's birthplace is listed as Barcelona!'

'Barcelona?' says Fiona, 'I didn't know that.'

Bella looks up in amazement. 'That makes me half Spanish. Why didn't Dad ever tell me that?'

'What else does it say?' says Fiona, peering at the document.

Bella says, 'Both Howard's and Alexandra's addresses are listed as Apartment 20, Florin Court, Charterhouse Square, London.

'That's the address I used to write to,' says Fiona. 'That's interesting. In those days, well-brought-up Spanish girls didn't have much opportunity to run off to London. Let alone live unmarried with a man who wasn't family. How did that happen?'

Bella looks at the certificate. 'There's only two witnesses here. Clara Monerayo for the bride, and Adeline Stephens for the groom. I suppose Clara was Alexandra's mother or sister. I wonder who Adeline Stephens was?'

'The name sounds familiar,' Fiona thinks.

'Ah, yes! he worked with her at Reuters throughout the war.' Fiona looks up. 'They might still be friends; we'll have to find Adeline to tell her Howard has died.'

'Maybe Storm can help,' says Bella as she lifts another document out of the box. 'Here's my full birth certificate.' Bella waves it in the air. 'I've never seen this. It's got Alexandra's birthplace too. If I'd seen this years ago, I could've asked him then.'

Fiona looks up. 'But didn't you need a full birth certificate for your passport?'

'No, up till now, I've used the Extract of Birth Entry that he sent me.'

Fiona hands the birth certificate back to her. 'I wonder why he didn't send you this?'

Bella gazes at the certificate. 'Why all the secrecy? It just doesn't make sense.'

Fiona sorts through the box. 'I have Howard's passports, university degrees, everything. All in order! If he was so methodical, why can't I find a copy of Alexandra's death certificate? Or divorce papers if that's what happened. They weren't easy to get in those days; they took years and were very messy.'

'Perhaps I need to search for those in London.' Bella makes a note in her notebook. Her list of tasks and questions is growing.

They continue working. Fiona empties the desk drawers; she places the contents in neat piles onto a long trestle table they've moved in.

Bella picks up the photographs she found in Howard's wallet. Now, in silver frames, they look at home with the other family pictures. Settled in as if returning after a long absence. It seems that Howard had another devotion, a private one. Was his love for this woman so intense, he carried her pictures, hidden from the world for over forty years?

She's looked at them under a magnifying glass, willing these small photos to give up their secrets. 'It's a bit odd; he kept two photographs but no proof of what happened to her.'

Chapter Sixteen

Yarra Glen

Since Howard's death, their peaceful life in tune with the farm, and the seasons, is undergoing a change of pace. At any moment, they might find a piece of paper that will change their beliefs about Howard forever.

Bella places the screen around the fire. 'Let's go for a walk, I need fresh air.'

Max and Mischa follow the two women as they walk through the gardens and then head for the vineyards. Bella often walks through the sleeping vines when she needs clear thinking space. It's almost as if the neat rows help order her scattered thoughts.

'Fiona, what shall we do with Struan? He needs a strong rider. He can't stay in the paddock looking after the girls. Should we find him a new home?'

'Bella! What an awful thought. We can't send Struan away...I'll have to think about it.'

A sudden rain squall darkens the sky and hurls needle-sharp hail at them. Bella whistles the dogs, and they turn for home. Back in Howard's study, Bella stokes the fire and closes the shutters. The late afternoon cold is rising from the paddocks to push through the glass.

'Sometimes my whole life feels like a fiction. My family is mysterious to the point of being ridiculous.' She reaches for a photo album on the coffee table. It is full of pictures of her with her horses and dogs. Her growing up years here at Yarra Glen. She looks up and says to Fiona.

'My mother, Alexandra, was never spoken about. Uncle Tom died and was never mentioned. The love of my life disappeared without a trace, and Howard never wanted me to speak about him either. No matter whether I fell off a horse or lost a lover, he always had the same advice.' Bella parodies her father's deep voice. "Stiff upper lip, Bella; don't cry, Bella, get back on that horse. You don't want him getting the upper hand, do you?"'

'Later, when horses gave way to boys in my life. Fiona, d'you remember him saying?' Imitating her father again. "Don't waste your time girl; he's not worth it, plenty more fish in the sea. We Clemens are made of sterner stuff."' Bella captures her father's deep voice so well that Fiona laughs.

'Fiona, we lived by his rules. There was a prescription for anything that befell my life. All to do with "getting on with it." Getting on with what? Rushing through life with armor plating and never feeling anything? Never let anything touch me?' Bella is wound up now; Fiona sits down.

'And what's more, that control meant that I was never able to touch on anything in life that may hurt me!' Even my pets were put down without me being here so I wouldn't see them die. I should've been with them.' Bella flops into the sofa. 'No wonder Eli's disappearance devastated me.'

'Howard's protectiveness was at odds with his own lifestyle, but he genuinely thought he was helping you.' Fiona kisses her and adds gently, 'Dear girl, I promise you, no animal ever died alone here.' She leaves remembering Bella's teenage storms and knows that she would be best left now.

Bella stares into the fire. Why didn't she push it with him? Demand to know more about their family. Because she didn't, she couldn't make him go to those places in his heart she understands now, were so full of secrets and, in this family, it wasn't done! The past weeks have turned her father into a stranger.

There were good things, too. He taught Bella to trust her intuition and treat it as her friend and ally. He imbued in her a respect for the world of nature and animals. He and Fiona ensured Bella had a good education and a strong streak of social justice. They'd ensured Bella understood the inequities of the world. His eyes and ears were everywhere, tracking her progress even if he was away from home. They travelled together, enjoying music, theatre, and art. They spent time volunteering during her holidays.

When Bella travelled alone, his letters addressed care of Post Restante found her in cities around Europe. Thinking about those letters from her father reminds Bella that she had never received any letters from Eli. He'd claimed once he didn't write in English, but now she wonders if he'd not wanted to leave any trace of himself. Theirs had been a relationship of shared thoughts felt and spoken but never written.

Bella knows she needs to stop wearing her father's mantle of work and words to the exclusion of allowing feelings to intrude. Since she's started to look at Scotty differently, she realises that after Eli left, she had suppressed her hunger for touch or sensuality. She pushes this insight away for now, though she realises she needs to look at it more closely. Her conversation with Fiona about Scott has unsettled her.

Next morning, while Fiona is cooking breakfast, Bella looks around the old kitchen. It hasn't changed in all her lifetime, the same long wooden table, and chairs. A huge dresser takes up most of one wall, the drawers and cupboards below are full of items that date back to Grandma Clemens' time. Nothing is thrown out unless worn out.

On the end wall is a wire screen door to the pantry, which has a cellar below it. Bella used to love going down the steps to the cool, dark place where meat used to hang in a Coolgardie safe. Butter and perishables lived in terracotta crocks, which sat in baths of cold water. It took a lot of persuasion before Grandma finally accepted the first Kelvinator refrigerator into the family.

The cellar! Howard's large wine collection lives down there. Another job: maybe Scott will help her? 'Fiona, what do you think if I ask Scotty to come and help me with sorting Dad's wine? Perhaps we could send some of the special bottles to his friends as a parting gift. I think Howard would approve.'

Bella can't see Fiona's smile. 'Good idea, Scotty can give Struan some exercise while he's here.' She turns around, waving the spatula. 'And that car, what do you want to do with it? It's a heavy beast, I won't drive it. I'm sure Scotty will.'

Game, set, match, thinks Bella. She must never underestimate her aunt when she gets an idea in her mind.

As Bella sets the table, she asks Fiona, 'Yesterday, I remembered you saying something to me after Balthazar died. At the time, I didn't ask why you said it.' Bella repeats Fiona's comment about Eli being called back to his world. 'Do you remember, and can you tell me why you said that, please?'

'Yes, I do remember,' Fiona replies. 'In those awful months after the home invasion and when Eli didn't return, I started to face the reality that Eli wasn't who we thought he was. I watched your fruitless enquiries all over the place. I watched you trying to relate to the ASIO agents. I even tried to make some enquiries myself. Nothing; it was like a giant eraser had completely rubbed out that man we loved and thought we knew. I was quite desperate watching your struggle, so I talked to Howard.'

'You did? What did he say? Why haven't you ever told me this?'

'I guess because Howard was so unhelpful.'

'Why? asks Bella, 'what on earth did he say?'

Fiona breathes in, her voice cracks. 'Howard said, "Leave it alone, Fiona. She's best off without him."'

'What! He said that?' Bella's voice rises. 'That doesn't make any sense at all. Howard and Eli were good friends; sometimes, I even felt a little left out!' Confusion washes over Bella. 'I'll never forget how he was so good with me at home here in those weeks after Eli left. I felt as if like you, he was grieving for him too.'

'I know, I remember seeing a side of Howard I wasn't used to seeing. Even worse,' Fiona's voice catches before she continues, 'he wouldn't let me ask any questions. He held up his hand at me in that awful final, end-of-conversation way that he had. He got angry with me, and I got very angry with him.'

'Oh Fiona, I'm so sorry. I know what he was like. Did you patch it up?'

'Bella, you know the Clemens way. Go out the door, and when you come back, nothing is ever said again. The worst part is, since then, I've become convinced he was hiding something from us. And now, he's gone, and that question won't be answered. It's so unfair, and I feel so angry and manipulated by him. I don't want to feel that about my brother right now or ever. I want to mourn him in a loving way.'

Bella is appalled to see her aunt so upset. 'This is terrible, I'm so sorry. We need to try to put the pieces together. I feel that he might've known something about Eli, too. Why didn't we talk about these family mysteries? Why couldn't I know about my mother? And what about Uncle Tom? Did Howard ever find out more about how Tom died? He's gone, and I realize I may never know the truth about anything.' Bella pauses. 'The worst part is Fiona; it seems Howard is the common denominator in every story.'

Fiona passes Bella some eggs on toast. 'Exactly, I've been thinking the same thing. Somehow, Howard seems to be at the centre of everything. You're right that we rarely spoke about emotions. It was bad form to pry, or show upset about personal things. Our parents expected us to be stoic. Back then, stoicism was a mark of a good upbringing. And now, I feel as if Howard has used this family trait for his own purpose.'

Fiona sits down. 'I'll tell you a story. It shows what we're talking about. When the telegram arrived with the news that Tom was missing, our parents went into the sitting room. They left me to wander in the garden with the dogs. I've never forgotten when the vicar came to call the next day. It was so awkward; they didn't want to talk to him about Tom at all. It was months before confirmation of Tom's death came. I guess they kept hoping that Tom would turn up alive.'

'Did they ever talk about Tom after they knew he was dead?'

'Not to me. They had friends around here who were in the same position; there were many men lost from this area. Maybe these poor souls only spoke about their losses when they were together.'

Bella looks at her aunt. 'Now dad's dead. I can't even think why I accepted such rot for so long. Without a single bloody question! Damn him and his secrets! I'm going to find out whatever I can.'

Chapter Seventeen

Solicitor's Office Melbourne

Fiona and Bella cross the worn stone-flagged foyer of the old Queen Street building where their solicitor Jock has his law practice. As they enter the ancient cage lift that clanks its way to the first floor, they smile at each other. No high-rise tower of glass and steel for Jock.

A family business passed from father to son for three generations means the gold lettering **McIntosh & Son** on the tall mahogany entrance door has never changed.

Bella whispers to Fiona. 'I hope Jock's daughter goes into the family business so he will have to change that sign.'

Fiona whispers back. 'And I hope I live long enough to see that!'

In his office, dressed in a smart three-piece suit with his rather wild red hair well and truly restrained; Jock once more looks the part of a family solicitor. No hint of the man with his coat off displaying his richly colored waistcoat and a broad grin as he danced a jig at Howard's funeral.

After reminiscing about the funeral, Bella places their copy of Howard's will on his desk, Jock looks at the date.

'Ah yes, when Howard came home, he made some amendments to this will. Here's the new one.' Jock places the document in front of them. He waits to give them a chance to read the two-page document. 'Whilst all his Australian bequests remain the same as the earlier will, he has left a lifetime interest in his London apartment at Florin Court to his long-time friend and colleague, Adeline Stephens.'

Bella and Fiona exchange glances and look at the address. It is the same as the address of the apartment that Fiona thought Howard had sold years ago.

Jock continues, unaware of the effect of this news on the women. 'On Adeline's demise, the leasehold will revert to Bella's sole ownership.'

'Adeline Stephens?' Fiona places the marriage certificate in front of Jock and points to the name of Howard's witness. 'When we found this in Howard's study, I remembered Howard worked with Adeline at Reuters. I haven't heard him mention her for years. He must have still been very close to her to leave her a life interest in the apartment.'

Bella asks. 'Has anyone told Adeline that Howard has died? Clearly, they were more than friends.'

'Yes, the news of Howard's death was given to Adeline by Howard's London solicitor.'

Fiona looks aghast. 'Oh, how awful; it should have been us. The poor woman.'

Bella says, 'Jock, why didn't you mention her to us before the funeral? We could've rung her to ask her if she wished to come out here.'

Jock looks uncomfortable. 'I didn't realise that you don't know her. Of course, I had to act upon Howard's instructions. When you didn't mention her, I knew that I couldn't, until the reading of the will. I am sorry.'

'How can we get in touch with Adeline quickly?' Bella asks. 'I don't want to wait for a letter to get to London and via her solicitor.'

'I can help you there.' Jock pushes a card across the desk. 'This is Howard's London business card. The fax number will get to Adeline. The solicitor advised me to use it to contact her directly.'

Bella takes the card and looks up. 'Oh, of course, I've got this too. I never connected it with anyone else. I wonder if they lived together at Florin Court! The old fox. What else has he kept from us, d'you think?'

'Now don't jump to conclusions,' says Fiona. 'Anyway, what would it have mattered if they were partners? After all, they were long-time colleagues and friends.'

'Of course. No, I don't mean it like that. I always wanted him to have a partner.'

She turns to Jock. 'Was there anything else from Howard? A letter, perhaps? Anything to explain…anything at all? We're finding out that we knew so little about his life. We're completely mystified.'

Jock shakes his head sadly and says, 'No letter, but I know Howard had a lot on his mind. He did say to me that he intended to clear up a few important matters whilst he was here. He had an appointment for last Friday.'

Chapter Eighteen

Adeline Stephens 1990

B ack in Howard's study, they send a fax to Adeline. Late that evening as she is sliding into an exhausted sleep, Bella hears the fax machine grumble into life. She pulls herself up, she knows she can't leave it until morning to see what is waiting for her. This machine is connecting her with her past, a bit like a time machine. H.G. Wells would've loved all this technology had he known about it when writing his stories. Pulling her woolen robe around her, she walks quietly to the study. Mischa, hearing her comes too, she whines softly as if asking why Bella is wandering around the house so late.

Adeline's reply although brief, is warm. She suggests Fiona and Bella could call early the next day as she is longing to talk to them. Early morning, Bella wakes Fiona so they can call Adeline before it gets too late in the evening in London. Bella stokes up the fire against the early morning chill. Fiona, wrapped in a large shawl over her nightdress, brings the tea tray and sets it upon the desk; she opens the curtains to let in the pale morning light. The ground mist is thick, giving a ghostly appearance to the trees, which are trying to push their way upwards through the fog to greet the sunrise.

'Look,' says Bella pointing to the beautiful scene, 'this is exactly how I feel. I'm trying to push through the fog toward the light, too.'

The three women have tears caught in their voices but after a couple of minutes, they are calmer. Bella speaks. 'Adeline, I'm so sorry that you had to hear about Howard from his solicitor. But you see, we didn't know about you.'

'Dear Bella, I understand completely. I chose not to go out to Yarra Glen for the funeral. I hadn't heard from him that he'd spoken to you and Fiona.'

'What was he going to tell us about, please, Adeline?'

A brief silence. 'Well, about him and…about Alexandra.'

'Ah, so there is a story about her.' Bella looks at Fiona.

'Yes, so when I hadn't heard from him, I decided it wasn't the time to start to explain myself.'

'We would've coped, I promise you. Anything would have been preferable to this, trying to unstitch my father's secrets.'

Adeline continues, 'Bella, could I ask you how much Howard told you please?'

'Nothing at all.' Bella tells the story of the Jaguar and finding the photographs in Howard's wallet.

'It's a tragedy he died so suddenly. The only comfort for me is that he was with you and Fiona. When he left here, we made an agreement that he would tell you the whole story about his marriage to Alexandra. It was time.'

'Way past time!' Bella exclaims. 'I was to have dinner with him the evening he died. Maybe he planned to tell me then?' Bella hopes this would have happened. If she holds on to that thought, she might be able to accept her father's choices. 'I need to come to London to see you, please Adeline.'

'Of course, you must stay here. Will you come soon, Bella? I would love to see you again.'

'Again?' Bella catches the question.

'Bella, of course you wouldn't remember. I knew you when you were a baby before your father took you to Australia.'

'So, you knew my mother, Alexandra?'

A brief pause, then Adeline replies. 'Yes, Bella, I did.'

Bella waits, but Adeline doesn't say anything more. 'Perhaps you will tell me everything you can remember when I come to London. Maybe you might find some more photos of her.'

Adeline replies, 'Yes, of course, I'll see if I can find any in Howard's study. It must be cleaned out anyway.'

'I hope there's not as much for you to deal with as there is here,' says Fiona as she looks at the boxes on the floor.

'I'm rather afraid there might be,' says Adeline ruefully.

Bella smiles, 'I'll help you when I come over.'

'Oh, dear Bella, thank you, but I think one of Howard's studies to sort out is enough, no one deserves two.'

Fiona asks, 'please will you tell us a little about yourself?'

Adeline replies. 'I met Howard before World War Two, I was working with Reuters as a researcher. I remember Howard as a rather interesting Australian who seemed to come and go with no questions asked. In time, we came to work on projects together and became friends and allies, our minds complemented each other. I had three brothers, so I was quite comfortable with Howard's Australian ways: and his sense of humour. I also met Tom on many occasions, he was great fun.'

'Oh' says Fiona, 'I love hearing that you knew Tom, I have so little to remember him by because he was so young when he left here.'

Adeline asks. 'I understand, Fiona, I have that feeling about my fiancé Robin too.'

The women pause as they reflect on loss not only of their loved ones but how memories, no matter how dearly held, can, in time, become elusive as well. Within hours, the fax machine delivers the next chapter for Fiona and Bella.

Dear Fiona and Bella

It is such a relief that we have spoken. I hope to meet you both as soon as it can be arranged. Until then, I'll tell you a little about Howard's marriage.

I saw the whole romance with Alexandra bloom. After Howard met Alexandra at the Ritz, he fell for her quickly and hard! She had graduated from Cambridge and was looking for work. Keen to help her and knowing her language skills—as well as English and Spanish she spoke fluent French and German. He secured her an interview through his contacts at the Ministry of Information, where she was promptly hired.

Soon after, Clara and Alexandra were bombed out of their London home, so Howard offered them his apartment here at Florin Court. Do you remember it at all, Bella? He was often away, so the place was empty, and he was happy to stay at his club when he was in London.

In December 1944, Howard surprised me with an invitation to his marriage to Alexandra. It was not long after my fiancé was lost at sea, so I was delighted to be part of a happy occasion.

That week, Tom was posted as missing on active service. Although Howard was desperately worried about him, he decided to go ahead with the wedding because Tom might return safely at any time. War heightens the need to make the most of every day. It was a very small registry office wedding. Howard asked me to be his witness. Only Alexandra's mother, Clara Monerayo, was there from her side. After, we had lunch at the Ritz. Where else? After all, they'd conducted much of their brief courtship there.

We finally learned that Tom's plane had crashed, but only the pilot's body was found. We hoped David and Tom could be trying to return to England because their names didn't turn up on Red Cross prisoner of war lists.

You were born in November 1945. A tiny, beautiful creature. Howard was, and remained, a doting father.

We didn't hear the whole story of Tom's death until David McKenzie, a friend of Tom's, saw Howard in London in 1946. This news devastated Howard.

Bella, I think the rest should remain until you come to visit us here. I will find an address for David so you can contact him. Between David and me, I hope we can answer most of your questions.

With fondest regards to you both.

Adeline

Fiona sits back, she reaches for her handkerchief to wipe her eyes. 'Poor Tom, I've never stopped missing him. I wonder who David McKenzie is? And it seems that Howard knew him. Oh, it would be so good to be able to talk to David and Adeline about Tom.'

'If David McKenzie told Howard about Tom's death, why didn't he tell you and Grandpa and Grandma?'

Chapter Nineteen

David McKenzie 1990

Driving rain and swaying trees along the drive, tell Bella not to open an umbrella for the short dash to the house. Bella is spending as much time as she can at Yarra Glen helping her aunt with the piles of condolence letters and a myriad of unforeseen tasks arising since Howard's death. Max and Mischa hear her footsteps; they burst through the screen door, turning circles in welcome. Fiona greets Bella and takes her coat. Hugging her aunt, Bella feels Fiona's familiar warmth; she is worried the last weeks must have taken their toll.

Fiona ushers Bella into Howard's study places a brandy in her hand saying, 'the first letter is a surprise. It's from the same David McKenzie that Adeline mentioned.' She smiles and leaves Bella to read the letter by the fire in peace.

Batiscombe House
Hastings East Sussex UK
30ʰ September 1990

Dear Miss Fiona Clemens.

I hope this letter from the past will not cause you distress. I saw the tribute to your brother Howard in 'The Times' and our Squadron News.

Tom and I were at Cambridge together. Tom spent many of our university holidays at home here.

My parents were very fond of Tom and considered him a part of our family. Howard often stayed here, too. Both he and Tom were such fine chaps, possessing that particular brand of courage and resourcefulness Aussies are known for. The two of them were very special men.

Tom and I flew that last mission together, and after the bailout, we were captured at Mézières Sur Meuse. By an incredible miracle, I survived the firing squad that killed Tom and several villagers. Although severely wounded, when I was found alive, I was taken in by a French family and hidden for many months before being repatriated to England.

It wasn't until 1946, after I'd mostly recovered from my injuries, that I was able to contact Howard. I fear the story I told him was the cause of his marriage breakdown, and I have carried that burden all these years. But this is old history, and I'm sure Howard told you the whole story.

I saw in The Times that Howard and Alexandra's daughter Isabella is a well-regarded journalist. Howard would be very proud of her. I do hope her life is a happy one.

Again, I wish to convey my sympathy to you and to Isabella. Howard was a very fine man and had a startling way of conveying images with words. And to apologize to you both for the contribution I made to your family's troubles.

Yours sincerely
David McKenzie.

Bella finds Fiona making supper in the kitchen. The warmth from the Aga stove and the tangy aroma of fish pie brings Bella back to the present. Waving the letter, she says, 'I've read it several times; I don't understand any of it!'

As Fiona turns towards her, Bella can see that the strain of the past weeks has caught up with her. She seems less robust, more lines have gathered around her eyes that seem to have faded from their deep cornflower blue and become greyer and, sadder. It's the first time Bella has ever seen any hint of frailty in her beloved aunt.

Fiona shakes her head. 'I'd never heard of a place called Mézières Sur Meuse! Oh Bella, what kind of bubble have we been living in, not knowing any of this?'

Bella puts her arms around her and draws her to a chair. 'More to the point, Fiona dear, what kind of bubble did Howard live in?' They sit with the letter in front of them and look at it in silence. The Aga cooker radiates warmth; the dogs lie in their baskets, gazing solemnly as if they sense Fiona and Bella's confusion.

Bella says, 'And, what does David mean about feeling responsible for Howard's marriage breakdown? I need to speak to him; I want to know more about my mother. He and Adeline appear to be my only chance now.'

'Yes dear, I agree,' says Fiona as she wipes her eyes. 'This has been as much of a shock as Howard's death.'

'At least we might be able to clear up this mystery he has left us with.'

They decide they will write to David. They're concerned that a phone call might be rather overwhelming for him. It's such a hard letter to write. Thanking David for his condolences and describing Howard's funeral is the easy part. They tell him they know very little about Tom's death. And Howard never told them anything about his marriage breakdown. Bella adds that she will come to England soon and would like to meet him. She has very little information about either her mother or father's life together. She includes the fax number here at Yarra Glen and suggests that if David has a fax machine, perhaps, he could fax them.

A week later, Fiona receives a fax to make a time for 4:00 pm on Saturday. David will call them. Bella decides to stay all week with Fiona and commute to work. She feels they both need each other's company whilst all this strangeness is unfolding.

Bella is working in Howard's study when another fax arrives. David writes about the events he assumed that Fiona and Bella know about; he's shocked they don't know. He's anxious to help put what he sees as his second major blunder, to rights. He wants them to have at least an outline of what he understands happened before they speak. He describes his meeting with

Howard after the war.

When we met up, I told him the story of our capture and Tom's death. I showed Howard a drawing I had done of a woman I saw in France with a German officer before we were captured. I felt sure she was Howard's Spanish girlfriend, Alexandra. I did the drawing for Tom and, so I wouldn't forget her face. He also thought it was her. But neither of us could fathom why she'd be in France. And with a German officer. Even worse, we saw the same woman at Mézières in the moments before we were shot.

I will tell you both the full story when we meet here in London, but for now, suffice it to say Howard was desolate when I showed him the picture I'd drawn. I didn't know until then that he'd married Alexandra, and they had a baby daughter. He intimated that he had reason to suspect Alexandra's loyalty to both him and the Allied war effort. The sketch may well have confirmed his suspicions. The realization that I caused Howard such pain has been a terrible burden to me. I refrained from contacting him again in all these years for fear of causing him further distress.

Another page follows. It is a charcoal drawing of a woman's face with a hat placed at an angle shadowing one side of her face. Bella smooths the paper out on Howard's desk and turns on the lamp.

'Fiona, come and look at this.'

Fiona bustles into the room and peers down at the drawing. 'It's you, she's so like you Bella.' Fiona reads the letter.

Bella stares at her own face reflected in the drawing. It's the first time she has felt any physical connection to her mother. What should have been a joyful moment of recognition is, instead, confusing. Was her mother really this person, a…she can't bring herself to say the words, some kind of war criminal. 'Fiona, why? I can't understand why Howard hid all this from us. It's awful.'

Fiona takes off her glasses to rub her eyes. 'If this is true, it would make Alexandra a traitor.' She looks up at Bella and shakes her head in disbelief. 'This could explain Howard's need to bring you here to grow up untainted by all this.'

Chapter Twenty

Yarra Glen

On Saturday afternoon, Fiona and Bella are at Howard's desk waiting for David's call. The drawing of the woman they believe to be Alexandra lies in front of them. Bella has spent a lot of time gazing at this likeness of herself. Who is the person behind the eyes that are fixed on some point over Bella's shoulder? David has captured a quality of detachment and hauteur in the woman's face. Fiona places two glasses of brandy and dry ginger on the desk. 'In case we need them,' she says with a wry smile.

At 4:00 pm, as the grandfather clock in the hall chimes its message, the phone rings. A crisp English voice introduces himself.

'David McKenzie here. Fiona and Isabella, I am so sorry if I have caused you further distress on top of losing Howard.'

Fiona leads off. 'David, we're so grateful to you for agreeing to speak to us. Neither Bella nor I, want you to continue to feel any upset about the past events. Or anything that comes out of this ...'

David replies, 'You're very kind, I...' His voice trails off.

Fiona and Bella wait; they sense that David is struggling with emotion, and why wouldn't he? A catastrophic event in his past that he clearly thought was behind him has emerged to revive bad memories.

'David,' says Bella, 'your sketch has a striking resemblance to the photos in Howard's wallet. We guessed the pictures are of Alexandra, but you've confirmed that for us.'

Fiona leans in closer to the phone. 'When you meet Bella, you will see it could be a drawing of her. You're a very fine artist, David.'

'Thank you. Yes, art is my life and my solace,' says David. 'Please tell me what happened. The notice only said Howard died in Melbourne.'

Bella tells him. 'It was very sudden,' she outlines, finding Howard sitting in a classic Jaguar that they had no idea he owned.

'Oh, that car! Was it red?' David asks.

'Yes! exclaims Bella, looking at Fiona.

'Howard used to try to break a land speed record driving from London to my home in Hastings. Tom and I used to find excuses not to drive with him.'

'Oh,' said Bella, sitting back in her chair, 'he was always so hard on me about driving within the speed limit.' She reaches for her glass and sips. 'So, finding out that Howard had kept the Jaguar here all these years was the beginning. Why did he hide it away from us?'

'We'll have to put that in the unanswered questions for now, Bella.'

The three fall silent as they contemplate the truth of David's statement. And all the other unknowns that, until Howard's death, no one dreamt of were waiting to be found.

Fiona continues. 'When Bella found the photos in his wallet, we were mystified. Who was the woman? without you and Adeline, we could've lived our lives without knowing. Where could we have started?'

Bella looks at David's letter. 'You said here *"that Howard had reason to suspect Alexandra's loyalty to both him and the Allied war effort."* Do you mean she was some kind of,' Bella exhales then breathes in to try to steady herself, 'war criminal?'

David says gently, 'I'm so sorry to tell you this but, yes, there was an internal security enquiry into Alexandra. My sketch rather set the cat amongst the pigeons. I'm sorry, I really don't know any more about that. It was kept very hush hush.'

'For heaven's sake!' exclaims Fiona, 'this is getting worse.' Fiona retrieves the brandy decanter from the drinks trolley and pours Bella and herself another hefty nip.

David doesn't want to upset the two women. Clearly, this is all a shock to them. 'I think it would be best to try to sort this from here in London. Bella, when you are coming?'

'As soon as I can arrange it.'

Fiona says, 'If he did find out Alexandra was guilty of some misdeeds, bringing Bella here to Australia was one way to avoid questions.'

'Yes, almost watertight, I would think,' says David. 'It was a smart move to distance Bella from all that.'

'Even so,' says Bella, 'Howard would never even answer basic questions about my mother, except that she had died in an accident.'

'Died? did she?' David pauses. 'Of course, she might have. I wasn't in contact with Howard after that day. Also, given it was post-wartime, and we know she was under suspicion, there might have been very good reasons he couldn't speak about Alexandra.' says David.

'I hadn't thought of that,' agrees Bella.

'We're still looking for any information here in his study.' Fiona looks about her.

'When you come over, please come to stay here at Hastings, I would rather tell you whatever I can in person.'

'That would be lovely, thank you. I'll spend some time with Adeline first.' Bella continues. 'David, Fiona remembers that the plane went down near Metz, but she's certain they never heard whether Tom was found.'

'Oh,' David sounds surprised.

'David, I need to hear about your capture with Tom and how you managed to escape. And...' Bella looks at Fiona, who looks devastated. Bella touches her aunt's hand and can feel her trembling. Fiona leans forward and says in an unsteady voice.

'I know you will find this hard to understand, but we didn't know anything about Tom's death in a place called Mézières. We've always thought he was missing but not found.'

'Good grief.' David reacts, 'I wonder what Howard was thinking of.'

'That's exactly what we're trying to unravel,' says Bella. 'David, we've put

106

you through enough today. I can't tell you how much you are helping us. Thank you so much.'

'Yes, David,' Fiona recovers enough to add. 'Please don't ever think you are doing the wrong thing by telling us whatever you can. We're truly grateful.'

Bella pours more strong drinks; dusk is falling. Fiona stokes the fire into life, for they need the warmth. Bella calls the dogs in; they flop onto the rug in front of the hearth. Their wagging tails make life seem almost normal. Fiona brings a large Atlas to the desk and reaches for the magnifying glass. They find Metz in north-eastern France, and nearly two hundred kilometers northwest of Metz, near the French border with Belgium, they find Mézières Sur Meuse.

'Well look at that,' says Fiona tracing the route with her finger. 'How did they get from there to there?'

Bella says. 'At least now we have found David; we have one reliable witness to this piece of the story.'

'As a well-connected war correspondent, Howard must've found out what happened.' Fiona pauses. 'The big question is, did Howard ever tell our parents about Tom's death in a place called Mézières Sur Meuse? The place names were redacted on the telegram and letter we received from Howard. I don't remember ever hearing Mézières ever mentioned.' Fiona looks at Bella. 'There is no way if my parents knew that they wouldn't have told me. I am sure of that. So why?'

'Why did the news come from Howard? I thought those telegrams came from the Australian War Office.' Bella taps her pencil on the pad in front of her.

'Howard was listed as Tom's next of kin because he enlisted in England. He didn't come home to enlist.'

'Do you remember what the telegram said? Bella asks as she looks around the study with piles of papers on every surface. 'Would they still be here somewhere?'

'Quite likely,' replies Fiona. 'I'm sure mum would've kept something like that, we'll look tomorrow. I can't deal with any more shocks now.'

Chapter Twenty-One

Yarra Glen

Next morning, the weather has closed in; rain and low clouds obscure the hills and paddocks. It's a perfect day to go through the filing cabinet. Bella finds the contents of the drawers in folders. Everything is labelled in Howards neat script. Two drawers are filled with Howard's photo negatives. Every folder has a catalogue of the contents. She feels a wave of sadness at this expression of her father's attention to detail. Examining these will be a task for another time.

The bottom drawer holds a trove of family records. These folders are labelled in Howard's neat script as well. She finds one marked Peter and Amelia Clemens and takes it to Howard's desk. Birth certificates for themselves and their children, baptisms, confirmations, wedding certificate, and their own death certificates. She's shocked to read the dates of their deaths were so close together and how comparatively young they were when they died; they had always looked so old to her. Such was the impact of grief on their lives.

Next is a folder marked 'Tom'. A large envelope yields school photographs, school awards, and sports achievement certificates. All the young life of the boy, Thomas Andrew Clemens. He grew up here, then left to finish his education in England. He would return home to take up his life as a lawyer, farmer, and, most likely, a family man. The natural order disrupted by a faraway war. No wonder her grandparents had faded into silent old age.

Howard, too, must have looked at this small, tidy summary of his brother's life and felt the grief he never showed to anyone.

Bella opens another envelope. She gently draws out two telegrams. She goes to the door and calls out, 'Fiona, I've found them!'

Fiona sits next to Bella at the desk. They open one telegram each and lay them out. One dated 15th December 1944 says:

Tom missing in action stop

More news soonest stop Take courage stop

Howard stop

'What does the other say?' It was short and, because of censorship, redacted.

I wish I could have better news for you stop

Tom's burnt out plane found at

[Redacted] on [Redacted] stop

No survivors reported stop Howard stop

'Is that all?' asks Bella.

'I guess we were lucky to get this.' Fiona turns it over. 'Mum has written received 24th March 1945.'

'Three months after he went missing. Such agony for them.' Bella takes the form and sees some of the print is blurred. Tears? She wonders. 'Is there anything else from later?'

'Not that I can see.' Fiona shakes the envelope; a small, yellowed newspaper clipping falls out. The picture is faded and very grainy. Bella places it under the lamp, and the two women lean in to examine it with the magnifying glass. The photo is of a man dressed in the uniform of an officer of the German army. The title reads Generaloberst der Waffen-SS Klaus Schoeffels—Verschwindet. The subheading is Nürnberg 20. Dezember 1946. The rest of the clipping is in German, so they are unable to read the content. Fiona reaches for the German English dictionary, and they quickly find that verschwindet means disappeared.

'Good heavens. I wonder if this is the same German officer David mentioned?'

'Must be,' replies Bella. 'Why else would it be in this envelope? I'll get it translated. Anything else?'

Fiona shuffles through the folder. 'I'm sure we did get one final notice after some months that Tom was still missing and presumed dead. She looks around the items on the desk. 'I can't see it here. I wonder where it is.' She gently gathers the aging pieces of paper together. 'So that's how it has stood until now.'

'Until David tells us that Tom died…was executed,' she pauses, unable to continue. The rush of emotion feels like it will choke her. She looks up, and her beloved aunt has covered her face with her hands, her body trembling. Bella picks up the telegram, 'in Mézières Sur Meuse in Northern France!' And, that he was with him!'

'And' Fiona adds, 'even worse than that, Howard knew all along.'

'What was he hiding?'

Fiona shakes her head. 'It could only be something to do with Alexandra.'

'Yes, David spoke about the woman they thought was her in France…at Mézières!'

'Good heavens! How awful.' Fiona shakes her head. 'If Howard had told us, I would've taken our parents to this Mézières place to see that Tom was properly buried.'

'At least that I'd think,' agrees Bella.

'Or to bring his remains home here. I know one thing I will do.'

Bella looks up. 'What's that?'

'I'm going to have his memorial plaque in the church, remade with the date and place of his death.'

'Will you come to London with me, Fiona?'

'If you don't mind, I'd rather stay here. You need to be able to move around without me to think about.' Fiona hesitates, then she surprises Bella with her next statement. 'Howard was my brother, and I loved him dearly, but I have to say, I'm torn between a desire to box his ears or to try to understand why he lived as two different people for so long. Right now, I'm pretty damn angry.'

'Exactly.' Her father is Howard to Bella now. She can't think of him as Dad. Now, he's a virtual stranger who happens to be her father. Bella feels a renewed sense of a double loss, first Eli and now Howard as the father she thought she knew! She can only hope that when she can peel back the layers of her father's secrets, she will return to the place of love for him she has always held in her heart. Bella understands that anger is a normal part of the grieving process, but this level of deception is hurting as much as Eli's abandonment of her.

Fiona and Bella sit at the kitchen table, each wrapped in their own memories. 'Fiona, do you remember all the letters Howard used to write to me?'

'Yes, they're all still here in the cupboard in your room if you want them.'

'If I look at them with fresh eyes, would there be any clues that we didn't know to look for?'

'Possibly Bella, but I don't think so. I'm starting to understand that Howard spun a web of obfuscation all these years, and I need to know why. What made him do this?'

Bella locates the box. Inside are wads of blue Aerogrammes held together with ribbon. So many of them! As she sorts through each bundle, she wonders if Aerogrammes or air letters still exist. The paper is so fine, and Howard always wrote with a fountain pen in those days. No crossing out or replacement of words. His use of language was so fluent and evocative.

His voice is clear as he describes his travels. In conflict zones, he describes the lives of displaced persons waiting for resettlement. She realizes that even then, in his own way, Howard tried to open her eyes to those less fortunate than herself. Hours pass; she's so absorbed in these letters from the past. Fiona is right in saying she doubts there would be anything personal in them. They all started with *My Darling Daughter* and end with *Love Dad*.

Bella feels that love and remembers how she waited to receive his letters at boarding school. She would take them to a quiet place and devour every word. That they are still here, kept together after all these years, speaks of their value to her. As she ties them together with the old ribbons to put them away, she plants a gentle kiss of love. She loves rereading them, but in doing so, she understands that Howard kept the cipher to his mysteries and memories: he died taking the key with him.

Chapter Twenty-Two

Meg examines the two photographs with a magnifying glass. 'This mystery mother of yours is beautiful, Bella. You look so like her.'

'I've looked for a resemblance to my father all my life; now I know why I couldn't find it.'

Scott comes in with his coffee. Meg hands him the magnifier; he looks at the photos.

'What a stunner! So that's where you get your looks.' He smiles; his face is full of a gentle sadness, an unguarded moment of longing, as he hands the photos back to Bella.

She catches his look and feels his nearness; a small tremor passes through her. She wishes she could overcome her reserve, touch his hand, or turn her face towards his and kiss him. Properly. What stops her? She knows the answer to that. Eli. As much as she wants to, she's still not sure that she's ready to put Eli behind her and move on with her life. Bella snaps her mind back to the task at hand, away from her inner confusion.

'Thank you,' she smiles at him but can't find any other words. She tells them about David McKenzie and Adeline. And what she knows about Alexandra. 'Something tells me that there's more to the story than her name was Alexandra Monerayo, and she died in London in 1946.'

She hands Scott the clipping about General Kurt Schoeffels; now pasted onto a sheet of paper, he reads the translation. Although short, it says General Kurt Schoeffels was found guilty in absentia for deaths of civilians in Mézières Sur Meuse in February 1945. His whereabouts are unknown.

Scott whistles, 'What're you going to do about this, Bella?'

'Not sure. Fiona and I are still sorting Howard's study. We're hoping we'll find some answers there.'

'Amazing. So do you think there's a connection between this badass man and your mother?'

'I'm sending this to David McKenzie. If anyone knows, he will. He described the woman at the shooting, whom he thought was Alexandra, as being with a German officer.' Bella places the paper in an envelope and says sadly. 'If there is a connection, I need to know. It might help explain a lot about my father.'

Meg starts their meeting. She has the layouts of the final draft in front of her.

'This's great. Stunning photos, Scott! They give such a sense of the mountains and how difficult it would be to find someone in those vast spaces.'

'And look at that dense bush below the snowline,' adds Bella. 'If you got into that, how would you get out?'

'You're lucky to still have me here after that shoot,' says Scott. 'Bella has no fear of heights, I do!'

'Come on, Scotty, you loved every minute of it,' Bella replies.

'It's alright for you to say. You weren't lying on your stomach facing down a perilous slope,' Scott grumbles.

She points to the photos. 'Simon's family found great comfort in seeing these. They said Scotty's pictures tell them a story in a way that they can understand.'

Bella points to a photo of Simon with the other guests in the lodge the day before he disappeared. 'What do you think of this shot, Meg? The family gave us these extra photos to help us.'

Meg examines the photo and says, 'He looks quite sad, doesn't he? Not like in the photo taken earlier in the week.'

'We feel that he looked alone in the group.' Scott passes them a blow-up print of the photo so they can see Simon's expression. 'He's with his lifelong friends enjoying their annual week at Perisher. So why does he look so sad?'

'So, what happened?' Bella asks.

'He looks as if he'd rather be anywhere but there,' Meg says as she taps her pencil on a paragraph in the interview transcript. 'This's interesting too. His sister commented that Simon left his belongings in good order when he went out to ski that day.'

Bella adds, 'his mother told us he never kept his room tidy.'

'Did that affect the family's view of Simon's disappearance?' asks Meg.

'Yes, it was so out of character, it made them wonder if he intended to disappear.'

Scott adds. 'It's already tough for his partner Lucy, without her feeling he meant to leave her. Her dreams vanished into thin air with Simon.'

'I know how she feels.' Bella says quietly, 'We've so many photos here of Simon taken over many years. The Spencer family are keen photographers. Every event or celebration is recorded. They were the easiest family to build a background for.' She pauses.

'So?' asks Scott.

'I wanted to make my own storyboard with a timeline like this. I hoped something might make sense to me. But I didn't have enough information; I only have two small photos of Eli. He never wanted his photo taken. Why?' Bella muses: 'Why didn't Eli like his photo taken? I realized the ASIO man was right; I had to accept that Eli was hiding something from me.'

Meg asks gently. 'You mean like Simon might've been hiding something from his family?'

'Yes.' Bella pauses. 'It's the same for every family. The thought of that subterfuge is so painful.'

They're quiet. Noises from the office outside intrude on their silent reflection.

'We need to wrap this up so you can have some real time off, Bella,' Meg hugs her.

'Now that I've found these photos of my mother and talked to Adeline and David McKenzie, I need to go to London to find out more about her. I need to be where Howard and Alexandra met, married, and parted.'

'Where did Alexandra die?' Meg asks.

'That's the problem; Howard told Fiona and their parents she was hit by a lorry at night in London. If he wanted to hide something, I can see he was trying not to create any more tangled web of lies than he had already.'

'I'm sure Storm will help you.' Meg smiles. 'He has a soft spot for you; he could help you with his contacts. But be careful; he'll try to get you to write a story about your parents.'

'Howard and Storm go back a long way.' Bella looks up, 'It was such a lovely surprise when he came to the funeral.'

'And, gave that marvellous speech,' adds Scott.

Meg says, 'He'll enjoy getting his old journalist's hat on. When I see him in London, I feel he's a bit isolated in his glass tower.' Meg thinks and then continues, 'Storm understands that time of Cold War spy hunting. He might still have contacts in the security services.' They both smile, thinking about Storm burrowing in the tunnels of MI6. 'Have you thought of asking Adeline and David to Yarra Glen?'

Bella replies. 'They'll come out at Christmas time.'

Meg smiles. 'Come on, let's see what we can do to get you to London. We'll send a fax to Storm.'

As soon as the fax goes, Bella feels guilty. And a horror of exposing her private, secretive father to public scrutiny. Could she get this through to Storm? Bella will take four weeks' leave. As Meg predicted, Storm asks Bella to send ahead any information she has about her mother.

'He's hooked!' laughs Scott, then as Meg answers the phone, he says quietly. 'Bella, do you really want to do this alone? I could come with you.'

'Oh Scotty, would you?' her heart twists. As Meg ends her phone call Bella whispers, 'can we talk about this later?'

Meg hasn't heard this soft exchange; she gets back to business. 'Has doing this story done anything to help you with Eli?'

Bella leans back into the couch, and Scott's hand slides closer to hers until they touch. Bella feels a warmth, a sensation like a blush creeping through her. She tries to focus on her reply.

'I know any knowledge that could help solve the mystery, even if it's conclusive proof of a death, would be a relief. I've met many others who share my helpless sense of loss. In every case that we looked into, the families were asking the same questions.'

'What's that?' Meg asks.

'Well, the main question is how does something that ends in a disappearance start? Maybe a chance meeting changed the course of a life. Or an idea started a chain of events that had devastating consequences.'

Meg asks. 'Has a pattern emerged for the families?'

'Yes, by digging deep, some of the families can find a beginning. A glimmer of light that shows them that at a point, the events started to unfold.'

'Has this happened to you, Bella?'

'Yes, in a way. I've started to understand that I'm an unwitting bystander in a still unfolding drama.'

Meg sips her coffee. 'How's that?'

Bella stretches her arms above her head. It's been an intense hour. 'If a life together finishes in death or the end of a relationship, there are rituals for those left behind. These enable their grieving and readjustment. Those left when a loved one disappears have nothing. That's the struggle we all share. Unless I find Eli, I haven't a choice but to accept his leaving as the finality.

Scott has been silent during this exchange between Meg and Bella; he chips in. 'So, this is the big difference in understanding the grief of those left behind. It's a void that can't be filled without answers.'

Bella is touched Scott understands. 'Yes. Everyone we've interviewed needs a key to a future without unsolved mysteries. The trick is to get on with life and, if the key arrives, that's a blessing.'

'What if that key brings further pain?' asks Meg.

'That's a risk we have to take.' Bella gathers up the storyboards.

III

Part Three

Chapter Twenty-Three

QF1 – Bahrain/London Sector October 1990

Although Bella needs to clear the layers of mystery covering her family history, apprehension, and excitement brush their wings across her. She catches her breath, thinking about her parting from Scott. A crowded departure lounge wasn't the ideal place to tell him of her growing feelings for him. They had both been quiet, their mutually unexpressed emotions making them unable to keep their normal flow of conversation.

He wanted to come with her, but she said no. Now, she realises that, once again, she has rejected his obvious care for her in her usual summary fashion. As the plane tears along the runway, an unfamiliar feeling washes over her. It's regret. With horrible clarity she realises that she keeps hurting this good man and, if she keeps doing this, one day, he might stop trying to get her attention. With equal clarity, she realises that, yes, she does want Scott to be here with her.

The plane lifts off from Bahrain, the force of the aircraft's thrust to get airborne mirrors Bella's internal agitation. She wonders if she is plunging down a dark tunnel in pursuit of ghosts. Yes, more than one ghost. There's a possibility she might find out about her mother, but also a slender lead that may help her, at last, to understand what happened to Eli.

The weeks leading up to her departure had been overwhelming. So many condolence letters to acknowledge, and further searching of Howard's files to find any scraps of information that might assist her search for the truth about her mother. Nothing emerged, but while reading and replying to the letters, Fiona passed one to her from Howard's Israeli friend, Ariel Achmed. The return address is Geneva, Switzerland.

Howard had first met Ariel during an assignment in Israel. The connection is almost too tenuous to contemplate, but could Ariel help her to find out anything at all about Eli? Why hadn't she thought about Ariel before? Then she remembers asking her father to talk to him, and later, Howard said Ariel hadn't been able to help. Bella wrote to Ariel saying she will be in Europe, and could they meet? She tells him she hopes to find any connection to Eli that might be possible. Ariel replied that he is aware of Bella's history with his compatriot. Some years ago, Howard asked him similar questions. Ariel says he put Howard in contact with an Israeli colleague at the embassy in London, but he heard nothing more from him. He closes the letter by saying if he can turn up anything at all, he will contact her at Power Press.

Bella is shocked that Howard may have been in contact with someone who knew Eli. Why would he do that and not tell her? This is as bad as finding out that he had told Fiona that Bella was better off without Eli. Putting these two pieces of information together makes her even more convinced that her father was hiding something from her. Impotent rage wells up inside her.

Apart from the letters, Fiona and Bella realized in the time before her departure, they couldn't hope to go through in detail, any of Howard's drawers of folders about his travels and assignments. Fiona found that the drawers contained files pertaining to Howard's war reporting from Malaya, Egypt, Korea, Vietnam, and the Arab-Israeli conflicts. Where are his writings from World War Two? They decided to ask Adeline. Logically, Howard could have kept all his European material in London. Was this for purely practical reasons, or could it be another way that Howard had kept the two halves of his life apart? She sent a letter of request to Reuters, Howard's employers since his early days in London until his retirement, for details of his years of service. Nothing else emerged from the files they have seen to give her any information about Alexandra.

A voice draws Bella to the surface of awareness. Raising her eye mask, she looks toward the speaker. 'Would you like breakfast, Miss Clemens? We'll land at Heathrow at 9:00 am.'

'Thank you.' She longs for this endless journey to finish and to breathe fresh air. Soft tinkles of fine china remind Bella she is in the first-class section and enjoying the extra comfort. The upgrade from Singapore was so welcome. Is Storm behind this gift of luxury? She glances at her fellow traveler occupying the window seat. Her bowed head might be in sleep or prayer. There's no way of knowing. Since the woman boarded the flight in Bahrain, they haven't exchanged a single word. Bella's companion is dressed in a black Burka. An impenetrable outer shell: Bella hasn't seen her hands emerge from the folds. She hasn't taken food or drink or left her seat. During the long wakeful hours, her head hasn't turned towards Bella. She hasn't even glimpsed the woman's eyes through the veil.

The steward leans toward her and speaks softly. 'Madame Al Soud would you care for some breakfast?'

No reply or acknowledgement. Madame, voulez-vous le petit déjeuner?

A small head movement indicates no, her stillness and silence are profound. Bella feels uncomfortable to be unable to match the woman's self-containment. Eating, drinking, turning the pages of her book, and moving about in her seat, make Bella feel she's creating an almost unbearable intrusion upon the woman. Bella has tried, without success, to reach inside herself to find a place of stillness, to try to settle her tumbling thoughts.

Howard's death has exposed a deep silence. Alive, his presence and energy distracted Bella from pursuing answers she understands he didn't wish her to seek. Now she realises his career, and his passion for traveling, always meant he could be somewhere else. If Bella can't understand her father's motivation for hiding so much from her, how can she continue to love him and value the memories of their life together?

Adeline faxed a letter about Alexandra's Spanish family, the Monerayos. She found out that a Señor Eduardo Monerayo is Alexandra's brother. Eduardo holds a position at Casa Milo Museum in Barcelona. He manages the exhibitions and activities held there. Casa Milo was the Monerayos' townhouse before the Spanish Civil War. This revelation astounded Fiona and Bella.

Bella has been there; it is one of Antonio Gaudi's masterpieces and would have been the home of very well-established people. This paints a picture of her mother's family. It also poses the questions of why they left this luxury home and how Eduardo became an employee of the trust that takes care of the historical treasure. Bella wonders if Eduardo had ever wanted to meet her, couldn't he have found her? Surely, he knew Howard had taken her to Australia after Alexandra died. Should the past lie untouched? She closes her eyes and remembers her first visit to Barcelona in 1974.

After Bella left her father in Rome, she travelled to Barcelona. The architect Antonio Gaudi's work had always fascinated her; she joined a day tour of Gaudi's treasures. Howard knew she was to visit Barcelona; how could he have stopped himself from saying.

"Your mother's family home was at Casa Milo. Write to your uncle Eduardo and ask if you could visit."

Bella remembers her visit to Casa Milo. The walls covered in pelagic blue and green ceramic tiles with pools of golden pink gave the effect of the sea shining in a sunlit dawn sky. She became speechless with a shadowed feeling of déjà vu; tears blurred her sight. Embarrassed, she turned away from the tour party. They might see her emotional response to this place. What depth of her inner ocean formed this unexpected wave of sadness; how to explain it?

Up a winding staircase, Bella touched the wrought iron balustrade with wonder. It felt familiar, too. The staircase opened onto a vast hallway with carved wooden doors leading off. In her memory, a woman opened one of these doors and invited her father to enter. Yes, she was with her father! She was very small; how old would she have been?

The tour guide came back looking for her and made her move on with the group. The moment was gone, but it left lingering thoughts that she couldn't place.

The aroma of fresh coffee brings her to the present. The passengers are talking and making restless preparations for arrival. The shadowed memories of Casa Milo are of Bella's mother's family home, and as Alexandra's daughter, it was hers too. Howard had never said a word. When Bella recounted her experience in Barcelona to him, he passed it off as her active imagination. How dare he edit out such vital parts of her life without her knowledge!

The still figure beside her moves. Bella wonders if her silent emotional storm had washed over her. Is she a wise woman, an elder of her tribe? Bella wishes Fiona could be with her. Fiona is a wise woman, the elder of their tribe. Bella began this journey hopeful that she could get the answers to her questions. Now she feels on unsafe ground. She feels unsure whether she should be disturbing Howard's hidden secrets. Was her father very wise in his choices or very foolish?

Reaching into her bag, she finds the letter from Eduardo Monerayo. The crested paper is fine vellum, the script precise and written with a nib and blue-black ink. Brief and non-committal, Eduardo Monerayo says he has business in London during the first week of October. Please telephone his solicitor to confirm the details upon her arrival. Bella feels the silent woman beside her move, she turns to see the woman looking down at the letter in Bella's hand. The woman raises her head and briefly looks at Bella before turning her head away. Bella feels very uncomfortable; she longs to get off this plane and away from this presence beside her.

Chapter Twenty-Four

Florin Court, Charterhouse Square, London October 1990

T he curved, concave exterior of the building with its iconic Art Deco featured windows and brickwork, stands tall in the morning sunshine. Bella enters the foyer through wrought iron and glass front doors. She pauses, hidden memories push at her. The expansive marble floor is inlaid with the Charterhouse coat of arms. The polished wood concierge desk with the glass top is still in place. A lot of effort and devotion to authenticity has kept this jewel intact. It takes her a minute to realize that there is still a concierge, and he is speaking to her.

'Good morning, madame. Can I help you?'

'Good morning, my name is Isabella Clemens, and I'm here to visit Adeline Stephens.'

'Miss Clemens? Oh, you're Mr Howard's daughter. My name is Jack; I knew him well. I am sorry, Miss Clemens. Miss Stephens told me. I'll ring through.'

'Thank you, Jack.' Bella wonders how many more people she will meet who knew her father, but she never knew they existed.

The lift doors open, and a woman moves towards Bella with her arms open wide.

'Isabella!'

'Adeline?' Bella moves forward,

'Isabella, it is you. How wonderful.'

They hug and pause to take each other in. Bella sees a slender woman of her own height. Adeline's gloriously curled hair seems to escape any effort of restraint by tortoiseshell clasps. Adeline clearly resists the urge to colour her hair, and so, it is still auburn but shot with glinting silver strands. Her eyes are a green that would have matched the exuberance of the deep auburn hair of a younger woman. The effect is matched by a smile that makes Bella feel she has found a precious jewel in the mosaic of her life.

They turn to the lift; Bella feels another frisson of déjà vu. Inside, the scrolled outer doors close, and the inner wire grill appears out of the wall. It clangs with a familiar sound. Adeline turns the brass handle to start the lift in motion. Bella recalls nanny would never let her turn that handle.

The lift glides upwards and halts with a gentle bump, bringing her back to the present. The doors open, and she emerges into her childhood home.

Without hesitation, she turns left and walks towards the tall window at the end of the passage. A river of wide, carpeted hallway stretches ahead, the walls have a geometric style frieze with wall lamps lighting the way. She remembers the hushed quiet and nanny's warnings not to run or make a noise. She's walking backwards in time, back through half remembered dreams and images. Bella stops in front of the last door to the right. She turns to Adeline, tears long constrained by her Clemens stiff upper lip fall. 'I'm home. This is where I last saw my mother.'

They enter the apartment. In the sitting room, light fills every corner. Bella moves to the windows and peers out, expecting to see Howard's car pull up outside. The purring Jaguar of her dreams is now a reality, sitting under covers at Yarra Glen. She is looking forward to sharing outings in it with Scotty. Lost in thought, Bella reflects that her journey has been long in time but, in truth, quite short. She only knew she had a journey to make after her father died.

Adeline brings her out of her reverie. 'Bella, I've put you in your old bedroom. Why don't you freshen up whilst I get lunch?' she smiles.

Bella leaves the sitting room, and in the hallway, she knows her room is the second on the right. All traces of her *'Winnie the Pooh'* curtains and bedspread have gone, but the room still feels familiar. She sits on the bed, almost expecting to see her knitted rabbit with his red waistcoat propped up on the pillow waiting for her. She remembers that when she felt lonely, she would talk to her toys. They were her friends and never got cross with her like mummy often did. Bella starts up. Where did that thought come from? She has never remembered anything much about her mother and certainly not that she was often cross with her!

They decide a Pimm's and soda with the sandwiches would be appropriate. While Adeline pours, Bella says. 'In the bedroom, I had a flash of memory about my mother. That never happens at home.'

Adeline replies, 'I guess that's because you never had any memories of your mother at Yarra Glen, but being here certainly could unlock them.'

They eat and chat as if they had known each other all their lives. Adeline has always known of Bella's existence, but Bella never dreamt all this awaited her. Adeline settles back into her chair; Bella waits for her to start.

Chapter Twenty-Five

Florin Court

'In April 1945, Howard announced that Alexandra was expecting a baby. When you were born, I took a present for you; I was so delighted for the new parents. Howard was a doting father.' Adeline pauses as if choosing what to say. 'After two minutes, Nanny Brown took you to the nursery.' Adeline looks down at her hands and pauses. There is some sadness in her next words. 'By then, with my fiancé posted lost at sea, I accepted that I might never have my own babies, so...'

'Oh, Adeline, you mentioned Robin the first day we spoke. How terrible for you.'

'Bella thank you, it's so long ago now and I've had an interesting life.' She smiles, 'Back then, I longed to cuddle you, to be a kind of aunt to you. This wasn't to be. Alexandra made it quite clear that she didn't welcome visits.'

'How extraordinary. Did you ever talk to Howard about that?'

'Not at first, it was a bit difficult.'

'What happened then?'

Adeline recounts that when peace finally arrived, Howard offered her a permanent job as his personal assistant. So much was happening with post-war reconstruction and the looming Cold War; Howard was away more than he was home, and he needed Adeline as a manager and anchor. He had no choice but to leave Alexandra and baby Isabella at home in London in the care of Clara, his ever-present mother-in-law. Adeline explains that despite peace, neither Clara nor Alexandra seemed keen to return to a war-torn Spain to show off the baby to the Monerayo family.

Outside, the autumn afternoon promises a cold night. Adeline lights the fire set in the grate. 'Howard sent despatches to me from wherever he was. I compiled his pictures and articles ready for editing and printing and researched any background information he needed.' She recounts that they had an office in the London headquarters of Reuters. Sometimes, when Howard was away, she needed to access files stored in Howard's study here.

'If you were alone with nanny, I tried to have some time with you. You were a beautiful, but rather serious child. After a few visits, I began to feel a bit sorry for Howard and, for you. I felt a lack of warmth towards you from your mother and grandmother.' Adeline looks sad as she tells Bella that she put away feelings of disquiet and got on with picking up the pieces of her own life, without the man she loved and planned to marry.

Adeline says, 'I became aware that Alexandra was often away. "Away" was never explained. It was always "Madame isn't home." You seemed to live a very solitary life enclosed with Nanny Brown. It didn't seem right to me, so I decided to mention this to Howard when he returned.'

Bella remembers Fiona describing when Bella first came to Yarra Glen, she was a serious child who didn't seem to know how to play with other children. No wonder. 'So, what happened when you told Howard?'

'He was stunned. He had no idea that Alexandra was often away from you. He admitted that he had concerns about the marriage.' Adeline concludes, 'That's how matters lay until David McKenzie met with Howard at the Naval and Military Club.'

Bella asks. 'Yes, David mentioned that to us. I'm looking forward to meeting him.'

Adeline looks pensive, then she says. 'I know it might feel like working backwards, but I believe it should be David who tells you about Tom and their capture in France. It is really his story.'

'Yes, I agree, He wants me to stay at Hastings, I'll see Storm first and keep my appointment with Eduardo Monerayo.' Bella asks softly. 'Adeline, you can't keep me in suspense for days. Please tell me what happened here after the meeting between David and Howard.'

Adeline continues. 'That meeting blew everything apart; Howard went home to speak to Alexandra, and the conversation wasn't encouraging. As soon as he could leave without raising her suspicions, he came straight to my home. Howard told me that Simon Day, from MI6, had approached him about Alexandra's activities a few months before. That was the reason that David's story of the shooting and the drawing of the woman had such an impact.'

Adeline continues the story. Howard was very shaken, he called Simon. They decided that Adeline would collect Simon to go with her to Florin Court; they intended their call to look as if they were passing by and hoped to be given a cocktail.

In the meantime, Howard went back to see if he could talk to Alexandra again. By the time Howard arrived, he'd been away less than two hours. Simon and Adeline arrived ten minutes later.

Bill, the concierge, looked stricken: all he could do was point. They rushed past him and up in the lift. The front door was wide open. Nanny Brown was trying to console a screaming Bella. It was as if she knew that something terrible had happened, and her world would never be the same again.

Howard was on the phone to Scotland Yard to get the aerodromes and ports covered to stop Alexandra and Clara.

Nanny Brown told them that after Howard left the flat, Alexandra and Clara went into overdrive. Suitcases were pulled out from the storeroom. Nanny heard the fuss and came out of the nursery; Alexandra pushed her back inside and locked her in.

Bill contributed the next part of the story. 'Mrs. Monerayo called down for a taxi. I went out and hailed one. Before I could telephone to say it was in the forecourt, Mrs. Clemens and Mrs. Monerayo came down in the lift and rushed past me, dragging suitcases. They were in the car and gone before I could say anything.'

Bill recounts that he thought something was amiss and rushed back upstairs to the apartment. He was confronted with a chaotic scene and could hear pounding from down the hallway. He found Nanny locked in the nursery with an inconsolable Bella. He was about to phone the police when Howard rushed through the door. Men from Scotland Yard arrived.

Adeline returns from the past, and Bella asks her. 'So, they weren't intercepted?'

'No, no sign of them.'

'Alex probably had an escape plan,' Bella muses.

'Almost certainly.' Adeline replies.

'So...what happened?'

'Well, nothing, it all went quiet.' Adeline explains. 'Howard's wartime activities with the Security Service and Alexandra's so-called legitimate activities for the MOI couldn't be discussed then.'

'Security Service?' Dad?' Was he...some kind of spy? Bella is shocked. 'Good heavens, I wonder if I can find out anything now?'

'Perhaps,' replies Adeline. 'It might be possible now that Howard is dead. I'll enquire for you.'

'Thank you.' Bella takes a breath. 'Adeline, I have to ask, you worked so closely with Howard, were you involved with this work too?'

Adeline looks away out the window and back. 'During the war, there were many people who played roles in the security services.' She smiles. 'I supported Howard's work. Okay?'

'Oh, of course. I apologize if I'm out of order.' Bella understands the message. 'You said Alexandra worked at the MOI. What was the MOI?'

'The Ministry of Information. It was the central government department responsible for publicity and propaganda. It was formed in 1939.'

'And my father helped her to get the job there? How ironic.'

'Yes,' replied Adeline, 'the question was, from her position at the MOI, did she insinuate herself into Britain's security services? Her actions seem to confirm this. The level of trust Alexandra managed to inspire in her superiors is surprising! But this could explain her apparent presence in France at the time of the shooting in Mézières.'

The two women fall silent. Bella feels far away from anything that is familiar to her as she tries to understand this isn't a story, but events that really happened to her father and...her mother.

Adeline's memory reaches back to those days. 'Howard had to accept that Alexandra was a German spy and that she had played him like a violin from the very first time they met at The Ritz. It seems Alexandra's handler was her German lover Klaus Schoeffels.'

'So, my mother really was a traitor or, at best, a double agent.' Bella shakes her head. 'It's a shock, but then... she's never been real to me..." Bella's voice tapers off as she sits in a muddle of emotions. She wonders how her father would have explained all this to her.

'We found a newspaper clipping in Howard's study about a Klaus Schoeffels who disappeared before he could be tried at Nuremberg. Until we spoke to David McKenzie, neither Fiona nor I could figure out why it was there. We never found anything else that related to it,' she pauses, 'except, of course, it ties in with David's story of the woman at the shooting with a German officer. I've sent him the clipping.' She thinks for a minute. 'Adeline, when Howard reported on the Nuremberg trials, do you think he was trying to get to Alexandra through contact with Klaus, but Klaus slipped the net, so that opportunity was lost.'

'No doubt about that,' Adeline replies. 'I remember how frustrated he was when Klaus disappeared.'

'Could this also have meant there was a mole in the service who covered Alexandra's tracks? Promoted her to a position where she could do even more damage?' Bella feels sick and fascinated.

Adeline says. 'Howard and I discussed this. If there was a mole, and that person was discovered, that information was far above our security clearance at that time or even later. This information may be available by now. After all, it's over forty years ago. Statutes of Limitations expire on some papers, the records might be accessible. Sadly, Howard isn't here to read the files.'

The two women are silent, then Bella says. 'Adeline, we can't find a death certificate for Alexandra. Have you found it here?'

'Death certificate? Why would Howard have a death certificate?'

'But...' Bella looks at Adeline. She can hardly say the words. 'That's the whole reason Howard took me to Australia. He told his parents and Fiona that my mother had been killed in an accident and her family couldn't look after me.'

Adeline presses her hands against her face. 'Bella, Howard told you this? When did he find out? He never told me.'

Bella jumps up; she doesn't know where to put the flash of rage she is experiencing; her heart is thumping. 'Did he make that up? My father made up a lie that has affected my whole life. I can't believe it! The...' Bella almost says "bastard" but stops herself. Instantly, she perceives that this terrible untruth is the reason Howard kept his English life and Adeline separate from Fiona and Bella. Adeline and Bella stare at each other in total confusion.

'Adeline, what was he thinking?' Bella feels as if she is drowning, waves of sorrow wash over her. 'It's so much to take in. And now, it's not only about finding my mother, but I need to find my father. My real father! Not someone who told lies and harbored secrets. As each day passes, I find that I didn't know him at all.'

Adeline recovers herself enough to say firmly. 'Bella, your real father was Howard exactly as you knew him. All this other ...' Adeline pauses, 'was to do with his wish for your life to be free of the past. It's no more complicated than that. Can you try to accept that, please?'

'Right now, I'm not sure. To accept what he has done is to go against everything he taught me about honesty and integrity.'

'I understand, Bella, can you give it time? This has been a massive shock to both of us.' Adeline says gently. 'It's possible that when you find out more about your mother, you might start to understand Howard's choices.'

'Y' know what upsets me, Adeline? You lost your fiancé and the possibility of your own family. Then, Howard keeps you separate from sharing his! I would've loved to have you in my life, for all my life.'

'Yes, at least I had the advantage of knowing of your existence and Fiona and Yarra Glen.'

'That's exactly what I mean! You knew about Fiona and me, but he kept you away from us! Why? What possible explanation could he have?'

'It was very simple. Howard didn't want to put me in any position where I could be a party to his web of evasions.'

'Oh, how very noble of him. Fiona and I also accepted him without question. It seems so wrong now.'

'Yes,' said Adeline. 'I admit I've had misgivings for a long time.'

'This's so sad.' Bella sinks back onto the sofa beside Adeline and takes her hand. 'Did you plan to contact us? After all, you've lost a lifetime friend and partner.'

'Bella, I expected that by the time Howard returned to London, he would've made a clean breast of the whole story, and you would come to live here whenever you choose. It is your home.'

They both fall silent as they contemplate the enormity of the revelations they are uncovering. 'Now, Bella, we must be practical and use your time here wisely. Apart from seeing David, how do you plan to find information about Alexandra?'

'Nothing is on the public record, which is curious. David only found a newspaper clipping about her being listed as a missing person. Nothing else. I'm hoping that when I see my boss, Lord Storm, he might help me. He's only a few years younger than Howard. He may have some history with the wartime security services.'

'Ah, Storm! Adeline smiles. 'Now there's an interesting man! Yes, Howard knew him well. I want to hear what he has to say.'

Bella shakes her head, another connection. How many layers are there for her to peel back? 'One thing confuses me, Adeline. By working with Simon Day from MI6, Howard was prepared to expose Alexandra. But after she bolted, he shut down and went to extraordinary lengths to suppress the whole affair. Why d'you think that was?'

Adeline muses, then gives Bella an unexpected reply. 'Could it have been male pride? Alexandra used him and then, out maneuvered him by escaping. That must have been very hard for Howard!'

'Oh dear, I see what you mean.' Bella thinks about her father's contradictory nature. The expansive host. The sportsman. The tireless reporter.

And to the outside world, a total extrovert. Bella wonders if, by protecting her from her mother's treachery, was he also protecting himself? Adeline is giving her a lot to think about. The idea that anyone could outwit Howard shocks her.

Adeline excuses herself to answer the telephone; Bella wanders over to a wall of framed photographs. Pictures of her everywhere! No wonder Adeline recognized her so easily downstairs! A picture of her university graduation day. Many more of Bella taken with Howard and Fiona at Yarra Glen. Horse riding with Howard. Traveling in Europe with Howard, Skiing with Howard. Bella feels the love of her father here, in this room, so far away from home. She can feel a soft side to her father that she never dreamt existed, when he was at home on the other side of the world.

The sun has moved from one side of the windows to the other. The shadows of the trees in the square outside are lengthening, reminding Bella she is in the northern hemisphere with early darkness promising winter. Adeline closes the drapes and switches on silk-shaded lamps that infuse a soft rose glow into the room. The décor is more feminine than the very practical furnishings of the old farmhouse at Yarra Glen. This room is elegant in an understated way, with soft furnishings in beautiful Sanderson print fabrics, comfortable sofas, and fine rugs. To balance this, the artworks and wall of bookshelves announce Howard's presence. Bella notices one of his pipes and a tobacco pouch on a side table next to a chair whose style and leather covering show it was his. Clearly, Adeline isn't ready to sweep all traces of Howard from their shared home. This pulls at Bella's heart. Despite their discoveries, Bella's internal scale is tilting towards love of her father, but managing her anger and confusion, isn't easy.

Bella shows Adeline the letter from Eduardo Monerayo.

'I hope, if my meeting with him this week goes well, I'll be able to visit him in Barcelona.'

'Yes, that would be perfect, but Bella, please don't try to rush him into this. I have a feeling that Eduardo will be very cautious about you.'

'Yes,' smiles Bella, 'after all these years, I guess he's got very mixed feelings about digging up the past. I want to meet Ariel Achmed in Geneva, too. I'm hoping he might be able to tell me something about Eli. Do you know him?'

'I know of him, but I've never met him.'

The next question tumbles out of Bella. 'Did you ever meet Eli here? Do you know whether Howard did?'

'Ah, Bella, I understand why you're asking, but no, it's the same as Ariel. If he did meet Eli, I wasn't present, and he never spoke about it.'

'I'm coming to understand that doesn't mean he didn't.'

'Yes, I agree,' says Adeline.

Bella is forming an image of the watertight compartments of Howard's life. His written words said so much without telling her anything about his feelings. He could, through his journalism, name, shame, declaim, and move mountains to be an agent of change. A masterful lifetime performance of creating a complete outer persona. So complete that everyone, even his family believed they knew the real Howard Clemens.

Few people would suspect the existence of the private, hidden person. Neither Bella nor Fiona dreamt it existed. The screen between one and the other was so tight-woven. She realises that her life, like his, is full of outer diversions. All created to delay the need to look inside her heart and soul. It's a trick to stop her from looking for the truth. Not to ever look at the reasons behind all this activity that leaves little room for introspection. And, she realises with remorse, this trait has stopped her from really seeing Scott as he wants her to see him.

The peal of nearby Church bells interrupts Bella's reverie. This reminds her to make the appointment with Eduardo Monerayo's solicitor in London. She picks up the letter and dials the number. A male voice answers.

'Good afternoon, Swanston Barry & Son. How may I direct your call?'

Bella, startled by the formal greeting, finds her voice and speaks. 'Good afternoon, I would like to speak to Mr William Pridham, please.'

The voice replies. 'Are you a client of Mr Pridham?'

'My name is Isabella Clemens. I have a letter of introduction to meet with him.'

The voice asks. 'May I enquire whom your referee might be, Miss

Clemens?'

'Senor Eduardo Monerayo,' she pauses and adds, 'I'm his niece.'

'Oh!' said the voice; 'I will connect you to Mr Pridham's junior, Mr. James Ogilvy.'

'Thank you.'

Another male voice speaks. 'Good afternoon, Miss Clemens. I am James Ogilvy; we are expecting your call.'

Bella feels encouraged by Mr. Ogilvy's more friendly tone. 'Good afternoon, Mr Ogilvy. My uncle has written, requesting that we could meet at your office.'

'Yes, Miss Clemens, it's all arranged. Mr Monerayo will be here to meet with you this Wednesday at 10:00 am. I trust this will be suitable?' Mr Ogilvy enquires.

Bella replies, 'Yes, of course, thank you, Mr. Ogilvy, I'll be there.'

'Very good,' says Mr Ogilvy, 'now you have our address, but are you a stranger to London? Can you find your way here? I ask this because Mr Pridham and Mr Monerayo are very precise about punctuality.'

Mr Ogilvy is giving her a message. 'Thank you, Mr Ogilvy, you're kind to enquire. I've spent a lot of time in London, I'll be fine.'

'Until Wednesday, thank you for your call, Miss Clemens.'

'Goodbye, Mr Ogilvy.'

They are ready for something stronger than coffee. Adeline pours each of them a large gin and tonic. She's also used to the Australian taste for ice; the first sip calms Bella. Until Howard's death, she believed that Fiona was her only family. Now, she has, if he will accept her, an Uncle Eduardo; she also has David and Adeline, whom she wants to be part of her life.

Later that evening Bella writes a long fax to Fiona, she needs to crystallize her thoughts. Most of all, she needs to process her feelings about her own father; what a complex man he was. She phones Scott at the office. The busy sounds in the background and his familiar voice make her realise how far away she is from him and his care of her.

'What's happening, Bella?'

'Scotty, I'll send you the fax I've sent to Fiona. That will give you the headlines, but oh…' her voice trails off. She wants to tell Scott she is missing him, but that's a big step for her. Suddenly, unbidden, the words rush out. 'I wish you could be here.'

Silence, a beat. Bella can hear the clattering and chatter in the background, and then Scott speaks with tenderness. 'I wish I could be with you too. You know I didn't want you to go alone.'

'I know, I realise that now. I'm sorry I didn't think it through.' Bella looks around the room in her father's home. 'It's lovely here, and Adeline is wonderful. She's helping me so much,' she pauses, 'but Scotty, I'm like Alice. I've fallen down a rabbit hole and found a whole world I never dreamt existed. I've found my father was two different people with two separate lives, and it feels like I am living in a tale with the story still to unfold.'

'I hope this doesn't turn into a Grimm's fairy tale with an evil witch Bella.'

'Scotty, you're making fun of me.'

'You're the one that mentioned the rabbit hole.'

'Scotty, I'm sorry I was so hasty when you offered to come with me. Until I left you at the airport, I truly thought this is a journey I had to make by myself.'

'Ah, Bella, you might wonder who your father really is, but I know you are truly his daughter with the same stiff-necked pride.'

'Oooh, am I that bad?'

A beat of silence from Scott's end of the line before he says with a softness in his voice. 'Bella, you need to be clear with yourself and with me about what you want. If I come to join you, it won't just be Scott and Bella on assignment somewhere.'

Scott's meaning is clear to her. It's time for her to make a choice. She can stay in her old world focussed on Eli, or she can take the hand Scott is offering and step into a new life. With equal clarity, she realises if she backs away again, he might not be around for her when she returns home.

'Scott, I want you to…I need you to come here if you can please.'

'I'll see what I can do.' They talk for a while longer before they say goodnight, both knowing they have crossed into a new place.

Feeling tired but with a calmness in her heart that she hasn't felt for many years, Bella goes to bed, but sleep eludes her. She realizes there's another question. She could ask Adeline this one: why did Howard die with two photographs of Alexandra in his wallet? She doubts that he died loving Alexandra as she thought. Were the photos a reminder to Howard that he couldn't ever let his guard slip? To expose Bella to the risk of learning the truth about her own mother. In doing this, he condemned himself and others to a lifetime of living in shadows.

Chapter Twenty-Six

Power Press Headquarters London 1990

The sullen autumn morning overlays its mood onto the streets and the people hurrying along. Slanting sleet ignores Bella's umbrella and attacks her side as she walks quickly to Vauxhall Bridge Road. Publishing houses flock together in this area; she can visualize vast basements with giant presses breathing print like live beasts. As she walks along the pavement, she imagines underfoot, she can feel a thrumming sensation like being in a hive of bees. A feeling she's arriving in the heart of a world where the art of using words and language is paramount. It's her world, and she loves every part of it.

At Power Press House, the façade and first three floors is a renovated red brick Victorian building. A soaring architectural glass shard-like tower rises from the historic building that housed the first publications. Bella's boss, Lord Storm's family, has owned the business for over a hundred years. The contrast in the architecture reminds her of two aspects of Storm. Underneath, he is a traditional journalist and a man from an earlier era of manners and style. Outwardly, he's a progressive publisher and forward-thinking company executive with a sharp mind and interest in the ever-changing world.

The lift gives her a sense of weightlessness; Bella's stomach feels a little unmoored. In the outer office, she takes a deep breath and smiles a greeting to Storm's PA Phoenicia; she is on the phone and indicates to Bella to go into Storm's office.

She knocks and, hearing a gruff 'come in,' she enters, closes the door, and waits for Storm to speak. He is standing in front of a large pin board with the galleys of the Missing Persons article laid out page by page. Even from her place by the door, she can see Scott's photography is masterful. The images are mesmerizing. The layouts look clear and uncluttered.

'Bella, welcome,' he turns towards her and smiles. She's struck by the sheer magnetism of the man with the piercing gaze out of a lined, leathery face. His reputation as tough and uncompromising, could easily overwhelm someone meeting him for the first time. Bella used to be a bit overawed by him whenever she visited London until he arrived unexpectedly at Yarra Glen for Howard's funeral. His gentle care and respect for Fiona and wonderful speech about her father showed his true kindness and humanity.

'Good morning, Storm,' ventures Bella. 'How do you like the proofs?'

He sits at his desk and waving Bella to a chair, buzzes Phoenicia for more coffee. 'It's very good, Bella,' he says, waving his cup towards the board, 'I've sent my comments to Meg. This is an international story. Missing people often make new lives in foreign countries. I really like these pieces about the people left behind. Gives the readers and, maybe the missing, something to think about.' His next comment winds Bella. 'Is your story of finding your mother to be part of this?'

Bella sits back; what does she say now? Her worst fear is exposing herself and her family to scrutiny. Has Meg told their boss more than Bella would have liked her to?

'Well…I don't know what to say. I'd rather keep my own story out of all this …' Bella trails off.

Silence as he taps his pen on the desk and regards her with his intense gaze. He's like a hawk circling at a great height. It sees her on the ground and sizes her up as a morsel for breakfast.

Bella continues. 'Meg, Scott, and I feel that this piece will start a discussion about missing persons. And those left behind.' Bella stops, and she watches him. More tapping of the pen, then silence.

Storm says. 'You're very persuasive. Are you saying that this first article is a teaser? And you hope more stories will come to you.'

'Yes… exactly. We will invite readers to submit their own stories. We believe this has legs as a series. We hope you agree.'

'Yes, it has got "legs," as you put it.' Storm replies. 'I can see a time when most people will have personal computers. This World Wide Web I've been reading about, is going to completely revolutionize how we, as human beings, relate to each other. TV, radio, newspapers, and magazines will only form a part of media.'

'Scott says that the Internet is going to link up people in a way we've never seen before. If people want to go missing, it will be harder for them to stay missing. He talks about us all leaving digital footprints. He's a bit obsessed about it all.'

'Smart man!' Storm taps his desktop. 'I'll talk to him about this. Come to think of it, I'll get Scott to come over with his edit of the documentary. I want him to talk about this stuff to my people here.'

Bella feels a surge of pleasure; she is missing Scotty more each day. Hearing his voice last night and their conversation, has changed everything. She can see Storm is satisfied with moving a human chess piece on his board to get the result he wants. In this case, Scotty is the piece to move across the game. It clears the way for him to come to London to be with her.

Storm walks back to the whiteboard; he's quiet for a minute as he looks at the proofs. He turns around and continues in a completely different tone.

'Bella, sometimes I miss coalface journalism. Life up here on the top floor is a bit removed from the buzz downstairs.'

Bella looks at this man who has always seemed such a towering figure to his employees. He has ink in his veins like the rest of us.

Storm comes around the desk and sits in the chair next to her. 'You must miss Howard dreadfully.'

Surprised, Bella can only say. 'I do,' and hope that Storm can't see the tears that have sprung to her eyes. 'It was good of you to come to the funeral. Fiona and I were so pleased to see you.'

Storm says, 'Howard and I go back a long way.' He hands her his handkerchief.

Bella is touched by his quiet gesture of care. She grows to like Storm more every time she meets him. She remembers the stranger in the dark suit at the funeral. She asks Storm if he knew him.

'Ah yes,' Storm replies. 'A retired army type from Canberra,' he says dismissively.

'But Howard wasn't in the army. Why would a retired army type turn up at his funeral?'

Storm waves a hand. 'Oh, um, I only spoke to him for a minute. I think Howard did some type of consulting on security matters ...'

Bella sees that Storm won't be drawn on this subject yet. 'Storm, I'm staying with Adeline Stephens, she mentioned that she knows you.'

Storm's face softens. 'Bella, we all operated in the same circles.' He smiles and then says. 'Interesting woman Adeline; what did she say about me?'

Bella smiles, 'she said you're an interesting man.'

'Is that so?' he says, looking pleased. 'I must look her up for lunch.' Storm regards Bella thoughtfully. 'What's this about your mother?'

'Can you tell me how to find out anything at all about her?'

'What do you know so far?'

Bella recounts that her mother was a suspected British traitor. She tells him everything she has found out so far from David and Adeline. 'Meg said you might be able to help me find any records about her work with the Ministry of Information during the war. And her disappearance in 1946.'

'Oh? Why would Meg think that?'

Bella dives in. 'Meg believes you may have had contact with MI6 in the past. And you may know someone who remembers the events surrounding her disappearance.' She stops, unsure how to read Storm's gaze. 'My friend David McKenzie has researched newspapers from that time. He can't find anything much at all.' She hands a copy of the missing persons clipping to him. And the copy of the clipping about Klaus Schoeffels. 'I think there's a connection.'

Storm reaches for the clippings, looks at them, and then says. 'MI6? Meg might be getting a bit ahead of herself there.'

Bella isn't convinced by his tone. She can see he's studying the grainy black-and-white photographs. Storm places the clippings on the desk and looks up at her. His face doesn't give Bella any clue to his thoughts, but she senses a tension in him. Is it like that frisson a journalist feels when they get a lead on a story?

He smiles at Bella. 'I admit your story interests me; I'll see what I can find for you.'

Bella gets up to leave, and as she reaches the door, she turns back. 'Storm, I need to find someone else.'

Storm looks up. 'For goodness sake, Bella, who would that be?'

'Eli Fossbach, my former partner, disappeared five years ago. I had given up on ever finding him, but since Howard died, I've found out that he might have been in contact with Eli.' Bella tries to stop the anger and emotion rising. She can't let Storm see the gut-wrenching feeling of betrayal she feels that her father might have known about Eli's whereabouts, and never told her.

'I plan to meet up with Ariel Achmed, a colleague of Dad's; he lives near Geneva. Howard met him covering the Arab-Israeli conflicts, they became friends. It's a long shot, but being Israeli, and a similar age, he might have met Eli. I'm hoping he can help me. Have you ever met him?'

Storm looks at Bella, 'I know of him, he's a first-rate investigative journalist. Let's deal with one thing at a time, shall we?'

Bella smiles as she closes the door. She hadn't known what to expect when she opened the box of her family's secrets to Storm, but he hasn't disappointed her, far from it. Tomorrow, she will meet her Uncle Eduardo. She suspects that today's meeting was the easy part. Whenever Bella thinks about the following day and meeting her mother's brother. She feels a twanging of her nerves like discordant vibrations from an untuned harp.

Chapter Twenty-Seven

London – Bella Meets Eduardo

Bella is shown into the conference room at Swanston Barry & Son. She takes her place at the table, where she can gain a first impression of Eduardo Monerayo as he enters. Only her third day in London, and so much is happening she is glad of a few minutes to reflect.

Now the time to meet Eduardo has arrived, Bella is thankful for Adeline's research into the Monerayo family. She had received material from Barcelona that had yielded distressing information about Eduardo's experiences during the Spanish Civil War. The translations revealed the tragic events that befell the family.

Bookcases line the room. Bella can smell the age and mustiness of the tomes squeezed inside the tall glass doors. How many scenes of hope or despair has this room witnessed? The soft chime of a mantle clock striking ten distracts her.

The door opens; Bella stands, her stomach churns, but she hopes she appears outwardly calm. Mr William Pridham enters and stands back to admit Eduardo Monerayo. The frail white-haired man is dressed in a black suit from another era; the severity is only broken by a starched wing collar, which in turn gives way to a thin, unsmiling, high-cheeked face with prominent cheekbones, black eyes, and a hawk-like nose. He gives an instant impression of a life spent without sunshine or joy.

Mr Pridham speaks. 'Miss Clemens, may I introduce Don Eduardo

Monerayo.'

'How do you do Don Eduardo.'

'How do you do, Senorita Clemens.'

Bella moves forward to offer her hand; he touches it as he inclines his head. Mr Pridham holds a chair for Eduardo at the head of the table. A flush of schoolgirl awkwardness catches Bella as she resumes her seat after he sits. Round one: formal.

Has she made a breach of etiquette already? Yes, she should've waited for him to offer his hand. Presumptuous of her to offer hers first, he would've noticed that. Bella decides not to speak until she is spoken to. She regards Eduardo with a calm and, she hopes, respectful gaze.

Don Eduardo appears to be aware of this gesture but then, it is nothing less than he would expect. His opening line still sets her back. 'May I ask what proof you have that my sister Alexandra is your mother?'

"Is" not "was," Bella catches the tiny floating feather this word represents. Her heart is beating hard. Can this stern-faced man hear her anxiety? Does it show on her face?

'I have Howard and Alexandra's marriage certificate and my birth certificate. Mr Pridham has copies. Also, photos of my father and myself.' Bella looks across the table towards Mr Pridham. He sits like a wax figure, his face and horn-rimmed spectacles a polished sheen. An irreverent thought flits across her mind. He matches this room full of silent, burnished furniture.

Eduardo moves the pieces of paper to one side. 'Pieces of paper, they could be forgeries or stolen. I have asked Mr Pridham to arrange for some further investigations. A DNA test if you will agree? I will consider the options when I receive the answers.'

Bella's anger at this man's presumption replaces caution. 'Why? How can you test for a DNA match if Alexandra is dead? Or is she still alive? My aunt Fiona and I couldn't find a death certificate amongst my father's papers or any record of a divorce.'

Eduardo Monerayo stands. Shocked, Bella realizes the longed-for meeting is over. Five minutes! She's travelled across the world to find her mother and he gives her five minutes! Blood rushes to her head, her heart thunders. Through a haze, she hears her stern-faced uncle speaking to her.

'Senorita Clemens, I understand you are a journalist. I need to be assured of your identity and your intentions. I do not wish to find you are here to ingratiate yourself to write a story about my family.'

"My family," not "our family." The knife, having made a cut, turns. Recognition of this startles Bella. She looks closely at this man, her blood relation. She tilts her chin slightly and gazes into his eyes. What she sees startles her; it is so unexpected. She sees fear. The elderly man's mask of arrogance conceals a deep-seated anxiety. This can only mean her uncle has something to hide. More secrets. Family secrets? Bella is not yet considered family, so she is excluded. She refuses to be intimidated. She stands as Eduardo turns towards the door.

'Don Eduardo, something about me has upset you; it wasn't my intention.' The part of her saying these words comes from deep inside her. She is speaking from a place of quiet truth. Don Eduardo pauses; his hand rests on the doorknob. She feels her father's presence supporting her. He would want her to see this through to get the best possible result within her power to do so. Bella takes a deep breath, and the steadiness of her voice surprises her.

'I'm sorry. Please will you stay? Yes, I'll agree to any tests you may need; when you mentioned the DNA test, I understood that my mother might be alive.' Bella takes a breath. Be calm, she tells herself. Eduardo doesn't move, so she continues.

'I believed that she died when I was very young. Please help me, Don Eduardo.' Bella hesitates. Unsure whether to continue, she says, 'I've spent my whole life with less than half a family.'

Eduardo half-turned. Bella scans his face for any hint of a softening, no visible change, his dark eyes inscrutable, giving her no relief from the anxiety crawling in her stomach.

'Yes, Senorita Clemens, I believe my sister Alexandra is alive.'

'Oh!' Bella sits down; she feels winded. She wishes Aunt Fiona could be with her right now. 'Don Eduardo, please can you help me to understand?'

Eduardo still has his hand on the door handle; his hand looks polished, too. His skin has a translucent quality. The skin of a man who lives a life sequestered with his books and his unhappy memories. She watches his hand, but it's still, it doesn't turn the brass knob that will signal an end to her hopes. Mr Pridham also seems like a crow hovering motionless in an updraft of air. Not going forward, just hanging, his wings waiting for a signal to follow.

Bella is quite sure Mr Pridham would only ever follow. Not take the initiative to lead her out of this tricky moment. Don Eduardo's response takes her by surprise.

'How much do you understand about the Spanish Civil War, Senorita Clemens?'

In the silence that follows, Bella can hear muffled traffic noises. They give an everyday quality of normality to a situation that grows more bizarre by the minute. Still standing, she wills herself to make an appropriate response. She feels the sleeping books have awoken, and all turned to listen. She chooses not to disclose what she knows of the Monerayo family's tragic personal history.

'A little Don Eduardo; in Australian education, the subject was not well-covered. I've read a lot of Hemingway and Martha Gellhorn.' She takes a deep breath; the pounding in her chest is subsiding. She says softly. 'That war was a tragedy. All war is a catastrophe, but if it's possible, a civil war is more so. Brother fighting against brother, families divided, many forever.' She falls silent.

Eduardo nods ... 'Please continue.'

'I'm interested in the stories of young English and Australian people who fought with the International Brigades. Most of them could hardly have understood the issues at stake; the politics were so complex.' Bella takes a breath. 'Don Eduardo, I'm curious about why you consented to this meeting at all. If this is all so difficult, you could've refused my request. I've come a long way, but I find this position you are putting me in quite difficult. I'm asking for your understanding. I don't wish you to treat me as an imposter or a schoolchild.'

'Your father's daughter, I can see.'

Bella thinks this is an interesting admission that he has met Howard. She says quietly, 'I'm not ashamed of that, Don Eduardo.'

Her uncle nods to Mr Pridham, who, at last, stops appearing to hang in the air and moves toward him. Eduardo takes an envelope from his briefcase. He hands it to Mr Pridham, who walks around the table and gives it to Bella. Eduardo resumes his seat.

Taking this as a sign of temporary reprieve, Bella sits. She opens the envelope and draws out a black and white portrait photograph. The stiff matte paper and deckle-edged backing shows its age. Two women gaze at the camera, their expressions serious. Bella tries to focus on the details, but she can't see. Tears fill her eyes. Normally quite stoic, now, she can't seem to control herself.

The younger woman is Alexandra. A small child sits on the older woman's knee. Now she can see why Eduardo agreed to the meeting. She understands his shock at meeting Bella face to face. There she is in the photograph. Yes, she is the child, but even more startling is her resemblance now in her own mid-life, to the older woman. The photograph opens another door in Bella's memory. She remembers Grandmother Clara in their home in London. Before her mother left Bella with nanny Brown. She points to the older woman in the picture.

'My grandmother.' Not a question; this is a statement of recognition.

'Yes, Eethabella, your grandmother, Clara Somers-Monerayo.'

The photograph and Eduardo's pronunciation of her name as 'Eethabella' in the Castilian style catches Bella's breath, relieved Eduardo has finally chosen to call her by her first name.

'Yes, my father Raymondo met and married Clara Somers in England whilst he was at university.' He half smiles, 'against my parents' wishes.'

'Clara was English?'

He looks at Bella with the first shadow of a smile. 'Yes, she came from a prominent family in Oxfordshire. Howard and Alexandra's Anglo-Spanish marriage was history repeating itself.' The old man sighs: he's shed the cloak of arrogance he wore into the room.

'Why did you say you wished me to have tests when you can see I bear such a strong resemblance to Clara and to Alexandra?'

'Eethabella, it's a shock to see you and, most of all, selfishness. I want to heal old wounds in our family, but in truth, I'm unsure if I have the strength to go through with it. Part of me hoped you would be discouraged and go away.' He smiles again. 'I should have known better. A daughter of Howard and Alexandra would not be put off by the bluster of an old man.'

Bella watches as Eduardo rises, looks out the window, then turns to her.

'Eethabella, a few minutes ago, you said you have lived your life with less than half a family. The story I am about to tell you will show you that I understand this more than you know. This is why I asked you about the civil war.'

He recounts the facts. 'When the Spanish Civil War erupted in 1936, Clara and Alexandra sided with the Fascists. My father Raymondo, and I, were Republicans; we didn't support Franco. Clara and Alexandra's, as we saw it, traitorous views horrified us. Raymondo sent Clara and Alexandra to England to enroll Alexandra at Cambridge University. And, as we thought, out of harm's way. We didn't understand then that Clara's English family, the Somers, were powerful supporters of Oswald Mosley. And the emerging British Union of Fascists who, in turn, had strong links to Hitler's Nazi party in Germany.'

'Fascists? The Somers were supporters of Mosley? I wonder what my father thought of that?' Bella shakes her head; she must keep listening to Eduardo and deal with this later.

Eduardo continues. 'In Spain, my father and I were imprisoned. It was a trumped-up charge of treason, and after a farcical court case, father — Raymondo was executed in 1938. I remained in prison.' He looks down as if reliving that time.

Bella wonders at the toll these tragedies must have taken on him.

He raises his head and continues. 'After Franco's victory in Spain, Clara and Alexandra secured my release. I was only spared by the work my mother and sister performed for the Fascists. I'm still ashamed I survived in that manner. At that time, I opted for life; I would have died had I stayed in the foul prison. I lived under house arrest in Barcelona throughout World War Two. I worked translating documents for the government; I had no choice.'

A quiet knock on the door signals the arrival of tea served in a silver tea service with porcelain crockery. Bella smiles, thinking about her office at home. The different atmosphere is greater than distance. The short break allows her to absorb the gravity of Eduardo's story.

Eduardo continues. 'In 1946, I finally met Howard after Alexandra and Clara disappeared. By then, we could see how much the contact with the Somers family, fed Clara and Alexandra's beliefs they'd brought with them from Spain. They immersed themselves into the lives of the upper-class British Fascists.' He pauses to sip his tea.

Bella takes a chance. She asks, 'Please, can I call you Uncle Eduardo?'

'Yes, of course you may Eethabella, but Eduardo will do nicely. Can I call you 'Bella? That is what you prefer?'

They smile at each other. Eduardo looks straight at her. 'Bella, please understand, I find it so difficult to think of those days. Let alone speak about them.' He falls silent. He contemplates the papers in front of him on the table. The silence is heavy.

Mr Pridham and Bella sit, not wishing to break into Eduardo's thoughts. Bella wonders if she should ask Mr Pridham to stop the meeting. She looks at Mr Pridham who, as if he is reading her mind, shakes his head. He gives her a slight hand gesture to tell her to give Eduardo time.

A telephone ringing outside the room interrupts the silence. Eduardo takes a deep breath: 'Bella, I understand that this must be as hard for you to hear, as it is for me to tell you. Your mother, Alexandra was, and possibly still is, a Nazi and Fascist through and through. After all, in the Civil War, Hitler and Mussolini supported Franco.'

Bella sits back, stunned. 'How on earth did she hide all this from Howard? I can't believe he was so taken in by her.'

Eduardo looks down at his hands and replies quietly. 'Since she was a child, my sister was a consummate and pathological liar. She would've spun a story about herself to Howard from their very first meeting.' He looks

150

up, 'I know Alexandra never let on about Clara's and her connection to the Somers family. Howard told me that.'

'Eduardo, would you say that, in fact, Alexandra had no allegiance to Britain at all? Would she have seen her alleged activities during the war as justifiable? Because her true allegiances were to Germany?'

Eduardo replies in a firm voice. 'Yes, exactly. Clara was also committed to fascism, but she became terrified of Alexandra's extremism. She stayed close to her, to keep her from committing crimes that would cause her to hang as a British traitor.'

Bella interjects. 'Except as Alexandra had no allegiance to Britain, she wouldn't see herself as a traitor.' Bella is horrified at these revelations about her mother. Her understanding of her father's actions is growing; he did spend his life trying to protect her. Bella continues. 'Howard may have been a marriage of convenience for Alexandra.'

'Bella, I agree. Alexandra knew how to get whatever she wanted from Howard. Later, after Howard left Barcelona, I could only hope she hadn't compromised him. He was a good man.'

It's Bella's turn to bow her head. Eduardo's acknowledgement of her father threatens to undo her composure. *Hold on,* she says to herself and then to Eduardo.

'Adeline told me that Howard knew of Alexandra's possible role as a spy and a traitor. He was already working with the security services.' Bella takes a sip of water. She feels completely drained, but she can't stop now. How must this old man be feeling? She asks, 'Where are Clara and Alexandra? What happened to them?'

Eduardo replies, 'In truth, Bella, I really don't know.' He recounts that after the war, Alexandra never adjusted to the defeat of her ideologies. The Somers, despite their fascist leanings during the war, rehabilitated themselves in English society by doing "good works." Eduardo allows himself another small smile. 'Today, we call it a PR whitewash. I realise my life could have been quite different if I hadn't refused to help your father when he asked me.'

'Why do you say that?' Bella feels a growing sense of attachment to him.

Eduardo stops pacing and sits down. 'I refused to help Howard when he brought you to Barcelona.' He recounts that at that time, he was still full of stiff-necked Spanish pride and arrogance. He didn't want to hear Howard's story. That would mean he would have to acknowledge to Howard, and in public, that his sister was a traitor, a Fascist, and most likely, a murderess. He pauses, then looks at Bella.

'No matter what they had done to me, I didn't want to help Howard to bring her to justice and see my sister hanged. I didn't know where she was, but I had a good idea she would have gone to be with the German officer. She'd been in love with him before the war, but they couldn't marry because his wife would not give him a divorce. I never met him, but I recall his name was Klaus.'

Bella exclaims, 'It must be Klaus Schoeffels. He was the officer David saw Alexandra with in France and,' she hesitates, unsure of the impact on Eduardo her next words will have. 'At Mézières when David and my uncle Tom were shot by a firing squad.' She places a copy of the newspaper clipping on the table in front of Eduardo, he reads it. When he raises his head and looks at Bella, she sees he is grief-stricken.

'Eduardo, did you ever tell Howard about her relationship with that man?'

'Yes, Bella, I did. He showed me the drawing and I couldn't deny it could be Alexandra. The likeness was extraordinary.' Eduardo bows his head. 'Howard left to return to England with you, and yes, I live without a family and without a heart.'

Bella moves around the table to sit next to him. He surprises her by taking her hand.

'Bella, I understand why Howard kept your family a secret. After I recovered from my fear of damage to our family name, I was too ashamed to contact Howard to make amends. I thought you were better not to; how do you say it? Have these skeletons in your family closet. Clearly, Howard felt the same.'

'Eduardo, my father died still carrying photos of Alexandra in his wallet. He never remarried. Perhaps he died still loving Alexandra? I'll never know.

I understand his moral dilemma about Alexandra. If he found her, he would have to turn her in for trial as a war criminal.'

Eduardo smiles. 'At least in that, your father and I had that in common. My reason was selfishness. His was to protect you.'

'Yes, I understand that now. I'm so sad for both of you.'

'Bella, it's the choice we made.'

Mr Pridham refills the water glasses. The tension in the room has subsided; sadness and a beautiful feeling of two souls related by blood but separated by tragedy finding comfort in each other replaces it. Her father made himself a prisoner of his past as her uncle Eduardo had.

'So, I'm curious,' Bella says. 'What happened next? Did Clara and Alexandra stay in contact with you?'

'Nothing from Alexandra, she disappeared. After some months, Clara came to see me demanding money. I made a settlement on her, providing she would never contact me again.'

Bella asks, 'Was Clara content with that?'

'Content? Neither of them ever understood that word. They always wanted more. They believed I should provide for them forever. Although, it's a few years now since Clara approached me for more money. She might have died; she would be well into her nineties.'

'Do you ever hear from Alexandra?'

'Not for many years now.' Eduardo is silent. 'Bella, would you consider coming to visit me in Barcelona? It would give me great pleasure to get to know you.'

Bella smiles. 'I was hoping you would ask me. Would next week be suitable?'

Adeline mixes Bella a stiff drink and waits.

'I don't know what to think.' Bella takes an unladylike gulp of the gin. 'Eduardo frightened the life out of me, but by the end, I liked him, very much. He's invited me to Barcelona so we can get to know each other.' Bella paces the room. 'I can't bear to think about the conflict Howard must have suffered. He never gave us any hint of this terrible burden. We only saw the successful journalist whom everyone admired.'

'Bella, you told me that he never discussed any feelings with you. That was the way that he kept his secrets.'

'How am I going to tell Fiona all this?'

'Ring Fiona later this evening and give her the headlines. She must be very anxious. When d'you think you'd like to go to Barcelona?'

'Monday if I can get a flight. I want to spend the weekend with David; he has so much to tell me.

The cold moon is high above the trees outside her window as Bella sits in the warmth of her room, talking on the phone to her aunt. 'Fiona, Howard lived in a world that I never dreamt existed.'

'I agree,' replies Fiona. 'But, apart from loving Alexandra beyond wisdom, I'm sure he didn't want you to grow up with a convicted traitor for a mother.'

Hearing Fiona's voice from so far away sharpens the loneliness Bella is feeling.

Fiona continues: 'Both Howard and Eduardo lived with this terrible unhappiness. Eduardo never married. No wonder Howard became the man he was. How did he keep up this pretense for so long?'

Bella has been thinking about this same question. 'I'm sure that's the reason he travelled so much; his work was a perfect cover for him. It was easier to avoid any situation or conversation that could cause his façade to slip. Or, for his secrets to come out.'

Fiona sums it up. 'It feels like he was hiding from us in plain sight.'

Chapter Twenty-Eight

Batiscombe House, Hastings, England October 1990

The two-hour train trip to Hasting delights Bella. The greenness of the countryside is startling. She's left home with southern Victoria already in the grip of a dry spring, the lack of good winter rainfall is causing Fiona great concern for an early bushfire season.

David picks her up from the Hastings station in an elderly Austin Estate car. It brings memories of Grandmother Clemens cruising up the drive at Bella's boarding school in her ancient English Wolseley.

As for David himself? If Bella were a casting agent looking for someone to play the part of a retired art teacher, she'd look no further. It seems fashion in all things has passed him by, whether cars or clothes.

It's his eyes and smile, she notices first; his voice is already familiar from their phone calls. His smiling face occupies the space between a brown tweed suit complete with leather patches on the elbow. A checked Viyella shirt, knitted woolen tie, and a battered houndstooth check hat that would be at home on the hallstand at Yarra Glen.

His eyes are those of an artist adept at seeing beyond the apparent. Bella can understand now that this is exactly how, in a time of danger, David was able to produce the drawing of the woman in the hat. The drawing that has brought Bella on this journey.

They leave Hastings on the coast road, traveling west towards St. Leonards.

Not far outside the town, they turn right up a laneway lined with hedgerows. The large, gabled house with a slate roof faces the sea. In the courtyard, Bella can hear the waves; the sharp sea air is a tonic. She can see past the house down a sloping lawn to a semi-circle of old beech trees. They screen the garden from the English Channel gales. She looks forward to rugging up and walking the cliff tops, her face towards France across the water.

From its size, she can see why during the war, David's parents had opened their home and their hearts to the men and women on leave from serving overseas. They must have loved filling this house with laughter, music, dancing, and conversations. She's curious about David's current family situation. In all their calls and letters, he's never mentioned a wife or family. Instinctively, Bella wants to let David tell her, not to be too Australian and 'upfront' before he's ready.

David shows her upstairs to her room and invites her to join him for lunch. On her way downstairs, she passes an open door into a cosy den. This is clearly David's private domain. On a wall, she sees a life-size portrait of a tall, slender man whose resemblance to Fiona and Howard tells her it must be Tom. The eyes and smile shine with an inner joy and love for the person he is looking toward, the artist…David. This picture tells her everything about why David doesn't appear to have his own family. Oh, how sad, how very sad, she thinks as she tucks this insight away to be shared with Fiona.

David folds his napkin, inserts it into a silver holder, and places it on the table for use tomorrow. She's touched by this familiar routine, it's another echo of her home.

'David, Adeline told me the parts of the story after you met with Howard at the Club, but she said the rest belongs to you. I wish Fiona could be here to hear it first-hand.'

David starts his story. 'That day in Mézières, we were in the wrong place at the wrong time. It's as simple as that. Until that day, we had the most extraordinary luck after bailing out of the Lancaster. Tom and I were on a sortie to bomb Darmstadt; did you know that Tom was a radio operator?'

'Yes! Fiona told me that when they were kids, Howard and Tom were always building crystal sets in the barn. They both loved to talk to people all over the world on what we call Ham Radio.'

David smiles. 'Ah, so that's where that skill of Tom's came from. They were both very good photographers, too.' The story unfolds.

Chapter Twenty-Nine

Tom and David December 1943

They were returning from the raid over Darmstadt. It was planned as a diversionary tactic to lure German fighters away from the main raid on Mannheim. After dropping their payload, the formation turned towards Britain. Enemy fire took out part of the Lancaster's tail, including the unfortunate rear gunner.

To the north of Metz, the pilot ordered the crew to bail out and 'hit the silk.' His aim was to get the plane as far away as possible from the crew's landing area. Without a crash to alert the Germans, they would have a better chance to survive. Once on the ground, it was every man for himself. At first, it was a relief to leave the crippled plane. David was sad about the likely fate of the pilot. For a while, he could see the other parachutes but lost sight of them as they lost altitude. He floated towards the ground before coming down on the edge of a forest. He unbuckled and ran into the forest to bury his 'chute and flying suit. Loath to shrug off the padded warmth, he knew that this suit would brand him. As he was on his knees covering up the hole, he felt the muzzle of a gun beside his ear. He hadn't heard a sound. He was gagged and a bag thrown over his head. Surprise and fear hit him. Was he going to be shot right here?

His hands were tied in front of him. Someone holding the rope led him along very rough ground. He was pushed inside a building. Hands went through his pockets, to search for any identity. They'd put all their personal belongings into canvas bags before they left on the mission. He had his survival kit; that was enough to tag David as a British flyer. Or, a German spy posing as a British flyer, trying to infiltrate the French underground. He touched his Omega RAF watch, pulling his sleeve lower. It was special to him; he would only ditch it as a last resort.

After the search, he was pushed onto a chair. Although no one spoke to him, after listening for a few minutes, he understood they didn't plan to kill him. They'd plenty of chance to do that already and to bury him out in the forest. David addressed his captors in fluent French; he stated that he needed to get in touch with someone to help him make his escape back to England. He answered many questions. He assured them that he and the rest of the flyers dotted around somewhere outside weren't German spies. The bag was lifted from his head. He looked around; he was in a barn with straw under his feet. He could hear and smell animals nearby. Three men were watching him, one, with a gun pointed at his head.

The door opened, and three more men arrived. They had another blindfolded, bound flier with them. It was Tom; relief flowed through David. The leader spoke in a low voice to the new arrivals; he gestured towards David. The first group slipped out the door, leaving David and Tom with these men.

After a few anxious days in hiding, Tom and David were separated to travel to their next destination along their escape route. Tom went off on a rusted bicycle with his guide, and David was placed on a cart and covered with hay to travel to Mézières Sur Meuse. In peacetime, the distance of 177 kilometers, would take two hours by car. As fugitives, this distance seemed almost impossible for them to cover. They hoped the Maquis there would help them to find an escape route across Northern France. Then, by an arrangement, they would cross the channel to freedom. They were too far north to attempt to travel the length of France and cross the Pyrenees to Spain - supposedly neutral territory. In truth, the Spanish government supported the Axis powers, so the dangers of that route were magnified.

In Charleville, the town nearest Mézières, his minder stopped, and left David hidden in the straw. David was very frightened, but what could he do? Clearly, his escort had business to conduct, and he had to sit and wait. David also understood that if the cart attracted any unwelcome attention, his minder would abandon him without a second glance. Although the cart was pulled into an alley, David had a good view through the straw to a café in the town square; it was patronized by German officers. Being a fine day, the outside tables were full, and the waitresses running to keep up with the orders of beer. At one table, sitting alone and judging by his uniform, a high-ranking officer sat tapping his gold cigarette lighter on the tabletop, his impatience obvious.

David had time to study his face; the man had the most startling blue eyes in a thin, tanned face with high cheekbones. Suddenly, he stood and clicked his heels. He was tall, over six feet. A woman joined him; she was so petite the officer had to bend over to kiss her on both cheeks and then, more intimately on her lips. Clearly, they knew each other well.

The woman was very well-dressed. In wartime, amongst these surroundings, she stood out from the shabby townsfolk around her. She was wearing a small burgundy velvet hat perched on an angle over dark cascading curls. More Paris than Charleville David thought. Something about the woman made him try to look closer; her face was familiar, very familiar; how could that be? Then she laughed. Horrified, David realized he knew that laugh. The woman was Alexandra, Howard's girlfriend. For the next five minutes, he watched and listened as the two conversed. She was speaking fluent German, but David knew that Alexandra spoke four languages, that's how Howard had got her the job at the Ministry of Information. As he watched the pair, he could see and hear enough to know that they are both very used to being with each other and that the officer was asking her a lot of questions, which she was answering. Without warning, the cart lurched forward, and David was on his way to hopefully, meet up with Tom and to be moved along to the next stage of their escape.

In Mézières, David waited where he was instructed and remembers the joy and relief he felt seeing Tom leaning an old bicycle against a wall. Tom's story of survival was like David's. They slept each night with 'helpers' along the way. David never forgot the courage and generosity of these people. They shared their meagre food supplies and a glass of wine as if they had plenty of everything. David had to wait until they were alone to tell Tom his news; he didn't want anyone to hear him speaking English. The waiting was awful, but he was too frightened to put them in further danger.

Wearing French countryman's clothing, they tried to blend in with the locals. This proved difficult. Tom's height and lean frame stood out. The local men tended to a short, stocky build and stooped shoulders that showed a lifetime of manual labor. It was hard to appear in the Mézières town square looking presentable. If they appeared as vagrants, they would attract attention from the ever-present German patrols.

They were briefed to sit on the fountain's edge between four and five pm that day. Their contact, Claudine, would approach them. At four fifteen, a woman carrying a baker's basket stopped and nodded. David gave the introduction code. Soon a man walked up to them, greeted Claudine, and gestured to the men to follow him. Claudine said to meet again in two days' time. The man took them to a hut on the edge of the forest. They would stay there and not come out until it's time for their next rendezvous at the fountain. David asked their minder for paper and charcoal.

The hut had a small, smoldering peat fire to keep them from freezing and a little food. Rough bunks, a table, and two handmade chairs made up the rest of their comforts. Sacking covered one small grimy window. After returning with the paper and charcoal, their minder left, ordering them not to show any light after dark. As David drew in the low firelight, he told Tom in a whispered voice, about the woman he saw in Charleville before he arrived here in Mézières. A woman he believed was Howard's girlfriend Alexandra but, she was with a German officer!

Tom looked at the drawing and was horrified. They knew that somehow, they had to get back to raise the alarm about Alexandra.

Claudine didn't arrive at the second rendezvous. They were worried but couldn't wait past five o'clock as they would infringe curfew. They would be arrested on the spot if they were caught out of doors. They would try the next afternoon. After an anxious night and the day following, they returned to the fountain at four o'clock. Claudine was waiting for them. She took them to sit at a table outside the adjacent workers' café and ordered coffee and cognac. In a hushed voice, Claudine told them of an incident the night before. Saboteurs had blown up a railway bridge between Mézières and the next town.

Blaring Klaxons drowned her words. They stood up, but two truckloads of soldiers had entered the square. Claudine told them to leave as she melted into the side alley. One truck stopped right at the café, leaving them no escape. The soldiers rounded up all the café patrons at gunpoint.

The townsfolk were bewildered at the speed of their capture. Pushed by the soldiers, Tom and David stumbled into the church across the town square. Soldiers tied them back-to-back in pairs. They were thrown on the stone floor to spend a freezing night of fear.

Conversation was impossible. David guessed the roundup was in reprisal for the bridge sabotage the evening before. No speech was allowed. This suited the two men: fugitives and now captives; they did not wish to answer any questions about their identity.

If the other townsfolk questioned the presence of strangers in their midst, they gave no sign. Their fears for their own safety and their loved ones outside the church occupied them. Cold from the floor, and the tight ropes binding wrists and feet, numbed their bodies as the long night travelled to sunrise.

The end of their ordeal was swift. As early sunlight slanted through the slatted shutters, sirens ripped the silence. The church doors flung wide, admitting extra soldiers. Foot bindings were yanked loose by bayonets. Dragged to their feet, the men and women were pushed towards the waiting daylight.

Stumbling on circulation-starved limbs, the group staggered outside. They tried to maintain a grip on the ice-slicked stones. Light reflected off hard-packed snow on the ground blinded them. Falling against each other, they felt themselves pushed against the church wall in two rows. Awareness came; they could see the terrified townsfolk corralled across the square, surrounded by soldiers. Tom and David, like the other captives, realized this was to be their last minutes alive.

David nudged Tom in his ribs. David whispered, 'That officer. He's the one I saw in Charleville with Alexandra.'

Tom heard David's words, then says, 'Bloody hell, look over there. Is that her, the woman you saw with him?'

David follows Tom's eyeline to the crowd behind the firing squad. Slightly to one side stands a young woman. Taller and better dressed than her neighbors, she is watching the scene before her. Around her, the unwilling watchers are starting to sway with silent grief. Not her, she is still, her shoulders square, her back straight. Her eyes reflect the grey stone church; she seemed preoccupied, thoughtful, detached from the unfolding tragedy.

'Yes, it's her.'

Tom replies. 'It IS Alexandra. I'm sure of it, you don't forget a face like that. She must be the …'

'I hope someone gets word of what happened here to HQ. I pray that Claudine got away yesterday.' David craned his neck and surveyed the shivering villagers. He realized the cold wasn't touching him; poor souls, he thought, they'll have to live with the memory of this. 'I can't see her here. I hope she's safe. So much depends on her.' The whispered exchange was so soft, it is more like transference of thoughts than speech.

Tom whispered, 'We're done for now. I love you…'

The two men leaned into each other, their shoulders touching.

The doomed hostages gave their last salute to their country and their lives by striking, as one voice, into the opening of La Marseillaise.

'Allons, enfants de la …!'

'Vive La…!'

Upon command, gunfire pierced the frozen air. At the instant the rifles cracked, David felt Tom, taller and broader than himself, rise off his feet in front of him as if flying for a ball to catch. Tom's weight, as he fell from the bullets, pushed David to the ground in their journey to oblivion. Their bodies and the lives of the onlookers shattered.

Chapter Thirty

Batiscombe House 1990

David and Bella return from that nightmare morning in the past. The fire has burned low, allowing the night chill to creep from dark corners. David looks so sad that Bella reaches out to touch his hand. She is acutely aware of the true depth of David and Tom's relationship.

'David, how awful. I'm sorry I've taken you back there; how thoughtless of me.'

'Not at all. You're the one person, apart from Fiona, who should hear this story. I still remember the day I told Howard. I believe telling him of his brother's death, was worse than being shot myself.'

She asks. 'Did the officer in the clipping I sent you look familiar?'

'Bella, the photo was very indistinct, but I would say it was definitely the man I saw Alexandra with in Charleville and,' he shakes his head slowly, 'later at Mézières.'

Bella reflects on the feeling of helplessness the two young men must have felt. 'What an extraordinary story.'

David, rising to stretch his legs, says. 'Would you like some coffee?'

'Yes, please!'

David goes to a side table where a silver Thermos jug sits on a tray with two cups. He pours, and they return to the fireside with their coffee.

Silence falls between them; Bella's mind turns to Howard and his secrets.

When she thinks she should say goodnight to David, he stirs the fire and adds another log of wood. This signals to her that he hasn't finished his storytelling. She can listen all night if he can keep speaking. She's waited all her life to hear about her family history and about Tom.

Bella pours another coffee. 'Before you tell me about meeting Howard, would you tell me what happened after the shooting?'

'Of course! I took two bullets that day; one grazed my skull and did some damage on the way through. The other went through my shoulder. It only missed my heart, because Tom fell on top of me; Tom was much taller and a bigger man. He saved my life.'

'David, what a terrible memory to live with.'

'The bullet that hit me in the head was a blessing. I was unconscious, so I never saw the aftermath. The villagers had to bury their own dead; they've had to live with that.'

David stirs his coffee. 'After the war, I went back to Mézières. I had to thank those people for saving me. They'd lost so much.' Silence, as they both ponder the horror of this statement. He continues, 'They told me the burial party of villagers found I was breathing. They managed to spirit me away in a wheelbarrow.' He smiles, 'They buried their scarecrow in my grave.'

'Is Tom buried there too?'

'Yes, Bella, we'll go there together one day. I'm sure Fiona will want to come too.'

Bella gasps; tears blind her and fall down her cheeks. 'Fiona and my grandparents should've been able to go there years ago! Damn you, Dad! How dare you do this!' She calms herself, not wishing to upset David.

'Of course, I didn't know Howard hadn't told his family,' says David, 'but I do know that he has helped those people a lot over the years.'

'Some consolation, I suppose.'

'Would another brandy help?' David enquires.

'Yes, please! What happened next?'

David pours two large snifters, hands one to Bella, and speaks. 'The Résistance wanted to get me home so I could tell the story of Mézières. After a lot of rough travel, I was hidden in a cottage near Boulogne for about six weeks whilst I was patched up.'

'What huge risks these people took,' says Bella.

'Of course, but freeing France meant everything to them.' He continues. 'I lived in a cowshed attached to a farmhouse near the sea. I became rather fond of those cows. They were so warm and comforting in such a dangerous world.'

'Had you recovered from your injuries?'

'Partly, I received excellent medical care from a vet! I was lucky; the bullet affected my speech, not my memory.' David adds. 'I still couldn't speak, but speech can be fixed more easily than memory.'

'Thank heavens for that!' Exclaims Bella. 'I've heard stories of escapes from Occupied France. I've never understood how it could happen under the noses of the enemy.'

'Yes, I know. They were ingenious and very daring, those Maquis. The British Navy, in small boats, plucked escapees from tiny beaches along the coast of France. Also, there was a French-Canadian Airforce unit based in Britain. They flew in to land wherever they could, pick up returnees, and drop weapons and supplies for the French to use. Those pilots had unbelievable flying skills and sheer guts!' David smiles. 'I was extracted with four others in the stinking bilge of a French fishing smack.' He wrinkles his nose. 'My ticket to freedom was to stink of fish.'

'A small price to pay!' Bella smiles. 'So, what happened after you made it home to England?'

'I had surgery, lots of physiotherapy, and the hardest of all, speech therapy. That took a year until I was fit enough to take up my old job here at Hastings Grammar. I couldn't resume my career as a teacher until I could speak adequately.'

Bella smiles at the thought of teenage boys' behavior. 'And all that time, you must've been trying to piece together what had happened. Was that woman Alexandra? Had you imagined it?'

'I went over it and over it. If Alexandra hadn't been such a beauty, if she'd been more ordinary, that face wouldn't have stuck in my mind.'

'Was your meeting with Howard a coincidence?'

'No, I was reading Howard's dispatches about post-war reconstruction. He was a marvellous writer. I sent a letter to the London office of Reuters News Agency.'

'Did he reply?'

'Yes, it took a while; I got on with my life. I was so happy to be working again. Then, in May 1946, a letter arrived suggesting we meet at the Naval and Military Club. The rest of the story starts from there.'

Chapter Thirty-One

Naval and Military Club. Cambridge House, Piccadilly London 1946

'Howard!'

'David! Good to see you! – Where've you been?'

'Ah, well then, it took a while to patch me up after I caught the bullets in France.'

'I'm sorry I haven't looked you up earlier. Let's find a seat. I want to hear all about it.' They made their way across the foyer to the lounge. Howard stopped several times to answer greetings from other members. And, to accept congratulations on his recent series of articles in Life magazine.

David realized that Howard's career had reached new heights since they last met. He wondered how, with Howard such a centre of attention, that he would get to talk to him about the tragedy of Tom's death. He felt sick enough about recounting the story. The constant interruptions from these bluff, hearty, back-slapping, hand-shaking types rattled his nerve. They seemed to think Howard was a film star.

They moved towards an area near the windows. Sunlight streamed in, giving that side of the room bright warmth; they sank into the leather chairs. A steward appeared; Howard ordered whiskey, sandwiches, and coffee. As they waited, neither man seemed to know quite how to start.

Howard could see that David had gone very quiet and appeared to be struggling with his emotions. 'I say, David, are you alright? You've gone a bit pale, old man.'

'Yes-y-yes, David stammered. W-w-would i-it b-be-p-possible to go-s-s-somewhere q-q quieter please?'

'Of course! Hang on a minute, David.' The steward arrived with their drinks; Howard spoke to him in a low voice.

'Yes, sir; please follow me.' The steward led them through a doorway off the lounge into a smaller room. The noise level dropped as soon as the door closed behind them. The room was furnished as a private sitting and dining room. Long windows overlooked Green Park; David stood looking out to calm himself.

The peaceful scene with children playing helped him to feel that the nightmare memories of the war were behind him. The feeling of panic he'd experienced out in the crowded lounge started to subside. Today, seeing Howard, maybe he could start to come to terms with Tom's death at Mézières and his guilt at his own survival.

The changes in David shocked Howard. He hadn't seen him since the last time he, Tom, and David were on leave together in London in 1944. He had seen this speech condition in many war wounded he had interviewed and knew not to rush David. They both produced their pipes and tobacco pouches. They proceeded to do the ritual tapping, filling, tamping, lighting, and puffing that give men a chance to figure out what to say next.

David took a deep breath. Then, his words came out in a rush. 'Howard, I wanted to see you today to talk to you about Tom. I'm so sorry that Tom was taken.' David cleared his throat, sipped his scotch, and spoke. 'What do you know about how he died?'

Howard was relieved to see that David appeared to be calmer. 'Very little,' Howard replied. 'Tom was listed as Missing in Action, late in 1944 after a bombing sortie over Germany. No trace of him was ever found until after the liberation of northern France, a woman from a town called Mézières Sur Meuse, in North-eastern France, handed a watch into the Americans. She told a dreadful story of a reprisal shooting. The watch was taken off one of the bodies. A body who wasn't a local, so they kept it to hand it into the authorities when it was safe to do so.'

David knew that watch; he knew it has the letters D&T engraved on the casing. He had the identical watch; they had bought them together. He eased his coat sleeve lower over his wrist. He realized that Howard must not know that David was with Tom on that mission. He didn't say anything but let Howard continue.

'The Germans supervised the townsfolk who had to remove the bodies, dig the graves, and bury their loved ones. Despite their grief, the townsfolk understood that two of the men were strangers to them, but they didn't let on. One of the men wasn't dead, so they spirited him away. The woman wasn't going to hand the watch in and risk another round of brutality.' He paused, closed his eyes, then turned to look out the window. 'So that's how I finally heard of Tom's fate.'

'Was he identified through the watch?'

'Yes, the watch was an Omega RAF watch, designed for aircrew; it had a serial number. Omega in London told the war department in charge of investigating such matters, which dealer had sold it and serviced it. The dealer had it registered to Tom's name at my address at Florin Court.'

'Howard, how awful for you and your family to have to wait that long.'

'Yes, it was hard. I was here, and they were so far away.'

He leant forward and said his speech had returned to normal. 'Howard, this will come as a shock to you. I was with Tom there, in Mézières. I was the man who survived the shooting and was hidden.'

Howard looked stricken. 'Oh, good heavens! No, we didn't know that!' He looked confused and upset. 'David, what happened? How did you escape?' Howard told David that after hearing where Tom was buried, he went to Mézières to see his grave. The townsfolk never mentioned the second man.

'I'm so sorry; I should've moved heaven and earth to find you earlier. Oh, damn it! You must've thought me a total cad.' He moved his head from side to side as if in pain. 'What about your poor parents? After all their kindness, they must've thought Tom's family are a bunch of lousy colonial rat bags!'

David had never seen the unflappable, urbane Howard Clemens in such a state. Now he tried to calm Howard. 'My family knows that war distorts the accepted niceties of life. They don't think badly of you at all. I'll tell them what happened.' David started the story. 'It was bad luck we were in that massacre at Mézières; that's a story for another time, we need to sort this out first.'

Howard nodded and rose to press the bell to call the steward. 'Would you like another scotch? I could do with it!'

'Yes, please!' David continued. 'When the couple realized I was still breathing, they managed to wheel me into a barn in their wheelbarrow. They buried their scarecrow instead of me. Of course, I didn't know anything about this. One bullet grazed my skull as I fell.' He tapped his forehead. 'It injured my frontal lobe, which affected my speech; that's why my rehab took so long. And sometimes it's difficult to get my words out.'

Howard said. 'You gave me a bit of a fright just now! I don't recall you or Tom ever lost for words.'

They both smiled. David felt better; something of their old relationship had slipped back into place.

The steward arrived with their drinks; Howard reached forward to relight his pipe. With that done, he said.

'David, I had no idea you were with Tom.' He stopped, unable to continue. 'Oh, Tom!' Howard said his brother's name with such anguish. After a pause to collect himself, he continued. 'I thought he was flying with the Australian group at Bottesford.'

'Yes, he was. Bottesford field went over to the Americans, so Tom put in for a transfer to join me at Spilsby. I'd moved there when the 207 relocated from Langar. We flew that last sortie from Spilsby.'

'But David, why wasn't your name on the missing list if you were with Tom? I didn't see your name. I would've contacted your parents straight away.'

'Yes, I'm sure,' said David. 'It's a simple answer. My whole name is McGillivray David McKenzie-Ogilvie. Not even my parents use that mouthful. The RAF enlisted me as McGillivray Ogilvy.'

'Ah, I see,' says Howard. 'That explains why we didn't know you were with Tom.'

'Yes! Exactly. You wouldn't have known David paused. He lowered his head when he spoke; his voice was unsteady. 'Howard, Tom leapt up in front of me. He looked like a footballer in your Aussie game going for a mark.'

Howard felt in his stomach the countless times his taller, fitter younger brother had marked a ball in front of him.

David continued, 'his height saved me from death. He saved my life.' He paused, the pain of that day still with him, 'I have nightmares about it. He had so much to live for; I'm so sorry.'

The two men were so absorbed, they didn't hear the steward place their sandwiches and coffee on the serving table. The aroma of coffee brought them back to the present; they stood up to serve themselves.

Howard moved to David and placed both hands on his shoulders. 'Thank you so much, I needed to hear this. My sister Fiona and my parents need to hear this. They'll be so grateful that Tom had his best friend with him right at the end.'

The generosity of this statement overwhelmed David again. Since the shooting, he'd been fighting with guilt about Tom's death and his survival. Now Tom's brother was thanking him for being with Tom! They took their sandwiches and coffee back to the table.

Whilst they ate, they were both in their own thoughts. David broke the silence. 'Howard, there's something Tom wanted me to tell you.' He took a piece of paper out of his pocket, unfolded it, and laid it on the table.

Howard leant forward; he looked up with a startled expression. 'Where did you get this?'

'When I was being taken to Mézières by the Maquis. I saw this woman with a German officer in Charleville. I'm sure it was Alexandra. I heard her speak, and her voice sounded...' his voice trailed off, anxiety washed over him.

Howard reached for it and turned it towards the light. He was silent, and David could see, shocked. He broke the silence. 'And Howard...I'm sure she was in Mézières that morning.'

Howard's head jerked up to look at David; his head moved slowly from side to side as if he was in pain.

David asked, 'But how could Alexandra be in France at all?'

'When did you draw this David?'

'After Charleville, when I was reunited with Tom, I drew it to show him. After the shooting, while the Résistance were hiding me, I kept drawing her so the image wouldn't escape my mind.' The grief on Howard's face alarmed David. He struggled with the next question. He felt his old enemy overtaking him again. 'D-do you th-think it is A-Alexandra? D-d-did you k-k-keep s-seeing h-her a-after w-we l-left?'

Howard passed his hand across his eyes. 'Yes, yes I did. Please can I keep this copy?'

'Of course! B-but h-how c-can it it h-help y-you?'

'David, I married Alexandra late in 1944. It was after you and Tom went missing, so he wouldn't have known.'

David's hands covered his face. Oh, w-what've I-I d-done? I-I m-must b-be wrong. It c-couldn't p-possibly have been Alexandra.' He paused and then blurted out, 'Why w-would she, h-have b-been in Fra-France with a G-German officer? F-forgive me, H-Howard, I'm a b-blundering i-i-idiot!'

Howard looked up from the picture, a sad smile crossed his face. 'David, you've given me a gift; Tom has too. There's something urgent I need to do. You've given me a vital piece of information.'

'I say Howard; I'm so sorry, I do apologize. I thought it might interest you.'

'Yes, it is much more than that, and I am very grateful. The people I need to show this to will be also. I apologize, but I must rush off: I have some urgent business. I'll keep in touch with you.'

David returns from the past into the fire-lit warmth. He stands up and places the brass fireguard in front of the flames. 'I expected I'd hear from him when he had something to tell me. After all, in 1946, we were still untangling the aftermath of war. Day-to-day living was a challenge to keep families fed, clothed, and warm.' He smiles, 'Enough for now; tomorrow if the weather's kind, we'll walk the cliff tops. I only have you here with me for one more day.'

Bella stands up, too, longing for the duvet to cocoon her from these sad stories. She gives him a kiss goodnight. How else can she thank this man who's helping her to unlock all the secrets of her past?

Chapter Thirty-Two

Batiscombe House October 1990

S unlight wakes Bella: she's slept for eight hours. She feels calmer here in this soft room, so close to the seat of her past. Instead of researching and writing other people's reality, she is on the path to discovering her own story. She wants to take David home to Yarra Glen, to fold him into the family that would have been, in different circumstances, his own. Fiona will be so happy to welcome him as a link to her beloved Tom.

She flings back the duvet and walks to the round dormer windows. These upper-floor windows are set attic style into the sloping slate roof. She kneels on the window seat, pulls her wrap around her, and opens the casement. Starch-crisp air focuses her attention.

Autumn is deepening towards winter; Bella is sure, for her to see this coast at its best. Russet colours here are stronger, more vibrant, and a contrast from the mostly olive green of the bush at home. Fortunately, the gardens at Yarra Glen were planted by her English ancestors so she can enjoy the beauty of the imported English trees in their autumn colours. She must remember not to call the fields paddocks here. The name doesn't suit the sea-softened green pasture so unlike anything at Yarra Glen.

As she dresses to walk with David, she muses that she had never dreamt that anyone in the world still lived except Fiona, who had known Tom. Bella has the strangest feeling of walking on stage in the third act of her own life. Players she didn't know existed have been acting behind the scenes all along. Each actor, like a mime artist, points to a scene to be written.

Does one scene describe Alexandra and her possible connection to the officer present at Tom's death? Will a scene be acted wherein Bella meets her mother? Eduardo Monerayo is the only possible author of that act. Now that Bella is here, in touch with her father's other life, a thought, one she had never had before, creeps in. What if she does find her mother? How will she feel? The answer to that is a dagger-sharp pain that starts in the pit of her stomach and shoots its way to her throat, closing her airway as surely as a steel claw has squeezed it. She breathes deeply several times to dissipate this sharp shock. Oh! Where did that come from? 'Oh Fiona,' she cries out, needing her beloved aunt to be with her to calm her as if she was a child who has fallen.

David and Bella walk along the seafront and up the hill to Hastings Castle, the remnant of William the Conqueror's stronghold. They find a seat looking out to sea. The sun-warmed stones of the ancient wall give them some protection from the stiff breeze.

'David, at the club, when you found out that Howard had married Alexandra. Did he say that it could've been Alexandra that you had recognized?'

David replies. 'He didn't deny it. He was so upset, and I sensed he wanted to end our meeting. I thought it must've been the shock of hearing my story of how Tom died. I know it would've shocked me if our positions were reversed. I felt like a blundering idiot.'

'Yes, but for him to ask you to give him the copy of the sketch, he must've recognized something in it.'

David lights his pipe, and between puffs, he says, 'I thought so too. I felt very strange about the whole incident. After a few weeks, I received a short note from Howard. He asked if I could visit his home in London the next Wednesday. He said that if he was unable to be there that day, I was to see his associate, Miss Adeline Stephens. I remember that day very clearly. It was August 1946, a beautiful summer, the first one of peace, and everyone was loving the sense of freedom that comes with warmer weather.'

David recounts that he went to Florin Court and met Adeline Stephens; Howard had gone away on urgent business. David was apprehensive about this meeting because he believed he had caused Howard terrible upset. Adeline was quick to reassure him that quite the opposite; what David had told Howard that day at the Naval and Military Club was of vital importance. She briefly filled him in about the whirlwind courtship and marriage. Isabella's birth and Alexandra's disappearance with her mother, Clara, after David's meeting with Howard. She told David that Howard had gone to Barcelona to try to see Alexandra's family. Howard wanted David to know that he must not feel he had done anything wrong. In fact, he had helped a great deal.

Bella listens and then says, 'I must say that surprised me; Adeline told me how quickly they married. From what we know now, what could he have really known about her?'

'Yes, That's the question, isn't it?

'How could Howard not have seen Alexandra's fascist sympathies?'

'Oh Bella, it was a terrible "live for the moment time" back then, I can understand Howard being swept off his feet.'

Since her arrival, Bella's feelings for her father, whilst still conflicted, are now tinged with compassion for a man who believed that his actions, or inactions, denied him the right to a whole life, for all his life.

David continues. 'My sighting of her with Klaus Schoeffels in Charleville; the drawing and placing Alexandra at the scene of the massacre in Mézières added up to enough evidence to bring her in for questioning.'

'But she escaped and has never been found,' says Bella.

'True, but you tell me she is still alive, so maybe her past will catch up with her.' David's voice becomes serious. 'At the time, I was cautioned by the Official Secrets Act. It would be a relief for me to have it over.'

'Oh dear! You too? Adeline talked about that.'

'That was enough to send me back here to Hastings and get on with my life as a provincial grammar school art teacher.'

'So, you never heard from Howard again?'

David smiles. 'After that day, Howard, for his own reasons, chose not to get in touch with me. That's how the whole matter stood until I read of his death in The Times.' David looks out to sea, remembering the years he tried to put the whole tragedy behind him.

Bella takes a deep breath. 'Did Howard know how much you and Tom loved each other?'

David looks up at her, his face suffused with light. 'Oh, Bella, you guessed. How did you know?'

'I saw your painting of Tom. It is beautiful. I hope Fiona will see it one day.'

'No, I don't believe Howard knew. I'm sure Tom never told him.' David says quietly, 'Those things weren't talked about then.'

'Well, you can talk about it now.'

'Yes, it's such a relief.'

Bella puts her arm around him and leans her head on his shoulder. 'David, I'm so sad that this dreadful story has followed you for so long. You are coming out to visit us, aren't you?'

'Yes, Fiona and I have spoken about it. I want to do that...very much.' David ties his scarf and pulls his hat on as they move from the shelter of the wall into the stiff sea breeze. 'Tom and I used to talk about me visiting Yarra Glen. Now, let's get home before this wind whips around and chills us both to the bone.'

Chapter Thirty-Three

Barcelona October 1990

On the flight to Barcelona, Bella reads the information Adeline found for her about Alexandra's English family, the Somers. The current head of the family is Hugo Somers aged eighty. The family tree shows the late Sir Peregrine Somers, was Clara's father, Alexandra's grandfather, and Bella's great-grandfather. Yes, there he is, his birth, marriage, and children. Clara and Charles. Charles has a birth date, and oh, he died very young, during the second war! So, no marriage and no children. Bella understands that the law of male progeniture still survives amongst the English aristocracy. On Charles' death without issue, the Somers titles and Somers Hall, according to Adeline, a building more like a castle, passed from Clara's family's grasp to her cousin Hugo who has three sons. Clara and Alexandra's need to get money from Eduardo makes more sense now. She reads on.

Clara's entry only has a birth date. No marriage to Raymondo Monerayo is shown! No children. There's no mention of Eduardo or Alexandra. No Alexandra means no marriage to Howard, so Bella doesn't exist! Some judicious re-writing of history has happened here.

Is Clara still alive? There's no date of death, just a dash and a space. This means, in family tree language, that person is still living. Eduardo will be fascinated by this news.

Bella checks the date of publication; Clara may have died since. No, the footer of the photocopied pages from Debrett's Peerage shows the entry is from the current issue. The text talks about the family's royal connections and the acquisition of the land and titles going back to Henry V111. There is, of course, no mention of the family's dubious connections with fascism. More revisionism! The landing announcement is made, so Bella packs away her paperwork and watches the Mediterranean city reveal itself below her.

Barcelona is the city of Bella's dreams. This place is embedded in her heart; part of her belongs here! She wishes she'd known this when she first visited here. Although they've come a long way since their first meeting, she feels Eduardo isn't ready for a newly introduced niece to stay at his home with him. Bella will stay at the Hotel Picasso in the El Born district. The exterior is in distinctly classical Spanish style whilst the elegant and functional interiors and facilities suit her perfectly. The El Born area is characterized by narrow medieval streets offering designer boutiques and cafes by day and cocktail bars and Samba at night. Not that Bella is looking to Samba the night away; she is looking forward to rediscovering Barcelona through Eduardo's eyes.

Bella visits Eduardo in his home overlooking the Arco de Triunfo de Barcelona. He lives in an old mansion that has been divided into separate residences. Eduardo's home faces the park and has a wide terrace and loggia with beautiful views towards the sea. The large rooms have ornate architectural flourishes in the baroque style. To balance this, Eduardo has furnished them with a genteel style to create a harmonious home. As he shows her around, she examines many family treasures and photographs. When he shows her pictures of the former Monerayo home at Casa Milo, Bella says.

'Y' know Eduardo, I went to Casa Milo when I first visited Barcelona. I remembered being there at your home with my father when I was a little girl.'

'Ah, Bella, yes, he did bring you to see me; what a memory you have.'

'It was more a half-remembered dream than a real memory.'

'Please come and meet Jose and Maria; they have looked after me and my family as did their parents and grandparents.' He introduces her to Jose and Maria and speaks to them in Spanish. He turns to Bella.

'I am telling them you are Alexandra's daughter who has come from Australia.' Eduardo says.

Maria looks at Bella but doesn't smile. Her black eyes glitter with barely-suppressed anger. Bella is surprised at the woman's expression, but she smiles back. Maria speaks volubly to Eduardo and nods her head towards Bella before she turns to leave, Jose following along behind her. Bella chooses not to ask Eduardo why Maria seems agitated. Does Maria fear this interloper from Australia who claims to be Alexandra's daughter? She understands that the old woman would have had a strong attachment to Alexandra. Maria may resent Alexandra's exclusion from Eduardo's home.

Eduardo and Bella sit outside on the terrace. Their conversation turns to Alexandra and his mother, Clara. Eduardo studies the copy of the Somers family tree entry. He agrees with Bella that if the entry is correct, Clara could still be alive.

'Thank you for this, Bella. I'll write to Hugo Somers. It's time I faced up to the question of my mother's welfare.'

Bella leaves after a delightful afternoon. She doesn't want to tire her uncle.

'So where to tomorrow, Bella?' Eduardo asks as Jose holds the car door open for her.

'I would love to revisit La Sagrada Familia Basilica, please, Eduardo. I have read a lot has been done since my last visit.'

'Buenos días, tío Eduardo,' as she slides into the back seat of the elderly but immaculate Mercedes the next day.

'Mi hermosa sobrina,' smiles Eduardo as he kisses her hand. 'My beautiful niece.'

She gives her uncle a warm kiss on the cheek. Every detail of Eduardo's cream tussore silk suit and the gleaming car with its blinds and tassels, leather upholstery, and even small crystal vases on each side with fresh flowers move Bella gently backwards to a time before the Spanish Civil

War and World War Two, devastated and divided the Monerayo family. To complement her uncle's style, she is dressed in a cream linen dress, stockings, and low-heeled shoes with a straw sun hat.

Bella delights in revisiting La Sagrada Familia Basilica. Although still unfinished, she can see the changes since her first visit. Eduardo takes the time to sit in quiet contemplation telling her he needs to save his legs. Bella circles each of the interior pillars that are created to resemble trees. When she looks up, their shapes constantly change, as real trees appear to do. There is also a tortoise and turtle holding up each of these pillars, representing both the earth and the sea. Satisfied with her tour that all is well with this sacred space, she finds Eduardo sitting in a pool of light from one of the soaring windows; she sits beside him.

'It's beautiful, and I'm so happy to be here with you,' she whispers.

He pats her hand.

As they leave, across the square, Bella sees a woman in a dark suit and wide-brimmed hat, talking to Jose beside Eduardo's car. It is too far away to see any detail other than a slender shape. The tilted hat obscures her face. Jose bows to the woman, who turns and walks away quickly. Probably someone asking directions Bella thinks, but a sensation like an echoing bell chimes inside her.

'We have a luncheon reservation at Café Cataluña.' Eduardo says as they settle into the car. Like everything else to do with Eduardo, the restaurant is a step back in time. A perfect example of Art Deco style, they sit together on a velvet banquette at a marble-topped table on a sculptural pedestal, complete with a glass and pewter lady lamp. Bella absorbs the atmosphere almost like an animal sniffing the air.

'I love coming here. It never changes,' Eduardo pauses and looks around. 'It takes me back to before the war when we were a family.'

As Eduardo speaks, Bella looks past his shoulder. She is startled to see, across the room and half obscured by a scrolled metal screen and a decorative palm, a woman staring straight at her. The woman's hat brim is tilted over one eye, and a veil obscures her face. Bella feels a strange sensation of recognition. Is this a coincidence? Could it be the same woman she saw talking to Jose? In a low voice, she tells Eduardo the whole story about the woman on the plane and now these two apparently unrelated but coincidental sightings.

When Bella looks again, the woman has disappeared, she says. 'I must have an over-active imagination. I'm seeing mysteries everywhere.'

Chapter Thirty-Four

Eduardo's Home in Barcelona

They arrive home tired but happy. Maria meets them at the door and speaks to Eduardo. There is a rapid exchange. Maria shrugs her shoulders and turns away. The happy look on Eduardo's face is replaced by a grim set to his mouth.

'Bella, this will be a shock to you. Alexandra is in the salon. Maria insists she didn't know she was coming here. Do you wish to meet her, or would you prefer to leave?'

'Alexandra is here? Why now?'

Eduardo shrugs.

'No, I'm not leaving.' She takes his arm, and they enter the salon together.

Alexandra's profile matches the drawing that started this whole journey. Bella ponders the chain of events that have brought her here to see her mother for the first time in over forty years. With total clarity, Bella understands the woman seated next to her on the flight from Bahrain and again across from her in the restaurant is here before her. But why?

Alexandra turns to face Eduardo and Bella; she raises the veil covering her face. In her mid-seventies, she's still beautiful. So European, delicate, her face is a perfect oval, her complexion is an ivory never touched by the sun. The only colour is deep red lipstick. Bella feels a flush of confusion at seeing the face that resembles her own. Slender and petite, Alexandra makes

184

Bella feel like a large kangaroo. She can see she has inherited something from Howard, his height. Alexandra wouldn't reach her shoulder. And yes, Adeline was also correct in remembering Alexandra's impeccable grooming and style. She is dressed in a black fine wool Chanel suit with gold buttons, dark stockings, elegant black leather shoes, and a signature Chanel handbag with a gold chain strap. Her dark hair is shot with silver and pulled back into a severe bun. There is no warmth in her face or, Bella feels, any emotional reaction to coming face to face with her daughter.

Alexandra doesn't rise to greet them. She makes no effort to embrace Eduardo or Bella. 'Eduardo, I see you have met your niece.'

Bella notices that she hasn't said, 'I see you have met my daughter.'

'I have met Isabella before, Alexandra. When she was a baby. The baby you left behind.'

'There were greater issues at stake.'

Is this woman her mother? She hasn't moved towards Bella. In turn, Bella can't move towards her. Bella feels like an invisible steel mesh lies between them. They take a seat facing Alexandra. Bella feels reassured by Eduardo's presence. She doesn't know how, if she ever had the opportunity, she would have managed this meeting on her own.

Eduardo takes the lead. 'Why are you here?'

'I want my inheritance.'

Eduardo replies in the voice of steel that Bella remembers from their first meeting.

'What inheritance, Alexandra? You know I settled Father's estate with Clara.'

Eduardo looks at Bella. She's pleased she's here to support him. He feels Bella's care and gives her a faint smile; he continues. 'As you weren't to be found, that included your share. Where is Clara? Go and ask her for money.'

Alexandra shrugged. 'Clara crawled back to her gutless family. She is spineless, like you.'

'So, you and Klaus are finding that crime doesn't pay.'

'I know what you have from our father. I demand my share. I don't like refusal.'

'My answer is still no.'

Alexandra snaps. 'Clara and I freed you from prison and restored our family fortunes. Otherwise, you would have nothing.'

This statement infuriates Eduardo; he leans forward. 'Restored our family fortunes? What rubbish. I had to sell off our properties. And our grandfather's art collection. I still work to provide for myself. Alexandra, your behavior, and Clara's foolish support brought disgrace to our family. Your evil, wrong-headed ideas imprisoned our father and me. He died because of your actions; you have a lot to answer for. Then, and for everything you have done since.' Exhausted by this effort. Eduardo slumps back against the cushions.

Alexandra isn't finished with him. 'We should have left you in jail. You will regret this.'

Eduardo stands up. 'Alexandra, this is a warning. You and Klaus will be brought to justice if it's the last thing I do.'

She shrugs. 'Here in Spain, I have committed no crime.'

'Alexandra, Britain, and Spain have an extradition treaty in place for people like you.'

Bella realises that Alexandra is partially correct. Spain's neutrality in World War Two means that she has not committed war crimes against the Spanish State. Her crimes were against the Allied powers. She will follow that up in London.

Eduardo says. 'You are despicable, Alexandra. I wish that Howard had turned you in to the British authorities.'

'What a colonial that man was.' Her face has a cold look that flattens her eyes to the colour of flint.

Alexandra's words wind Bella; she stands up. 'How dare you speak of my father like that. You have no right ...'

A withering look from Alexandra meets this outburst. The look that Bella hoped she might receive from her mother if she ever met her isn't love. Her heart fills with gratitude for Fiona's love that filled every empty space. She sinks down onto the couch beside Eduardo.

'Why did you marry Howard? You didn't love him. You didn't want me in your life.'

Alexandra repeats. 'There were far greater issues at stake, Isabella.'

As she watches her mother, she sees the woman on the plane. Bella remembers her discomfort at being so close to her through that long night.

'And … why are you following me?'

Alexandra ignores these questions. She inspects her nails, then says. 'Before you judge me, find out about the relationship between your father and your precious Jew.'

The shock that shoots through Bella's body is so intense it takes her breath away. 'How do you know about my relationship with Eli? You abandoned me, and now you've been spying on me. Why?' Before Bella says what's on her mind. She wants the answer to the question that Alexandra has laid out for her. 'Is he alive?'

Alex crosses her legs and scoffs. 'Eli? Oh, is that what you call him?'

Bella watches her mother say this as if it is no more important than discussing the weather. 'What is his name? Have you ever met him?'

'We had an encounter. As to his name, I really can't remember.' She shrugs as if this is of no importance.

Who is this woman? Who is she in her heart? What pleases her, makes her laugh, moves her to tears, or to feel—anything? Bella pushes these thoughts away, her need to ask the next question is so great; she must pass over this shocking answer.

'Do you know where he is?'

'How could I?'

'Where was this encounter with him? How long ago?'

Silence. Is Bella going to have to beg? Bella controls her feelings of rage mixed with fascination. She is determined to use this interview to find out all she can. She hopes it will be the last time she ever sees this woman. She hears her voice rise; she can't call her Mother, or Alexandra. Damn her, damn her to hell. She doesn't know she's echoing her father's dying words.

She says, 'And, what do you mean about finding the truth about Howard and Eli's relationship?'

'I don't have to tell you anything Isabella.' She pauses and then seems to relent. 'I encountered the man you call Eli in Tangier two years ago. I've no way of knowing if he's there now. As for your father.' She shrugs her shoulders again; clearly, this is her habit when she chooses not to say anything.

Bella waits; she's alert to Alexandra's inference that Eli is not his name, but she understands this anyway. She feels as if Alexandra is weighing up whether to say more. The silence is so deep, Bella can hear a clock ticking on the mantelpiece. Then, as if Alexandra has shut down the blind that had opened a crack, she says.

'Isabella, you don't belong with that man; he is a Jew! You are pure Aryan.'

Bella cries out in rage and frustration. 'How dare you, with your record, you have the gall to speak about him like that and to say he doesn't belong with me? What is his name?'

Alex inspects her perfectly manicured nails before she replies. 'It could be anything by now.'

With her head full of the roar of a bushfire, Bella is beyond discretion; she cries out at her mother. 'Who are you? What are you?' Silence. For the first time she feels Alexandra is looking at her daughter.

'Isabella, you don't understand anything about me. Go back to Australia. There's nothing for you here.' She pauses, and then, as if finding somewhere inside herself some compassion for the child she bore and then abandoned, she says in a quieter voice. 'I left you because I wasn't able to take you with me.' She turns away from Bella.

After forty years, the moment of attention from her mother has passed. The nearness of Alexandra threatens to suffocate her. She moves to the window to hide her tears; if she'd imagined any scenario at all about her first meeting with her lost mother, she could never have conjured this scene.

Did Howard live with this coldness? Or did she get away before he could see the iced heart that drives the blood through her veins? Bella doesn't hear the angry words spoken between the brother and sister. A door slams. Silence: she has gone. She has left Bella again. Without a word of goodbye.

Chapter Thirty-Five

Barcelona

Bella watches from the window as Alexandra leaves the building and enters a black car. It's too far away to see the number plate. She turns around to find Eduardo with his head in his hands. Forgetting her own upset, she sits beside him. He is pale and very shaken. 'Oh Eduardo, was she always like this?'

'Yes, Bella.'

'Why did Howard spend his life protecting her?'

'He wasn't protecting her, Bella; he was protecting you.'

'So, he didn't try to bring her to justice. He shut himself down.'

'It would seem so, Bella. I am so sorry to put you through this.'

'Please don't feel that. Once I get over the shock, I'll be able to get on with my life without the burden of my unanswered questions.'

'You are very strong, dear Bella.' He touches Bella's cheek.

'I'm curious why she chose today to come here. She could visit you at any time to demand money. I realise she has followed my movements but...' Bella pauses. 'I can't understand why as clearly she didn't want to make any amends or connect with me.'

'Ah sadly dear Bella, I don't know the answer. One thing I do understand is that Alexandra never does anything without a purpose for her own gain.'

Eduardo summons Jose and Maria. Jose looks worried, but Maria stands with her head up, her expression defiant. As a rapid-fire conversation takes place, Bella can't understand a word, but the tone is obvious. Jose and Maria are denying any foreknowledge of the visit. Eduardo does not believe them.

They move out to the courtyard, both needing to free themselves from the atmosphere indoors. The breeze from the harbour refreshes them. It moves the leaves on the trees, creating a soothing whisper. They gaze out to the turquoise sea shimmering in the sunlight. When Maria brings a meal, she will not meet Eduardo's eye or Bella's. She feels a steady current of hatred from Maria as she serves a meal of sardines, fresh tomato and basil salad, and a sheep's milk cheese with bread and a jug of sangria. The chilled red wine drink starts to relax them a little.

'Eduardo, what sort of life does Alexandra lead that she can know so much about people? What kind of people does she associate with?'

'I would say they are people from the wartime who never let go of their reprehensible beliefs.' He sighs. 'I'm sure Klaus and Alexandra are involved in the same misdeeds as they were then. These days, it's called by different names: extortion and terrorism.'

Bella is struggling to understand any of this. It all feels so far from her world. But then, she thinks, as a journalist, why is she so surprised? Bella can still feel the pain that went through her when Alexandra threw out her poisoned barb about Eli.

She asks Eduardo, 'Could she know where Eli is? Is Eli...' Bella pauses. Tears well up, and she tries to speak. 'Was she saying that Eli is like her?' More tears flow before she can say. 'A terrorist?' She reaches for her handkerchief. The pain this possibility brings her is overwhelming.

Eduardo leans forward to take her hand. 'I don't know, but my sister could know his whereabouts. And she is keeping that piece of information to use to her own advantage at another time. Dear Bella, we haven't heard the last of her.'

This tenderness from her uncle calms Bella, she says with feeling. 'I hope we do!'

'Why is that?' asks Eduardo.

'We can hope she'll make a mistake and will get caught.' Bella says grimly.

'It doesn't matter if she's exposed now; Howard doesn't have to protect me any longer.'

'She's a very dangerous woman, Bella.'

Bella strokes Eduardo's hand gently and speaks to him. 'I'm not frightened. My mother doesn't think I'm important enough to be of any use to her!'

Eduardo is silent. He seems to be weighing up what to say. 'Bella, I know that if you or I can be a pawn in any game Alexandra chooses to play, that is exactly what she will do.'

Bella leans back into the cushions. A reaction to her encounter with her mother is setting in. It's an effort to gather her physical self. She's shivering and unsure whether she is cold or feeling the effects of shock. She takes deep breaths; her concern is for Eduardo; how much more of this sadness and upset can this already frail, gentle man take?

'Eduardo, where to from here? We can't do anything about the past, but we might be able to right some wrong by trying to bring her to justice now,' Bella speaks slowly. 'Before I came, I asked Storm to find out anything he could about my mother. I had no idea that I'd meet her here. Do you mind if I tell him about today? I'm sure he will help me.'

Eduardo nods. 'Yes, you must. And tell Storm I wish to offer any assistance that I can. It's time. If he wants you to see the security services. I will come too.'

Bella nods; she feels gratitude to her uncle. 'So, Eduardo, please think back to this afternoon: did Alexandra leave us any clues to Eli's whereabouts? You don't know where she lives, do you?'

'No idea at all.'

'Why do you think she wants to live such a clandestine life?'

Eduardo replies. 'There is no doubt that Alexandra knows that in Britain, at least, she is guilty of war crimes, Klaus also. He disappeared at the end of the war to escape the Nuremberg trials. I have sometimes wondered if that is why Alexandra waited until she did to leave you and Howard. She probably thought she was safe enough there and was waiting to hear from Klaus.'

Bella changes tack. 'Do you remember much about Howard visiting you with me?'

'Yes, I do. I wish I had taken a different course. I was so ashamed of Clara and Alexandra. I wanted to shut the door on the whole thing.' Eduardo pauses, chewing before he continues. 'Howard must have had some misgivings about her. He told me he felt committed to the marriage until that day he found out the truth about your Uncle Tom's death from David. He tried to move on her then, but it was too late. She, as you might say, "flew from the coop."'

Bella smiles at Eduardo's version of the English phrase. She feels today has brought trust between them; she asks. 'What do you think about me contacting the Somers? After all, I'm Clara's only grandchild. We don't know if Clara is alive or what happened to her. Although Alexandra did say, "She is spineless." Not, "she was spineless." She also said that Clara had crawled back to her family. If anyone knows about Clara, the Somers might.'

Eduardo nods. 'I will contact Hugo Somers after you go back to London.'

Bella reaches out to take Eduardo's hand. She doesn't think touch or physical comfort has featured in his life; there are tears on his cheek.

'Finding Alexandra is out of my hands. There are greater reasons for the security services to find her...and Klaus! She needs to answer for her presence in France with him.'

'At least that,' agrees Eduardo.

Bella smiles, 'Today has closed that chapter for me. So, Eduardo, you have done me a great favor.' Despite everything that is happening, Bella feels peaceful here with her uncle.

'Bella.'

'Yes?' she comes back to the present.

'I agree, it's best for the security service to find her. I think it's essential that you meet the Somers. But with the time you have available, what's more important to you? See them if you can but, there is no way they could help you with finding Eli; he isn't anything to do with them.'

Bella considers Eduardo's words. Even if the Somers know where Alexandra is, they're unlikely, even now, to lead Bella to her. Especially if they understand that Bella will bring her to justice. They've spent over forty years trying to distance themselves from that scandal. Eli is her focus now. 'Yes, you're right, Eduardo. I need to get to work.'

Bella looks up and catches sight of Maria. She's standing in the shadowed part of the loggia, almost hidden by the vines creeping up the pillars. Bella has a fleeting feeling that the woman has been standing there listening. Why would she do that? As far as Bella knows, Maria doesn't speak any English.

Chapter Thirty-Six

Geneva

Bella tidies her hair and checks her makeup as the plane lands in Geneva. The mirror shows her how much her hair colour is like her mother's and, even her choice of deep red lipstick. Where do these preferences or tastes come from when a child has been separated from her mother for most of her life? What else does she share with Alexandra? After such a brief and difficult encounter, Bella doesn't want to delve into that. She is overwhelmed by a rush of love for Fiona and her homesickness for everything that is dear to her at Yarra Glen. She's only been away for two weeks, but it feels much longer.

Ariel Achmed meets Bella at Geneva airport. He's aged since she last saw him at Yarra Glen, but his smile and hug bring tears to both as they remember Howard. Five years have passed since her last trip to Geneva en route to Verbier with Eli in January 1985. At that time, she had no hint of what was to come only a few months after they returned to Melbourne.

Bella is flying to London late afternoon, so they will lunch at the Grand Hotel Kempinski as Ariel's home is in Thonon-les-Bains, a forty-five minute drive around Lac Leman. He couldn't know that this hotel was Bella and Eli's usual place to stay in Geneva. Bella feels she's walking through a dream as they cross the familiar foyer and turn right into the restaurant; their table has a view of the lake and the Jet d'Eau. Exactly where Eli and Bella would breakfast before they set off for Zermatt or Verbier. She can feel Eli's presence; she focuses on the menu and her pleasure seeing Ariel again. After their orders are taken, Bella tells him about her visit to Barcelona, meeting her mother, and the shock at Alexandra's mention of Eli and an "encounter" in Tangier. 'Do you have any idea what she could mean by that?'

'Tangiers? Ariel queries, 'That is interesting. Bella, since you wrote to me, I have, through a contact, spoken with people who knew Eli and worked with him in the past.' Seeing Bella's face, he stops and touches her hand. 'I'm sorry, but no one can or will tell me exactly where he is.'

'You say "where he is." Ariel, are you saying Eli is still alive!'

'Yes, it seems so, Bella.'

Bella turns her face away. The impossibility of this situation, so close on the heels of meeting her mother, leaves her breathless. She turns to face Ariel.

'Please, Ariel, tell me anything you can.'

He tells Bella that Eli is very well-connected. Ariel is sure that he is not being told the whole truth about him, and certainly not his real name.

'I wasn't exactly helped, but my enquiry wasn't entirely blocked either.' Bella searches his face for any further clues.

'The contact implied that his service acknowledges the partnership between Eli and Howard and services rendered by Howard. He will pass on my request for information or, hopefully, an opportunity to meet Eli.'

The news of clandestine activities shared by Howard and Eli shocks her. It was bad enough to think of this possibility, but the reality sears her brain and her heart. Again, she feels a surge of anger at her father's secrecy.

'I don't want to raise your hopes, Bella, but I understood this request would not be considered if Eli is still fully operational. It's possible that his age or physical limitations may mean he is retired.'

'Thank you, Ariel. I'm astounded that Howard and Eli might have worked together.' She hopes Ariel can't see her feelings reflected on her face. 'It's the first glimmer I've ever had. I hope that someone, hopefully, Eli, will contact me.' Bella pauses. 'Why did you say Alexandra's mention of Tangier is interesting?'

Ariel asks. 'What do you know about his family?'

Bella shrugs. 'I'm sure his story about his wife and children was false. So why would he be truthful about his family history?'

'You have a point, but tell me what you remember anyway.'

She recounts what Eli had told her. 'His mother, Sofia, married the man she met after she arrived in Palestine. Eli told me that his stepfather had arrived in Palestine after the First World War.'

'Do you remember where the stepfather came from, Bella?'

'Oh!' she exclaims. 'It was Tangier, the family came from Morocco! They were wealthy businesspeople. Import-export. Eli's Grandfather left Morocco to move to Palestine around 1920.' She pauses whilst the waiter tops up their wine glasses. 'They would have been well established in Palestine, years before the European refugees from Hitler started arriving there.'

'Interesting; my contact mentioned Tangier. So, Bella, nothing solid to go on but enough I feel, for you to go there. As soon as you have your travel details, I'll pass them on. Okay?'

Bella nods. It is hard to sit in this elegant room when she needs to run outside into the cold wind that blows down from the Alps. Anything to cool the pain she feels at her father's duplicity. How could he have done this to her? Instinctively, Bella knows to leave it at that. Further questioning wouldn't be useful. After lunch, they walk around the lake; they have so much to talk about. When Bella leaves, she gives Ariel a bottle of Howard's precious Penfold's Grange Hermitage, vintage 1971.

Chapter Thirty-Seven

Florin Court London

At five o'clock, Bella calls her aunt. She knows Fiona will be awake and ready to start her day at Yarra Glen. Bella tells her about Barcelona, Eduardo…and her meeting with Alexandra. She has trouble finding the words.

'Fiona, I've never met anyone like Alexandra. I can't understand how Howard fell in love with her.' Bella's voice breaks, 'she's quite evil.'

A brief silence over the phone before Fiona speaks. 'Yes, I struggle to understand how Alexandra deceived him so completely. It doesn't fit with the Howard I know. I can only say it was wartime. We were so protected here at Yarra Glen compared to what Howard and Tom,' she says softly, '…especially Tom experienced.'

'Y'know Fiona, I've never had any real connection with my uncle Tom before now. He was always such a remote figure. Now I feel so close to him. Especially after spending time with David.'

'Ah yes, David and I talked about Tom,' Fiona pauses … 'About he and Tom.'

'Oh Fiona, how do you feel about that? Did you ever understand that about Tom?'

Fiona's voice speaks wistfully. 'Not directly, but I guess as his sister, I had a better sense of him than Howard. He was away so much when Tom was growing up. I never spoke to Howard about it. I don't know why really.

How do I feel? Well, I am happy. Happy that Tom and David knew such love.'

'That's how I feel too.'

'But getting back to Alexandra. How do you feel about her?'

'I rang Storm from Barcelona and faxed him a report. I know I'll have to deal with my feelings, but for now, she's an assignment to me. It helps me to keep going to put it in that perspective. And Eduardo, Adeline, David, and Storm are all great support.'

'I'm thankful for that,' replies Fiona. 'I can tell when I speak to each of them how much they care for you.'

'I know, I feel that,' replies Bella. 'We are making a family of friends with these good people.'

'So precious, Bella, especially when you think that Eduardo, David, and Adeline have no real family of their own.'

'Extraordinary, isn't it? I suppose we can thank Howard for our newly extended family.'

'We can,' replies Fiona tartly, 'if we put aside that we should have been able to know and care for them years ago.'

She tells her aunt the security services will take over the search for Klaus and Alexandra, she concludes. 'However, Alexandra has unwittingly sharpened my resolve to have a go at finding Eli whilst I am here.'

'Is that helpful, Bella? Can't you let that rest?'

Bella can hear Fiona's unsaid concern for Scott and thinks before replying, 'It's one last shot, I promise. So much has happened since Howard died that shows me the futility of hanging on to the past.' She thinks about Scott. 'You're right, Fiona, it's time to move on.'

'Well, that is good news,' her aunt says with a touch of irony.

Bella delivers another surprise to her aunt. 'It's possible that Eli and Howard were working together in clandestine work.' She recounts her meeting with Ariel Achmed in Geneva.

Her aunt's shock is palpable. 'No! How could that be? Bella, this is simply too much for you to bear alone. I must come to be with you.'

Bella replies, 'Please don't worry about me; Scotty will be here soon.'

Before her aunt can reply, she says. 'Do you know what is hardest for me? Howard ensured that I had a strong moral compass and a commitment to fair play and honesty.' A tear catches in her throat. 'Where was my father's moral compass that he kept so much from me? From us.'

'Adeline gave you the answer. She believes that Howard came home to tell us everything,' her aunt pauses. 'So, you see, his moral compass was set to true north. Without being able to hear him tell us, we need to accept that he made his choices out of love.'

'Do you accept that, Fiona?'

Her aunt hesitates, 'Yes, I believe I have, and I hope you will, too. Unless we find a letter from him, we have little choice.'

Before dinner, Adeline and Bella walk around the square outside Florin Court. Darkness falls early; a damp cold is settling, and the winter-naked trees silhouetted in the lamplight look like sentinel ghosts. Bella pulls her coat around her and turns to Adeline. 'I struggle to understand my mother.'

Adeline replies. 'Sometimes during the war, we came across these people. They were very dangerous.'

'Eduardo told me about Clara's family's connections to Oswald Mosley.'

Adeline nods. 'Yes, that is quite likely. Many of Mosley's supporters were well-known people with important jobs and connections. They aimed to prepare the way for Hitler to invade Britain. They believed they would be rewarded with positions of power in the new regime.'

Bella shakes her head in disbelief. 'I think about my father's political views. Fiona and I wonder how Alexandra took him in so completely.'

'Yes, I thought it was quite extraordinary at the time.'

'I want to try to meet the Somers family before I go home,' says Bella as they turn back to the warmth of home.

'Oh?' says Adeline with a question in her voice.

'Yes, I just want to try to fathom where...' Bella pauses, unsure of what she is trying to express.

'You wonder if Hugo's family shared Clara's family's beliefs.'

'Yes, that's it,' replies Bella. 'They are first cousins. It was a twist of fate and British family law, that Hugo inherited the title. He might've struggled with the Clara's family history as much as I am.'

'Ring him and ask if he will meet you.' Adeline hugs Bella closer to her as they walk arm-in-arm across the darkened square. In the hallway Bella hangs up their coats, she thinks about her feelings for her mother; she can't grasp anything. It's all so elusive.

She feels forces building pressure inside her, squeezing her, making her breathless. It's impossible to tell whether those forces will resolve in clarity or further confusion. The phone rings, and Adeline tells her it's Storm's PA, Phoenicia. She puts that sharp-edged thought away to examine later.

'Hello Phoenicia.'

'Isabella, welcome back. Lord Storm will see you tomorrow at ten o'clock.'

Whilst Adeline serves supper, Bella stokes the fire and turns her back to the warmth. The question about her mother is answered, but that meeting opened more. Damn Alexandra, Bella thinks. Her evil words about Eli have stirred up conflicting emotions. Is he a good man or a very bad one? There's the question of trust. Was her trust entirely misplaced? How would she feel if he walked through the door at home in Armadale? He could; Bella has never changed the lock. Deep down, she always hopes he will return. Because, of course, she still loves him. Does she still love him? Really? Or is she more in love with the memory of him? Is this yearning because she doesn't like unanswered questions; why did he leave?

As a child, she would plague Aunt Fiona, or her father to answer her questions. The reason why. She always must know the reason why. So, is her longing really her love for Eli, or is it her thwarted need for answers? Bella asks herself what her real motive is for trying to find him. Why can't she accept that he left her? After all, he did leave for something or...someone else. The call of the "else" was stronger than his desire to stay with her.

She wants to ring Scott; she really needs to hear his voice. Bella feels Scott's anxiety for her on each phone call, feels the depth of his care. 'Oh,' she exclaims as she picks up the phone. 'I've been so...' The phone answers, his voice clogged with sleep softens when she speaks. 'Scotty...'

Chapter Thirty-Eight

Power Press London

Next morning, Bella joins the commuter crush. In the office, a letter has arrived from MI6 in response to her enquiry about Howard. She makes an appointment.

Also, a thick envelope from Reuters detailing Howard's years of service as a foreign correspondent. Tears blur her eyesight as she reads the pages of assignment details. She wonders where her Clemens' stiff upper lip has disappeared since Howard died.

For forty-five years, Howard had put himself in the face of danger with devastation and personal privation, his regular diet. What can MI6 possibly add to this? She can see from this litany of travel and Howard's presence in the trouble spots of the world, that he would have been an ideal observer for intelligence gathering. Phoenicia summons Bella to the top floor. Storm greets her.

'I want to hear about Barcelona. Your fax was intriguing.'

'Yes, I have a lot to tell you, but my priority now is to find Eli. Please will you help me?'

'Isn't finding your mother and her partner more important?'

'I think Eli might help us to find them.' Bella holds her breath; she sees his expression change.

Storm buzzes Phoenicia. 'Please request a light lunch for us.'

Bella tells him about meeting Alexandra. She includes Eduardo's assessment of Alexandra and Klaus's life as international criminals since World War Two. She finds it difficult to describe her feelings to Storm.

Storm says. 'You asked if I could find anything about her from my old network.'

'Did you? Anything would be helpful.'

Storm fills her water glass. 'The file is still open on Alexandra Monerayo Clemens. Your mother is still a wanted person, and not only here in the UK. Apart from her war crimes, your uncle is correct. Alexandra and Klaus are implicated in a variety of unsolved crimes across Europe. These cover extortion, kidnapping, murder, and more.'

'How extraordinary! They must have a significant network.'

Storm smiles. 'SMERSH and SPECTRE might not be figments of Ian Fleming's imagination.' In a more serious tone, he says. 'Both Scotland Yard and Interpol are very interested in your search for your mother.'

Bella knows she needs to do this. For her father, for herself, and now, for Eduardo, too. Not to mention the victims of Alexandra's post-war crimes.

'I know I speak for Eduardo; he agrees that it's time to bring them in.'

'Good!' says Storm. 'So, you're happy for me to give this information about Alexandra to Scotland Yard then?'

Bella nods. 'Yes Storm, do it please.'

Storm asks. 'And Eduardo doesn't know where Alexandra lives?'

Bella shakes her head. 'Until this week, he hadn't seen her for years.'

'If she pops up around Europe, it's unlikely that she and Klaus would be living too far away.' Storm sips his coffee and continues. 'Many Nazis escaped any criminal charges when they found havens in South America, especially Argentina.'

'Yes, I've read a lot about that. Extraordinary, wasn't it? Thousands of Nazis were smuggled out through Italy and Spain by a system called the rat lines to make new lives and escape retribution for their wartime activities.'

'Yes,' Storm adds. 'Incredibly, the Catholic Church aided many of these escapes.'

Bella shakes her head, 'I can't get my mind around that. Howard worked at Nuremberg during the trials. I'm sure he was trying to trace Alexandra through Kurt Schoeffels. You know the German officer in the clipping I showed you? He escaped and was never tried so that ended any possible lead to Alexandra.'

Storm nods. 'Yes, it seems so.'

'And,' Bella takes a breath, 'I saw Ariel Achmed in Geneva.'

Storm laughs. 'Nothing stops you, does it?'

Bella smiles. 'We've been writing to each other about Eli since Howard died. He was very discreet, but he is communicating with someone about my quest.'

'Go on,' says Storm.

'It seems Eli and Howard were connected.' Bella gives him a short summary of Ariel's comments; she leaves out her feelings about this.

'Now that is very interesting.' Storm drums his fingers on the desk. 'Tell me more about Howard and Eli.'

She describes Howard's friendship with Eli and their long conversations in Howard's study. Working together around the farm and the vineyards. Their mutual love of horses, including trail rides in the Yarra Glen hills, just the two of them.

'So, I've been thinking,' says Bella. If Howard knew Eli's background and his work. He might've told him about Alexandra.'

Storm sits back in his chair. 'Yes, that's possible. He must've made Eli promise not to tell you. Eli must have found it difficult to keep that undertaking.' Storm regards her for a minute. His normal flintiness is softening. 'You must have mixed feelings about Howard taking these decisions about your life, without your knowledge.'

'Sometimes I feel I'm going to choke with anger. When I can manage those feelings, I feel it's sad that he couldn't let go of the secrets locked inside him.'

'Death has the final word, Bella.' Storm says gently.

She reflects on the truth of this statement.

'So, to find Eli, where would you start?'

'Tangier.' She tells him about Alexandra, saying she had "encountered" Eli there.

'Interesting. Do you believe her?'

Bella shrugs. 'Who could know? It's a starting point, and Ariel's informant suggested it also.'

Bella falls silent; she looks up. 'I would try older parts of the city and near the seaport.'

'Why is that?' Storm asks.

'Eli told me his family were seafarers and traders. Also, he loved the sea.'

Memories of hot summer nights sailing on Port Phillip Bay catch her unawares. Sitting in the cockpit of their Couta boat, sharing supper and a bottle of wine. Moonlight trailing across the water, waves lapping against the hull as she gazes at the myriad stars. Breathing in the smell of him mixed with the warm, heavy salt air.

'My problem is…if he hid so much from me, why would I believe anything he said about his family's history in Tangier?'

'That is a hard one,' Storm replies, 'perhaps even Eli needed to ground himself in some reality. Given his profession, though, he was taking a risk. Where would you start there?'

She laughs. 'Not with a telephone book, I can tell you that much.'

'Why not?'

'I don't know what name he might use. And he had an aversion to directory entries. Except for the business premises in Melbourne, at home, he always insisted on unlisted numbers.'

'That's interesting.' Storm looks thoughtful. 'He really did prefer anonymity. It all points to a covert life.'

'Eli's life, like Howard's, consisted of a series of watertight compartments. One did not link to the other. I'm certain his name wasn't Eli, but,' she shrugs, 'in the absence of any proof otherwise, he can only be Eli to me.'

'Yes, if Eli was a foreign government agent and he knew no one in Australia. His whole persona could be fabricated.'

She tells him about the ASIO officer's view that Eli's family story was a cover. They didn't exist!

'Bella, it seems to me that Eli could have many reasons for you not to find him.'

Bella nods. 'Yes, I had to accept that after my search for him got nowhere.' She thinks back to the years of living with Eli; was he only real in a physical sense? His name and persona are a mystery.

Storm says. 'You should research businesses in Morocco that fit with Eli's family's activities. If they were traders, they would have lived near the port. I am giving you Tarik Mehenuin, our local journalist, for a week.'

She smiles at Storm, 'That's great. I'll go downstairs and start.'

'Good luck, Bella.'

'Thank you.' Bella leaves before he sees the tears she feels trying to escape.

Downstairs, the senior editor, Sam Stryker, arrives in front of Bella's desk. Storm has briefed him. 'Well, Bella, you've charmed Storm.' Sam hands Bella a note with Tarik's details.

Next, Bella calls Scott. He's leaving Melbourne tomorrow night, flying to London via Singapore.

'Not long now, Bella,' Scott says softly. 'I miss you.'

'Yes, I miss you too.' Bella says this from her heart; saying the words makes her feelings real and present. She explains the possible connection between Eli and Alexandra. She tells Scott about their trip to Tangier. 'Scotty, this is the last lap.'

'Really, Bella?'

She can hear the question in Scott's voice. 'Yes, I know it, I feel it.'

Scott doesn't reply, so Bella, so she says. 'I need to identify what Eli might use as a business front.'

Scott asks. 'Apart from skiing and sailing with you, what interests did he have here?'

'Work, work, and work.' Bella replies, remembering the weekends and weeks he would be away.

'That's no help. Would he get into engineering and road building somewhere else?'

'No. If his primary existence was undercover work, he wouldn't want the infrastructure that he had in Melbourne. I've been told it was an army maneuver, to dismantle that yard. Whatever he was doing living in Australia, he intended to be there for longer than he was. Otherwise, I'm sure he wouldn't have built up that business.'

'Would he get a job in an established company?'

Bella thinks before she replies, 'Possible, but I can't feel it. If his lifestyle or job required freedom to move about, being an employee wouldn't work for him at all.'

'Agriculture?' enquires Scott.

'No, he would not want anything that needed feeding or looking after. I know that.'

'Antiques?' says Scott. 'He could be an antique dealer. All he would need to do is to store them and have a gallery. Those items appreciate with age, and dust adds to their charm so low care.'

'He did love Spanish or Middle Eastern furniture, woven goods, colored tiles, artefacts. Spanish chandeliers, anything like that! He bought me that beautiful fountain for the courtyard at home.' Bella thinks about the unusual fossil bowls from the Atlas Mountains.

Scott laughs. 'I know the one. And the malachite chandelier. I always thought it was a touch well...' he laughs, 'over the top.'

Bella says, 'I'll call Tarik to see if he can start to identify some possibilities. I'll see you at Heathrow on Monday.'

'I'm looking forward to it,' says Scott softly.

'Oh Scottie, please could you go to Armadale? On the bookshelf is a photo album of all the collectibles. Eli made them for insurance. It might be useful.'

She rings Tarik to book him for this assignment. She promises she will send a brief as soon as she confirms her travel bookings. Tarik will meet them at Ibn Battuta Airport. Would she please fax a photo of Scott and herself to him? He will find them in the arrival hall.

'So, Tarik, it's possible the friend I am looking for may have an artefact export business. Can we spend a couple of days looking at those kinds of businesses?'

Tarik's French-accented voice elevates when he hears her question. 'A couple of days Eeezabella! I could have a long grey beard and thirty grandchildren before you look at all these in Tangier. This is not a neat and tidy place like Oxford Street in London. This place is a total schmozzle.'

'Bear up Tarik. I've a hunch that we're looking for a smaller business. Not one of the tourist traps with salesmen offering coffee and cakes.' After a moment, Bella adds. 'Not carpets, they'd still need more care than he'd want to give.'

'Eesh! Can you send a photograph of him, please?'

'Yes, Tarik, I'll fax you everything tomorrow.' She pauses. 'Scott is bringing photos of the artefacts I think he might deal in. Would that help?'

Chapter Thirty-Nine

MI6 Headquarters London

Bella enters the foyer of MI6 headquarters at Century House. At the desk, she shows the letter then she crosses the foyer to sit in a leather armchair. She looks around the anonymous space; it is a tribute to the bland architectural style of its era and gives no hint of the work carried out here. A tall, grey-haired woman appears, introduces herself as Elizabeth, and ushers Bella through a door into a small room. The only furniture is a wooden table with a black telephone and a chair on either side. Excitement flushes through Bella.

'Please take a seat, Miss Clemens.' Elizabeth opens a folder and places a document in front of Bella that, like the one she received from Reuters, brings a lump to her throat. It states that the security services acknowledge the contribution of Howard Clemens in his role as a Covert Human Intelligence Source or "Agent." Agents are described as people who can provide information about a target of an investigation. It is noted that Agents are not MI6 employees.

Bella looks up in surprise. 'Oh, for heaven's sake! How long did he do this for?'

Elizabeth points to a line in the document. The length of service is listed as 1940 - 1988. Again, as with the Reuters report, Bella feels humbled by how much Howard put himself in the way of danger without apparently, much thought to his own safety.

Elizabeth tells her. 'Your father's travels on reporting assignments overseas enabled him to gather external intelligence. If this information was relevant to internal security, this was shared with MI5. This work was vital in developing foreign contacts and gathering intelligence that helps to make the UK safer in times of war and peace.' Elizabeth pauses to give Bella a moment before she continues. 'His post-war work assisted the fight against terrorism and in the resolution of international conflict.'

Bella shakes her head. She can see exactly how Howard's secretive nature enabled these activities. 'Thank you so much for this, but are there any details of his actual assignments?'

'No, we can't give you any of that information, Miss Clemens. This is an acknowledgement of service as you requested.' Elizabeth relaxes slightly.

'In an agent's role like Howard's, the pieces of information contributed to a bigger picture that enabled actions to be planned and taken as necessary. His role was vital.'

Bella thinks again about the hidden sides of her father. And Eli. What were the chances of two of the major influences in her life being men of this type?

Elizabeth continues. 'Your father's job as a Reuters correspondent gave him mobility in Europe during the war and in the years since. It positioned him perfectly for information gathering. He was welcome in every strata of life around Europe or wherever he travelled.'

Fascinated, Bella listens as Elizabeth explains that Howard had a chameleon-like ability to blend into his surroundings. From palaces to marketplaces, people talked to him, and he listened. At parties, as alcohol loosened people's tongues and told him things they ought not, his sharp memory stored every detail for transmission. He was able to gather some hard intelligence as well as some personal quirks and indiscreet remarks of prominent people. At the other end of the scale, people told Howard their stories out of desperation or a need to find a way for injustices to be addressed.

'So, Miss Clemens, that's about all I can tell you. Your father's length of service from 1940 until his recent retirement is a staggering commitment.

He was one of the longest serving agents in the history of the security services.'

Bella reflects that this work occupied more than half his life; she says, 'Thank you again. I have another question, please. I'm looking for any information I can find on my mother; her name is Alexandra Monerayo-Clemens.'

Elizabeth looks down at his folder. 'I don't see a request form or a copy of her death certificate here. Is she still alive?'

Bella's heart is banging so heavily, she's sure Elizabeth can hear it. 'Yes.'

Elizabeth is silent, then looks up. 'I'm sorry, I cannot give you any information on her, at this time.' She closes the folder and stands up to show Bella out.

En route to her next stop, Bella posts a copy of the report to Fiona. Oh, how she wishes Fiona had been with her this morning. It would've put so much about Howard into focus for her.

Chapter Forty

The Naval & Military Club London

Bella looks at the writing on the back of Storm's business card. The IN & OUT. Is this a joke? The cab whirls her over Eccleston Bridge, hard right into Grosvenor Place. Around Hyde Park Corner and pulls up outside 94 Piccadilly. Set back from the road sits an imposing building. Two sets of gates allow access and departure via a driveway and forecourt. Yes, one set of gates marked IN in large letters and the other OUT. She pays the cabbie and opens the door. Opposite lies the beautiful Green Park. Bella wishes she had time to sit there and sort out her thoughts, but a summons from Storm isn't ignored.

At the entrance, she realises she's at the famous Naval and Military Club. Why couldn't Storm have said that instead of the silly IN & OUT business? Curiosity moves her past the doorman and into the foyer. She tells the concierge her name and whom she is here to see.

'Ah yes, Miss Clemens. Lord Storm is waiting for you in the small drawing room on the first floor.' He calls an attendant to guide her upstairs. As she thanks him and turns to leave, the concierge says. 'Miss Clemens, please accept my condolences on the death of your father. He was well known and liked here.'

Bella utters her thanks. Howard would have been a member here; there are reciprocal membership arrangements with Melbourne Clubs. She's surprised because, when she visited Howard in London, she usually met him where he stayed at another club. Are these separate clubs more of Howard's watertight compartments? She follows the attendant up the stairs. He opens a door, and Bella enters the room. She can see the park through the long windows. Without knowing, Bella is in the same room where the meeting between her father and David McKenzie in 1946 changed the course of her life. And started the journey that brings her back to exactly here today.

'Bella!' Storm stands up and, to her surprise, hugs her.

'What's this silly IN & OUT business?'

'Ah well, Bella, it's a bit of an in-joke to do with earlier residents of this building. It's kind of stuck as a nickname. Make yourself comfortable; we've a few minutes before my other guests arrive.'

Bella looks around. 'Why are we here? What other guests? What's all this mystery Storm?' She adds tartly. 'I'm getting a bit worn down by mysteries.'

'Patience Bella. We're here to meet the people who are investigating Alexandra. They want to talk to you before you go to Morocco.

A waiter returns with a tray; Bella is pleased to see a plate bristling with sandwiches. While they eat, she tells him about her meeting at MI6.

'After Elizabeth gave me the report on Howard's service, I asked her about Alexandra, and she stopped the conversation right there.'

Storm smiles. 'I'm not surprised. She would be aware of your meeting with Alexandra; you've got them quite excited. It's the first confirmed sighting reported since her disappearance in 1946.'

'I hope Adeline will be able to tell me about her part in all this. Sadly, in his efforts to conceal my mother from me, Howard made her a partner in his conspiracy of silence.

Storm replies. 'I understand. I'm meeting Adeline for lunch whilst you're in Morocco. I'll be able to talk to her then.'

The door opens, two men enter. The older man is dressed in a navy reefer jacket with gold buttons. White hair, a trimmed moustache, and his bearing make him, despite his age, still look very military.

Storm turns to her. 'Bella, I'd like you to meet Simon Day.'

He steps forward and gives her a firm handshake. 'Good afternoon, Miss Clemens.'

'How do you do, Mr Day,' replies Bella. Simon Day, could he be the same person Adeline spoke about? She turns to the younger man; he holds out his hand.

'Fergus Campbell, unsolved case consultant from MI6.'

Storm takes the lead. 'Bella, Simon was part of the original investigation into your mother's activities. He was with Howard the day they went to Florin Court to detain Alexandra. Simon agreed to come out of retirement to help in any way he can.'

Simon nods. 'Miss Clemens, may I call you Isabella?'

'Bella, please, after all,' Bella smiles, 'I understand you've known me for a long time.' They all smile, and the atmosphere in the room lightens.

Simon says. 'How do you feel about your mother Bella?'

'Dreadful!' she replies with passion. 'In a way, I can understand Howard keeping me away from her. I'm devastated to find that my mother is a traitor and a criminal.'

Storm speaks. 'After Bella's meeting with her mother in Barcelona. Alexandra's brother Eduardo and Bella both agree that Alexandra should be brought to justice.'

She speaks. 'Yes, Eduardo and I both want this to happen.'

Fergus speaks. 'Has Storm mentioned to you that Scotland Yard and Interpol want to work with us?'

Bella nods. 'Even better. Eduardo is happy to meet with you here if he can help in any way.'

'Excellent, thank you.' Fergus continues. 'In the meantime, Bella, we need to get you as far away from Klaus and Alexandra as possible.'

'Oh? Eduardo and Storm both say the same thing. I can't see why they'd bother with me.' Bella stops; confusion is making her feel at a loss. These men and this situation are testing her mettle. This was her father's world, not hers. She tells them about her suspicion that Alexandra was on the flight from Bahrain.

Fergus says. 'Bella, this is vital information. Do you still have your flight details?'

'Yes,' she reaches into her briefcase and passes the boarding pass across.

Fergus looks pleased. 'Excellent, Bella.' He goes to the telephone and speaks in a low voice. He explains. 'I've requested the passenger's name and booking details for the seat next to Bella. Every scrap we get helps. But I have to say, I don't like this, and it confirms my concerns about your safety.'

Storm adds. 'We all want you out of her reach. For Alex to appear in Barcelona demanding money makes us feel they are desperate for funds.'

'Who are they? This supposed syndicate.'

Simon explains that they believe many former Fascists who hadn't integrated into post-war Europe had, over time and financial need, turned to major crime to support themselves. Art and jewelry theft is their most benign activity. Their talents and experience enable them to use kidnapping and extortion on a very sophisticated level. He says, 'Klaus Schoeffels murdered innocent civilians during the war. He is a very dangerous man.'

'Bella,' says Fergus. 'This task force has opened up access to information from other agencies. All small pieces, but they help build a picture.' He tells her that this criminal cartel, whom they believe control Alexandra and Klaus, have had projects misfire. Two recent kidnappings went wrong; people have died. No ransoms were collected for the cartel's coffers. Intelligence sources believe that they're not planning their moves as well as they used to. It could be their age combined with changing technology. Their mistakes will trip them up. He concludes. 'If you're correct about Alexandra's presence on the flight from Bahrain, then her sudden arrival in Barcelona, she has been following you, which concerns us greatly.'

Chapter Forty-One

Somers House, Witney Oxfordshire

B ella telephoned Sir Hugo; she was informed he is away. She left
a message, but Sir Hugo hasn't returned her call. As her time in
London is short, Bella decides to visit with Adeline and David.
The bus drops them at the gate. They've arrived too late for the house
tour, but they can walk in the gardens and have afternoon tea. This is good
news; Bella still feels she is spying on her relatives by visiting without an
invitation. She's happy to be an anonymous tourist. After the intensity of
the last weeks, this day out is good for her.

They set off with a map of the gardens. It's a beautiful autumn afternoon.
The air has a crispness and clear, sunlit sky rarely seen in London. The
map tells them that Capability Brown designed and set out the park and
the gardens during the 1760s. Bella looks around, admiring the beauty,
and hopes she can bring Fiona here one day as a welcome guest. David
and Adeline know a lot about the plants and are happy pottering around
together. Bella decides to leave them; they agree to meet for afternoon tea.

On the way to the teashop, Bella passes through the old kitchen garden.
The raised beds are full of vegetables and herbs. The warmth of the sun
reflecting off the stone walls brings out aromas of Lavender and Rosemary.
Bella sniffs the air and feels homesick for Fiona's herb garden at Yarra Glen.
A faint memory tells her that there should be another gate in the far wall.

How could she know this?

Yes, there is another gate. Opening it, she finds a large rose garden. Concentric circles of rose beds have an elegant fountain as the centerpiece. There are stone benches in arbors punctuating the rose beds. Enchanted, she sits down to enjoy the tranquility and finds her memories of playing in this garden. The bushes still have late blooms but will be pruned for winter soon. Bella remembers hiding under a bench whilst Nanny went around and around looking for her. Other images push forward. A garden swing, a building with a conical roof made of timber shingles. Inside, picnics happened on hot summer days.

It's obvious that the Somers family take pride in preserving their heritage here. The ancient stables and outbuildings are well-kept. Bella grew up with horses at Yarra Glen, but their stables whilst first-class, weren't like these equine mansions. At the carriage door, she remembers the whickering of the horses when she brought carrots to feed them. The groom had to lift her up to reach their whiskery mouths. She realises she took her love of horses from here to Yarra Glen. She stands for a few minutes, willing more memories to come forward from the places hidden inside her. She isn't prepared for the sadness she feels. Why? Does her sadness about her mother go back so far? Oh Dad, she thinks. You tried so hard to protect me, but memories will undo all your best intentions. Now she has met Alexandra; she feels more sympathy for Howard and his choices.

Next door, Bella finds the teashop. At one end, there is a wide fireplace; could this have been the Blacksmith's forge? Sunlight fills this welcoming space. Tall windows in the south side flank two sets of French doors leading to a terrace that runs the length of the building. Bella can see that great care has been taken to keep this space in harmony with the original buildings. As she orders her tea, she finds a tourist magazine about the area. Excellent, this will give her the reason to sit and linger until David and Adeline join her. Choosing a sunny table on the terrace, Bella opens the book at the section about Somers House.

The sound of a woman crying interrupts Bella's thoughts; she looks up. Close by is a very old woman in a wheelchair. She is reaching out her hand towards her, calling to Bella; no one is near, so Bella goes to her. Close up, she can see the poor woman has suffered a debilitating stroke and she is very agitated. Bella takes the woman's outstretched hand and leans closer to hear what she is trying to say, then steps back in shock. Over and over, a broken sound is coming out of the drooping mouth. It sounds like Shhhandddra! Is she trying to call Bella Alexandra? Could this poor woman be her grandmother, Clara? Does she recognize Bella's likeness to Alexandra? A likeness Bella has only recently come to understand. Is she alive and here at her family home? Alexandra's words, "she crawled back to her gutless family," make sense.

Bella doesn't know what to do. To calm the old woman, Bella strokes her cheek and finds a handkerchief to gently wipe the tears from the wrinkled face. Bella looks closely into the faded grey eyes; she can see a faint resemblance to the elegant woman in Eduardo's photographs. She looks around her to find someone to help.

A woman in nurse's uniform bustles up to them. 'There there, Madame! Don't take on so. I was only gone for a minute.' She looks around to Bella. 'Thanks, miss, I don't know what upset her so.'

Bella tries a wild guess. 'She was calling out to me as if I reminded her of someone called Alexandra?'

'Oh dear,' says the nurse. 'She's having one of her bad days. Sometimes, she gets muddled and calls out for an Alexandra. She thinks she had a daughter.'

Bella can't resist, she asks. 'What happened to Alexandra?'

'That's the problem, dear. Sir Hugo told me when he hired me, that the poor lady never married. And she never had a daughter called Alexandra or anyone else come to that.'

Bella has only enough breath to ask. 'What is her name?'

'Miss, I don't know who you are.' replies the nurse. 'Sir Hugo wouldn't welcome you hanging around here asking me questions. And upsetting the old lady.' She bends over to wipe the old woman's face.

Bella sits quietly; she's not going to let the nurse turn her away. 'Please, can I sit with her? She seems calmer now.' She can't get this close to her grandmother; she's sure this is Clara and not stay for a minute. No matter what sort of person Clara might have been. Bella's revulsion for everything this family stood for is temporarily overcome.

'Well, yes I suppose it'll be all right. Only for a minute while I get her a drink,' the nurse says.

Bella sits next to the woman and strokes her crippled hand. Did this hand used to hold Bella's little paw as they walked in the park in London? Did Clara ever read her stories? Bella's memories are too locked away; she doesn't know. The curtains that are drawn over that time are too firmly closed. If she is Clara, they both share the act of abandonment by Alexandra. How else would she be here?

Bella speaks to her softly. 'Clara, are you Clara?' The old woman nods slowly, not taking her eyes off Bella's face. Bella continues. 'I'm your granddaughter Isabella. Eduardo doesn't know that you're here.' Bella looks up. David and Adeline have come to the terrace; they stand back as if they sense a moment of high drama is happening.

'Ella, Ella.' Clara is trying to say Bella; tears fall down her face; Bella cries too. The two women sit holding hands and smile through their tears.

The nurse hurries back to them. 'Have you upset the poor old thing again? What did you say to her? Come on, darlin', I'll take you inside.'

Bella stands up and releases Clara's hand. 'No nurse. I can promise you, she's very happy.' She touches Clara's cheek and whispers, 'I'll see you again.' The nurse is busy with the chair, so Bella says. 'Nurse, this is Clara. How long has she been here? I need to know.' Bella says this in a tone of voice that makes the nurse look around at her. 'If you can't tell me, I'll ask Sir Hugo myself.'

Fear crosses the woman's face. 'I'll tell you, miss, but you must go before Sir Hugo comes out and sees us talking. I don't want to lose my job.'

Bella holds that piece of information that Hugo is here and not away as she was told, until she can look at it.

'Yes, her name is Clara, she's a relative of the family. She has been here for about three months.'

'Like this?' Bella enquires.

'Yes,' the nurse replies. 'Sir Hugo brought her here in this pitiful state.' She looks around. 'I shouldn't be talking to you.'

Bella watches the nurse wheel Clara to the house. She joins David and Adeline. They order tea. She tells them what she learned from the nurse.

'Clara has been living here for three months...I must tell Eduardo.'

David dollops cream on his scone as he says. 'Perhaps Alexandra asked the Somers for money before she went to Eduardo?'

'If Hugo Somers said no,' Bella exclaims, 'maybe Alexandra abandoned Clara.'

'Every likelihood of that,' confirms Adeline.

'Did I do the wrong thing speaking to her?' Bella asks.

David speaks first. 'I don't think so. You may have given her some small comfort.'

Adeline says. 'Does it suit him to maintain the story that Clara is confused and childless?'

'I agree, but apart from the specter of the money-grabbing Alex, I can't understand why he might go along with this.'

'You might be the problem, Bella,' says David.

'Me? Why on earth would I be a problem?'

Bella is interrupted by a very angry, elderly man who appears beside them at the table.

'You will leave now and not return!'

Bella stands up and looks at the man. She sees a tall, strongly built man dressed in a three-piece country squire-style tweed suit. Above the starched collar and tie is a large, red, belligerent face, topped by a shock of white hair. A face that is used to issuing orders and having them obeyed. The stick he carries reinforces that impression. Made from knotted wood, it has an ebony knob that, in his current mood, Bella feels he wouldn't hesitate to use as a weapon. She realises it is Hugo Somers. She's about to hold out her hand to introduce herself when he bursts out with.

'How dare you come here asking questions and cause upset to my family and my staff. I suppose you're from the gutter press trying to rake over old coals.'

The man is in such a rage, he doesn't realise if that was the purpose of her visit; he has made a huge mistake referring to the past. Bella smiles at Hugo; this makes him even angrier. She can see that underneath the anger, his eyes are full of fear. He takes her arm and pulls her to the door. Caution prevents Bella from attempting an explanation. Another time, she needs to talk to Eduardo first.

Five minutes later, they're at the bus stop. Bella is shocked by the sudden ending to their afternoon. David continues as if he wasn't so rudely interrupted. 'As I said, Bella, you might be the problem.'

'Clearly, I was today, but as I didn't even get the chance to introduce myself. How can I be a problem?'

'Because you exist! From his reaction, I think he knows who you are. Like Alexandra, he might have been keeping tabs on you. You might have some legitimate claim to an inheritance.'

'How extraordinary,' Bella shakes her head.

It's Adeline's turn to offer a piece of this puzzle. 'Howard went to Barcelona to seek help from Eduardo after Alexandra and Clara bolted. I'm sure he came here too.'

'I would've gone to both sides,' agrees David.

'So, Eduardo refused to help Howard because he went into damage control after Alexandra's treachery. Wouldn't the Somers have the same reaction?' Adeline asks.

'Makes sense,' adds Bella. 'They were already having to re-invent themselves after the Mosley debacle. They wouldn't want to have a hanged traitor in the family to add to their problems.'

David says. 'This means the Somers and Howard had a shared goal to keep Alexandra out of the newspapers. Unless she was caught and brought to trial, and they had no choice?'

'Yes!' Adeline says. 'I know that if Alexandra had been caught, Howard would have seen it through to see her charged. I'm sure about that. She wasn't caught, so he wanted you as far away as possible.'

'I understand that now.' Bella looks out the window; a late afternoon mist of rain is coming across the soft green fields, casting a grey shadow which reflects her sadness. She is devastated at the outcome of her visit and wishes she hadn't gone to Somers house. 'So, Hugo, Eduardo, and Howard each maintained their own fiction.'

David says, 'Each of them had a part in this story of a fractured family across two generations. They would've jumped at every headline that said, "Traitor Apprehended."'

Bella decides she's going to assign this question of Clara's existence at Somers House to Eduardo. Later that evening, she writes a fax to him, including her travel itinerary for Tangier.

IV

Part Four

Chapter Forty-Two

Tangier Morocco

As the flight approaches Tangier, Bella and Scott gather themselves. They haven't had any time alone together yet. Her pleasure at seeing him at Heathrow was complete, she still feels the moment she saw him in the crowd. Head and shoulders above most people, she saw his familiar, well-worn Akubra hat first. Close up, she could see he hasn't made any wardrobe concessions to arriving in chilly London. He was still clad head to toe in his everyday RM Williams gear. Checked shirt, moleskin trousers, and elastic-sided boots. When he wrapped his arms around her, she breathed him in, and they stood so close together she could feel his lean body. His warmth sent a shiver through her as she realized they had never held each other this close before. Why not? she asked herself. Then he held her back at arm's length and they gazed into each other's eyes. Bella had never noticed what a deep blue Scott's eyes are. She was still taking in the familiar but also new, closer details of a face she understood she has until now, taken rather for granted. He kissed her. This was not the kiss of greeting from a friend and workmate. Bella understood this was a kiss of promise.

They had rushed to the office to meet Storm who gave them a quick briefing on the Barbary Lion project for them to do some initial research in Morocco. After a delightful dinner with Adeline at Florin Court the long flight from

Australia caught up with Scott, he fell asleep in Howard's study. He brought letters from Fiona and Meg for Bella. She devoured every word and felt real pangs of homesickness for her aunt and her friend.

At Ibn Battuta Airport, Bella and Scott find a smiling Tarik holding up a sign with their names in the arrival hall. Tall and loose-limbed with a mass of curly hair only partially constrained by a woven kufi; Tarik is dressed in an embroidered shirt over flared jeans patched with multi-colored fabric, he looks like a genuine throwback to a 1960s hippie. He welcomes them as long-time friends. They collect their luggage and exit the terminal building. The air hits Bella with the force of a sandbag hitting her stomach. After cold, damp London, this warmth and salt-laden air, feels like Queensland. She and Scott peel off their jackets and pull hats from their backpacks.

Tarik leads them to his open-top Land Rover. It looks as if it did desert service here during World War Two; it still bears traces of camouflage paint. Bella laughs with delight and gets into the front seat, 'Tarik, we have a Rover like this at home.'

'As old as this?' Tarik's face splits in an even wider grin.

'Easily, but a bit less battered,' Scott answers as he loads the luggage, climbs into the back seat, and hangs on to an overhead strut as Tarik takes off.

Tarik weaves through thick traffic along the Boulevard des Forces Armées Royales, the openness of the Rover and squealing tires in the narrow adjacent traffic lanes, makes Bella feel they are driving at frightening speed. She's too excited to close her eyes; she must see everything.

What is it about these places with Moorish influence that moves her so much? It must be her Spanish blood. Yet, Alexandra doesn't seem to be part of this world. Her cold haughtiness doesn't speak of any Mediterranean heritage at all. Bella thinks how amused her friends will be to find out there is a reason for her occasional voluble outbursts when she feels a need to express herself.

Tarik has booked rooms in the *La Maison de Tanger* for them. Inside the gateway, it's everything she could wish for. Beauty surrounds her; from the elegance of the entrance foyer, through interconnecting courtyards, sitting, and dining areas, all open to the luxuriant gardens and cooled by sea breezes, to the rooftop terrace overlooking the old town and out to sea.

They can't waste a minute of their time here, so they head off to visit some dealers on Tarik's list. She shows the first two shopkeepers the small photo of Eli. She understands the head shakes and the replies. 'Non-mademoiselle. Je ne sais pas cet homme.'

The variety of shops seem endless, Bella has the file of photographs from her home, she watches as Tarik shows each shopkeeper the pictures and discusses where similar items might be found. The shopkeepers stand outside their premises and point in various directions, describing volubly to Tarik how to find the next shop. As Tarik had warned her, it's not like Oxford Street here. Streets are haphazard, and the numbering system, if there is one, doesn't make any sense to Bella.

They park the Rover and walk into the market areas through the narrow lanes. The colours, sights, and sounds dazzle her. Bella thinks of the staid, almost uniformly grey CBD in Melbourne; nothing compares to this place. Barcelona, even with all its own richness and style, seems monochrome in comparison.

They walk or, rather, push their way through the crowds. Vendors of every imaginable item, either living or dead, approach them; Tarik waves them away. Bella is thankful for his presence. The sights, sounds, and smells saturate her senses. Spice shops overwhelm her with their perfume and variety. She's still struggling to adjust to the heat. She feels the unfamiliar cobbles under the thin soles of her espadrilles. In the crowded souks, she wonders if the overhead canopies will fall and drown her in colored fabrics. Silk has always been a favourite of Bella's, now she sees rolls of fabric in fabulous vibrant colours and patterns, unlike anything she has ever seen. Bleating sheep and goats, quacking ducks in market enclosures, and music from wandering musicians create a cacophony of sounds that somehow manage to blend into a synchronous whole.

By late afternoon, all their enquiries have drawn blanks. They have been to two places where Bella found items like Eli's collections. It gives her a strange feeling of déjà vu to touch them. Bella feels a kind of suspicion emanating from the traders. A silence as they size the trio up. Rapid-fire questions are asked of Tarik. Much shrugging of shoulders and palm gestures say more than understanding the words. She wonders if, even if they did recognize Eli, whether they might close ranks and not tell these foreigners anything anyway. She asks Tarik.

'Do I get a sense that these people might not tell us even if they do know Eli?'

'Yes, it's possible,' he replies. 'I'm sure there is a very profitable black market in items that shouldn't be exported. These dealers wouldn't want to give anyone away, even if they are a competitor. It would be, how you say? bad for business.'

Bella feels weary. 'What we're doing isn't going to work, is it?' She sits on a stone bench; Scott sits beside her and gently rubs her back; she leans her head on his shoulder and closes her eyes. Confusion fills her; why is she here? Why can't she accept that Eli has gone and allow her growing fondness for Scott to take the place in her heart that it is asking her to allow?

Tarik gives her some water, and after a few minutes, Bella feels better. 'Tarik, you know that I wrote to you about Eli's adoptive family living here?'

'Yes, but that was a long time ago Bella.'

'I know. Question is, was there a Jewish area of the old town? Like the Marais in Paris?'

'There is the Ancien Medina, it's a part of the old town nearer the harbour that is a walled city; it was the trading centre of Tangier before the city outgrew the walls. We will start there tomorrow.'

Scott asks, 'Bella, do you have many business cards with you?'

'Yes, I brought a new box, why?'

'I think we need to try something different. I want you to write our hotel address on some cards, and we're going to drop them in to as many dealers as we can. Even some of the ones we visited today.'

'Ah, yes! interjects Tarik. 'Then the card might get passed along, but no one is compromising their unspoken code.' He claps his hands. 'Very good.'

On the way back to the hotel, they go to a photographic shop. With Tarik's help, Scott explains what they want, and later, they emerge with contact-size proof sheets with multiple copies of Bella's only small photo of Eli and herself together. This added touch was her idea as she hopes, deep within herself that if Eli does see this, he will respond to seeing her face.

At the hotel, they spread out on a table and create the cards with the photo of Bella and Eli attached. Bella writes the address of the *La Maison de Tanger* on the back of each card.

'Voila!' cries Tarik. 'I'm going to drop some of these around now. I'll be faster by myself, and maybe, um, maybe without foreigners, it would be better.'

Chapter Forty-Three

Tangier Morocco

They bid farewell to Tarik and decide to dine in. In a place as beautiful as this, why would they need to venture back out into the crowds? Bella still has so much to tell Scott about her time in London. After a swim in the turquoise tiled pool, they are served mint-flavored cocktails in beautifully etched flutes as they watch evening fall from the rooftop terrace, relieved that sunset takes away the strident heat. The sky changes colour from azure to rose gold, then finally to a star-strewn indigo.

Downstairs, dinner is served in a courtyard lit with lanterns and candles set in wall niches. The light is soft, as is the evening air. The peace is palpable after their afternoon in the noisy Kasbah. Bella looks at Scott across the table; there is no one she would rather be sharing this journey with.

Small entrée dishes are served with a crisp local Sauvignon Blanc from Domaine des Ouled Thaleb. Bella remembers the first meal of similar food she shared with Eli at Mt. Buller and delights in these local delicacies. Next, a succulent chicken tagine cooked with apricots and almonds on a bed of fragrant rice. They are offered a sublime Ksar Bahia Syrah or, as they would recognize, a shiraz, to drink with this. To finish off, they are served the best pistachio ice cream she has ever tasted.

Bella tells Scott about her time with David McKenzie and meeting Eduardo. She tells him about her extraordinary encounter with her grandmother, Clara, at the Somers family home. He listens without too many questions until she comes to describing her meeting with her mother and the subsequent revelations from Bella's meeting at the Naval & Military Club.

'Bella, what did Alexandra manage to do in her espionage work?'

She explains. 'Howard unwittingly got her a job at the Ministry of Information; Alexandra was able to commit many acts in breach of wartime defense regulations. She surreptitiously copied details of military operations and equipment from her employer's papers.'

'Extraordinary,' Scott shakes his head.

'She made sketches of the security arrangements at factories she visited.' Bella looks at Scott, her face hardens. 'Now that I've met her, I can see how she would've manipulated Howard, bosses, colleagues...' her voice tails off.

Scott says, 'I read about these fifth columnists. She was not alone; other British fascists were found to be equally keen to pass important information to Germany specifically to undermine the Allied war effort.'

'I know, Adeline told me. I find it all so hard to understand.'

'So, what happened then?' Scott asks.

'Over time, observant co-workers started to find her behavior odd, and slowly, far too late, she was put on a watch list. The security service approached Howard about her not long before he met with David and heard about Tom and David recognizing her in France with the German officer. So that's where the story got to until she escaped.'

'It explains a lot about Howard, doesn't it?' Scott reaches over and takes her hand.

'Explains maybe, but I can't forgive him for hiding the truth about Uncle Tom's death from his parents and Fiona.'

'Bella, I'm not excusing him at all. Perhaps he couldn't face up to accepting that it seems his wife was present at his brother's murder at Mézières.'

Bella is silent. She looks at Scott, sitting opposite her. She has come so far to see someone who was so close to her. Is so close to her, she corrects herself.

'Even if your father hadn't hidden all that from his family, he still couldn't have talked about any of his secret life. In that way, he was no different from countless others who chose to work in those roles.'

'You're standing up for him!' Bella says with a touch of petulance.

'Well, yes…I guess I am,' says Scott, smiling. 'This world of espionage and spies is as old as history.'

'I know that.'

Scott continues, 'I believe Howard saw that he could contribute to the greater good by using his skills and experience like this.'

'Yes, when I look at the parallels between Howard's career at Reuters and his years of service for MI6, he was a natural fit for that level of undercover work, wasn't he?'

'Yes, he was.' Scott tops up their wine glasses. 'Was Howard any less of a father to you because he led a covert life?'

Bella sips her wine and thinks about her father and their life together. 'No, in truth, he wasn't.'

'Well, there you are,' replies Scott. 'Can you start to go a bit easy on him now? Maybe think about his contribution to fighting evil.'

'Adeline says the same thing. Maybe I'll get there. It has all been such a shock.'

'Of course, it is. You've gone from being a journalist working on a missing persons assignment to mingling in a nest of spies.'

'Damn you Scotty, why are you so rational, you drive me crazy.'

'I need to be; someone has to be a realist in this relationship.'

They look at each other; Bella remembers another candlelight dinner so long ago where the evening changed her life forever. She feels the same sense of crossing a threshold, a doorway from one life to another. She feels gratitude that Scott has both led her to this moment and cared enough for her to let her come to it in her own way.

'So, do you think I'm chasing a ghost here?' asks Bella.

'A few weeks ago, I would've said yes. But now, I can see that if you find

Eli and get resolution about your mother, it can only be a good thing.' He adds softly, 'not only for the justice of stopping Alexandra and Klaus but for you to be able to leave the past behind and look to a new future.'

Bella takes a deep breath, 'with you?'

'Yes, with me.' He stands up and gives his hand to Bella.

She rises, takes his hand and they walk through the hotel together.

'How have you put up with me all this time?'

'Tenacity is my middle name.'

'Did you ever feel like giving up on me?'

'Often.'

'I'm glad you didn't.'

Chapter Forty-Four

The Search Continues

Next morning, at breakfast on the terrace, they are quiet. Both know they need to find a new way to be with each other that embraces their old relationship and this new one as lovers. Their lovemaking in the soft candlelit evening was both tender and joyful. The tenderness was their crossing to this new territory to explore together. The joy was the depth of their delight in each other. Bella feels an echo of the falling sensation in her stomach when she felt his touch and the unexpected softness of his skin clothing his lean muscled body. He has a sensuality she had never suspected.

They prepare to leave with Tarik. At only ten o'clock, the sunlight reflecting off the buildings creates a fluorescent glare. Tarik drives to the Ancien Medina area. They enter through an arched gateway of bright white stone set in the ancient wall that surrounds this fabled area. Tarik parks the Rover at a market square. As they prepare to leave, Tarik says.

'Bella, there's a man on a Vespa. I noticed him a couple of times yesterday. He's been following us since we left the hotel. He seems very interested in us. He makes me feel a bit uncomfortable.'

Bella starts to turn around to look for the man.

'Don't look, Bella,' Scott says urgently as he takes her arm. 'Tarik, Bella, and I will follow a step behind you. If you can, when you turn around to talk to us, nod your head if you can see him. okay?'

'Sure,' agrees Tarik.

'Scotty, who could it be? We don't know anyone here.'

Scott is quiet for a moment. He doesn't want to either alarm Bella or raise her hopes. 'Bella, the worst answer is that Alexandra is for some reason, still following you. The best answer could be that Ariel Achmed has, by some means, contacted Eli, and someone is quietly checking you out before he makes his move.'

'How would Alexandra know I'm here?'

'Bella, I can't answer that, but from what you've told me, Alexandra has been tracking your movements for a long time. Anything is possible. I think we need to be very careful and, above all, stick together.'

The streets narrow as they walk into the heart of the Medina. Colours on doors and tiled walls everywhere contrast with the whitewashed buildings that reach upwards out of the shadowed streets to a sky of kingfisher blue intensity. Bella takes in every sight as she walks hand in hand with Scott. His presence reassures her feeling of alarm that someone might be following them. The buildings jostle together in shapes and forms that defy gravity; layers of filigreed balconies make these buildings look like art forms. From time to time, when Tarik turns to speak to them, he shakes his head so they know he can't see the man. Today, Tarik talks to the shopkeepers and Bella hands them the photos and card kits. She senses the merchants are a little less suspicious of them by using this approach.

At noon, they collect the Rover, emerge from the medina, and cross the wide boulevard Avenue Mohammed VI to find somewhere to sit in the fresh sea breeze; they find a quayside café at the yacht harbour. Whilst Tarik orders their lunch, Bella and Scott wander around the quay. The boats in the harbour reflect the diversity of the population of this trading crossroads. Bella hears Tarik call; he is walking towards them.

'Bella, there's a boat here with your name on it.'

'Oh, how nice, where is it? We'll take a photo to send home to Fiona.'

They join Tarik near the café. Bella sees an Arab dhow tied up. She looks down to the waterline and sees *"Isabella"* painted on the stern. The name is painted in cursive English script, which seems rather unusual here in this setting; the other craft have names in Arabic. This is not an old fishing smack. It is beautifully restored and maintained. Clearly, this beautiful sea creature is used for recreation. Although a larger craft, it's very like Eli and Bella's own Couta boat at Sorrento Sailing Club. Scott sails that now; he maintains it with as much care as Eli did. Bella makes excuses not to join him; her heart has never quite felt up to it. She makes a quiet promise to do so when she gets back to Australia.

Bella asks Tarik to take their photograph beside the boat. She starts to shiver in the hot sunlight as she sits on a bollard, gazing at the gold lettering on the polished wood stern. Memories wash over her of the years she has searched for Eli, yearning to be near him once more. She feels the lost years of trying to forget him. She becomes conscious of the sun beating down on her; she cannot move. She has an extraordinary feeling of his presence. Maybe she is getting sunstroke. She sends a silent thought to him; 'Eli, I feel so near to you. I need you to know...' Bella stops mid-thought. Tangier and the whole atmosphere of this extraordinary place must be getting to her. She looks at Scott and understands she wants to tell Eli that she has found peace.

Scott is examining the boat. There is a sign on it; he asks Tarik what it says.

'It is for sale.'

Bella cries out, 'Tarik! I need to find out who owns this boat. Can you help me, please?'

They follow him to the marina office and stand back as a conversation in low tones takes place. Bella sees folded money changing hands, and looks away. This is the local way of doing business. They leave, and she contains herself until they are much further down the pier.

'Who is it? Tarik. I will give you the money. Please tell me the name.'

'Bella, a man called Mr. Bruno Bruin owns it.'

'BRUNO BRUIN!' Bella shouts. Scott catches her arm before she topples backwards into the water. Bruno Bruin or Brown Bear was her nickname for Eli. He was so like a large brown bear! She cannot believe this.

'Were you able to get an address, Tarik?'

'Yes, I told the man in the office that you are interested in purchasing the *Isabella*. Mr. Bruno Bruin lives in the old town. It's not far from where we have been this morning. Would you like to go tomorrow?'

'Tomorrow? I've come this far and waited five years, and you suggest tomorrow?'

They roar away from the marina as fast as the traffic allows. Again, they need to leave the Rover and proceed on foot. Once more, they walk through a bewildering maze of streets.

Tarik checks the houses; he stops outside a large wooden door painted deep burgundy red set in a windowless wall. Up to shoulder height, the wall is faced with richly colored, tiles. Bella wonders why our Western tastes are for plain walls. Silence, the noises around her recede as she waits and looks about her.

In the deeply shadowed alley, she notices the engraved brass plate on the stone wall above the tiles.

Bella points, 'What does this say, please Tarik?

'Lumeah Enterprises.'

The name strikes a chord in Bella's memory. She remembers hearing Eli speak of the kibbutz he lived in. Or was it a house? Something was called Lumeah. She is sure he has mentioned this name to her. The trouble is, she reflects, she doesn't know if anything he told her about his early life was true. But she reasons, maybe even Eli was human enough to have a need for some anchor points in places he knew. She holds that thought as weightless as a leaf. Will this be the final piece of her puzzle? The last-colored fragment to complete the mosaic? The strangled streets of Tangier, saturated air and tension close about her, squeezing her nerves.

Scott is quiet beside her; she glances at him; his eyes are on her; she's grateful for his presence. She pulls the bell pull, noting with interest that the brass bell and the nameplate gleam against the ancient stonework. This clue revives her nerve; Eli never could stand mess or dirt. A young man in a snowy white Jellaba and crimson Fez opens the door.

Bella speaks. 'Monsieur Bruin s'il vous plait. Je desire un rendez-vous avec Monsieur Bruin.' She tries to peer around him to the shadowed interior, but in the low light, she can't make out any detail beyond the tiled foyer.

The young man says, 'M Bruin ne sera pas à la maison pendant deux jours.'

Scott moves closer. 'What did he say, Bella?'

She turns, 'he says that Monsieur Bruin is not at home until two days' time.'

The young man says 'souhaitez-vous laisser un message mademoiselle?'

Bella gazes at him, speechless. Is she so close to the end of her journey? And now, she needs to wait two days?

'Bella, what do you want to do?' Scott enquires.

Close by, she hears a muezzin call to mid-afternoon prayer. The young man looks up beyond her, and she knows he wishes to conclude this conversation.

'Merci, je vous laisse cela pour lui donner.' She leaves one of her cards with her photo attached and the address of the *La Maison de Tanger*. It could, of course, be a series of bizarre coincidences, but having come this far, it is also possible that this Bruno Bruin is Eli.

The emotion of the past hour makes Bella feel weak and shaken. Scott holds her firmly as Tarik guides them back to the Rover. Despite her fatigue, she drops his hand to look at one of the stalls.

'I'll be a minute.' She purchases some rosewater-flavored sweets and glace fruit, then turns to catch Scott and Tarik, who are at the car. Without warning, a push in her back sends her sprawling. She lands hard on the cobblestones. The force of her fall pushes her head to the ground so that her hat, sunglasses, and bag all fly off and under the feet pushing past her. She's wearing a fine cotton shift; her legs are unprotected. Pain shoots through her knees. 'Scotty, Tarik, help me!'

Scott turns back and kneels beside her, his arms around her. 'Bella, what happened?' He lifts her to her feet.

'I don't know, Scotty, I felt someone close behind me and then...' She's shaking, and her head throbs, her knees sting, the skin broken and bloody. She looks around; a woman hands her the sunglasses and hat. There's no sign of her bag; it's gone. Tarik guides them across the square to a seat. A stall holder gives him a cloth and water to clean up her wounds.

A glass of water is placed in her hand; Bella nods her thanks and drinks. People are speaking to her, talking over each other, gesticulating in every direction. She can't understand a word. The pain in her knees and head blots out all else. This accident, was it an accident? Bella can't help but wonder if Storm was right about her safety. Tarik is questioning the onlookers to see if anyone saw what happened. Headshakes from everyone. 'Non, non-Monsieur.' One said he saw a man running away, pointing to another street.

Losing her bag is a disaster. Apart from the brief about their Barbary Lion assignment, it holds her pocket recorder and notebook with notes she has made about her mother. The loss is a catastrophe! Fortunately, her passport is in the hotel safe, with most of her money.

Already hot and tired and now bruised and distressed, she wants to get back to the hotel. She is overwhelmed by the events of the day.

Tarik says, 'Bella, I'm so sorry this happened. We'll go back to the hotel; you need attention.' He spreads his hands with a rueful gesture. 'I don't think we have much hope of finding your bag. This is Tangier.'

Scott and Tarik help her limp back to the Rover. At the hotel, Soula, the manager's wife, tuts and clucks. She insists on taking charge of Bella.

Tarik says, 'Bella, I'll leave you to rest. I'll call you later to see what you want to do. Okay?'

Soula bathes Bella's knees and applies a cream that smells of herbs. Bella lies on her bed and falls into an exhausted sleep. She stirs; the light has moved from the room, and she realises it's late afternoon. Scotty is sitting close to her bed; he's watching her. Bella lifts the light blanket covering her, and Scotty slides onto the bed beside her, his body sculpting itself around her. She loves the feeling of his skin and his kisses; she falls asleep in his arms.

The sound of running water wakes them. The bathroom is open to their private courtyard oasis with a fountain and lush greenery. The bath is filled with warm water and aromatic oils; the fragrance of rose and jasmine fills the steamy air. Bella and Scott luxuriate in the warmth, their limbs entwined as they face each other. The peace she feels tells her that no matter the outcome of meeting Mr Bruno Bruin, her heart has found its home.

Scott lifts her out of the bath, dries her, and redresses her wounds. He helps her into a caftan made of gossamer fine white cotton and embroidered in a spectrum of her favourite greens. Silver thread woven through the embroidery gives a shimmering effect.

She looks at it and says, 'where did this come from, it's beautiful.'

'I rather thought it matched your eyes,' says Scott as he brushes her cheek and plants a gentle kiss.

Bella feels ready to face the world. She takes the phone to the terrace and places a call to Storm.

'Bella! Have you found your man?'

Bella looks at Scotty; has she found her man? Yes, she has. She puts the phone on speaker. 'I think I have, but he is away until Friday.' She tells Storm about her fall. She's sure someone pushed her. And the loss of her bag. 'Storm, it's a disaster. All my work! I'll have to rebuild everything from my memory!'

'I'd rather that than you are hurt, Bella.'

'Maybe Eduardo is right about Alexandra being a danger to me. If she's behind this, I'm afraid she has our travel itinerary, my tapes, and notes of my search for Eli.

Storm replies. 'I'll report this to the Scotland Yard team. I've a little bit of news about Eli, though it may not be relevant now.'

'What've you found?' Bella asks. 'Don't keep me in suspense, Storm.'

'Your instinct about Tangier was good. About two years ago, an operative fitting Eli's description was in the area.'

Bella exclaims, 'That fits with Alexandra's comment. Anything else?'

'Nothing concrete, but MI6 told us there was a kidnapping and murder of an operative near Tangier about that time.'

Nausea washes over Bella. Realization hits her that the man she loved really does come from a world beyond her understanding. 'So…it seems as if Eli could be who the ASIO people said.'

Scott draws her closer with one arm whilst he gives her water with his free hand.

Storm's voice continues through the speaker. 'Anything's possible, Bella, but I understand this man, we'll call him Eli, was trying to rescue the operative. You can't do much until your Mr Bruin returns to Tangier, so I want you, Scott, and Tarik to go down to Chefchaoen tomorrow morning to meet the people about the Barbary Lion story. I want you out of Tangier.'

Bella is loath to leave if Eli is close by, but she's confident that now he knows she is close, he will come to her. And, after all, it's only a day trip to Chefchaoen; they'll be back by evening. She looks at Scott and decides. In two days, her life has changed forever, she says. 'Yes, we'll go tomorrow.'

Chapter Forty-Five

Ambush

As the sun, a large golden orb radiating a pink halo rises in a cerulean sky, they leave Tangier to drive to Chefchaoen, two hours away in the Rif mountains. Tarik and Scott ride in the front of the Rover. In the back, water, cameras, a first aid kit, and provisions in a cool box surround Bella. The morning breeze on her face and blowing through her hair, is soft and welcome as she knows that soon the heat will become stifling.

Whilst they're driving along the highway, Tarik says, 'This is a great assignment, tell me more about it.'

Bella replies. 'Storm wants us to meet the group interested in the reintroduction of the Barbary lions into a wildlife park for breeding in the wild program. It's a very long-term story, but we're doing some groundwork because we're here.'

'Ah yes,' replies Tarik, 'I've read about this. The barbary lions were hunted into extinction in the wild in the early 1920s.'

Bella adds, 'They intend to use breeding stock from the lions in the Rabat Zoo. These lions are directly descended from the original Barbary strains.'

'Amazing isn't it,' says Tarik. 'The Rabat Zoo lions are descended from the animals that were hunted and then given as gifts to the king for his private collection.'

'We're going to meet the principals of the project and shoot footage of the open range habitat the lions will be reintroduced into.'

'I could do this as an ongoing assignment and gather material as developments occur.' Tarik offers.

'Great idea, Tarik,' says Scott. 'You can shoot video as well as I can. I'll talk to Storm when we ring him tonight.'

They talk more about hunting wild animals, and Tarik tells them he is bringing up his children to be very conservation-minded. He hopes that both his oldest boy and twin girls will make careers in this field.

Off the main highway, the Rover starts to climb into the Rif Mountains; the road becomes rough. Bella folds Scott's jacket to cushion her backside from the jarring ride. As they climb and Tarik is crunching the gears on the hairpin bends, it's impossible to hear what Scott and Tarik are talking about, so Bella watches the scenery and daydreams about the shift in her relationship with Scotty. She hadn't seen how much love he has for her; Aunt Fiona was right. She smiles to herself and cherishes the memories of their nights together.

As they round a bend, a large khaki army truck overtakes them at a dangerous speed.

'Whoa!' shouts Scott as Tarik swerves to avoid being run off the road. 'What kind of idiot driving is that?'

Tarik says, 'That truck has been following us since we left the city. I didn't think much of it until they turned off the highway when we did.' He stops the Rover. 'There are lots of bends here, so I'll let him get well in front. He must be going to the next town.' Tarik jumps out and unfurls the canvas sun top, securing it to the struts and windscreen. 'There you are, Bella; it's getting a bit hot.' He laughs, 'I don't want you baked like a Turkish Baklava.'

'Thanks, Tarik,' Bella smiles; she can't imagine how she would have known where to start her search for Eli without him. She offers a silent thank you to Storm as Tarik drives off.

They round another bend; the army truck is blocking their way. In front of the truck, rocks have been placed across the road. Tarik shouts, 'Hold on!' as he brakes hard; the front of the Rover slews hard to the left, hitting the rocks. A loud clunk underneath and a sudden list on one side tells them an axle has broken. Bella falls forward and hits the front seat. As she sits up, to her horror, she can see that the rear right-hand wheel of the Rover is hanging out over a drop. She carefully pulls herself closer to the left-hand side behind Tarik.

The Rover is disabled; they can't turn around. Four armed, masked men come from behind the truck and run towards them. They are completely covered from head to foot in dark robes. Their head coverings leave only their eyes exposed, and they are obscured by wrap-around mirrored glasses.

'Scotty!'

'Quiet, Bella,' Scott answers without turning his head. His eyes fixed on the men; he holds out a hand for Bella to clasp.

The men surround the Rover with guns pointed; two men wrench the doors open. Tarik, Scott, and Bella are pulled out. The Rover door is on an angle, Bella falls. Scott tries to help her and is pushed aside. On the roadside, they're told to turn around and put their crossed hands in front of them. The men tie their wrists. They also tie Bella and Scott together and tie the rope to a strut on the Rover, pulling their arms up above their heads. Bella looks at Scott; he mouths 'shh!'

Tarik is trying to speak to these men. It sounds as if he's trying to reason with them: to find out what they want. To please set them all free. Bella holds her breath. From her limited vision Bella hears rather than sees, that a scuffle breaks out. She whispers to Scott, 'What's happening?'

Scott shakes his head. Tarik has been knocked to the ground. He can see one man raises his rifle butt and brings it down on Tarik's head. He doesn't want Bella to see this. 'Don't look, Bella!' He tries to move his shoulders to block Bella's view.

'What's happening? Is Tarik hurt?'

Scott twists around to face Bella. 'Don't look over there. Bella, look at me! Only at me! Got it?' She does this, and they hold each other's gaze.

Scott starts to speak. 'Silence!' A voice near them shouts.

Bella cries out. 'Who are you? What do you want from us?' This brings a swift reaction from the guard. Something hits the back of Bella's head, crashing her forehead against the side of the Rover. Winded, her already bruised head explodes with pain. Blood trickles down her face. She is barely able to stay on her feet.

'Leave her alone!' Scott shouts. He receives a blow to his head; he sways but keeps to his feet. He tries to crook his elbow towards Bella to steady her. He is belted from behind again. This time, she feels his knees buckle, and he falls to the ground, his arms wrenched above his head as the rope tightens.

Bella can't tell how long she stands here in the sun. Her arms ache, but her concern for Scott outweighs her discomfort. She feels him move; he can't get up unaided, and she can't help him. Any movement might make their captors beat them again. Pain, the heat and thirst, and the horror of the ambush wash over her. She sways and leans against the Rover.

Renewed fear clutches at her as she hears the men approach. One unties the rope that secures her. As he pulls her away, she stumbles and falls half on top of Scott. He's barely conscious; he's taken a harsh beating. She's grateful for even a minute's closeness. She leans her head forward to touch him. It's all she can do for her friend and now, her lover.

Strong arms pull her to her feet and push her forward until she reaches the army truck. She is lifted and hauled into the truck and falls, winded, onto the floor. Another thump, and Scott arrives beside her; he doesn't move. Foul-smelling sacks are pulled over their heads. The suddenness of this and the instant claustrophobia makes Bella gag. She fights to get some oxygen; a wave of panic overtakes her. The steel mesh tail gates crash into place. She's quiet until the truck starts moving. Still bound, she can only roll and hope she will find Scott. She manages to do this, and rests nestled into his back.

No one yells at them or kicks at them, so they must be alone. After a few minutes, the road becomes rough and winding. Scott comes to, he whispers.

'Is Tarik here with us?'

'No, they must've left him with the Land Rover. I hope he's safe.'

'I don't think their business was with Tarik.' Scott comments.

'I can't think, I'm so angry!' Bella tries to wriggle into a more comfortable position so she can whisper to him.

The hood muffles Scott's voice, 'Bella, it must be Alexandra.'

Chapter Forty-Six

Kidnapped

Time passes, the rough road, heat, discomfort, fumes, and the hoods make breathing difficult and a constant fight against nausea. Finally, the truck stops. More voices—raised voices, excited voices: Bella and Scott are the bounty. They endure more rough handling as they're hauled off the truck. She can only see down through the hood to her feet. They're pushed through a doorway. Bella stumbles sideways into the opening and feels pain shoot from her elbow to her shoulder. Thumps follow as some items are thrown in after her.

Scott grunts as she feels him shoved in, too; her hands are untied. The door bangs behind them. With her hands-free, she removes the hood, breathing gulps of air to quell the vomit rising in her throat. Scott is sprawled on the floor, helpless. She unties him and helps him to sit up with his back against the wall, he looks very bruised. She sits beside him; he puts his arms around her and holds her close. Bella can feel his thudding heart which matches her own.

Their prison is a concrete-walled room; the door is steel. Above them, a pitched tin roof. Their gear from the Rover is strewn around the floor. In the low light, they can see there is only a high barred window. No obvious means of escape.

Scott kisses her gently and says, 'You don't look too good; that's a big lump on your forehead. We'd better try to wash that if we can find some water.'

He reaches into a pocket and finds a white handkerchief. Bella thinks that only Scott could produce such a pristine item in a situation like this.

She finds the first aid kit, water canisters, Thermos flask, and the cool box and pulls them over to Scott. The tea in the Thermos is still warm. They drink it gratefully before spending a few minutes attending to each other's cuts and bruises. This quiet closeness calms them. Hungry now, they eat the sandwiches. They feel stronger after food and tea.

Bella asks Scott, 'If it is Alexandra, and who else could it be? How long do these things take? We could be here for a while.'

'Don't hold your breath, Bella; you know the Australian Government doesn't pay ransoms.'

She is silent as she ponders the truth of this statement. 'Where's your passport?'

'In the safe at the hotel—where's yours?'

'Same place, they can't be stealing our identity to use for some espionage job.'

'Now, Bella, that is such good news!' Scott is recovering his sense of humour. 'We should try to rest for a while. We don't know what will happen later.'

'Scotty, how long do you think it will take for someone to realise something's happened to us?'

'Quite quickly, Bella.' Scott looks at his watch. 'If Tarik doesn't come home by early evening, his wife will ring his office. They probably tied him up and left him with the Land Rover. I hope he managed to flag down a passing vehicle.'

Bella hopes Scott's assessment of Tarik's situation is correct and that he's not badly injured.

Scott asks. 'What time is Storm expecting us to call tonight?'

'Six pm London time. Seven pm here, gives us time to return from the mountains. If he doesn't hear from us, I guess he'll call the hotel. If we haven't returned, he'll want to know why.'

They find a groundsheet amongst the gear, and with their coats under their heads, they turn to face each other. Scott folds Bella into his arms;

the closeness comforts them. Despite their fear, exhaustion takes over, and they fall asleep.

They awake late afternoon: the hut is stifling from the sun on the iron roof and the poor ventilation. Scott finds the Thermos; the tea is still warm, and some cake and fruit from the lunchbox revives them. They take an inventory of their gear and create some order in the stone cell.

Scott says, 'My camera gear isn't all here.' He rifles through a bag and smiles as he holds up his Swiss Army Knife. 'They've gone through everything else but missed this; it might be useful.'

After they've sorted their possessions, Scott says. 'We need to see what this place is.' Even though Scott is tall, he can't see over the high window ledge. He makes Bella climb on his back and onto his shoulders to look out. They start laughing; despite their situation, they can't help their shared sense of humour breaking through.

'Oh, Bella, you've been eating too much; you've put on weight,' he gasps as she perches on his shoulders.

'Rubbish, I've never sat on your shoulders.'

'I've hauled you up on your skis often enough to be able to tell. What can you see?'

'Someone's coming! Help me down, we'll do this later.'

The door pushes open; two men enter. Dressed like their earlier captors and masked, it's impossible to identify them. One bars the door and points a gun at them.

Scott pulls Bella to his side. 'Who are you, and how long will we be here?'

The second man looks at their stuff on the floor and kicks at the bags. 'Until we say otherwise.'

Scott tries a bluff that could either get them freed or sign their death warrant. 'We are Australians. Our government does not pay ransom to kidnappers. You may as well let us go now.'

The man ignores this. 'You will have food and water brought here. If you try to speak to anyone, you and they will be shot. There is no escape.'

His English, though lightly accented, is faultless; Scott and Bella look at each other and take note. This afternoon, they decided to create notes of every single piece of information.

After this speech, he throws down two blankets, and leaves. His companion has the gun trained on the prisoners until the door slams. At twilight, Bella climbs up to look out. They hear a generator starting; dim lights appear in various windows. The single bulb flickers in the prison room, so Scott lets Bella down. They don't want her to be silhouetted against the window. If they are seen, their captors will board up their only glimpse of the outside world.

'I think we are in an old farm complex.' She points at the rough concrete floor. 'This could've been the dairy.'

'Yes, something like that,' says Scott, rubbing his shoulders. 'If power comes from a generator, not mains—we could be anywhere, not near a town.'

If this is so, escape on foot, even if they managed it, could be a death sentence. What to do? Bella finds her notebook and adds notes and descriptions of the men to the events of the day. Old habits and discipline bring a slight feeling of normality; she does this every day in a journal anyway. The past few months have filled many pages. If they ever get out of this place, she'll try to make sense of it all.

'Bella. Did you bring your Polaroid camera with you?' Scott usually scoffs at her use of this camera. Bella likes to use it because she can take quick snaps to remind her of details of a face or a place for stories.

'I've done better than that. I have Howard's Minolta Minox; it was in his study at Florin Court. He used to call it his spy camera.' How close to the truth was that? Bella thinks. 'He's had it since the war. I bought some film for it in London. I hope they haven't found it.' The kidnappers haven't gone right through her backpack. The tiny camera is still inside the gloves where she had put it for protection.

'Fantastic! Thanks, Howard.' Scott takes the little camera and turns it over to inspect it. 'Well done, Bella. We'll have to eke these out to try to capture as much as we can about this place. Will room service arrive soon?'

Later, the door opens and two tin plates with maize meal porridge are put on the floor. Bella notes that the food is delivered by a shorter, rounder man, possibly the camp cook? But the same guard holds the gun.

'Better eat it, Bella. Beggars can't be choosers,' Scott reaches for the unappetizing food, has a taste, and says. 'No worse than bivouac rations at cadet camp.'

At 10:00 PM, the bulb fizzles into blackness. They lie on the tarpaulin, pull the threadbare army blankets over themselves, and Scott folds Bella in his arms as they wait for sleep to come.

'They're a strange bunch of kidnappers,' whispers Scott.

'What do you mean?' asks Bella. 'How many times have you been kidnapped to know?'

'They aren't professionals. They didn't go through our stuff very well, did they?' Scott whispers. 'That means that someone else should arrive to take charge.'

Bella thinks, then says. 'I thought that the security people were being a bit dramatic when they said they wanted to get me away from Alexandra.'

No answer from Scott. Once again, Bella wonders how men can sleep anywhere, anytime. Eli did this when they slept in swags under the stars in the outback. She can hear the night sounds through the high window. Her mind travels back to 1944, to the capture of her Uncle Tom in Mézières. Does lightning strike in the same family twice? Was he as angry as she is now?

Chapter Forty-Seven

Tangier Morocco

The man returns to his home, places his bag on the floor, and picks up the card that is sitting on the foyer table. He holds the small photo toward the lamplight to see it better. His life experience has tempered his feelings to fine steel; he's not given to waves of emotion rising to catch his breath in his throat. His feelings betray him; tears spring unbidden to his eyes. 'Ahmet, Ahmet,' he calls. The young man appears and bows. 'Monsieur?'

'D'où vient cette carte?'

'La mademoiselle était là hier, elle l'a laissé pour vous,'

'Hier?'

Ahmet nods his head.

The man picks up the phone and dials the hotel number on the card. A message tells him that due to a local exchange outage, the number is unavailable. He rushes from the house, throws up a roller door along the alley, and wheels out a motorbike. He kickstarts it with vigor and weaves the growling machine through the choking late afternoon traffic until he reaches *La Maison de Tanger*.

The concierge tells him that Miss Clemens and Mr Sinclair went for the day to Chefchaoen but are expected to return later this evening. The man gives explicit instructions for Miss Clemens to contact him as soon as possible. He hands a card to the concierge. He is assured this will happen pronto. If the phone is not restored, they will drive her personally. He retraces his journey to his home. The man Bella knows as her lost love, Eli, is coming out from a life undercover. It's time.

After dinner, Eli can't settle, he paces the rooms willing the telephone to ring. Two hours pass but no word from Bella. Where is she? Distractedly, he half watches a news flash on the television about an accident on the road to Chefchaoen. He moves closer to the television set and turns up the sound; this is the place the concierge at Bella's hotel said they were traveling to. The news presenter continues to say that a passing truck had found a wrecked Land Rover and stopped to render assistance. A local journalist, Tarik Menuhin was found unconscious, injured with a head wound, near the vehicle. When paramedics were able to revive him, he told police his two Australian colleagues were abducted after he was assaulted. Mr Menuhin's injuries are serious but not life-threatening. He was flown by helicopter to Mohammed V Hospital, where he will remain until he is able to assist police with their enquiries.

Eli reaches for the phone: the local exchange is still out of order. He goes to a locked cupboard and retrieves an army-issue Iridium satellite phone. He dials the private number of the local police chief, who confirms that Bella and Scott are the kidnapped Australians. After listening to Eli, the chief assures him that all his requests will be actioned in readiness for his return. Next, he telephones Power Press. He's connected directly when he tells the telephonist he wishes to speak to Lord Storm about Bella and Scott. From experience in these matters, Eli knows he has a small window of time, possibly forty-eight hours, to get to London before the real task of resolution of a kidnap for ransom will require his 24/7 focus here in Tangier.

He dials another number and speaks in Hebrew; the conversation is short and to the point. His last words in English are. 'I owe it to her. And we all owe her father that she is safe.' He replaces the phone and glances at Bella's business card and photo on the desk. He picks it up and touches it to his lips. So much sadness fills him; he has never stopped loving Bella.

He telephones directories and asks for a number for Eduardo Monerayo in Barcelona. He already knows the number for the farm at Yarra Glen, but he'll save that call until he has spoken to Eduardo, and knowing Fiona's astuteness, he doesn't want to ring her without anything productive to say. Storm had undertaken to get Fiona to London so Eli can meet her in person. The thought of seeing Fiona again brings another rush of emotion and love for these two women.

The telephone rings. An unfamiliar voice is speaking to Eduardo in heavily accented Spanish. When he understands the caller is Bella's lost love, Eli, he's shocked but alert. After introductions, Eli says.

'Can I speak frankly?'

Eduardo replies. 'There is a problem, could we converse in French?'

'Bien sûr,' comes the immediate response.

Eli tells Eduardo of Bella's kidnapping and his plans to go to London today to meet Storm to offer his assistance.

Eduardo is desperate to help and doesn't waste time with questions. He tells Eli about the meeting with Alexandra and his fears for Bella's safety.

'Thank you, Eduardo, that's valuable intel. I'll relay that to the police.'

'Eli, I'll meet you in London. I need to see Alexandra's English family. I may be able to get more information about her.'

Eduardo prepares to fly to London. This kidnapping might be his worst fears about Alexandra come true. But how, he tries to rationalize, would Alexandra have known where Bella was going on assignment? Intuition and recent events at home prevent him from telling Jose and Maria his plans.

Fiona watches with horror as the morning television news breaks a story of a kidnapping in Morocco. The names have not been released yet. Fiona's knowledge of Bella's movements tells her that her beloved girl is in this area. The phone rings, and she jumps to answer it.

'Fiona Clemens speaking.'

'Fiona, it's Meg Petersen.'

'Meg. Have you heard this news? Please tell me that Bella and Scott are safe.'

'Fiona, please be strong. Storm has rung me to tell me that Bella and Scott have been kidnapped.'

Fear and anguish make a potent cocktail and attack Fiona with full force. 'Oh no! I will contact Foreign Affairs.' Fiona tries to quell the panic rising in her throat. Her heart is pounding; she feels weak with dread.

Meg replies. 'You don't need to. Storm has taken charge completely. Power Press is doing all the official channels because Bella and Scott are on assignment.'

The dogs, hearing Fiona's raised voice, have come in to see what is happening. She reaches out to scratch their heads. 'That's some relief.'

Meg continues. 'Storm wants to fly you to London as soon as possible. Can you do that?'

'Yes, yes! Meg, I will ring Adeline, David McKenzie, and her uncle Eduardo Monerayo.'

'Yes, Fiona, it's best if you are all together in London. Because of Howard's history, Scotland Yard and MI6 want everyone present.

Fiona absorbs this, but realizes questioning Meg isn't useful right now. 'Has anyone contacted Scott's family?'

'Yes, we will keep them informed,' she pauses, 'Fiona, this news will be another shock. Eli rang Storm. They are going to meet.'

'Eli! But Meg…why?'

'I don't know any more Fiona; Storm wouldn't elaborate over the phone. Except I know, he seems very positive about this.'

As Fiona hangs up, she looks around, trying to focus on her priorities before she packs her bag. The dogs, the animals. As she makes calls, waves of dread make her breathless. Bella, her dearest girl, is in terrible danger. Another thought rushes in. Eli! What has he to do with this? Bella had shared her fears about Eli's possible involvement with terrorism. She says aloud. 'Eli, If you're responsible for this, I'll…' She doesn't finish the sentence as fear washes the breath from her body.

Chapter Forty-Eight

In Captivity – Rif Mountains Morocco

A t dawn on the second day, they're awakened by shouts and dragging noises. Scott lifts Bella up to look. 'What's happening?'

'They're enclosing our hut in a wire mesh fence and hoisting camouflage nets across the top.'

'Damn!' says Scott as Bella clambers off his shoulders. 'That'll be to discourage any aerial search to find us!'

The door unlocks. They're led to a bucket shower where Bella must shower in the open. Scott places himself with his back towards her to shield her as much as possible from view. They are put in the screened outdoor enclosure; food and water arrive.

All they can do is pace the perimeter, try to see through the mesh, and then sit under the lone tree in the middle. It's a beauty, with wide-spreading branches. At least the tree, and now the netting, gives shade from the relentless sun. Scott brings the tarpaulin from the hut. Despite their worries, they manage to doze when the heat makes the air thick and breathless.

They take note of any vehicles arriving and try to place the origins of any sounds that they hear outside their enclosure. Bella makes a chart and writes everything they can identify into her notebook with the time of day. They're trying to define any routine in this place. They've also started a map of the compound to work out if escape is possible. Their ears strain to hear voices and to identify the accents. At five o'clock, they're escorted back into their shed; the same cycle of the night before repeats.

They know that Storm will do anything possible to rescue them. The Australian Government policy of not paying ransoms to kidnappers takes on a new meaning. They never expected to experience the fear this knowledge brings. Their usual belief in this policy dissolves into an overwhelming desire for a ransom to be paid so they can leave this place.

Reporting on a situation like this and being captives are two different feelings. Gut-wrenching empathy replaces their normally objective sympathy for their subjects. They feel desperate; they're completely helpless. Bella's greatest fear is for Fiona and how she must be suffering from this dreadful development. Scott is quiet but stoic; Bella knows he's worried about his own family.

Evening falls, and with it, the temperature drops. The mountain air is different here; cool nights follow the hot days, which are very different from the salt-soaked air of Tangier. Despite the lack of comfort, they can sleep. Scott has a map of the area they were to visit for their assignment. From this and the climate change, they've decided they must still be somewhere in the Rif mountains.

He looks up from his notes. 'We might be able to figure out how far away from the ambush point we are. Look at this.' Bella looks at the map; Scott has marked the place they left the Rover. He continues. 'When the truck left, how long do you think we drove before we arrived here?'

Bella tries to remember. It's important she does, because Scott was barely conscious from the beating; his recall would be less than hers. 'The ambush happened about eleven thirty am, right?'

'Yes,' says Scott. 'I looked at my watch.' He writes that down and asks. 'How long were we by the roadside?'

Bella replies. 'It seemed a long time, but it can't have been. They needed to get us away; we were very exposed there.' She thinks. 'Not more than twenty minutes.'

'Good!' says Scott. 'So, say twelve noon. We were thrown into this shed here around one o'clock, weren't we?'

'Yes,' replies Bella. 'Ah, I see. If we can figure out the truck speed, we can figure out an approximate distance.'

'Correct!' Scott starts writing.

'We only travelled on that road for a short time. Possibly ten minutes, then we turned off onto a much rougher road. From the way the truck lurched, it felt like a bush track. And we climbed; the road was very winding. I could hear the driver changing gears a lot.'

'Yes, that's about when I started to come to. The truck didn't make much more than twenty kph once we hit that track. So, that means we could be within hmm,' he jots some figures on the pad then says, 'a radius of thirty to forty km from the ambush point!' Scott pumps the air with his fist.

'Well, that's useful to know if we get a chance to escape.' Bella falls silent. They've no idea what physical challenges would face them outside the bounds of their prison. Could they survive an escape bid? They're both reasonably fit, but...

Scott is protective and thoughtful of her. They're both fearful of the possible outcome of this abduction. When Bella starts shaking with fear and anger, Scott holds her. He tries to keep Bella focused on their daily notetaking. Bella misses her pocket recorder that was stolen in Tangier.

They have created routines and jobs to get them through each day. Bella will never tease Scott about being Mr Neat again. Keeping their kit and themselves clean and in good order creates shape. And a feeling of defense against their vulnerability.

They're sure that their captors are hired jailers. There is a man in charge, but they have no sense that he handles any planning or ransom negotiations. He and his cronies are foot soldiers following orders. Bella muses that this is the last thing Aunt Fiona could have dreamt of when she suggested that Bella should spend more time with Scott.

Chapter Forty-Nine

Power Press Headquarters, London. Day 3

Storm and Eli meet. They shake hands, then a moment's silence as they regard each other. As men like these do, they gauge their level of trust and respect by some internal barometer. Both find that place in a beat; Bella is their mercury. If Storm is bemused at Eli's sudden appearance, it only takes him minutes to realise that Eli is exactly the person to drive this search and rescue. Eli's only comment to Storm regarding his sudden appearance is to repeat his words to Eduardo that Bella's safety is his total priority. End of subject. Eli has briefed Storm about his suspicion that Alexandra is involved in Bella and Scott's abduction. He adds.

'Storm, I only want to be in London until I can see Fiona; I'll meet her at Heathrow. I must return to Tangier to drive operations from there.'

Storm nods his understanding; he, too, is highly concerned about Fiona and wants her here near him instead of at the end of a very long telephone line to country Victoria. 'Understood. Fiona will arrive early tomorrow. She is on a direct flight from Singapore.'

Eli smiles. He can only imagine Fiona's reaction to being enclosed in an aircraft for that long, when her preferred transport is riding her beloved horse in the open air. He also knows that Fiona's anxiety for Bella's safety, will make that exhausting trip insignificant.

Storm continues. 'Re Alexandra; Scotland Yard and MI6 want anyone to do with that part of Howard's life here in one place. That includes,

Eduardo Monerayo, Adeline Stephens, and David McKenzie.' Storm briefs Eli on Bella's meetings with each of them since her arrival in Europe. 'Any information they might be able to offer, especially about Alexandra, if put together could help.'

Eli listens quietly, and quickly absorbs the interrelationships and impact on Bella from meeting these people. All previously unknown to her. Once again, he feels distress about Howard's lack of transparency about his life, with the people he loved most. He tells Storm. 'Eduardo Monerayo will go to Alexandra's cousin Hugo Somers in Oxfordshire. Despite past family rifts, he's appealing to Somers to help find Alexandra. If he has any news, he'll telephone us here.'

'Excellent,' says Storm. 'I believe Fergus Campbell from MI6 has contacted you?'

'Yes, I'll see him after this meeting. He'll return to Tangier with me and be my direct liaison with all agencies.'

Thirty minutes later, Storm, Eli, and two Scotland Yard officers, Jock and Paul, are in conference. They are part of the multi-agency task force assigned to the Alexandra Monerayo case after the meeting with Storm, Bella, and MI6. They settle down to assess the information they have about Scott and Bella's days in Morocco. Tarik Menuhin's statement details their movements from arrival to the point of kidnap. Including the robbery of Bella's bag, and the man on the Vespa who appeared to be shadowing them.

At noon, a cycle courier arrives at the concierge desk downstairs. The rider places an envelope on the table. He leaves before the concierge can finish with the previous enquiry. The concierge rises to his feet. He calls out 'wait!' Too late, the rider has disappeared through the revolving door. This is enough for an immediate security alert. The envelope is addressed to Douglas Storm. Two words, nothing more.

The security officer approaches the desk; they clear people from the area. With tweezers, one places the envelope on the marble floor. They scan the envelope with a hazard detector. Nothing shows.

Jock and Paul have left the boardroom to watch these proceedings from the mezzanine floor. The guards give the all-clear; Paul descends the staircase. He dons surgical gloves, picks up the envelope, and takes it to the boardroom. He opens it with a penknife and using tweezers, draws out a letter. Without touching the paper, Storm, Eli, and Jock read it. It is, as Eli had predicted, a ransom note for the release of Scott and Isabella.

$USD10,000,000 for the release of Scott Sinclair and Isabella Clemens

Deadline for receipt is 3:00 pm Friday next.

Details for money transfer will be sent.

Hostages will be released 24 hours after confirmation of receipt of funds.

Do not contact police.

Failure to comply will mean death to the captives. No negotiations.

Jock says. 'Storm, do you know that the British Government won't pay ransoms?' he adds, 'neither will Australia, for that matter.'

Storm replies, 'I know that. I have insurance for staff, and I would resource anything else myself.'

Eli says, 'We hope it won't come to that.'

Storm looks up from the letter. 'It's exactly as you said, Eli. If these people are Klaus and Alexandra, they've made their first move.'

'I can't claim credit for that. It was Alexandra's brother, Eduardo.'

With a grim nod, Storm says, 'Bella told me her family history before she left for Barcelona. Otherwise, I wouldn't believe this could be possible.' They sit thinking about this situation, and the events leading up to it.

Storm says. 'These kidnappers aren't wasting time, are they? What does that tell you, Eli?'

Eli replies. 'I believe it's a small operation. Not a larger terrorist group. It's another pointer to Klaus and Alexandra. It shows their need to get out of this quickly.'

Jock adds. 'I agree. A larger group would have the resources to keep Scott and Bella longer. They'd wait for desperation to make us agree to their demands. I think this lot don't feel quite in control.'

Storm says. 'Should we pay the ransom to get them back?'

Eli replies. 'Storm, I understand your concern, but please could you let us try our methods first?'

'But what are your methods, Eli?' Storm stands up; clearly, he is very worried. 'Can you tell me, please, how you would rescue them?'

Before Eli can reply, Jock says. 'Colonel, I would consider it a great favour if you would head up this mission. We're lucky to have you with us; I thought you'd retired.'

'I have retired from active duty, but I have a personal interest in Bella and Scott's safety. And an equal interest in bringing the two suspected kidnappers to justice.'

Storm looks at Eli, so his informants about Eli were correct, even if they didn't give any details. 'Colonel? And who are you apart from Bella's lost partner?'

'I am that Storm, but I've had other responsibilities.'

Jock intervenes. 'Eli is reluctant to disclose his CV. I can assure you; he has experience in hostage resolution.'

Eli smiles as he looks around the table. 'Thanks for that, Jock. I spend years flying under the radar, and you out me in one go.'

Storm sits back in his chair. He will do anything in his power to find his two journalists. But he realises for once he is not the one issuing the orders.

Jock rises to leave. 'I'll take this to the office for fingerprints. What time tomorrow?'

Storm gathers his notes. 'Nine o'clock here, I'll have anything you need set up. We can work for as long as we need to.'

06:00 am, Eli waits at the Heathrow arrivals hall. Fiona emerges carrying a small bag. She is a head taller than most passengers; he moves toward her. They meet and stand face to face, each one taking in every detail. Eli's heart feels Fiona's sadness at Howard's death and now, her fear for her beloved Bella.

Fiona sees the man she had cared for deeply. She corrects herself; she still cares for him. Close up, she can see signs of age have settled on him. He doesn't look as strong as she remembers. 'Eli...'

'Fiona,' he wraps the older woman in his arms, and they stand silent, oblivious to hundreds of people weaving their way around them. The emotion he feels at reuniting with this dear woman, makes him feel like a drowning man who sees his life flashing before his eyes. The distress he feels at the pain he has caused her and Bella, too, makes him totally unsure of the life choices he made. Leaving them without explanation was the hardest thing he has ever done in a lifetime of tough decisions.

Fiona unwinds herself; she looks into his eyes. 'Does your presence here mean I can discount the possibility that you are in any way responsible for this disaster?'

Eli bows his head. 'I deserve your doubt, Fiona. I promise you; I would give my life for Bella.' In a way, he had already given his life for her, but now is not the moment to tell Fiona this.

Fiona arches an eyebrow. 'Really?'

'Truly.' He takes her arm gently and guides her through the crowd.

After a few paces, Fiona says in a low voice. 'I hope it won't come to that.'

Chapter Fifty

Somers Hall, Oxfordshire

Eduardo arrives at Somers Hall. He telephoned Hugo Somers before leaving Barcelona, outlining the reasons for his visit. Somers told him to come as soon as he could. He meets Eduardo at the door and holds out his hand.

'Please call me Hugo.'

'Thank you, Hugo,' replies Eduardo. 'The time for formality is long past.'

Hugo nods his agreement and shows Eduardo to his study. He opens the conversation. 'I regret that I was less than polite to Isabella when she visited here.'

Eduardo says. 'I understand. She worried about visiting here without speaking to you first.'

Hugo nods. 'I'm a fearful old man who wanted the past to stay in the past.'

'I understand that too, Hugo. Before we talk about Isabella, I do need to find out how it happened that you have my mother, Clara, here.'

Hugo replies. 'Clara was dumped at a public hospital in Paris. She'd already had a stroke. She was very weak and unable to speak very much.'

A moment's silence as Eduardo absorbs this callous act. Hugo didn't need to say who had dumped her. Alexandra and Klaus were running true to form.

Hugo continues. 'She had a note in her handbag giving her name and address as here, at Somers Hall. When she realized her plight, she had another stroke; this left her incommunicado. I went to Paris to rescue her. We were unable to find out from her, where she lived or with whom. We have tried physiotherapy and speech therapy, but her age and debility are against her.'

'Hugo, I'm grateful for your care. I'm curious as to why Alexandra didn't send Clara to me?' He pauses and then says, 'After all, Clara is more my responsibility than yours.'

Hugo looks up and shakes his head. 'I don't know the answer to that. Except maybe spite because I have always refused to give Alexandra money.'

'You too? So, she has come to both of us over the years,' he pauses. 'Would you have contacted me?'

'Yes, I intended to do that quite soon.' Hugo sips his coffee. 'I must admit, though, I hesitated because I was unsure whether I could face another exposure to our family's fascist past. I've tried for years to overcome all that.'

'I understand completely, Hugo; I've lived a very secluded life for the same reasons.' Eduardo pauses, then he says. 'So, you thought it might be easiest to keep Clara here and not open any old wounds.'

'Yes.' Hugo tells his side of the story. After the death of Clara's brother Charles and Hugo's family inheriting the title and estates, they were horrified to learn they were associated with Charles's side of the family's fascist leanings. Clara and Alexandra's flight after the war was a relief and sealed their exclusion from the Somers family. When Howard visited Hugo in 1946, they agreed it best to take Bella to Australia. And close the door on any further association that might hurt either Bella or themselves.

Eduardo tells Hugo that when Howard came to him in Barcelona, he had reacted the same way. 'I regret that if both of us had helped Howard and each other, Alexandra might not have been free to get to this point.' He tells Hugo about his recent meeting with Bella, and he concludes by saying. 'Hugo, I must tell you how much Bella means to me. I will do anything I can to help find her.'

'I understand, but how can I help?' asks Hugo.

Eduardo outlines his suspicions that Alexandra and Klaus are behind the kidnapping.

'Extraordinary,' exclaims Hugo.

They're silent; they contemplate that Alexandra would dump her mother and kidnap her own daughter for money.

Hugo breaks the silence. 'If it is Alexandra behind this, how would she know Bella's movements? Especially in Morocco?'

'Sadly, Hugo, I'm sure that leak came from within my own household.' He repeats the story he told Eli on the phone; he concludes by saying. 'I am hoping that you might know something, anything at all, about how to find Alexandra.'

Hugo's face brightens. 'Six months ago, I didn't. But now,' he rises, goes to his desk, opens a drawer, and removes a sheet of paper.

Eduardo clasps Hugo's shoulder, with tears in his eyes, he says. 'Amazing! How on earth did you get this?'

Hugo replies. 'I'll tell you that story later. It's time to take you up to see Clara.'

They go upstairs to Clara's room. Hugo and the nurse leave. Eduardo enters the room and closes the door.

Chapter Fifty-One

Power Press Headquarters London

Fiona, Adeline, and David enter the boardroom at Power Press. Storm, Jock, and Paul sit opposite them. After the introductions, Storm takes Fiona by both hands. 'We'll find them.'

Eli enters the room; Storm gestures to Eli to take the chair at the head of the table. Eli opens the conversation. 'Gentlemen, Fiona and Adeline. Now that we have a ransom note, I'm returning to Tangier. I needed to be here to meet Storm and,' he looks at Fiona, 'to take care of a private matter.'

Fiona returns his gaze. During the drive from Heathrow, Eli had given her the answers to all her questions. She prays that Eli can meet Bella; Fiona needs her to feel his love and care as she does. And to understand the terrible situation that caused him to leave. Fiona told Eli her concerns that Bella can't move on with her life. She remembers the pain in Eli's eyes as he listened to her.

Eli speaks. 'We can't presume that the kidnappers are Alexandra and Klaus. However, with their history and their association with Bella, it's a good place to start.'

The phone interrupts them; Storm presses a button. 'It's Eduardo Monerayo, I've put him on speaker.' Storm makes the introductions.

Eduardo's voice comes through clearly. 'I am at Hugo Somers home. Alexandra called him recently demanding money. After the call ended, Hugo pressed the last incoming call recall and wrote down the number.' He laughs, 'Alexandra wouldn't have thought of that.'

They all thank Eduardo; a different energy charges the atmosphere in the room. What seemed to be an insurmountable task to find Alexandra and Klaus, now with almost ridiculous ease, they have a clue. Paul leaves for the Yard to open a conversation with Interpol, to find the location, and, if it is a private residence, start phone tapping and put a tail on the pair if possible.

Storm asks. 'Would the kidnappers have smuggled Bella and Scott to another country?'

'No,' replies Eli. 'That would add extra expense and high risk to the plan. In Northern Africa, there are always mercenaries. They do the kidnap and keep their captives hidden until instructed to take them to a release point or...' he looks up and, seeing the women's white faces, doesn't finish the sentence.

Across the table, Fiona reaches for Adeline's hand; the two women have become close.

'The ransom payment,' says Jock, 'is to be a wire transfer, so they won't have to put any actual collection plans in place. Or risk traceable notes given to them.'

Eli continues this thought. 'Yes, it adds up to a small-scale operation. They're containing risk of exposure factors. As well as not stretching their resources.'

Storm asks the last question. 'Eli, what are your plans?'

Eli replies. 'A colleague with experience in these matters will meet Fergus and me in Tangier this afternoon. We have a lot to do.' He smiles.

Now, there's an understatement, Storm thinks as he nods at Eli. He can see exactly what attracted Bella to this man. He turns to Fiona, Adeline, and David. 'Please come to stay at my home in Windsor. It's within easy reach, and I can assure you the communications are first-rate. Eduardo will join us there.'

Chapter Fifty-Two

Rif Mountains Morocco

I n the inky black light between moonset and sunrise, Eli and his partner Shimon hide their 4WD off the dirt track. Wearing night vision goggles, they walk silently through the scrubby vegetation. They move with a surety of long practice in rough terrain. After thirty minutes of cross-country hiking, Eli checks his army GPS and gives Shimon the forward signal.

Ten minutes later, through the trees, they see a high razor wire-topped fence. The sky is turning to deep grey. Eli needs to find the entrance and survey the road access before dawn. As they circumnavigate the perimeter, they can see the buildings and layout of the camp. One stone building looks more secure than the others; Eli guesses that is where Scott and Bella are. He stands looking at the building and feels dreadful anguish that the woman he loves so much is in danger. He had left her to protect her from this kind of terrorism that is his life, but it found her anyway. He pushes these thoughts away and reverts to his commando training. Time is running out; the ransom is due to be paid tomorrow. He won't give Klaus a chance to take matters into his own hands.

They move away from the camp into the scrub and continue around the fence line until they find tall steel gates. A narrow access track leads from these gates into dense scrub. Shimon points to a wire that runs through the fence and up a tall mast. Telephone or radio? They will cut off communications when they return. Their hike to the road is shorter via this track, and when they get to the end, they can see why it wasn't obvious on their drive past. A wooden frame with camouflage and greenery blocks the entrance. Back at their base camp. Eli and Shimon brief their Moroccan counterparts. Then, before catching some sleep, Eli uses a scrambled radio telephone to report to Storm.

Chapter Fifty-Three

In Captivity

It's early evening and the seventh day since their capture. Scott and Bella are in the outdoor enclosure, listlessly picking at their meal of the usual maize porridge. During these days of waiting, Bella alternates between feeling hopeful of rescue and, without warning, she plummets into despair. What is happening in the outside world? Surely, someone is negotiating their release. Two days ago, photos were taken of them with a folded newspaper showing only the date. They understand this is a proof of life and part of a ransom negotiation. This gives them hope that negotiations must be happening. They hear an unfamiliar vehicle come into the compound; they've grown used to the sounds of the usual traffic.

Scott looks up. 'Powerful engine but not a large vehicle,' he whispers. They wait, and the new arrivals go out of earshot. They sit still and strain to hear any sound. Bella is facing the fence; a small flap in the mesh outside the wire is raised up; she rushes to the wire. In the fading twilight, she can barely see the pair of eyes peering out of a burnoose at her.

'Who are you? What do you want with us? I demand you release us immediately.' With her face against the wire, she is so close she can see the stranger's eyes. Amber flecked with green. Why are they so familiar? It must be the heat driving her mad; is she hallucinating? The stranger holds her gaze; seconds tick by. A bird screeches above her head, and the moment is broken. She shakes her head and looks back at the gap in time to see the eyes still looking at her but is she imagining it? Is there a hint of a smile in those eyes, surely not but there are crinkles at the corners, it's impossible. Bella knows those eyes; she has gazed into them with love. She's woken up to see them watching her in the morning stillness. She puts her face right up to the mesh. 'Eli?' she breathes, not even a whisper. A soft sound emanates from the face, 'shhhh…' There is another man beside him. Bella knows it isn't safe to speak. The flap closes. The moment the face with those eyes is gone, she starts shaking; her legs seem to have lost their ability to keep her upright, and she crumples to the ground. Eli? could it be Eli? Why? How? Did she imagine seeing him?

'Bella, what happened? Are you okay?' Scott kneels, puts his arms around her and holds her. After a minute, he gets her to stand and moves her to sit under the tree.

How can Bella tell Scott what happened? She can't even begin to think it's possible; is Eli here? She whispers. 'Scotty, I think that man could be Eli!'

'What?'

'That man's eyes, I was so close to him. His eyes were so like Eli's. Strange flecks in them …'

'Why would he be here? You don't mean he could be…'

'I can't think.' Bella's fingers rub her temples. She feels as if she's been shot in the head. 'Why is he here? Is Eli a kidnapper? Oh…I wonder if Alexandra was right about him. This is horrible,' she groans.

After they've been locked inside, two men enter; one is their normal guard holding his gun. The other is tall and broad-shouldered. Dressed in khakis, his face is mostly covered with a burnoose; only his eyes are showing. Bella looks down; he has placed one foot in front of the other, his arms behind his back. This stance is so familiar to her. All she needs to make sure it is Eli is to see his hands. But, for his own reasons, he keeps them out of sight. She looks up and stares straight into his eyes. They hold each other's gaze in silence. Bella reads the message in his eyes to be silent just like she's read so many expressions in his eyes before. It's only a few seconds, but she feels both black fear and white hope run through her. Scott stands beside her; he draws her close to him as if to say: "don't come any closer. I will protect

272

this woman with my life if necessary."

Mr Burnoose speaks to them. 'You will leave here tonight. A meeting is arranged to hand you over in exchange for the ransom for your release. Only take one bag each. Leave the rest.'

Bella is glad she has remained silent. It is Eli! Voices don't lie; she slumps in Scott's arms. Relief that they are to be free washes over her. Horror replaces it as quickly. Is Eli the cause of all this? Vomit rises in her throat, threatening to choke her; she fights for breath. How else could he get in here? He couldn't walk through the gates, she reasons, unless he was running this whole operation. The men leave.

Scott whispers, 'Is it him?'

'Yes, it's him…his voice. I don't know why he'd be here, Scotty. What if he's one of the kidnappers?'

'Bella, I don't know what to think.' Scott doesn't want to share what he thinks with her; she's upset enough already.

They sort their belongings and pack one backpack each. The Minox goes into Scott's pocket along with the Swiss Army knife. Bella takes all their notes; they wait.

At nine o'clock, the door opens, they hope, for the last time. Their captors tie their hands. A stranger, not one of their normal guards, escorts them at gunpoint. They move across the compound towards the gates. They pass four men sitting at a table, on it, an open case of Scotch whiskey; each man has a bottle to his mouth. Bella recognizes their guards. Has Eli brazened his way in here? Told the guards some story and ensured their compliance with whiskey. And money! Could this really be a plan to rescue them?

They are led to a rugged 4WD. Scott and Bella are pushed into the rear seats; harnesses are put over their heads and buckled in. They're in for a rough ride; the driver guns the engine.

Bella and Scott turn to look out of the rear window and see the compound gates close. Relief floods through Bella, but where are they going? Is Eli their rescuer, or will he become their killer?

They drive along a narrow road, jolting, bumping, and swaying. She's thankful for the harness holding her; this ride is bruising enough. Scott and Bella look sideways at each other. Bella can't help herself. Above the growl of the car's engine, she shouts out.

'Eli!'

Eli turns towards them; he takes the burnoose off. 'Bella.' He smiles and nods at Scott. 'Just give us a few minutes, I'll explain. We need to get away from here.'

Bella can only see his face in the glow of the instruments. She reaches forward to try to touch Eli, but the harness holds her firmly in place, and she can't reach him. She wants to touch him.

Scott draws her back. 'Bella, it's alright.' He takes both her hands in his and says in a low voice. 'We can trust Eli; he is here to rescue us.'

A two-way radio on the dashboard crackles. Above the engine noise, Bella hears Eli speak and listen, he says to Shimon in Hebrew. 'That was base. Klaus is heading this way in an armored Humvee. We need to get ahead of them.'

'Eli?' Bella calls out. 'What's happening?'

Eli turns and reaches out his hand; she clasps it briefly before he withdraws it.

Shimon replies. In a low voice. 'If we get to the crossroads first, we can turn left and get away. Are the police following them to the hideout?'

'Yes, but at a distance. They'll meet up with our team. It'll work out, but we need to get Scott and Bella out of this now.'

Minutes later, as they reach a crossroad, headlights swing in from the road to the right. The lights are coming towards them. Fast. Not another ambush! Bella clutches at Scott. Her eyes fixed on the road in front. There is nowhere to go, but try to pass this vehicle on the shoulder of the track and try not to crash into the trees.

Like the last ambush, the oncoming vehicle brakes to a halt, blocking the Benz's path. Shimon stops hard. This time, the full harness holds her. Her arms flail. Scott grunts as her arm connects with him; he holds on to her. Armed men come to the windows. Scott and Bella have guns pointed at them again.

The men gesture to the four to get out of the car and to follow them to the vehicle in front. High and large, as they get closer, she can see it is armor plated. What kind of people drive around in a mobile fort; she wonders? They stand in a line. Eli, Shimon, Scott, and Bella. Eli has replaced his burnoose.

A tall man climbs down from the high cabin. in the dark, it's hard to see his face, but judging by the stiffness of his movements as he walks towards them, he is quite old.

'Bella,' Eli whispers. 'It's Klaus.'

Klaus walks up very close and looks at Bella. As her sight adjusts, she sees the coldest pair of eyes she has ever seen. Even in this moment of danger, she reflects that her uncle Tom saw these eyes in his last moments. She is face to face with the man her father wanted to expose. Bella tilts her chin. She is determined not to show fear to this man. 'You bastard Klaus.'

Klaus slaps Bella across the face. Scott and Eli lunge at him, but the armed men hit them both with their guns. Klaus strikes Eli across the face with a short cane; the blow knocks off Eli's burnoose.

'Ah, Fossbach, I might've known you'd try to rescue her. We will demand three ransoms now. This is a good day.'

'Won't happen, Klaus,' says Eli.

Without turning away towards his guards, Klaus says. 'Kill the driver. One of you can follow us in that Benz. It might be useful.'

One guard starts to pull Shimon away. In the dark, horror-filled silence, Bella senses a movement behind Klaus's shoulders; two silent figures have captured the guards positioned behind him. Two more move forward and prod Klaus in the back with their guns. A rope noose is slipped over his head and pulled tight across his chest, his cane clatters to the ground.

Eli speaks to the two silent captors. 'Thanks, comrades, good timing.'

They return to the camp; Eli's commandos have the guards in chains in the compound. They lock the kidnappers into Bella's former prison.

Chapter Fifty-Four

Tangier

At dawn, Shimon drives them to Tangier in the captured Humvee. In the back, Scott and Bella sit facing Eli; Scott holds Bella's hand. She senses that, in his quiet way, he's sending a message to Eli. It doesn't go unnoticed; she knows that look of quiet observation.

Eli produces a thermos of coffee and sandwiches. In the morning light, Bella can see him close. She looks into his eyes, what she sees shocks her. His tawny gold lion's eyes seem faded. In this light, his skin looks quite grey. She's used to seeing his clear golden complexion, she fears for his well-being. She wants to lean forward and take off his cap to see more of him but knows this isn't the moment.

She says to Eli. 'How did you know about the kidnap, and where did you appear from?'

I came home and found you'd arrived in Tangier. I saw the news story about the hijack and Tarik's rescue. It said two Australian colleagues of the journalist were missing. It could only be you. The police chief confirmed your names. I had to act quickly.' He leans across and takes her hand. 'I rang Eduardo and then Storm who told me you were out here looking for me.' He smiles, 'Bella, you came very close to finding me.'

Bella says in a tight voice. 'We'll talk about that later.' She has quite a lot of things she wants to talk to Eli about later. 'How did you find us?'

Eli continues. 'After I rang Eduardo, we both flew to London, and I met

Storm at Power Press.'

Bella wishes she could have been there to see the two meet; they would make a formidable team.

Eli recounts that forty-eight hours after they were taken, a ransom note arrived at Power Press. This was quite a short lead-time, so he knew that the kidnappers had done this before and had their plans in place.

'Eli, have you done this before?'

He smiles. 'Several times, Bella. It's part of my job.'

Bella bows her head. What, if anything at all, does she know about this man she wanted to spend her life with? 'I've been sick about Fiona, and Scott's family too.'

'Fiona's in London staying with Adeline at Storm's home. I met her at Heathrow. David McKenzie and Eduardo are there with her.'

Bella can imagine Eli's reunion with Fiona, she could see both with their arms wrapped around each other. Not much need for words.

Eli says to Scott. 'Scott, your family are being taken care of.'

'Thank you, Eli.' Scott says. 'But how did you find Alexandra and then the camp?'

Eli repeats the story about Eduardo obtaining Alexandra's phone number, which was traced to a house in Lisbon. 'Bella, I need to tell you that it was Alexandra who made it possible to rescue you.'

'Oh! How did that happen?' Bella feels a strange twist in her heart. Almost like it has missed a beat.

'She and Klaus had fallen out over money with the people who control them. They weren't paying their dues. This kidnap was Klaus's attempt to get some money.'

Bella remembers Fergus Campbell's theory that Klaus and Alexandra's masters would unload them if they became a liability to the organization. 'Yes! The security people were talking about that in London.'

Scott says. 'So, you think they'd been following Bella to find a way to extort money from Eduardo?'

'Yes,' says Eli, 'either Eduardo, Storm, or both.'

Bella says, 'I think it goes back further than that. Maybe they planned to extort money from Howard; his sudden death meant they had to look elsewhere and quickly.'

Eli tells them that Alexandra and Klaus had argued badly about their situation. Klaus left. Later, two men came and demanded she give them the money owed. When she tried to get out of the house, she was shot, and the men fled. 'Alexandra told the police about Klaus and the kidnap.'

Scotty says. 'Even though Alexandra unwittingly enabled your rescue, I believe, and I'm sure Eli will agree, you should divorce yourself from her, in every way.'

Eli nods, 'I agree. Fiona is her real mother.'

How could she disagree with them? Her recent visit to Barcelona has given her a lot to think about. Still angry with Howard for concealing the truth from her for so long, Bella knows that she must be fair to him and asks herself how she would have dealt with the knowledge of her mother and her activities.

Scott asks, 'But how did Klaus know we would be in Morocco?'

'Maria listened to Eduardo's phone calls and reported to Klaus and Alexandra. They were able to keep up with Bella's movements.'

'I thought there was something shifty about Maria when I visited there. I was sure she listened to our conversations. I didn't think she spoke any English, so I put her out of my mind.'

Scott says. 'So how did you connect up with the kidnappers' hideout?'

'Ah, that was easy,' Eli smiles. 'After Alexandra was taken to hospital, we monitored calls to the house. Whilst Klaus was traveling to Morocco, the kidnappers tried to ring him. It traced back to the hideout.'

'How did you get there before Klaus? That could've gotten very messy.' Bella shudders to think of it.

'Interpol had him held up at the airport for a few hours.' Eli laughs, 'I heard he was very angry.'

'What a psychopath.' says Bella, feeling her bruised cheek.

Scott asks. 'How did you talk your way into the stockade?'

'That wasn't difficult. I can do a reasonable imitation of Klaus's voice. They'd never met him in person.' Eli smiles.

CHAPTER FIFTY-FOUR

'Who pulled this rescue together?' asks Scott. 'It's a massive effort.'

'Storm set up a campaign headquarters at Power Press. I was able to call in a few favors from former colleagues; you've seen some of the ground crew and Shimon here.'

He pours another coffee and continues. 'Bella, your friend Simon Day briefed me about the cold case on Alexandra reopening because of your meeting her in Barcelona.' Bella nods. Eli continues. 'So, the timing of your kidnapping brought everything together to give a joint operation with MI6, Interpol, and Scotland Yard a real chance of success.'

'I was so shocked when I looked through the fence, and there you were, so close to me. I thought you'd kidnapped us.'

'Ah, Bella, I'm sorry about that,' Eli sips his coffee.

Bella isn't sure he is sorry; she has a feeling that he likes this kind of activity. She decides not to pursue this now. Bella looks out of the window at the harsh terrain. She realises, how close she could have been to losing her life, and because of her, Scotty could have died too. She turns back towards Eli. He smiles that smile that started the whole thing that day in a blizzard at Mt Buller. They hold each other's gaze without speaking. She understands, at last, that even if his life took him away from her, he does care. She puts this insight away to examine later.

Scott breaks into her thoughts as he asks Eli. 'Is there enough hard evidence of their past crimes to bring Klaus and Alexandra to justice?'

'Yes, there is. It's way past time.'

At Tangier police headquarters, Bella draws Eli aside. 'I need to see you alone, please; I have so much I want to ask you. Please don't disappear again.'

'I promise, Bella. Come at ten o'clock tomorrow. We can talk before you fly back to London.'

Eli places one hand on Scott's shoulder and holds out his hand. Scott says, 'thank you Eli.'

After Eli leaves them, Bella asks if news can be found about her mother, Alexandra, in Lisbon. A policewoman takes Bella and Scott to a private office, finds the hospital number, calls, and asks for a medico in charge. Bella is connected with Dr Francesca da Silva, who speaks English.

'Dr Da Silva please can you update me on Alexandra Monerayo's condition?' Bella pauses before she adds awkwardly. 'I am her daughter, Isabella Clemens.'

'Good afternoon, Miss Clemens, forgive me, but we have no record of you being next-of-kin. In fact, we have no immediate family contact. It would be helpful if you could assist, but I need verification of your identity, please.'

Bella looks at Scott before she speaks. 'My mother has a brother in Barcelona, Eduardo Monerayo. He is currently in London. I can give you a telephone number, but I would prefer to speak to him first.'

'Ah yes, it would not be good for him to be caused a shock from a stranger.'

'Yes, exactly. For me to do that, it would be helpful if you could tell me how she is, please?' Bella hopes the doctor will agree to her request.

The phone hums with an echo before the doctor replies. 'I understand. Ms Monerayo is in a critical condition. She has two gunshot wounds. Due to her age and the nature of the wounds, her prognosis for recovery is not hopeful. I would suggest that if a family member can attend, it should be as soon as possible.'

Bella thanks the doctor and hangs up. 'Should I go to Lisbon?' she asks Scott.

'We'll go to the hotel and contact Eduardo. I think it best that he decides. Okay?'

'Yes,' she says and looks at Scott. 'My life is with you now; Alexandra is not part of us.' She pauses, 'Saying goodbye to Eli is.'

Chapter Fifty-Five

Bella and Eli, Tangier October 1990

Today, Bella is expected. 'Attendez voûs ici s'il voûs plait, mademoiselle Clemens.' the young man indicates a carved wooden bench. It sits in a foyer between the outer door and beautiful filigree metal gates that lead from this area into a courtyard.

She sits down. After so much yearning for this moment, it has arrived.

The tiled foyer is entirely enclosed. The designs and colours are luminous. It is lit by slants of colored light through high, stained-glass windows set back from the street facade. Bella looks up and around at the beautiful space. Dominating the area is a cascading chandelier. Refracted shards of light play upon the octagonal walls. She recognizes the copper, amethyst, and malachite treasure. It's like one she and Eli purchased in France now at her home in Armadale. Under the chandelier, a polished table carries a huge bowl of flowers, another touch of familiarity. At home, they'd walk to the Prahran market every Saturday; Eli always chose the flowers. He used to tell her how much pleasure it gave him to fill their home with flowers. His childhood on the kibbutz meant that every piece of arable land was used to grow food. No spare land or water was available for flowers.

Across the foyer inside the gates, she can hear the restful rhythm of water falling and splashing. Memories of the home they had made together remind her that Eli creates an oasis wherever he lives. Already, Bella feels at home here. She knows she could move through the rooms with ease, as if reconnecting with cherished friends. But, around the walls, there are open packing cases. Eli is moving somewhere and quite soon.

A familiar clearing of the throat tells her he's here. She turns totally unsure what to say or do. The pause feels very formal; he hasn't held out his arms, or even a hand to shake. How does one greet the person you loved so extravagantly that you thought you knew every part of him? Did he ever love her in the same way? What is he thinking? The silence becomes unbearable.

'Mrs Bear, Biénvenu.' His private name for Bella startles her with its familiarity.

'Mr Bear, or should I say Monsieur Bruin?'

He doesn't reply to that question. 'Would you be comfortable if we sit in the courtyard?'

'Yes, thank you, I'd like to be near the fountain.'

He puts his arm around Bella and gently draws her to him, he holds her close, for a moment. Long enough for Bella to feel that under his clothes, he's a much thinner man, less robust; his hair is peppered with grey. Then he releases her and takes her hand. He's dressed in a long white djellaba and sandals, the clothes of the region, further camouflage.

Bella remembers that no matter how well-tailored Eli's western-style clothes were, he'd always looked constrained by them. Echoes of the past rise unbidden from the locked steel box in her heart. The box contains memories that if left to run wild, will be impossible to manage. What of this man had been real? Or was it all, including herself, a disguise to suit his needs at a time and place?

They walk across the foyer to the courtyard; more crates are here too. Bella will ask Eli why, but there are more important things to discuss first. He is silent as she takes in the beautiful space. She remembers the first night she went with him to his chalet at Mt Buller and how she loved the home he had created. They sit on a cushioned chaise, as they would have on summer evenings before, in the other courtyard, in the other lifetime.

Eli pours her a glass of lemon water. Bella needs to break this silence that threatens to open the years of pure grief. There's no need to make any small talk about his business. It's another of the strands of his life that has a purpose but leads nowhere in this picture.

'Bella, I was sorry to hear that Howard died. I am so sad for you and for Fiona.'

'Thank you, Eli, but how did you know?'

'I heard from a mutual friend when I was in London.'

'Did you ever meet Howard after you left me?' Bella shocks herself with this direct question. It came from that angry heart. The one she's been trying to overcome since Eli left her.

'Yes.'

'What possible reason could you and my father both have to betray my trust in that way?'

'There were many reasons, Bella. I understand that none of them might be acceptable to you.'

'Well, Eli, I have the time and the need to listen to those reasons.'

'Bella, I know this isn't what you want to hear, but I ask you, can you trust me please? I can't tell you everything you might wish to know. I am constrained.'

'Constrained?' Bella asks, 'constrained by what?'

Eli answers with another question. 'Did Howard tell you anything about himself before he died?'

'No, he didn't! Is there anything you can tell me about any work you and he did together? And, whilst you're at it, you could explain yourself too.'

'I can't tell you much, Bella; the Official Secrets Act cautions me.'

'Not you, too.' Bella snaps. 'Howard's partner Adeline said the same thing to me in London.'

'I am afraid there's no getting around that one, Bella. Not even for those you love.' He pauses and says almost to himself. 'Most of all, for those you love.'

'Eli, that's just not good enough.'

He looks at her without speaking. She remembers that when she was angry, he used to wait until she had let off steam before he would respond to her, just like he is now. She understands this and with an effort, puts the angry voice away. Silence sits gently between them like it always had. They never felt the need to fill silences with words. Bella had learnt the beauty of stillness from this man. She feels her skidding heart settle when Eli puts his arm around her shoulder and draws her closer to him. Her face feels tears on his cheeks, she feels his love. Her tears fall now; they fall for her lost life with him. They fall naturally and, she realises they are tears of relief.

Sitting close to him, she can feel although his warmth feels the same, that she wasn't imagining he's thinner under his djellaba. Despite herself, a shiver of longing for him, suffuses her whole body. 'I've missed you so much, every part of me, misses every part of you.'

'I know my beauty,' he whispers, 'I still dream of us together.'

'What good is that?' Bella sits up and glares at him. 'Nice to hear, I s'pose, but no real answer for me, is it?'

He pulls her back towards him and kisses her hair, her face, and her tears. 'Bella, my darling. That's all I can give you for now.' He sighs, knowing that this short time is all he'll be able to give her for now or forever.

She needs to try to find the cause of this secrecy. 'Why did you leave me without even a letter? After ASIO came to search the house, I felt as if our time together was all lies.'

'I understand, and I'm sorry.' Eli looks down at her hand resting on his knee. He thinks of living without her and, wishing to send for her to join him. He picks up her hand,, kisses it gently, and puts it down. 'I couldn't tell you the truth.'

'Tell me now.' Bella's voice tells Eli it's more a command than a request.

'I can't, the story is too long, and I'm too old.' He smiles at her.

This nettles Bella's angry voice back into the conversation. 'Rubbish, I've waited too long and come too far for that lame excuse.' She feels a little more like herself, she puts her head back on his shoulder. He brushes her cheek, another touch so familiar to her. Bella pushes on; she needs to drive this encounter. It's happened almost by a miracle, and she needs to wring every moment for the information she needs.

'If you weren't prepared to answer my questions, you wouldn't have agreed to meeting me today.'

'That's true. I couldn't send you away. Towards the end of our time together, I was close to telling you about my life. Then, when it came time to leave Australia so quickly, matters were taken out of my hands. I promise you, Bella, I've always wanted to explain the real reason we parted.'

'Why did you leave that way? Why didn't you take me with you?'

He ignores the first question and gives an enigmatic, Eli-style answer to the second. 'At that stage of your life, you weren't ready.'

'*Not ready*! Not ready for what?' Anger rises from deep inside her.

'My life.' He replies sadly.

'You were cruel. Have you any idea how I felt?' A feeble lob, arguing with Eli, had always been a useless pastime.

'Yes.'

Has she come all this way for these answers? This conversation is like a tennis rally.

'It was better that way.' he speaks these words with the same soft voice that had caressed her in the moonlight.

Bella almost whispers. 'I was just…devastated.'

'Yes, I know. And angry. Are you still angry?'

'Yes! What do you bloody well think I am?' The pent-up emotions fill her. He puts his head to one side with that well-remembered look. As if he's waiting for her to explain a piece of illogical thinking.

Her voice steadies. 'You could've written.'

In a quiet voice, Eli counters her demand. 'Bella, I have to ask you to accept that I couldn't.'

'I don't buy that Eli. You must have been doing something wrong for ASIO to be chasing you!'

'Please don't be angry. I took you with me in my heart. You're still in my heart.'

'You're so selfish. How did you expect me to live, to make another life?'

'I could only hope you would.'

'I can't believe I'm hearing this. What about passion, romance! You took that too.'

'Not true, my love. I can feel it's all still inside you.

He's teasing her! After all this, he's teasing her as if they hadn't been apart for longer than a day!

'Eli, you're so arrogant!' She refuses to laugh; she turns her face away from him.

'You're strong, brave and wise now.'

'How would you know who, or what, I am?' Her voice rises; she feels nettled. 'And I want you to tell me the absolute truth. Was it completely by chance we met at Mt Buller? Or were you trying to get to Howard, and I was an easy way in?'

Eli laughs out loud. 'Oh, Bella, where did that come from? No, I can assure you it was completely unplanned. I looked up that day in the tow queue and saw you standing there dressed in your red Bogner ski suit. You looked as beautiful as any woman possibly could in a blizzard. I had to get to know you.'

Forgotten memories of conversations like this one crowd into the courtyard around them, jostling to join in. She can't help it. Fresh tears fall down her cheeks. She turns her face away from him.

He hands her a handkerchief; she slows her breathing and inhales the longed-for scent of him. When she feels able to, she asks him.

When did you first know about my mother, Alexandra? Did Howard tell you?'

'Yes.' Eli looks at her and looks down. 'Bella, I've played this moment in my mind so often. I'm so happy to be with you again. This isn't easy to tell you, Howard told me many years ago.'

'My father told you! This is insupportable! He told you about her, and he didn't tell me?'

'He was trying to protect you.'

'Eli. I've heard all that from others. It doesn't wash with me. Sorry to be so blunt!'

Eli laughs. 'And when were you anything else but blunt, my love?' He takes both her hands, raises them to his lips, and kisses them before he continues.

'Klaus and his associates are the kind of people we try to keep under very close watch. It's been difficult because until now, no-one has penetrated their organization.' Eli is silent for a minute before he continues. 'I'm sorry this must be very hard for you. You can understand why Howard wanted so much for you to live a life free of her. Free of knowing your mother as a person committed to reprehensible choices.'

'And what did those thugs who broke into my house mean when one said you were on one of your Mossad witch hunts? ASIO believe you are a spy.'

He is still, his eyes closed. He opens them and looks at her. Once again, she's saddened by the change in their clarity and depth of colour. She realises that his eyes are full of pain.

'Bella, I know how it must look to you. I can only tell you I've spent much of my life working towards a world free of the type of evil we saw during World War Two.'

'Maybe so, but what were you doing in Australia? The ASIO man said they believed you were working against Australian government interests.'

'Ah, in their position, I guess they would say that.' He shakes his head. 'From the time the first European refugees arrived in Australia after the War, their number included hundreds of active fascists, Nazis and collaborators escaping from Europe.'

'But how could that happen?' asks Bella. 'How did these killers slip through the screening process, which was supposed to weed out any war criminals from genuine refugees?'

'Seems hard to understand now, but back then, the most important factor was the political climate. It was about communism. There was a huge fear amongst Western nations of communism.'

'Yes, I do know a bit about that,' Bella muses. 'So that means that the war criminals may have been mass murderers, but they were anti-communists and therefore acceptable. Disgraceful.' She says with fervor.

'Exactly!' says Eli. 'When the Australian government was forced to investigate suspected war criminals, they relied on ASIO for information. Many fascists and Nazis slipped through because they were considered a lesser evil than the communists!'

'Unbelievable, but you still haven't told me whether you are a spy. What were you doing in Australia?'

'I can't tell you much, but...,' He tells her that he was tasked with identifying suspected war criminals from information given to him and he would send back information about these people to his employers. As simple as that. No, he wasn't any kind of assassin or character from a spy novel. That is why he travelled extensively within Australia and overseas. Yes, his infrastructure business was legitimate and yes, the traveling he did for that was genuine.

'So, Bella, if you want to call that spying, I guess I was spying. But there were very clear reasons why, post-war, there was little help from the Australian government or security services where war criminals were concerned.'

'But when I met you, it was thirty-five years since the end of the war. Was it useful to keep going?'

'Oh yes, that kind of evil needs to be rooted out. If these people aren't found and brought to justice, they will keep infecting future generations with their poison.'

Bella thinks about news footage she has seen of young Neo-Nazis strutting their abhorrent stuff and knows Eli is right. 'Well, okay, I can see why ASIO didn't approve of your activities, but who were the thugs, and why did they break in and search the house?'

'This is where Klaus and Alexandra come back into the story.' He tells her that their activities had been known about for many years but not where they were hiding. In Eli's travels looking for other criminals, he was ideally placed to pick up any information about them that might surface.

'In fact, it was our mutual interest in Klaus and Alexandra that literally threw Howard and I together. Klaus was the main person of interest because of his war crimes record.'

'And Alex?'

'She was only wanted in Britain for spying, whereas Klaus's crimes were committed in Europe. It's their post-war crimes that put them in the same criminal jurisdictions.'

Eli tells her that he believes that the break-in at Armadale was Klaus's associates trying to find any records of Eli's investigations. 'I believe that because of your association with me, they kept a close eye on you after I left.'

Bella shivers. 'Yes, I understand that now. Why did you leave so quickly?'

'I don't want to upset you, but the truth is, I had direct threats that unless I desisted, your farm and Armadale would be firebombed, Fiona and the dogs would be tied up in the homestead and burned alive. All the animals would be slaughtered, and you would be ...' He kisses her hair and says in a low voice that is near breaking. 'I couldn't run any risk of harm coming to you or Fiona.'

This thought makes Bella shiver. 'Oh, Eli.' She simply has no way to understand or deal with this type of evil.

'How could you get away without leaving a trace? And clearing your workplace?'

'I had a contingency plan and help.'

'Ah, so the ASIO man was right about that.'

She looks up at him. 'So, what did Alexandra mean when she said she had encountered you once, here in Tangier?'

'Just that, it was an encounter about two years ago. My associate and I arrived at the scene of a kidnap handover; that's part of our work. We try to negotiate safe resolution of abductions.' Eli remembers. 'We were unarmed; that was a condition of the negotiated handover of a British agent. Klaus drew a gun, wounded me, shot my colleague and the agent dead, and he and Alexandra escaped.'

They sit in silence for a minute, and then Bella asks. 'Do you think that my mother could've made different choices all those years ago?'

'I believe that Klaus has always been the driver of their activities, and Alexandra had little option but to go along with him. She had made her life that way. However, people like Klaus are the old guard. Time and natural attrition are taking care of those people, but nature abhors a vacuum. There are new kinds of people driving new kinds of evil, emerging all the time.'

'Unbelievable. Yes, Storm says the same thing; he calls it terrorism.' Bella says again as she thinks of global humanitarian tragedies and acts of these new kinds of terrorism. 'Do you think you're making any progress?'

'No one person can. But there's an international community who try, by exchange of information, to help each other. It's difficult to believe we've had any success when you look at the world today. What you don't see, of course, are the tragedies that, with luck and some good management, are averted. That's our motivation.'

'Was Howard involved with this organization?'

'Not at first, but during my time with you, I realized Howard was well-placed to help us.'

'How? Through his journalism?' Bella outlines her meeting at MI6 and the information from Reuters.

'Yes, I'm aware of all that; it was a natural progression for him to, with the agreement of the British MI6, share intelligence with us. Howard had a high international profile. He could move almost anywhere with an immunity like the Diplomatic Corps enjoy.' Eli says softly. 'You know Bella, he was a very special man.'

'Yes, that's exactly what I've learned too. How little I know of my own father. I'm sad about that.' She asks, 'Was Ariel Achmed part of this 'circle.' I really had the feeling he knew far more than he was prepared to tell me.'

'Ariel did initiate the contact to set up a meeting with you. I was a day late getting to you. I came back to town and found your card only hours after you'd left the hotel.'

Eli continues. 'Even though Klaus and Alexandra are out of action, there's a network of their associates still at large. This work cannot stop.'

They sit in silence; Bella understands everything he's saying. Instead of holding on to the hurt in her heart, she feels a stirring of interest in the wider picture. Her preoccupations with her past had limited her ability to see so much of the world in front of her.

Eli says. 'I am sorry Howard died without telling you about your mother.' He holds her hand to his heart before he continues. 'Bella, I've never been able to make up my mind about the right or wrong of Howard's decision, but he made me promise. It amounted to emotional blackmail.'

'Yes, I'm sorry too.' The silence is softer now. The familiarity of his presence is replacing her anger; she feels calmer. Bella finds it impossible to stay angry with him, although he is responsible for so much heartache. Or is he? She asks herself. Aren't we responsible for the state of our own hearts?

'When I met Adeline in London, she told me she believes that Howard intended to tell me when he came home. She said he felt it was time.' Bella pauses, then says. 'Time? How about thirty years past time! He might even have told me about you! Damn it, he died!'

'Yes, Bella, when I heard he'd died, I wondered what he'd told you.' Eli looks away at the fountain before he turns back and says to her. 'Believe me, I made a promise to you that I would find out. And, if he hadn't, I would find a way to be able to tell you what I can.' He adds, 'before it's too late.'

'Eli, are you unwell?'

'Yes, I need to go to Switzerland for treatment immediately.' He waves his arm at the packing cases.

'What is it? Do you have Cancer?' The word that, most often, means death, not life. 'Bloody hell, Eli. Where?'

He pulls her tighter. 'Pancreas, and now, it's spreading.'

As Eli says this, Bella turns his face towards her; she's stricken to find him like this. She wonders if he's alone. Who takes care of him? If she is given time to learn more about him, she might be able to accept that he has a complete life without her.

'Bella, I've often thought of us meeting again. I'm so happy it has happened.'

Her heart is home where it has wanted to be for so long. From the warmth of his arms, Bella can only feel that Eli feels the same. 'I have one last question.'

He kisses her hair. 'As long as you live, you'll always have a last question.'

She takes a breath. 'What is your name? I need to be able to remember you as a real person. Not some secret service construct.'

'Bruno Bruin,' he smiles at her.

'Stop it! that's how I found you. What other name do you use?'

'Bruno Bruin.'

'Don't be ridiculous; no one uses a name like that for real.'

'You always told me I was like a large brown bear; I think it quite suitable.' He smiles and tickles her ribs. 'How do you know I'll tell you the truth?'

Damn this man! He's laughing at her even now! Nothing changes. Their last few minutes together, and as always, he's teasing her! She can't believe it! She looks away from him. He whispers a name in her ear.

Before they return to London, Bella returns to Eli's house with Scott. She hopes for them both to see Eli once more. Ahmet answers the door; he shows them to the courtyard, and he hands her a letter addressed to Armadale, it's the first she has ever received from Eli. She sits by the fountain to read it. Attached is a card with the name of a Swiss clinic. Although he must go to Europe for treatment, he must leave immediately. Klaus has compromised his security. Eli doesn't want their syndicate of criminals to know where he is, so great are their powers of destruction. He asks her to resume her life and leave all this behind. The last paragraphs make her tears flow, he wrote.

> *"Bella, I know you wanted to ask me if I'd found another partner. I needed to say many things to you yesterday. The answer is, like you, I've been alone. You were, and still are, the love of my life. I couldn't make another relationship and live with what I did to you in leaving as I did. And to face the possibility, I might have to do it again.*
>
> *When we met, I told myself that I had a right to a life with you. It was all I wanted. I mistakenly thought I could leave my past behind and start again. Fate and some very evil forces in this world decided otherwise.*
>
> *I'm so sorry. I've lived every day with the pain of our parting and the loss of our life together. Now, my greatest wish is that someone else will hold you in his arms in the moonlight. I hope you'll choose Scott; he's a good man. I'll die in peace with that thought."*

After reading it, there's nothing left for Bella here. Her mother has given her an unintended gift; she's free from the past. Her father's secrets no longer have any power over her. She's free from Eli's choice to pursue his own star and not be her Antares, the heart star of her constellation. She shows Scott the letter.

'He got that bit right,' says Bella.

'Which bit?

'You're a good man.'

The next morning, Eduardo rings her from Lisbon. He sounds older and very frail. 'Bella, I was able to see Alexandra before she died last night.'

'Oh Eduardo, are you all right?'

'Yes, my dear, despite everything, I feel peaceful that she did not die alone.'

'Was she able to speak to you?'

'Not really, she was sedated. The only word she spoke was your name.'

'Oh!' Bella looks at Scott, her face stricken.

'I told Alexandra that you were safe. You know Bella, I think that was what she wanted to hear; she died an hour later.' He is silent, then he says, 'It's better this way.'

Scott holds her in his arms. She feels overwhelmed with sadness that her life has been rather like a marionette. Others have pulled her strings since she was a small child, her father the chief puppet master.

Chapter Fifty-Six

London October 1990

Storm spirited Bella and Scott home from Morocco to London in a private jet. A helicopter picked them up from Heathrow and deposited them on the lawn below the terrace at Storm's home at Windsor, on the Thames Riverfront. The irony of this effort to evade the press doesn't escape them.

Storm's home whilst large, is warm and welcoming. Fiona, Adeline, and David are waiting for them. Eduardo arrives from Lisbon, where he has finalized arrangements to bury Alexandra. Bella watches Eduardo with Adeline and Fiona; she sees the charming, sociable man that he could've been if tragedy hadn't dogged his life. David is basking in attention from Fiona and Adeline, too. Afternoon tea is served in the library. There is more Pimm's and champagne flowing than tea or coffee.

'I'll never eat maize porridge again,' says Bella as she eats a smoked salmon sandwich.

'Why would you?' says Scott with a mouthful of sausage roll. 'These are as good as yours, Fiona.'

'They are Fiona's. We took over Storm's kitchen,' laughs Adeline. 'We had to do something. Fiona was like a caged lioness marching up and down the terrace waiting for you.'

Bella and Fiona move away from the happy group. They sit watching Storm playing a genial host with ease. Fiona says, 'I think we could ask

Storm to Yarra Glen for Christmas with everyone.'

'Good idea, I think he would like that. He doesn't seem to have much family either.'

'Widowed long ago and no children,' replies Fiona. 'I've enjoyed getting to know him this week.'

'Ah, sad.' Bella thinks about Storm and Howard, two amazing men who were more similar than different. She thinks Howard would be pleased that Bella and Fiona will weave these strands of his life together. Creating a picture that, if his life had taken a different path, Howard would have been very happy to be part of.

'Did you spend some time with Eli?' Bella asks.

'A little, not enough. After I threatened to kill him if he didn't rescue you, we were fine.' Fiona smiles at the memory. 'Y'know, Bella, having someone like Eli in our lives was an amazing experience. I am sad that people like him, who have a calling to fight evil, most often must give up so much.'

'Everything.' Bella tells Fiona a little of Eli's revelations to her in Tangier. They sit, remembering the life they had shared with him. 'The hardest part is accepting that I was a small part of his life. To me, he was my whole existence.'

Fiona says, 'he left you because he loved you so much.'

'He left both of us because he loves us.' Bella takes Fiona's hand.

'And Scotty?' her aunt enquires.

'I can't promise the patter of little feet at Yarra Glen, but I can promise you he will be with us and won't disappear.'

'Good, that's all I want to know.'

'I wonder what Howard would have thought about this?'

Fiona draws an envelope out of her pocket and hands it to Bella.

Bella turns it over, and the sender says. Howard. 'Where did this come from?'

'I found it in his suitcase.'

'Hidden in plain sight after we combed his study.' She withdraws the fine onionskin airmail paper sheets covered in Howard's distinctive italic script and reads.

My darling daughter...

What I am about to tell you belongs in the pages of fiction, not in a letter to you. My need to protect you from the outfalls of the events I will describe to you is the only excuse I can offer. Bella, you are the heart star of my constellation: my raison d'etre.

This story will expose your father as a man with feet of clay. I have spent over forty years hiding these flaws from you and Fiona. I can promise you; I have paid a terrible price for this life of deception. Had I understood this price, the cost to you, Fiona, and others long ago, I hope that I would've found the courage to make different choices. I can only explain the choices I made as truly, 'une folie majeure.'

The story has two parts: my story and Eli's story. How are they synonymous? By a further twist of fate and to my deepest regret, my darling, they are, but I will start at the beginning.

I was meeting your uncle Tom and David McKenzie in the Rivoli Bar at the Ritz Hotel in July 1944. They were on final leave before re-joining their squadron...

Many minutes later, Bella places the letter on the cushion between them. 'He could never have imagined what happened with Alexandra.'

Fiona says. 'I think he did. I believe understanding her drove every choice he made.'

'The saddest part is his anguish at leading a double life.' Bella feels fresh grief for the father she lost without a chance to say goodbye. She almost lost him again through doubting his integrity.

'Howard's choices put him outside living a normal life in the same way as Eli. No wonder they had so much in common. 'Did you receive one too?'

'Yes. I'll show you later.'

'Did he say anything about Tom?'

'His death or...?' Fiona glances over towards David.

'Tom and David.'

'No...I don't think he understood. If Tom had lived, I'm sure he would've...
' She pauses and looks affectionately at David, who is laughing with Storm

and quite obviously enjoying himself. 'We've talked a lot. David has given me so much to treasure about Tom and I think, finally, David has found peace.'

'Good. He's been carrying so much grief by himself for too long.'

After two joyful days, Eduardo leaves for Barcelona. He will resettle Jose and Maria in a retirement community. He doesn't want any legal action taken against them, but he doesn't want them in his life either. And he will be spending time in Australia every year now.

Scott and Bella watch how the companionship and new friendships are enlivening Fiona, Adeline, David, and Eduardo. Such an extraordinary journey they have made to find each other. David suggests that before Scott, Bella, and Fiona return to Australia, they could all go to Mézières.

Chapter Fifty-Seven

London

In the back of Storm's car, he presses a button to close the panel between the passengers and driver. Storm asks, 'How do you feel about Howard now?'

Bella thinks, how does she feel? 'Relief, but I still need to accept that he couldn't tell me all about his life.'

'That's a tough one, Bella.'

She continues. 'I realise there's something in me that must have answers. I don't like mysteries.'

'Not many of us do, Bella, but some people are able to move on.'

'Maybe it's my father's genes that drive me. He always turned over every stone to see what lay underneath.'

'And a good thing, too. That helped you to become the journalist you are.' After a minute's silence, he says. 'You're very like Howard.'

Bella feels confused by this statement. Which Howard does he mean? The gregarious professional? Or the closed, secretive, controlling man? Lost in her thoughts she feels emotions rising.

'Bella.'

She raises her head to see Storm looking at her. She hopes he doesn't see the internal waves threatening to beach her.

'Are you going to write about this, to publish?' asks Storm.

Bella has been waiting for this question. This has been foremost in her mind, and she's still unsure how to answer it. She feels that Storm, if he gets hold of this, would squeeze every paragraph inch out of it that he could.

Bella answers in a firmer voice than she feels. 'No, not yet ... maybe never.'

Storm is looking at her in his unnerving way. She holds his gaze, silence, Bella waits.

'I'm pleased you've decided that.'

Just that. Nothing further. 'Storm, I didn't expect that response.'

'Bella, would you think about continuing the work that was so important to your father and Eli?'

Surprised, Bella turns towards Storm and says, 'Why would you ask that?'

'Bella, terrorism is on the rise.'

'Yes, I understand that. It's a new form of guerrilla war. It was the threat of terrorism that drew Howard and Eli together.'

'The threat is growing.' Storm is silent as he ponders the past twenty years.

Bella thinks about the reports from Reuters and MI6 and understands how Howard was able to serve two masters seamlessly. She can see how she and Scott could work in a similar way.

'Storm, I'll talk to Scott. It's a shared decision now.'

'Yes, I can see that.'

Bella looks out at the Thames Embankment. Her sad years grieving for Eli are behind her. The future with Scott is full of promise.

Epilogue

Melbourne November 1990

A t the Iris office, Scott and Bella have a happy reunion with Meg. After the tears, hugs, and chatter, Meg hands Bella a newspaper cutting.

Perisher Valley Ski Resort.

Forestry crews were clearing firebreaks recently when they found the skeletal remains of a skier in undergrowth at the base of a sheer rock face.

The remains are identified as Simon Spencer, who went missing at Perisher Valley in 1987. It is thought he became disorientated in the blizzard and fell down the escarpment. A deep injury to his skull showed that he may have been unconscious and died of exposure.

Meg says. 'The family asked not to mention in the press that an airline ticket was found in Simon's wallet.'

'So, he meant to go?'

'Seems so,' Meg replies.

'Even sadder,' concludes Bella.

'Are you okay, Bella?' asks Scott.

She replies, 'Never better,' as she puts her arms around him.

Acknowledgements

Utmost gratitude to Ian Kirk and John Kearney of White Hot Productions. They have encouraged and supported me every step of the way since I wrote the first outline of the story.

Many thanks to my editor Alison Arnold. Her guiding hand and experience was invaluable.

To my agent Sally Bird of Calidris Literary Agency - thank you. Your patience and unwavering support kept me going through the trials of 'The Covid Era' and beyond.

Heartfelt thanks to my friend and author Suzanne McCourt who has throughout, given me the gift of her friendship and considerable experience as we walk on our nearby beach with her beloved dogs Barney and Louis.

My thanks also to Verena Rose, Shawn Reilly Simmons & Deb Well for including me in the Level Best Books Family.

Thank you to Carol West for her calm guidance through the unknown territory of marketing my story.

And Andrew Morse whose rationalism and care keep me grounded.

About the Author

Evelyn Cronk lives in Melbourne, Australia. She is a member of Writers Victoria and the Society of Women Authors Victoria and a life member of The Australian Screen Editors.

Prior to falling into the world of words, she enjoyed a productive career in the Australian film industry as a film editor and post-production supervisor. Evelyn moved from actively editing to become manager of Roar Digital, a specialist film & television post-production house. This company is a subsidiary of film production company, White Hot Productions. As part of the team, she read and discussed many of the scripts that were submitted to White Hot Productions for consideration.

Evelyn proffered a story synopsis, thinking that the script supervisor might like to take her outline and turn it into a film script. The supervisor loved the story, the producers loved it. Before embarking on the TV series production, they encouraged Evelyn to develop the story as a novel. In *Without Question,* she has done that.

SOCIAL MEDIA HANDLES:
   Email: author@withoutquestionbook.com
   Facebook: /evelyn.cronk1/

AUTHOR WEBSITE:

www.withoutquestionbook.com